The Secret of Life

The Secret of Life

Paul McAuley

TOR®

A TOM DOHERTY ASSOCIATES BOOK
NEW YORK

THE SECRET OF LIFE

Copyright © 2001 by Paul McAuley

Edited by Ellen Datlow
Designed by Lorelle Graffeo

A Tor Book
Published by Tom Doherty Associates, LLC
175 Fifth Avenue
New York, NY 10010

www.tor.com

Tor® is a registered trademark of Tom Doherty Associates, LLC.

Library of Congress Cataloging-in-Publication Data

McAuley, Paul.
  The secret of life / Paul McAuley.—1st ed.
    p. cm.
  "A Tom Doherty Associates book."
  ISBN 0-765-30080-X
    1. Women scientists—Fiction. 2. Mars (Planet)—Fiction.
  3. Pacific Ocean—Fiction. 4. Fungi—Fiction. I. Title.

  PR6063.C29 S43   2001
  823'.914—dc21
                                              2001027121

First Edition: June 2001

Printed in the United States of America

0 9 8 7 6 5 4 3 2 1

This is for Georgina

Acknowledgments

Ideas in this novel were derived in part from books and articles by John Barrow, Robert Cook-Deegan, Peter Coveney and Roger Highfield, Paul Davies, Richard Dawkins, Armand Delsemme, Murray Gell-Mann, James Gleick, Stephen Jay Gould, Anders Hansson, Bruce Jakosky, Stuart Kauffman, Kevin Kelly, Christopher Langton, Lynn Margulis, Michael Parfit, Jeremy Rifkin, Ian Stewart, Edward O. Wilson, and Robert Zubrin, and from the articles collected in *Mars*, edited by Hugh Kieffer, Bruce Jakosky, Conway Snyder, and Mildred Matthews.

Some races increase, others are reduced, and in a
short while the generations of living creatures are changed,
and like runners relay the torch of life.

—Lucretius, *De Rerum Natura*

PART ONE

LIFE ON EARTH

Shanghai, Chinese Democratic Union:
March 2, 2026

All human life is here.

It is almost midnight, yet dozens of barges still plough the black waters of the Huangpu Jiang, hazard lights winking red and green, passing either side of streamlined robot cargo clippers that swing at anchor in the midstream channel. The tall white cylinders of the clippers' rotary sails are fitfully illuminated by fireworks bursting above a rock concert in an amphitheater on the Pudong shore, close to the minaret of the Oriental Pearl TV Tower. Nets of white laser light flex against the dark sky. The howl of massed guitars and the throaty roar of the audience carries over the river to Shanghai, where, along the waterfront avenue of the Bund, beneath tiers of neon, crowds swirl past stalled lines of traffic.

Most of the old colonial department stores and banks have been torn down, replaced by skyscrapers with organic facings like muscle fibers or wood grain seen under a microscope's lens, or coralline skins fretted with porous knots and hollows and veins. The human crowds at their feet are like columns of ants scurrying around the buttress roots of forest giants. People stream out of the Cathay Theater. Waiters in starched white shirts move among the crowded tables of terrace cafés where roaring gas heaters keep out the night's chill. Teenage police officers lounge sullenly at intersections, tugging at their white gloves as they watch opposing streams of vehicles inch past with blaring horns and glaring headlights. Huge signs are flooded with new advertisements every twenty seconds. Corporate logos burn sleeplessly inside glass-walled malls piled with electronics, silks, and exotic biotech.

Behind the Bund and the commercial sector, the gridded

streets are narrower but no less crowded. Traffic is jammed in a complex one-way system. Pedestrians and cyclists pour around little three-wheeled trucks, bubble cars, the limos of high-ranking government officials or entrepreneurs or gangsters. Electric scooters tow trailers piled high with flat TV sets or melons or cartons of cigarettes. Bars and clubs flaunt their wares in video loops cut to the hectic beat of slash funk. Hawkers thrust animated adsheets into the hands of passersby. Stalls sell ramen or noodle soups, spices, tacky souvenirs, bootleg spikes, cages of live birds, exotic tweaks. Here's an old woman tipping a handful of fish heads into sesame oil smoking in a blackened wok. Here's a beggar with an extra head that lolls idiotically on his left shoulder. Here's a crowd of shopgirls tripping along under a bouquet of colored paper umbrellas. Tucked away in narrow alleyways are chop shops for stolen motorcycles, the offices of gray biosurgeons and baby farmers, workshops where customized chips are hand-etched, traditional medicine shops with dusty glass jars of bark or twigs or dried berries, a shop selling cloned tiger penis and vat-grown ivory.

Anything that can be bought can be bought here, in Shanghai.

Pan and scan the restless crowds.

Here's a man ambling along with a slouch hat angled over his face. An American, a businessman—peacock blue suit, rouged cheeks, blue eye shadow. He plunges down reeking steps into a cellar bar and orders a beer he does not drink, watching the reflection of the bar's entrance in the mirror behind the pairs and trios of naked dancers who, in cones of smoky red laser light, mime fucking with the dazed compliance of sleepwalkers. After an hour, the American checks his discreet Patek-Philippe tattoo and moves on, anonymous in the crowds. There are many businesspeople and tourists here, many *gwailos*. He passes a Cuban bar, a German bar, an Icelandic bar where customers are handed fur-lined parkas as they enter—the inside's all ice. Another bar, this one a shack so small its half-dozen customers sit side by side, serves only whiskey; more than a hundred bottles are racked up behind the bamboo-and-rattan counter. The American waits until a stool is free and sits and orders a Braveheart on the rocks—despite the name, it is made in Kenya. He doesn't drink but turns the tumbler around and around in his long, manicured fingers. Three drunken salarymen are watching a postcard-size TV that shows baseball live from Tokyo, betting on each pitch in a flurry of fingers and coins.

The bar squats under a sign advertising the Peking Disneyland.

This is the American century.

A young, skinny Chinese man sits beside the American and orders a Rob Roy. They don't talk, but when the American stands up and leaves the other man gulps down his shot of whiskey and follows him into an alley, where the American suddenly turns and embraces and kisses him.

The Chinese man is startled and angry and tries to push away, but the American holds him tight. "They might be watching, so make it real," he says, and kisses the man again, tasting the whiskey on his breath.

They hire a room in a short-time hotel and go up the rickety stairs, stepping between the sleeping bodies of an entire family, from shrunken grandmother to fretful baby.

The room is tiny and overheated, smells of disinfectant, mold, and sex. It is almost entirely filled by a gel slab bed covered in purple, vat-grown fur.

The young Chinese man sits down and strokes the coarse fur and says, "My company makes this." His long black hair is brushed back from his round face; his skin is sallow and shiny with sweat. The width of his smile is a precise index of his discomfort.

The American tosses his hat onto the bed and says impatiently, "Let's do it."

The Chinese man, his eyes fixed on the American, slowly pulls a pair of flat-ended tweezers from the inside pocket of his snakeskin jacket. He uses them to lift up the nail of his left thumb, picks a glass capillary tube from the pink bed of artificial flesh, and drops it into the American's palm.

The American stares at the sliver of glass. "What's this shit?"

"It is in there. Alive."

"I wanted the code."

"That is not possible. I tell you already it is not possible. This is the second generation, but it has the essential property of the Chi. It is alive. You can sequence it yourself. Your people can. I do not cheat you."

"If you're fucking with me."

"I have no access to the sequence libraries. I tell you that already. Not the sequence libraries, not the Chi itself. I get you the second-generation lab prototype. I smuggle it past the sniffers. Very hard to do, very difficult. But I do it. I bring it to you."

The American's hand closes over the capillary tube. "I can verify nucleotide sequences right here. I can't verify this."

The Chinese man's smile is very wide now. "You sequence it. You see I do not lie. It is the essence of the Chi."

"Second generation."

"Yes."

"And also a prototype."

"It is fully tested. It splices genes, self-selects at a very high rate. Evolution with a fast-forward button."

The American stares hard into the Chinese man's fixed smile and says again, "If you're fucking with me."

"No, sir. I do not. This is for my family—"

"Yeah, yeah." The American knows the story—dissidents exiled to a mining village in Antarctica, a massive bribe needed to release them, blah blah blah. He says, "Before your family can wave bye-bye to penguin land, we'll have to check this out."

Now the Chinese man allows a hardness to show in his face. "Perhaps you fuck with me."

"Here, we shake on the deal. Okay? It's an American custom."

The Chinese man doesn't look at the American's hand. He says, "No. No, I don't think so."

The American scratches his nose. He's amused. "Suit yourself, Charlie. Maybe you want to fuck instead. We have the room another twenty minutes. Plenty of time for a quick in and out."

The Chinese man stands. "You will sequence the organism and you will pay."

"You've already been paid."

"You will pay the rest."

"Yeah, sure. We done here? Fuck off then."

The American lies back on the fur-covered bed after the Chinese man has gone. The handshake doesn't matter because the kiss did it; his saliva contains a toxin derived from puffer-fish liver, a toxin to which he has been made immune. It will shut down

his victim's nervous system in about twenty minutes: clonic sei-
zures, suffocation, heart failure.

The American leaves the room when the ayah taps on the door
to indicate that the hour is up. He strolls through the crowded
streets, brushing off touts and pimps and beggars, toward the Bund.
He sits at a table in a terrace café and drinks a latte, watching the
crowds from beneath the brim of his hat. Waiters begin to stack
chairs on the empty tables around his, but he takes his time, and
it is four in the morning when he takes a taxi several blocks, enters
an infobooth in an all-night mall noisy with rock music, and sends
a dozen ecards, all but one to random addresses. He spends an
hour in a games arcade, moving restlessly from machine to machine; then, as the day's first measure of light pours into the sky,
hails another taxi and goes to the airport.

Shantytowns full of displaced peasants slope away on either
side of the ten-lane freeway. Palms planted along the center divider
have died from a viral infection. Under a floodlit advertisement
for the floating pleasure palaces of the South China Seas, a ragged
boy is beating a water buffalo with a stick.

The American meets the government courier in the American
Airlines first-class lounge. Two minutes, in and out. He's on the
way back to Shanghai when the cherry lights of half a dozen police
cruisers begin to flash behind his taxi and he realizes who has
been fucking who.

The government courier carries only a diplomatic pouch, its
lock sealed with a roundel of security plastic embossed with the
eagle and shield of the U.S. government. There's a slight delay
after he has boarded the scramjet, something to do with a baggage
count. In dawn light, on the wet concrete beneath the courier's
oval window, men with white gloves sign each other's slates while
a truck with a flashing amber light goes past.

When it happens, the scramjet is climbing high above the
Pacific. The courier has settled into his calf-hide first-class seat, is
trying not to stare at the TV anchorwoman across the aisle. Stew-
ards are taking back glasses in readiness for the interval of free fall
at the top of the scramjet's suborbital arc.

And in the hold, the device planted by one of the baggage

inspectors fires a single microwave pulse that fries every processor in the scramjet's neural net. All power goes out. Cabin power, power to the fuel pumps of the air-breather motors, power to the control surfaces. The scramjet tumbles in an uncontrolled dive, the spine of its overstressed airframe shattering, the pressurized cabin exploding along welding seams, breaking up a kilometer above the Pacific.

Over the next three days, U.S. Navy ships gather from the ocean's heaving skin luggage and life vests and seats and clothing, carbon fiber shards from the scramjet's wings and fragments of its titanium hull, and bodies and pieces of bodies.

The tiny glass capillary tube, its seal broken, drifts more than twenty kilometers north before it finally sinks.

Oracle, Arizona:
October 12, 2026

When she arrives home, Mariella pulls on her sheepskin-lined denim jacket, saddles her bay mare, Twink, and rides at a trot along the dry riverbed. A kilometer out, she turns the horse and urges her up a trail that climbs between scrub pines and junipers to the top of the ridge.

It is not quite six in the evening of this unseasonably chilly October day. Across the desert basin, beyond the Batamonte Mountains, the huge sky is laddered with red clouds. Twink is sweating with the exertion of climbing the trail, her flanks steaming gently in the cold, dry air. The pungent odors of saddle leather and horse sweat mix pleasantly. Mariella twitches the reins when Twink drops her head to investigate a patch of engineer grass. A scurf of snow clings to the shady side of rocks and ruts. The air pinches Mariella's face and ears and fingers; she wishes she'd thought to put on her hat and gloves. She can feel cold in the barbell through her left eyebrow, the copper wires sewn along the rims of her ears.

The lights of Oracle are scattered below the ridge, trailer homes and the translucent bubbles and interlocked glass-and-steel cubes of newer houses. Lines of eucalyptus and acacia trees define unmade streets which generally follow the contours of the low hills over which the little town sprawls. To the south, Tucson twinkles like a pile of diamonds; in the middle distance, the perimeter lights of the Arizona Biological Reserve define three hundred square kilometers in the darkening desert. The long tented trench of Gaia Two is so brilliantly illuminated it seems more intensely real than anything around it, an interstellar ark floating in primeval darkness. Vapor from the tall steel chimney of the liquid-nitrogen plant catches its glow, a feather of white pinned against the darkening land. Beyond the northern end of Gaia Two are the lights of the commercial research laboratories, each separated from its neighbors by landscaping and concrete ditches and revetments and wire fences, and in a checkerboard pattern beyond the laboratories are the concrete blockhouses that cap the shafts, built to the same design as ICBM silos, where frozen biocores are stored. Constellations of red warning lights wink among the panels and cableways of the big solar energy field.

Mariella sits on her horse and watches as the sky darkens and the first stars come out. Thinking about the phone call from Washington. Thinking, not for the first time, that she has come full circle and that it's time to break out, time to move on. She can't let this chance go.

The sliver of the new Moon is setting in the west. And there, in Leo, close to the bright point of Jupiter, is what she has come to see.

Mariella rises in the saddle, reaches out with her right hand as if to clasp the red star of Mars to herself.

"Got you!" she shouts. "Got you at last, you bastard!"

Washington, D.C.:
October 13–October 14, 2026

Before dawn, Mariella drives her battered pickup to Tucson International Airport, collects her tickets at the South Western desk, and moves from business class lounge to scramjet with a sense of huge wheels invisibly meshing around her. All she carries is her slate, a set of clean underwear tucked into one of the pockets of its sand-colored canvas case. She is wearing her best clothes, a magenta bias-cut suit and a yellow silk shirt with pearl clasps she bought in Paris last year at the UNESCO conference on sustainability.

The flight is shorter than the wait at the airport, an arc that briefly takes the scramjet out of the atmosphere, half of the continent spread below, and then down, gliding in over the interlocked curves of the Potomac Barrier to Reagan National Airport, where it is already noon.

A limo is waiting for Mariella at the airport, and takes her to a hotel overlooking the river: the Watergate. Where she discovers that her appearance before the special ad hoc subcommittee has been delayed until the next morning. She can't get through to the NASA guy, Al Paley, but fuck it, it's just some bureaucratic glitch, the old hurry-up-and-wait routine. That's what she tells herself. Don't make a scene, don't screw up. Be a good girl and maybe they'll let you go to Mars.

She buys a toothbrush and makeup in the vending machines in the hotel lobby, showers and hangs her suit and blouse in the steamy bathroom to remove their wrinkles, chooses something from the room service menu and tries to do some work. There is always work. There are a couple of slash clubs she knows about in the central D.C. area—Studio 7, The Meatlocker—but she can hardly go tom-catting in her business suit, and she will need a clear head for the next day.

Sometime in the night, she is awakened by the throb of engines. She gets out of bed, tells the room to dim the light it considerately switches on, crosses to the tall window and parts the drapes and looks out through the armored glass. An attack helicopter with a shark's sleek profile hovers in the orange sky above the river's dark bend, at about the same level as her hotel room. Muzzle flashes star the opposite shore — a string of even, deliberate shots, the sustained crackle of a semiautomatic. The helicopter probes the shore with threads of red laser light, then suddenly stands on its nose and stoops in low and fast, disappearing between two megalithic office blocks.

Welcome back to civilization.

At seven, Mariella is awakened from uneasy dreams by her alarm call. Wearing unaccustomed makeup like a mask, she is met in the lobby by a Secret Service agent. That is how the woman introduces herself.

"Glory Dunn, Secret Service. I'm here to look after you, Dr. Anders."

"I didn't know I needed protection, Gloria."

The African-American woman is as tall as a basketball player, bulges with obviously enhanced muscles, and wears a severely cut suit: a cartoon superhero poured into corporate tailoring. Hair cut short in a bristly wedge, dyed the same red as the frames of her data spex. She cracks a frosty smile and says, "That's Glory, Dr. Anders. Not Gloria. It's a common mistake. This way please. Are you enjoying your stay?"

"It's nice to see where my tax dollars go."

A black limo is waiting outside, a gas-powered stretch Cadillac probably fifty years old. Mariella wrinkles her nose at the half-forgotten yet instantly familiar stink of carbon monoxide and half-burnt hydrocarbons. Like California, Arizona has air-pollution laws so strict you need to buy a license before you can fire up a barbecue. Agent Dunn holds the door open and climbs in after Mariella, folding her long legs like a stork. As the limo purrs off, Mariella asks about the gunshots last night.

"There was a helicopter, too. Chasing something on the other side of the river."

"Probably a sweep against draft dodgers. Some people would rather die than work. I understand you're easier on them in Arizona."

"We certainly don't shoot at them, Agent Dunn."

The limo's tinted windows darken the crisp fall sunlight. Huge white buildings, the shoulder of the Potomac's levee and the arc of a bridge float past in ghostly procession. A construction crew is working across from the White House, returfing a raw wound in a level stretch of grass. Where that light plane crashed a week ago, shot down by a handheld stinger missile fired from the White House roof. The plane flew up the Potomac under radar, a wildman suicide bomber sitting on a hundred kilos of plastique. The President went on TV to tell the nation that he refused to be intimidated, that unlike his predecessor he would not move inside the heavy fortifications of Camp David, but it hasn't stopped the rumors that he sleeps in a Cold War bomb shelter two hundred meters underground.

The special ad hoc subcommittee of the Science, Space and Technology Committee is meeting at the labyrinthine Rayburn House Office Building, which houses the staffs of most of Congress's standing committees and subcommittees. There's a complicated negotiation at the security barrier involving retinal scans and passing a chemical sniffer and a metal-detecting wand over Mariella's body, then a ride in a small, slow elevator. She has been here several times before, for it is typical of Washington that committees assess programs under their control by considering reports prepared by outsiders, and she knows to ask the secretary who takes her name at the reception desk on the second floor about briefing documents.

"This is just an informal session, Dr. Anders. Would you prefer coffee or iced tea?"

"Could you rustle up some hot tea?"

The secretary is a slender, immaculately groomed man with a prissily formal manner and silver eye shadow. He purses his lips and says doubtfully, "I suppose we could try."

Mariella has suffered numerous cultural misunderstandings over the proper way to make tea and long ago learned to accept that Americans willfully fuck it up, probably because they still unconsciously resent British colonialism. They make it with ice; they make it with hot water from the tap; worst of all, they flavor it. Her first Christmas with Forrest's family, she made the mistake of asking for a cup of tea. A dusty canister of tea bags was triumphantly produced after her mother-in-law noisily ransacked the kitchen for ten minutes, and at last the steaming cup was brought in and presented to Mariella with as much ceremony as if she was Queen Bess and it was the first potato. There was no milk and she asked for some, producing puzzled looks and another flurry. A measure of milk was stirred in. She took a sip. It was peach tea.

So she says now, "Never mind. Coffee. Black, two sugars."

"I'll bring it directly. Would you please sign this?"

Several pages of close-printed paragraphs of legalese. The secretary points to the dotted line at the bottom of the last page.

"What exactly is it?"

"A document of nondisclosure, Dr. Anders."

"Perhaps I should consult my lawyer."

The secretary purses his lips again. "Well, you could, of course, but it would considerably delay proceedings."

"I was joking."

"I see. Sign here, please, and initial the other pages. Here, yes, and here. Thank you, Dr. Anders. You'll have to leave your slate with me, but don't worry, it will be quite safe. I fix this seal, just so, and you press it with your thumb. That's right. Now no one but you can open it without the seal discoloring. This way please. The subcommittee is ready for you."

It is the same room where she gave evidence about the viability of a permanent Moon colony a few years ago. Low ceilinged and windowless, although floor-to-ceiling drapes at the far end make a pretense that there are windows, worn blue carpet, the air vibrant with the subliminal hum of air conditioning, the lights bright, a long table with three men and two women seated behind it, and more than a dozen secretaries and advisors and chiefs of staff crammed behind them like courtiers in a medieval throne room.

A flag furled on a staff to the right, a woman at a stenographer's table to the left. Cameras up in the corners of the room, on metal brackets under the white acoustic tiles. A straight-backed chair in front of the table, to which the secretary ushers Mariella.

Mariella knows the NASA representative, Al Paley, and the white-haired African-American woman who chairs the subcommittee—Senator Mae Thornton, chair of the Science, Space and Technology Committee, a notable champion of the space program and a regular on talk shows and government infomercials—but not the others. There's a congressman from the Energy and Commerce Committee, a member of the White House Science Coordinating Committee, the director of the congressional Office of Technology Assessment. One of the advisors is nursing both a slate and a young baby, and Mariella remembers afterward how the baby fretted throughout the meeting.

There are the usual formalities, her swearing in, the polite thrust and parry that establishes that yes, she really is Dr. Mariella Anders, that she is forty-one, that she is a recognized expert in microbial ecology, that she is presently working at the Arizona Biological Reserve, that although born in Britain she has been a citizen of the United States for fifteen years, naturalized by marriage but widowed, currently single.

And then they get down to the point with astounding frankness.

What she learns then is not the only shock of the morning. When she comes out, Penn Brown is waiting in the spartan foyer, sitting in a high-backed metal-framed wheelchair. He scoots over as she takes her slate from the secretary, the four fat-tired wheels of his chair leaving tracks in the carpet's thick pile.

"Here we are again, Mariella. Like Darwin and Wallace."

"Or Huxley and Bishop Wilberforce."

"I guess they're taking us in alphabetical order. How are you, Mariella? Still working in Arizona? That wire sewn into your ear is new, isn't it? I'm sure it impressed the subcommittee."

Penn Brown's crewcut head rests in a kind of brace, his polished Oxford brogues on a footplate. He fiddles with a stick control on the armrest and with an electric whine the chair raises him slightly.

Mariella is still thinking about what she has been told. The slick. The Chinese spacecraft is already on its way to Mars in a long Hohmann transfer orbit. The window of opportunity. Life. Life on Mars.

She feels as light-headed as if she has been breathing helium.

She says stupidly, "I thought you were on the Moon."

"I was, for the last six months. Excuse me if I don't get out of this contraption. I've been down less than twenty-four hours and I seem to weigh far too much."

"Sorted out the phosphorous cycle yet?"

"Getting there. I hope you still don't hold that grant rejection against me."

"It's your problem now."

Penn Brown looks at her as if she is a laboratory specimen pinned to a dissecting board, and he is considering where to make the first incision. He has very dark eyes, shuttered by heavy lids. He says, "Cytex is going to make a lot of money from it, and not just on the Moon. There are plenty of people willing to pay for sealed, minimal-input home environments. In the twentieth century the rich wanted privacy and security; in the twenty-first it's protection from environmental extremes."

"I remember the environmental extremes of your system, Penn. I hope Cytex has good lawsuit protection."

"I'm surprised to see you here, Mariella. I would have thought you'd be far too busy at the zoo, saving the world bit by bit. Do you know how many people they've called? Quite a few I would imagine."

"I have no idea, except that the minimum number is two."

"Certainly more. NASA redundancy protocols. They're obviously talking to all potential candidates on this thing, no matter how unlikely. Who's your commercial sponsor?"

"I beg your pardon?"

"I'm representing Cytex, of course. You don't have one? Then I suppose your presence is down to Al Paley's very twentieth-century attitude that this has to do with pure science. As if anything NASA ever did was purely about science. Or is Senator Thornton making trouble? That woman will squeeze hard to wring every drop of publicity from a situation like this."

"Why do you think one breast is acceptable on a man, but not two?"

Penn Brown looks puzzled for a moment, then says smoothly, "It's functionality, of course. One baby, one breast. As it is a character imposed upon natural morphology, there's no reason that it should display the redundancy that symmetrical embryo development imposes. You're babbling, Mariella. What did they tell you in there?"

"You mean you don't know?"

"Did you, before you came here?"

"Well no, not exactly," Mariella confesses, and is grateful when Glory Dunn smoothly interposes herself.

"I'll take you back to your hotel, Dr. Anders," the agent says.

"Of course. You'll have to learn about it for yourself, Penn. Break a leg," Mariella says, and in the elevator tells Glory Dunn, "Thanks for that. The bastard was enjoying himself. He knows something I don't."

"I did notice that there is a certain tension between you and the gentleman in the wheelchair."

"It goes a long way back. We have different ideas about the way science should be conducted. Once upon a time I proved him wrong and he didn't like it, so he got me bumped from a research trip to the Moon. He didn't have an escort. I mean, someone like you. I guess that doesn't mean anything."

"That's not for me to say, Dr. Anders."

Mariella is pacing about her hotel room, waiting for the limo that will take her to the airport, when Senator Thornton's chief of staff phones. He introduces himself and says, "Are you alone, Dr. Anders?"

"Why shouldn't I be?"

"Agent Dunn is not with you?"

Mariella lifts the slate and swings it around, then tells him, "As you can see, I'm quite alone. What do you want?"

The chief of staff is a handsome young man with a nice smile.

He says, "Senator Thornton would very much like to have lunch with you."

"I have a flight in two hours. I'm just now waiting for my limo."

"It's all in hand, Dr. Anders. I have already rescheduled your travel plans, and there's a car waiting downstairs."

The car takes her across the river to an Italian restaurant in the old town of Alexandria. It is on the second floor of a narrow, nineteenth-century townhouse. Despite the Potomac Barrier, Alexandria has been badly affected by the rising sea level: hardly anyone uses the first floors of the old buildings, and most new structures are raised on stilts.

The restaurant has the calm, ponderous atmosphere that only old money can generate. Blinds are drawn against the crisp fall sunlight. Candle flames burn above their reflections in crystal glasses and silver tableware laid on starched white linen. The maître d' leads Mariella to a booth in the back, where Senator Mae Thornton sits on the leather banquette like an enthroned queen, surrounded by a small retinue of staffers. Her chief of staff makes the introductions while a woman sweeps Mariella for bugs, and then the whole crew considerately vanishes.

"I've taken the liberty of ordering," the senator tells Mariella. "This is one of my regular haunts. It's very discreet, if you take my meaning."

Mariella blurts, "Did I get the place?" and, dismayed at her horrible rudeness, feels herself blush.

Senator Thornton pours golden wine from a tall green bottle into one of the glasses in front of Mariella. Silver bracelets tinkle at her frail wrist. Candlelight sparkles like frost in the coils of her white hair. "You're as direct as your reputation, Dr. Anders. Do try this. It's Swiss. Fendant de Sion. A favorite of James Joyce, do you know. He called it Archduchess's pee."

Mariella says, "I'm afraid I'm not very good at conspiracy. And this seems, if you'll forgive me saying so, pretty conspiratorial. I suppose we can't talk about the . . . discovery."

"I'm afraid not. I brought you here because I wanted you to be seen with me, which I can assure you will do you nothing but good. This place is discreet in the sense that its staff will not tip off the press, but it is not secure."

"The Chinese lied, didn't they? Their first expedition must have found—"

Senator Thornton raises both hands in a warding gesture. "Please. We really can't talk about that here."

"I need to know everything."

"I understand. Politics is to information as the Barrier is to the flow of the Potomac. I'm sure it's frustrating to a scientist, but perhaps you'll acknowledge that control of information is sometimes necessary. If this thing became widely known, it would disappear in a feeding frenzy, with every committee, national laboratory, and company with genome-related interests trying to get a piece of it. I'm on your side, Dr. Anders. I hope you'll pay me the courtesy of believing me when I tell you that."

There is a silence as, with ceremonial flourishes, waiters bring dishes of tortellini al brodo and a basket of bread, administer Parmesan and black pepper. The senator savors a spoonful of broth and says, "There's a certain rivalry between you and Penn Brown, I believe. Is it personal or professional?"

"Even in science it's sometimes difficult to disentangle the two."

Senator Thornton dips up another spoonful of broth and says, "Let's make a bargain to cut the bullshit, Dr. Anders. Like I said, I'm on your side. As a matter of fact, I was the one who pushed for your selection, against the considerable opposition of advisors from what you might call the scientific establishment. And of course from biotechnology companies who would like to grab this for themselves. I suppose that it will do no harm to tell you that Penn Brown was one of the dissenting voices, while at the same time pushing his own self forward. I defended you vigorously. I know about and admire your role in solving the Firstborn Crisis. I know there's talk that you might win the Nobel Prize for your work on the origin of life. I know about your work on genetic diversity and microbial ecology, and the fact that the goal of one of the research proposals you submitted to NASA was the very thing the Chinese may have done. All of that makes you a prime candidate for the mission, and I put that point of view forcefully. You may think I'm some good ol' gal Southern senator, concerned only with keeping up my profile to ensure re-election, but I like to think I know something about science, and I like to think I'm a friend of science. A harsh critic of certain excesses it's true, but what's a friend if she can't speak her mind openly? I know you and Penn Brown have differing views and something of a contentious history. He spoke about that this morning. I'd like to hear your side."

"I'd like to know what he said."

"Now, now. I'd be pissed too, but I wouldn't be pissed at the bearer of the news."

Mariella blushes. "I'm sorry."

"Apology accepted. He said you lacked experimental skills. Considering the training you'll receive, that's hardly to the point. He also said that your entire scientific approach is flawed and at odds with the requirements of the mission, but we won't talk of those requirements, or of any other details now. Instead, you can tell me about yourself and Penn Brown. It goes back to the First-born Crisis, I believe."

In fact, it went back to the workshop meeting in the Death Valley motel, a year after the discovery of the Moses virus and the beginning of the end of the Firstborn Crisis. The time when Mariella established her reputation while still grieving the death of her husband, his murder really, although in those confused and violent times the distinction between being murdered and being a casualty of war was tremendously blurred. She lost Forrest, that was what counted, lost her husband and a whole way of life. The little house in Silverlake that was no bigger than a double garage, its bedroom so small that they slept on a futon mat they rolled up each morning Japanese style, but which stood on a big lot with a steep terraced slope shaded by mature orange and lemon trees at the back, and a landscaped cactus garden to the side. Despite the hard work and pressures of trying to win tenure, those few years were the happiest of Mariella's life, when decisions seemed to flow naturally, and every moment might be graced with unexpected harmony and beauty. All the fame and success that flowed from her contribution to ending the Firstborn Crisis can't bring that back; even after all these years, she still has ambivalent feelings about it.

Over salad and pizza rustica, she tells Senator Thornton about the Second Synthesis group and Penn Brown's attacks on it.

The Firstborn Crisis, the spread of a genetically engineered disease that caused the spontaneous abortion of male fetuses, affected Mariella's generation of biologists as strongly as the Trinity project affected the careers of physicists in the second half of the twentieth century. As with the physicists and mathematicians who had been recruited to design and build the first atomic bomb, only the brightest and best biologists were selected for the Human Fertility Task Force. Mariella, newly widowed, was prominent among them, and a year to the day after the press conference at which the discovery of the Moses virus was announced, she and two dozen former members of the task force held a workshop in Death Valley. The meeting more or less spontaneously self-assembled. It took over a motel, with seminars in the restaurant or out by the swimming pool, once even *in* the swimming pool. People carpooled, packing the trunks with beer and wine. Someone with a lovingly restored Rambler station wagon brought a projector and a smartboard. They made an eight-hole golf course among the rocks of the lunar-like landscape, with squares of astroturf for tees. They wanted to catalog and define every fundamental biological problem still unanswered, to set the agenda for the next fifty years of biological research. They were hopelessly ambitious and naive, but they were full of energy and hope.

At that time, biological research was dominated by neo-Darwinist reductionists, whose central belief was that organisms were merely protoplasmic robots that acted as carriers for genes, just as chickens were merely the means by which eggs made more eggs. The reductionists claimed that every characteristic of an organism was determined by its genes, and that every characteristic helped to maximize adaptation of the organism to its environment, to ensure survival and replication of the genes it carried. This approach, championed in the last quarter of the twentieth century by Dawkins, Maynard Smith and Williams, had proven to be a very powerful way of analyzing how organisms work. An alliance of neo-Darwinian evolutionists and molecular biologists had dominated biology since the beginning of the Human Genome Project, and because they were the majority voice on grant-awarding committees and the boards of scientific institutes and journals, most funding was channeled into research projects that reinforced their view.

"Well I'm not saying it's right," Senator Thornton says, "but I do appreciate the commercial applications of genetics and molecular biology. I suffered from lymphoma some years back, and I was cured by a drug tailored to attack the cancerous cells. They grew the drug in one of those genetically modified soybean plants and fed me its magic beans. A wonderful thing, that you can pluck the cure for cancer from a plant like the apple of knowledge. A little girl, the daughter of one of my team here in Washington, was born with a metabolic dysfunction. She was infected with an engineered virus that cut out the bad gene and replaced it with the correct version in every one of her cells. There was a big debate thirty years ago about the morality of modifying the germ-line cells in such cases, but that little girl won't pass on the bad gene to her children."

"The Second Synthesis group has never denied that genetic modification is an important and useful technique," Mariella says. "But we disagree strongly with reductionists who want to explain everything in terms of actions and interactions of individual genes. You cannot isolate a single element—an organism, a gene—from its context and expect to understand how it is integrated into the whole."

Essentially, the reductionists at the helm of biological research are driven by physics envy. Twentieth-century science was dominated by physicists who, by building on the foundations laid down by Newton and combining the theory of relativity with quantum chromodynamics, were able to explain the origin of the Universe and the fundamental forces that shaped it, from the nature of elementary particles to the structure of stars and of galaxies. For a while, many physicists believed that it would be possible to derive a single mathematical statement describing the entire physical Universe, a Theory of Everything. But even as biologists set out on a similar path of rigorous reductionism, physicists realized that a single theory could not explain all that the Universe contains because much of the history and many of the structures of the Universe are derived from nondeterministic interactions. It cannot be otherwise, for indeterminacy is at the heart of quantum mechanics.

That was the path the Second Synthesis group wanted biology to take, the path Penn Brown so vehemently opposed. To move away from reductionism and the tyranny of the gene. To rediscover the organism and the context in which genes operate. To consider simplicity and complexity, chaos and emergent order, self-similarity in complex adaptive systems, Kauffman models and much else.

Mariella gave two presentations at that first workshop. One was a routine talk about her theoretical work on the evolution of the genetic code. The other was a disaster. She tried to sketch out a method of untangling the complex interactions between every gene product of bacterial communities and the environment in which they lived. She was not particularly successful. Many of her colleagues were baffled by the vagueness of her aims, and no one could follow the phase space mathematics she deployed. Finally, Penn Brown stood up and said, "This is well intentioned, but it is simply the Gaia theory in another guise. As such, its scientific virtues are in inverse proportion to its use as a pacifier for a public that prefers to believe in supernatural intervention rather than in actual physical laws."

People laughed, and Mariella could not regain their attention. After a few minutes she sat down, feeling hopeless. Later, at lunch, Penn Brown wandered past Mariella's table and smiled and said, "I don't mean to be cruel, but I really don't believe that science should be driven by public opinion. It inevitably leads to self-congratulatory foolishness, like the subjective analytical studies championed by feminist separatists. I'd hate to see you going down that path, Mariella."

"Do you really believe that, or are you saying it because I'm a woman?"

Penn Brown's smile was engaging. "Of course not. But I do

believe that I detect an unjustified eagerness to overturn the so-called 'hierarchical scientific norm.'"

"I have nothing against hierarchies, scientific or otherwise, as long as they are valid hierarchies."

"In that case, I'm sure you accept that we all must work by consensus. And I'm afraid that you failed to convince anyone of your approach."

Bridget York, who was sitting across the table from Mariella, said, "Consensus means that the parties concerned have reached an understanding by common agreement, Penn, not that one is better at playing clever word games than the other."

"Perhaps, but ideas must prove their worth by surviving informed debate. If you want to overturn the established point of view, Mariella, perhaps you should begin by tidying up your ideas. Then at least your colleagues might be able to understand what you are trying to do." Penn Brown smiled again, and wandered off toward the people clustered around the beer cooler.

That was the beginning of the rivalry between Mariella and Penn Brown. Like her, he was a biomathematician, although he had cultivated his speciality from the beginning, instead of drifting into it as Mariella had. His academic credentials were impeccable: a first degree at Yale; graduate work at the Harvard Medical School; tenure at Princeton. He had published important insights on the knotty problem of microbial competition for nutrients in soils, had done much useful work on the recalcitrant operation of introduced genes, had written several well-received popular science books. He had several lucrative consultancies with biotechnology firms, including one that earned him share options in Cytex just before it announced the lymphocyte-based cancer treatment that made it the hottest and fastest-growing biotech company in the States. He was rumored to be writing an account of the search for the Moses virus, and several people at the workshop were openly currying favor with him, in hope of good publicity.

After the workshop, Mariella spent a couple of months considering a slew of job offers, and at last chose the least likely, a sinecure post at the Arizona Biological Reserve, which paid her a salary but provided little else. She refined her arguments about a holistic approach to biological research, and tried to apply it to her own work. She spoke about it at scientific conferences and gained some converts, but the Second Synthesis group was still small and mostly invisible. Another workshop was held a year after the first, at a conference center in New Mexico which had been built by the author of the Little Iva cartoons. Penn Brown, who seemed to have appointed himself as Mariella's nemesis, did not attend, but wrote an excoriating article in which he dubbed the Second Synthesis group the Biological Underground, the last redoubt of scientists interested in solving problems for their own sake rather than in enriching humanity. After Mariella published a rebuttal, he invited her to debate with him at Princeton; she declined, fearing a setup. A few months later, she applied for a visiting research position at the Copernicus Lunar Research Station, with the intention of setting up a microbiological biome to improve the quality of the station's air and water recycling systems. She passed the initial selection stages, but then her project was rejected; she learned that Penn Brown had been on the NASA grant-approvals committee. She wrote more project proposals for NASA: all were blocked. She had acquired an enemy, and now she is going with him to Mars.

By now, Mariella and Senator Thornton have reached dessert—white-truffle sorbet—and coffee. The senator considers what Mariella has told her, and says, "So it's not just science. It's also personal."

"It's about personal reputations. Penn has staked his career to one view. I happen to disagree with him."

"But you don't let that get in the way of science?"

"I don't let it get in the way of seeing the truth."

"I hope not. That was the basis of my argument for including you in the mission."

For a moment, everything seems to fall away on all sides. Mariella says, "Well . . . thank you."

"You'll stay overnight in Washington, and fly out to Houston tomorrow for a briefing. I know it's short notice, but I'm sure you know that when politics gets involved in science everything is either stop or go."

"I think that's possible. I mean, of course it is."

The senator smiles. "Now I'm not asking you to think that you're in my debt, Dr. Anders, but I would like you to consider that we are on the same side. Because Penn Brown is one of the most prominent members of the scientific establishment, he is also at the center of a political cabal. And of course he is affiliated with one of the largest of the biotechnology companies. Certainly one of the most ambitious, and one that underwrites much fundamental research. Now, I can't deny the tremendous benefits that commercial sponsorship has brought to NASA, but there are tremendous dangers, too. What we cannot speak of is, of course, one of those dangers. Perhaps the greatest of them all."

Mariella sees at once what she means. For many years Senator Thornton has advocated increased political control of science, and tighter regulation of the biotechnology companies. It is a platform that has given her national attention and perhaps, according to some commentators, even a shot at the presidency. And she has had some successes, including a bill outlawing the kind of wholesale copyrighting of raw DNA sequences that bedeviled the Human Genome Project.

Mariella says, "Penn Brown is going too."

"Cytex offered a very generous financial incentive, and I have no doubt that it will be accepted. We may be in the middle of a new economic boom, but the federal government is failing to collect taxes from more than half its citizens, and ambitious programs are in danger of being closed down. I am concerned that Cytex will want to get control of this project by using the old trick of pleading commercial confidentiality. So I'd like you to keep me informed as to your opinions of the way the project is being run. If you have any doubts, any criticisms, any insights about its wider significance, please let me know. Don't think of it as being an advocate for me, but as being an advocate for the truth. Will you do that?"

Mariella has a hangover that Bayer's magic can't quite quell, and is sore and tender in intimate places. She got lucky at The Meatlocker, and spent an energetic few hours with her new friend at a capsule motel before returning to the Watergate. Welts on her back from her friend's long fingernails, bruised lips and stretched muscles, an animal contentment. Waiting for her flight to be called in Reagan's business-class lounge, Mariella drinks two shots of her father's old remedy, tomato juice and Tabasco sauce, and thinks about the work she has to do, about what she needs to find out to do that work.

She makes a couple of calls, and gets part of what she requires from Maury Richards at Woods Hole. He confirms that, yes, something is happening out in the middle of the Pacific Ocean. Satellite surveys show changes in the photosynthetic pigments with which phytoplankton, microscopic algae that are the primary producers of most marine ecosystems, turn sunlight into chemical energy, yet there is an overall increase in biomass. Something strange is growing there, Maury says.

"The slick."

"Where did you hear that?"

"I can't say."

"Hmm. Anyhow, a survey ship has been on station for the past five weeks, but I don't have access to its data. They're claiming processing problems or some such horseshit." Maury's wise old face twists in a grimace of distaste.

"The Navy?"

"Sure, but also Cytex. I hear there was an open bid on the research contract, and they offered a notional dollar."

"Have you been out there?"

"No. Not yet."

"But you are involved with it."

Maury was drawn into the Second Synthesis group through his work on carbon fluxes in marine ecosystems. He has been working on oceanic productivity for more than thirty years, is one of the leading authorities in his field.

"Sure. But so far only from remote sensing data. Why the sudden interest, Anders? Anything to do with the Mars thing?"

"How did you know about that?"

"There was a press release this morning."

"Shit."

"So you're going to Mars at last."

"Apparently. Me and Penn Brown."

"Cytex money there too, huh?"

"They have a lot of interests."

"What's the connection, Anders? Has someone tried to slip something past the San Diego protocols?"

"I don't know."

"You mean you don't know, or that you do know, but you can't tell me?"

"I don't know. I'm operating in mushroom mode."

"Dark and bullshit."

"Right. So what can you tell me?"

"Well, I don't know. It's kind of classified."

"We're both working for the government, Maury."

Maury thinks about that. He says, "I made a few naive calculations from the satellite data. At the rate the slick is spreading, it'll reach the Chilean coast about the middle of next year. If that happens, it could hit the fishing industry there harder than any Grande Niño. And it could be into Antarctic waters before then, although given that the plankton there is already badly fucked up by global warming, it won't make much difference. I'll tell you what, Anders, the easiest thing is if I send the raw data."

"You can do that?"

"They put me in charge of the remote sensing program, so I figure I can choose to bring you aboard. Besides, the satellite pics aren't classified. Just my work on them."

"Oh shit, my flight's being called. I have to go. But I'll look forward to seeing the data when I get on the scramjet."

"Where are you?"

"I really do have to go, Maury."

"You can level with me, Anders. You said you were working for the government, so let me guess, you're just now in Washington, D.C., going home after a head-banging session with a bunch of pencil-necked policy geeks."

"It's something like that, but this isn't the time or place to explain everything. Listen, Maury, maybe you can do me another favor. I might want to go out there."

"What, take a look?" Maury grins. "That's an interesting request."

"Who can I ask?"

"You can ask me. Let me call in a few favors."

On the scramjet, Mariella gets another tomato juice and Tabasco from the steward and opens and decrypts the file Maury has sent her. She calculates the rate of spread of the slick, plugs it into standard productivity models, and gets some scary results. Normally, phytoplankton use energy derived from sunlight to fix carbon dioxide into organic compounds. Zooplankton—protozoans, tiny crustaceans and fish larvae—graze on the phytoplankton, just as cows graze on a grassy meadow, and are eaten in turn by larger animals. Ultimately, almost all of the carbon fixed by phytoplankton photosynthesis is recycled back to the atmosphere as carbon dioxide.

But this is different. There is plenty of carbon fixation, but from the rate of spread of the slick it is apparent that there can be almost no cycling of fixed carbon back to carbon dioxide. Everything is going into the growth of the slick, and as it displaces the normal phytoplankton population, it will remove the base of the ecological pyramid through which fixed carbon flows from the microscopic primary producers to zooplankton, fish, squid, whales, and, ultimately, man.

Drumming her fingers in counterpoint to the delicate guitar of Mississippi John Hurt in her earphones, Mariella works out worst-case scenarios in her head, oblivious to the businessman who's flicking through news channels in the seat next to hers, and the flattening of the cloud-flecked curve of the Earth beyond the port as the scramjet descends toward Houston.

It is unexpectedly hot in Houston, sunlight vertical, humidity stifling. Mariella is grateful for the limo's air conditioning, although it is compromised by puffs of hot, smoggy air that come through the window the driver keeps open. Dense traffic moves at frightening speeds along the narrow lanes of the highways. Every other vehicle is a pickup truck with a rifle rack behind the cab. The limo driver switches lanes with casual skill, one hand on the wheel, the other resting on the sill of the open window, fingers tapping to the plangent twang of some corny country song. Smog hangs in brown layers between the crowded glass towers of the downtown financial center. It seems that using gas automobiles is mandatory in this once oil-rich state; Texans are big on tradition, still insist that Texas is a republic, fly the Lone Star flag everywhere, hold the frontier belief that it's your right to do anything you want on your own land.

The Johnson Space Center is a long way past downtown, in what was once a pleasant, wooded community, but which is now mostly overbuilt with strip malls and gated villages and the low ziggurats of hurricane-proof condominiums. Water towers stand like Martian fighting machines among clumps of trees. Billboards revolve atop steel columns. Most of the buildings are new to Mariella — she was last here eight years ago, for the preliminary training for her flight to the Moon, before Penn Brown conspired to cancel it — but there, in the rocket garden alongside NASA Highway One, are the tethered columns of an old Titan and an Atlas booster, and the long white carcass of a Saturn V. One of the old space shuttles, *Atlantis*, sits like a giant's toy inside a big transparent dome.

The scattered buildings of the old Space Center stand behind a road and a belt of trees, dominated by the gleaming glass pyramids of the new administration complex. The long, half-buried hangars of the Mars Sample Return Facility stretch beyond, aligned with the tarmac ribbons of the runways of the little airfield.

Mariella checks into the hotel that anchors one corner of the administration complex, buys a set of underwear from one of its shops, showers, emails her calculations to Maury Richards. There is a message on her room phone; Penn Brown is down in the bar. Well, she has an hour before the briefing starts. Maybe she can learn something.

The free-form lobby, six stories of construction-diamond spider-web and glass, has won several awards, although it looks to Mariella much like that of any modern five-star hotel. It's divided in two by a tinkling stream that winds among mossy boulders and ferns and bamboos, bridged here and there by red-painted wooden arches. Concrete islands are planted with trees and sword-leafed palmettos. There were once wing-clipped ducks in the stream, but they crapped slippery green-white duck turds everywhere and have been banished back to the lake in the old center, now the campus of NASA's space university. A capsule burnished with re-entry heat stains hangs high overhead, one of the old Mercury capsules, a metal holster from the time when NASA's astronauts were white knights going head to head with the Russians.

The bar that overlooks the lobby is famous, its counter a long, narrow crescent of raw iron carved from a chunk of asteroid 2004 KD alpha, which was moved into lunar orbit eight years ago. It is polished to show the flowing grain of stress patterns caused by ancient impacts, and gleams with dull, heavy highlights.

Penn Brown, no longer in his wheelchair, elegant in a crisp white short-sleeved shirt and pleated trousers, is nursing a beer at the far end of the counter. Mariella orders a vodka and tonic; they move to one of the booths under a video display running a live transmission from some lunar rover of a rolling, sunlight-saturated plain. They talk in low tones, a conspiracy of two. She compliments him on his fast recovery, but he waves it aside.

"I'm still fragile and I should still be in that wheelchair, but the hell with that. Amazing what they can do about bone replacement now, but it'll still be a week before I can run up stairs. I assume you've heard there's a third person going on this trip?"

"No. No, I haven't."

Brown hunches forward, serious and intent. "Woman by the

name of Anchee Ye. She's a NASA employee, so she'll have the inside track."

"I don't know the name." Thinking that Penn Brown, with his close association with Cytex, has the inside track too.

"She's a biogeochemist who's already done one tour on Mars, and that puts her square in the ballpark as far as NASA's concerned. I think she'd be better off selling hot dogs in the stands than playing on the field, but NASA is pushing to make her team leader, with us as her assistants. We should get together on this one, Mariella. Push back. Push hard for a real microbiologist to be put in charge. Me or you, it doesn't matter who."

Mariella smiles. She is pretty sure it matters to Penn Brown.

He says, "There's a tremendous amount of commercial funding behind this, but even so the NASA brass still want to call the shots. That's why they want one of their people to lead the team, even though they don't have anyone with the proper expertise."

"This is about science, not politics. As long as the work gets done, does it matter who gives the orders and who takes them?"

"You have to go through the politics to get to the science. NASA did a turnaround in the nineties with their faster-better-cheaper philosophy, and they've been building on that image ever since. But it's still the big missions that count because they bring in the big money. And big money means political clout. The space station, the base at Copernicus, the base at Ares Vallis, they're as much about prestige as science. I mean, look at the space station. It's pure politics, a way of uniting American, Russian and European space efforts while making sure that America keeps control. And it's an endless pork barrel for NASA. No one really needs more research into microgravity, but every company wants a piece of space because space is as hot now as the Internet was in the nineties and noughties. NASA has been playing them along, but pretty soon the debts will be called in."

This is the same line Brown has spun out in countless interviews. Impassioned, yes, but essentially a slick bit of performance. He is a snake-oil salesman who has come to believe his own pitch.

He says, "This thing is no different. If we don't push the envelope we won't have any freedom. We'll just be taking orders from

NASA. So are you with me? We push hard enough, and one of us gets to call the shots once we're there. Otherwise the whole thing will be run by NASA from the ground. They might as well send chimps."

The ice in Mariella's glass rattles when she drains her drink. She says, "The classic prisoner's dilemma."

"Sure. And it's solved by cooperation. We've had our differences, but this is more important than that. Commercial freedom, scientific freedom, it's the same thing in the end."

"Is it?"

"Don't think you're above this. Where do you think all the money supporting your zoo comes from?"

"I know where it comes from, Penn. And it isn't a zoo."

Brown ignores this. "The government chips in what it can afford, which isn't much these days, and there's about ten percent from tourist money and private donations. But the bulk is from commerce, mostly biotech companies who are in effect paying for access to the gene bank that the zoo maintains. It keeps the zoo in liquid nitrogen and it feeds pure research like yours. So really we're in the same business."

"I don't think so." Mariella decides not to tell Penn Brown about her calculations. Let him think that she's stuck on the outside: he might throw her some useful tidbits.

"Of course we are. You want a piece of the action as much as I do. What I'm proposing will make sure that we both get what we want."

Brown's smile is no more than an upturning of the corners of his mouth.

"Perhaps we should hear what they have to tell us before we start squabbling about dividing up the spoils."

"Oh, hell, this won't tell us anything we don't already know. It's just the start of a long road paved with administrative bullshit."

Mariella realizes then that Penn Brown already knows what the briefing will be about. Yes, the inside track.

The briefing is held in one of the anonymous, windowless rooms in the core of the administration complex. It has a classroom air.

The walls are decorated with blown-up photographs of nighttime launches of big lifters; chairs with sidearm rests are scattered in a rough semicircle around a smartboard and a lectern decorated with the NASA badge. Half a dozen men and women file in. Al Paley walks up to the lectern, a woman in a drab suit a couple of steps behind him. A man leans by the door at the back of the room—the White House staffer on the ad hoc subcommittee, Howard Smalls. Mariella finds a left-handed chair, listens sleepily as Al Paley makes the introductions.

Three astronauts form what Paley calls the Gold Crew: Colonel Martin McCord, the mission commander; Bernie Thomas, the flight engineer; Gus Plafker, the payload specialist. Superfit middle-aged men in smart off-the-rack leisure suits, white shirts and ties, highly polished shoes. Complicated chronometers on their wrists, quick and easy ring-of-confidence smiles, down home, aw-shucks attitudes. Career astronauts. Corporate men who look like golf or tennis pros. They are essentially highly qualified truck drivers, but they still think of themselves as knights of infinite starry space. Then there are the researchers who will spend varying times at Lowell Base. Alex Dyachkov, a NASA photodocumentarist, a compact, neatly groomed man in a black turtleneck and expensive white jeans. Betsy Sharp, gray-haired, with a no-nonsense air, dressed like Mariella in a suit whose cut is several years out of date, an atmosphere chemist going out for the full two-year tour with her colleague Ali Tillman, a striking young woman with pale porcelain skin, and a crest of white feathers growing through her red hair. They are going to study laminated polar deposits for clues about Mars's ancient climate.

Al Paley explains that three scientists from the Russian RKK Energia company and two from the European Space Agency have been bumped for the new science mission, and everyone turns to look at Mariella, Penn Brown, and Anchee Ye when he introduces them as the specialists who will be working on the microbiology project. Ye is a slight, composed woman who meets everyone's eye with a flash of determination that Mariella notes with foreboding. She is not the simple placeholder Penn Brown believes her to be.

Paley shows a slide of the mission badge, a roundel of Mars's battered globe with the triple-armed swirl of the south polar icecap prominent. There is a smattering of polite applause, and after the drab-suited woman has handed out mission statements and crew profiles in blue folders stamped with the NASA badge, the astronauts and the other members of the mission file out after her for a separate briefing.

The man by the door, Howard Smalls, comes forward. He hands out more folders, each sealed with security plastic, takes the lectern and introduces himself. He looks very young, his black skin shining under the lights, beads in his hair, a gold chain looped several times under the collar of his white shirt.

"You can open the folders," he says. "There'll be time to study them here, but you won't be able to take anything away with you. We have to operate under unusually tight security. I know you'll probably resent it, but this is a highly unusual situation."

Anchee Ye starts to say something, but Smalls cuts her off efficiently, tells her that there will be time for questions after he has outlined the problem.

"We already know what the problem is," Mariella says. "The question is, what do you think the Chinese found on Mars? And why are they going back?"

"That's exactly what I'll address," Smalls says. "Let's go through what I've given you."

The folders contain a sheaf of glossy photographs. Smalls talks them through the first one, a satellite picture of what he calls the dead zone, taken in infrared so that the slick shows white against the dark open ocean. Long streaks like fat in a slice of bacon, each three or four kilometers long, overlaid by arrows and numbers showing the direction and speed of expansion. Mariella does a quick calculation in her head; growth is bumping at the upper limit of her calculations, which is both satisfying and dismaying.

"It does not seem to be a true extraterrestrial organism," Smalls says. "Its metabolic pathways and many of its genes appear to be of terrestrial origin. However, it does also contain some novel DNA sequences which may be the basis of its unusual behavior."

Mariella feels a shiver of excitement. Smalls's remarks imply that the organism shares the same genetic code as life on Earth. A common ancestor then. Or perhaps life on Mars was ancestral to life on Earth. There is some reason to believe that because life arose so quickly in Earth's early history, probably as soon as the crust had cooled to allow liquid water to accumulate, it must have come from somewhere else.

She says, "Has the entire genome been sequenced? Have library matches been made?"

Brown says, "These people don't need to know that, Howard."

Al Paley clears his throat and says, "With respect, Dr. Brown, we don't know what might or might not be significant."

"There is a commercial agreement," Brown tells him.

"I'm aware of it."

Mariella says, "What agreement? With Cytex?"

There is a pause. Penn Brown says, "We really don't need to continue down this road."

Howard Smalls says sharply, "I can handle this."

Brown settles back in his seat, arms crossed. "You had better be sure that you can, Howard."

Anchee Ye has been watching the exchange with unruffled composure. She says, "I know that Cytex is involved. Perhaps you could explain just how deeply."

Smalls does not look at Penn Brown. He says, "Cytex has sequenced the genome of the organism which is the basis of the slick. It will not violate commercial confidentiality to tell you that we still don't know what it all means."

That is to be expected. It usually takes only a few minutes to read the nucleotide sequence of a gene, and a few days and several thousand gene readers to patch together the sequence of a complete genome, but thousands of hours of research may be required to discover the function of the product of a single novel gene. Cytex may have sequenced the genome of the slick, but the Thornton Bill prevents patenting of any gene until the function of the protein for which it codes has been determined. No wonder Penn Brown is nervous.

Mariella says, "It has to have come from the Chinese. Something they found on their first expedition, even though they said they found nothing at all. And presumably that's why they're on their way to Mars again even as we speak. Or did one of the European or Russian guest workers slip something past containment?"

Smalls gives up a tiny smile. "We do not yet know everything we want to know, Dr. Anders. The leading hypothesis is that this is a genetically modified organism incorporating novel gene sequences, and that those novel genes may have been derived from live organisms isolated on Mars."

Brown says, "I think we've gone far enough, Howard."

Mariella holds up the handful of photographs. "But there is no documentation here to support that hypothesis."

Howard Smalls says, "No, Dr. Anders, there is not. We cannot at this stage give you a complete picture. For instance, I can't tell you who we suspect may have released this organism. There will be plenty of time for speculation later. Let me tell you what you need to know at this stage."

Smalls refers them to the rest of the photographs. Satellite pictures of the Martian north pole, a segment at the edge of the polar ice cap outlined in yellow, a sequence of photographs zooming in until at the grainy edge of resolution structures can be seen nestling in an eroded crater. A half-buried dome, a drill rig, a couple of tiny white rectangles that might be vehicles, an abandoned landing stage.

"This is the first Martian expedition of the Chinese Democratic Union," Smalls says. "It spent thirty days on Mars, just over four years ago. I guess you all know what was made public. It made a series of deep drills using new technology, brought up core samples from at least two kilometers down. We believe that it found life beneath the ice cap. We believe that it brought back either living organisms, or extracts from which gene sequences were made. At present I cannot tell you any more than this, and you must understand that there is no causal link between the Chinese expedition and the release of the organism in the Pacific."

The NASA scientist, Anchee Ye, is watching Smalls intently, a hand curled under her chin, the photographs fanned but unregarded in her lap. Mariella is suddenly convinced that this woman already knows all about this. Inside information: inside track. And Penn Brown knows too. She's the outsider. She has a lot of catching up to do.

Brown says, "You know, one thing has always puzzled me. NASA made a series of deep drills with exactly the same purpose. Why didn't they find anything?"

"I can address that," Al Paley says. "One of the primary goals of the Martian research program was to discover if there has been and if there still is indigenous life on Mars. In one respect we have been stunningly successful, with the discovery of fossil structures indicating that microbial life existed on Mars roughly three-and-a-half billion years ago. Unfortunately, the search for existing life forms has not yielded positive results, even though much of it was concentrated at the north pole. Drills made into the ice cap found nothing, despite hopes that lakes of water might exist beneath it. The last attempt, four years ago, suffered a variety of problems. The drilling equipment malfunctioned. So did a robot probe. It was the end of the season and a dust storm blew up, meaning an early retreat. More importantly, the Chinese expedition sank their drill shafts in a deep valley—we believe into the rock underlying the icecap. Our last expedition was sited several hundred kilometers to the west, and at that time we did not have access to the proton-drill technology that the Chinese deployed."

Howard Smalls says silkily, "We are not here to apportion blame. It's possible that life on Mars is localized in only a few reservoirs. Perhaps even only one reservoir. An underground reservoir of liquid water, most likely, kept warm by geothermal heat and insulated by the ice cap. Perhaps it is life's last redoubt on Mars."

"It's a shame my proposal was never taken up," Mariella said. "We could have resolved this years ago."

"You're here because of your proposal, Dr. Anders," Al Paley says. "The point is not that we didn't find life, but that someone did. Say what you like about this crisis, but the fact remains that it is an epochal discovery."

Mariella says, "And yet the Chinese have kept this epochal discovery secret."

Smalls says, "I should remind you that the expedition was not funded by the government of the Chinese Democratic Union, but by a consortium of three companies. In fact, we suspect that all three are part of a single commercial entity that has split itself up to avoid antitrust legislation on its holdings abroad. But financial records in the Democratic Union are hardly transparent, and we can't confirm that."

Al Paley says, "We think the hypothesis of a Martian origin for the slick significant enough to send a microbiology team to Mars, to the same area as the Chinese expedition. I assume you don't object to that, Dr. Anders."

"Of course not. But I would like to know if anyone from the permanent base has been there since this situation arose."

"No. It's only just spring on Mars, and conditions were not ideal. There are localized dust storms around the pole each winter, and temperatures are extremely low. More cogently, there is the risk of contamination by untrained personnel. That is why we want to send three highly trained specialists instead of personnel already emplaced on Mars."

And of course there are other considerations, Mariella thinks. Commercial confidentiality. Profits, kickbacks. She says, "And the slick. What will be done about that while we are away?"

Howard Smalls says, "There's plenty of work being done on it right now. Don't think that we are not concerned. I agree with you that it has the potential to become as serious as the Firstborn Crisis."

"Which makes it even more important that I see those gene sequences," Mariella says.

"At the moment we don't consider it necessary," Penn Brown says. "We are developing an assay based on our sequencing work, and as soon as it is working satisfactorily, you'll be taught how to use it."

Smalls says, "Dr. Paley will have something more to say on this in a moment. I think you'll be satisfied with what he proposes."

Mariella knows that she is being given the runaround, and says stubbornly, "And if the assay doesn't work in the field? We'll need to know everything about it, I think, not just which buttons to press."

Smalls ignores this. He grips either side of the lectern and takes a breath and addresses them all. "So far we have been lucky.

The Chinese do not have the ICAN motor, so they must rely on rocket technology, the kind used by our first three Martian expeditions. They left in August and will arrive in the middle of March next year. A low-energy Hohmann transfer orbit outbound, with a transit time of one hundred eighty days. Our intelligence sources tell us that they'll spend thirty days on Mars, then return using a Venus flyby to slingshot back to Earth, an inbound time of four hundred thirty days. Luckily for us, that happens to coincide with the earliest possible arrival time using the ICAN flight profile, departing at the beginning of January next year. We needed to bring the planned flight schedule only a little forward so that your mission will overlap with that of the Chinese."

Anchee Ye says, "Are we engaged in a spying mission, then?"

"We hope that you can do two things," Howard Smalls says. "First, establish a successful drill site of your own, and retrieve living organisms. And second, wait until the Chinese leave, and then examine their drill site. They will have to leave before you to catch the launch window for the inward bound part of their mission. That's the golden moment of opportunity, and you will have to make sure that you will be in a position to exploit it."

Mariella says, "Suppose they have booby-trapped their site?"

"The complete details of all contingencies will be given to you later on," Smalls says. "Now, I have to draw a line beneath the need for complete and total secrecy. You will all sign documents of nondisclosure, and you will be made aware of the severe penalties for violating those agreements. At present, the crew and the other members of this mission do not know about this aspect of your mission, but they will be told if it is deemed necessary. You will certainly be questioned by them, and of course by members of the press and by your colleagues. The cover story is very close to the truth, that you are part of a definitive search for life on Mars, looking for reservoirs of water beneath lava flows. Dr. Paley here will give you a briefing on the cover story before you leave. If you run into any problems about this please refer to me at once any time, day or night. I'll give you all my card. And please also refer any potential problem to me. Especially if you are approached by someone outside official channels.

"Finally, I'd like to thank you for your immediate dedication to this mission. I hardly need stress its urgency and importance. As scientists, I know you will question the need for secrecy, but believe me, it isn't because anyone in government is anxious to cover their ass. There is a risk that premature revelation of this danger could lead to an adverse public reaction. We all remember the antiscience riots during the Firstborn Crisis. Any reaction at this stage could well be directed at scientists and scientific institutions as much as at the government.

"You are part of a very large ongoing scientific investigation. What you may find on Mars could be the key to the solution, but I won't lie to you it may well be irrelevant. We cannot know for sure until you go there. Finally, I am here to pass on the best wishes of the President. Godspeed, and God bless."

Al Paley announces that they will attend a preliminary medical examination before he briefs them about the cover story, and begins to collect and count the photographs while Smalls comes over to each of them and shakes their hands and gives them each a plastic card with his universal phone number. Mariella holds on to Smalls's hand and says quietly, "I'd like a word in private."

Smalls glances at his antique Rolex. His starched shirt cuffs are fastened with gold and onyx links. He says, "I guess you can spare a couple of minutes from your medical."

"In confidence," Mariella says, maintaining eye contact. "Not with Penn Brown listening in. Just you."

"As you like."

When the others have gone—Penn Brown shooting an appraising look at Mariella—she talks quickly, sketching out her rough estimates of the speed and consequences of the slick's spread.

Smalls listens intently. When she is finished, he says, "I'm glad you're on board, Dr. Anders. You're as formidable as your reputation implies."

"I have to get up to speed on this very quickly. Do my calculations agree with those of the people who have been working on the slick?"

"I'll have to check. May I ask how you arrived at these estimates?"

Mariella is reluctant to give up Maury Richards's name. She says, "There are vectors on the satellite photographs you handed out."

"You did the calculations in your head?"

"Why not?"

It's not exactly a lie.

"Okay. I'm impressed. Just don't say anything about this to any of your other colleagues. In fact, it would be best if you forgot about the slick. You'll be busy enough with your mission training."

"This is how science is, Mr. Smalls. It doesn't work if it is compartmentalized."

Smalls's handsome face is unreadable. He says, "These are exceptional circumstances. And by the way, it's really *Dr.* Smalls. I have a Ph.D. in molecular biology. At one time, I knew more about the *Halobacter* arginine transport gene than anyone else in the world."

"Well, Dr. Smalls, I'd like to know more about the slick. If possible, I'd like to see it."

"I'll be frank with you, Dr. Anders. You're asking the wrong man."

"Who is in charge of the research? The government or Cytex?"

"It's a collaborative effort."

"I want to talk to someone who knows more about it."

"I think you'll be busy enough with this end of the project, Dr. Anders."

"I see."

"Good. Now I'd better leave you to the tender mercies of NASA's medics. You've a long road ahead of you. Do your best."

Wondering whether or not she has earned a black mark, Mariella is led by an intern to the clinic, where she exchanges her suit for gray sweatpants and a white T-shirt. She is put through a heart-lung capacity test on a fixed bicycle. She is given a CAT scan. What seems like half a liter of blood is drawn from a vein in her elbow. Cell scrapings are taken from the inside of her mouth. She has to provide a urine sample. She spends an hour answering questions put to her by an expert system with a motherly synthesized voice; a human doctor gives her a brief physical, tells her that she will have to remove her eyebrow barbell, the wire in her ear, and her nipple and navel rings, but doesn't comment on her coital scratches. In short, it's nothing she hasn't undergone before, when she thought she was going to the Moon. She's sure that there will be worse to come, but after the physical she is released by the medics and, in front of two NASA lawyers, reads through and signs the contracts for the mission.

After a briefing on the mission's cover story, Al Paley takes the three scientists to dinner in what he claims is his favorite down-home restaurant on the NASA side of Houston. It turns out to be a faked-up fishing shack on stilts in the middle of a tourist village of similar reconstructions, built around a pontoon marina just out-side the thirty-kilometer concrete seawall that protects low-lying Houston from storm flooding. A hyperreal fantasy of a piece of Americana that never was, like a set for a production of *Porgy and Bess*. Still, Mariella thinks it is pleasant enough to sit on the res-taurant's long wooden balcony and watch pelicans fly heavily across the darkening sky beyond the tinkling masts of yachts bob-bing at anchor, and wonder at the energy with which Americans constantly recreate their world, an idealized fiction in which every-one collaborates, everything controlled and made safe.

Since they can't talk in public about what has brought them together, there is strained small talk over the huge platters of steaks and shrimp and lobster tails. Penn Brown is withdrawn, almost sulky, as if he suspects that he has overplayed his hand at the briefing but is not quite sure how. Mariella learns a little more about Anchee Ye. She did her thesis work at the UCLA Planetary Science Department, actually overlapping with Mariella's tenure in the Biology Department, although neither remembers meeting the other. She is married, plans to have children when the mission is over. She maintains a quiet reserve, as if operating within a circle she has drawn around herself. The only open enthusiasm she dis-plays is when Mariella asks her about her time on Mars. She was there for a three-month tour, working on isotope ratios in deposits of undifferentiated fossils in ancient lake beds in the tablelands of Deuteronilus Mensae and along the edge of the huge basin of Vastitas Borealis.

"So flat," she says, of the latter. She has a Midwestern twang;

she was born and brought up in Kansas. "Flatter than any place on Earth, but with its own subtle harmony. It took a little while, but at last it opened out to me. I don't know, perhaps I don't describe it very well. You have to be there to understand it, I think."

Brown says, "But you never got to the north pole."

"No. That is why I took this challenge." Anchee Ye adds, with a hint of a smile. "Like you, I think, Dr. Brown, and like Dr. Anders."

"You all have something to bring to this," Al Paley says.

"I like the idea of the revealed harmony of a landscape," Mariella says. "But I suppose you would think it might be some kind of mysticism, Penn."

"I think the problem needs focus, if that's what you mean. I've never said there wasn't a place for your kind of holistic thinking, but it's only useful for integrating sets of data, not attacking specific problems. And I think we can agree that this mission addresses a very specific problem."

"We do not yet know what we address," Anchee Ye says.

"Which is about as far as we can take it, I think," Al Paley says. He changes the subject, tries to interest them in arrangements for the beginning of their training, but the conversation over coffee and dessert, and on the ride back to the Space Center, is full of icy lacunae, the three scientists retreating into their own thoughts.

Arizona Biological Reserve:
October 16, 2026

Mariella sees the balloons as she parks her pickup truck, and says out loud, "Oh shit."

There are at least a hundred of them. All sizes and all of them red. Red balloons tethered from window frames, red balloons hung in an arch around the main entrance of the research building, bobbing and rustling and squeaking in the chill early-morning breeze. A banner is stretched between two windows: WAY TO GO, DR. A.

As she gets out of the pickup, someone driving past toots his horn. One of the cryo team, cheerfully waving.

"Oh shit," she says again. She is beginning to realize just how much her life is going to change. That it is no small thing to have been chosen to go to Mars.

She has already wasted most of the morning in her trailer, answering her email. Even though it was screened by her agent, there was still a lot. It seems that every single one of her former colleagues wants to get back in touch, to offer congratulations, to ask about the kind of work she will be doing. The only really important message is from Maury Richards. He agrees with her ideas about the consequences of the spread of the slick, and mentions the names of three people she might want to contact.

She makes some tea and does some phoning, ends up talking with an admiral, no less: Admiral Crystal Collingwood, the no-nonsense woman in charge of the Navy's oceanographic program. She knows Mariella has been selected for the NASA mission and is sympathetic to her request for more data on the slick.

"But I can't discuss it on an unsecured phone line," Collingwood says. "One of my people will help you set something up, then we'll talk."

It takes Mariella only a few minutes to configure the software Collingwood's aide sends her, but then she has to wait until the admiral is free to talk with her again. She makes more tea, tries and fails to read a paper she's been asked to referee, feels a solid thump of relief when the admiral finally calls back, because by then she's half-convinced herself that the woman wouldn't.

Collingwood listens patiently to Mariella's tirade about the foolishness of sending people to Mars with an incomplete idea of what is happening on Earth, and says, "You have to understand that I can't tell you anything myself. I don't have the authority and you don't have the clearance."

"I know that you can't exceed your authority, but—"

"I'm also covering my own ass, Dr. Anders. I'm very good at that. It's how I got to be an admiral."

"This isn't a sight-seeing expedition. I'd like to talk with the people who are working on the slick. They might have insights they haven't properly assimilated, things they haven't put in their reports because they can't explain them."

"And you think you can?"

"It's what I do for a living. We didn't discover the Moses virus and develop the MT54a gene by partitioning everyone from everyone else."

"That was a fine piece of work, of course, but you were all working in a secure facility then, and certainly didn't talk to the outside world about what you were doing." There is a pause so long that Mariella begins to think that the security software has thrown a glitch. But then Collingwood leans into the camera and says, "Maury Richards recommended you very highly, and I always listen to his advice. What I'll do is this: I'll try and bring you inside. I'll have to send it up the chain, and it might not even come to anything, but I'll do my best."

"I can't ask for anything else."

"I'm glad you're aboard, Dr. Anders."

Mariella takes Twink out for a brief canter along the dry river bed, thinking about Mars and the calculations she made on the flight back from Houston, playing around with worst-case scenarios, stretching the parameters of the NASA data, reminding herself of weather patterns and oceanic currents. The standard models are pretty inaccurate because of instabilities in the Southern Hemisphere caused by Grande Niños and by deflection of currents around the lens of meltwater that floats on top of the coastal Antarctic waters for five months of the year. In turn, these instabilities affect the Northern Hemisphere through the trade winds, where energy is transferred by wind cells pushing back and forth across the equator. And then there is the increase in heat retention caused by greenhouse gases, meaning more energy in the system . . . simple parameters interacting in complex and unpredictable ways.

But all this is no more than an aside to the main question posed by the slick, that of the nature of life on Mars. The slick possesses DNA, and apparently Martian genes can be combined with those from terrestrial organisms, suggesting that Martian life shares its ancestry with life on Earth, that perhaps both evolved from the same universal ancestor. It is possible that something very similar to DNA could have evolved elsewhere in the Galaxy, but it is unlikely that DNA evolved twice on two planets of the same Solar System, and inconceivable that two separate evolutionary paths could have developed the same genetic code. No. Either terrestrial organisms were the ancestors of Martian organisms, or Martians were the ancestors of life on Earth, or both have a common ancestor which arose elsewhere. On or in a moon of Jupiter perhaps, although evidence is still ambiguous about whether or not life once existed or still exists in the salty sub-ice oceans of Europa and Callisto.

In any case, it is clear that life has persisted for billions of years somewhere beneath the freezing, bone-dry deserts of Mars. It leaves Mariella breathless with amazement every time she thinks about it.

People often say that the Arizona desert, with its litter of fractured rock, its crusty soil, its rust-red coloration, resembles the surface of Mars. But there is a big and immediately obvious difference, for there is no life at all in the Martian deserts, and life is everywhere around Mariella as she lets Twink set the pace on the trail home. Creosote bushes, ocotillo, nopal, yucca, mesquite, brittlebrush, paloverde trees, even a few stately saguaros which have managed to survive the bacterial rots caused by increased rainfall. The plants seemingly evenly spaced across the red, rocky ground, winnowed by competition for moisture. It is easy enough to generate convincing distributions by using measurements of rainfall, movement of nutrients through soil, and the moisture requirements and root spread of the different plant species. Mariella has taken the work of ecologists and simplified their calculations into a two-line algorithm that, drawing data for species selected at random, can grow a virtual desert landscape in seconds.

And yet the reality is so much richer. There is a cactus wren, its swift jinking flight tracing low loops between stands of mesquite. Hummingbirds zoom around a flowering ring of creosote bush. Turn over big rocks and discover rattlesnakes or lizards; turn over smaller ones and find scorpions or millipedes or a thousand different kinds of beetle. Ants make little craters in the sandy soil, and the soil itself, although seemingly infertile, teems with life. Each handful contains millions of bacteria, fungi and algae from countless species, and the protozoans, springtails and nematodes that feed on them.

Life everywhere on Earth in blooming buzzing confusion, yet nowhere on the surface of Mars is there any trace of even the most simple forms of life, except for fossils billions of years old. But it seems that people have been looking in the wrong place. It is there after all, deep beneath the ice cap of the north pole, and perhaps all life on Earth is derived from it.

When Mariella returns to her trailer, she finds that Joe Sandeval, the Reserve's director, has called. He wants to talk to her about her trip to Mars, and so she drives down to the Reserve and finds the balloons and the banner. The world won't leave her alone.

"It might be good and it might be bad," Joe Sandeval says, "but in any case you can be sure of my support."

"How could it be bad?"

Sandeval's office is a wide crescent with a sweeping floor-to-ceiling glass wall that juts out above the western end of the tropical ocean biome of Gaia Two, a tank a kilometer long and two hundred meters wide. Mariella and Joe Sandeval are standing at this big window, looking down at water surging in white arcs of foam across purple and brown masses of coral. Sunlight strikes through the hexagonal panes of the roof, glints on the fretwork of pencil-thin construction diamond girders, sparkles on the white-topped waves that roll in over the reef, over the reef, over the reef. Behind them, a robot the size and shape of a horseshoe crab is vacuuming the carpet, unregarded and unregarding.

Sandeval is a short, acidulous man, not a great or even a particularly good scientist, but deft in political maneuvering and juggling of federal, state and scientific interests. He is wearing a lime-green suit and a lemon-yellow shirt slashed open to show the abundance of gray hair on his barrel chest. He dyes the hair on his head jet black, and it is slicked back and teased into long greasy curls weighted with silver beads. He always makes Mariella feel dowdy, a peahen to his peacock. Male display significantly increased after the Y chromosome was so horribly compromised by the Moses virus. She is wearing her usual outfit, a red-plaid shirt, blue jeans and cowboy boots, her fleece-lined denim jacket: a tough desert broad with sun-bleached hair and a lined and deeply tanned face.

Sandeval says, "I got a visit from the state's ecological commissioner in the afternoon. An inspection, he calls it."

"I remember the memo."

"Everyone will have tidied up their labs and put out their research posters, but this guy isn't interested in any of that. As far as he's concerned, this place is a big barrel of pork, and he's come to get a taste. We already have more than a dozen of his nephews and nieces and cousins working here, all with cow shit crusted on the toes of their cowboy boots and all dumb as posts."

Mariella laughs.

Sandeval growls in mock anger, "Yeah, and this guy's found another relative under some desert rock and has promised him a nice federal sinecure. Maybe I can give him your job while you're away."

"I'll still be in and out."

"We'll talk about that later. You think you'll have time, but NASA likes exclusivity. They see you sneaking off, they'll organize a field trip to Antarctica or a ride in, what do they call it?" Sandeval clicks his stubby fingers impatiently. "The Comet. The Vomit Comet."

"They haven't used that for twenty years now. If you need microgravity training they take you straight into low orbit."

"Yeah, or I guess they could just let you ride the East Coast shuttle a few times. So many people barfing around me at the top of the arc, it nearly puts me off my peanuts and bourbon. Anyway. How do you feel about it, Mariella? Excited? Apprehensive?"

Joe Sandeval turns to look at her, emitting a cloud of piny cologne, candid and concerned. His face is jowly and rumpled but he has a vivid, direct manner, redeeming his ugliness with pushy vitality, the sense that he has his thumb on the engine of the world.

Mariella says, "I haven't really thought about it."

"You can tell me. Just this once overcome your fucking English reserve."

"How many times do I have to tell you I'm from Scotland?"

"It's all one little island."

"Anyway, I haven't been back for ten years."

Her mother's funeral. And her father's before that.

Joe Sandeval says, "Maybe so, but you still complain about the way we make tea here. Look, I got to put a good spin on this for when the press come asking about you, so I need to know whatever you can tell me. I know you can't tell me everything, but tell me what you can. Okay?"

"Of course. When I know something I'll tell you."

"I read the piece-of-shit official press release. This isn't just a blind shot, is it? You're going after something they know is there."

Here it is already, only a couple of days after the briefing. The secret pressing to be told. The data are not yet complete, this is what she has to tell herself. The excuse she uses when people come to her for help with a problem, an important piece of work they hope will make their names, and get upset when they realize that she has already worked it out several years before but has never bothered to publish. *The data seemed to be incomplete*, she has learned to say, to appease them.

She remembers what Sandeval said earlier and asks, "Why is this a bad thing?"

"*Maybe* a bad thing. You know how people talk. We fucked up the Earth and we aren't content with that, now we have to go and fuck up the rest of the Universe. And you can't blame them, in some respects. You saw D.C. Dykes, levees, coffer dams, and still the water's rising. They're talking of moving everything inland, like that place in Egypt. Luxor. And the desert here, the cacti rotting, engineer grass growing everywhere, Grande Niños just about every year. You work with those alternative-culture types in their communes, you know what they say. Think they'll be happy you're going to Mars? There are plenty of people like them who'll hate the whole idea. What about Tony May? You told him yet?"

Mariella smiles. She is used to Sandeval's abrupt conversa-

tional shifts. Talking with him is sometimes like being subjected
to a police interrogation in which the same person plays both good
cop and bad cop. "Not yet. I suppose he already knows, like everyone else."

Tony May is her graduate student, the only one she has at the
moment. She tries very hard to put off people who want to work
with her, but Tony May was very persistent, and so far has been
true to his claim that he likes to work on his own.

Joe Sandeval says, "Talk to him. Get things sorted out here
before you go zooming off into the wild blue yonder."

"It isn't for that long. A few months training, but I'll be in and
out, as I said. And then four months for the actual mission."

"And the decontamination. How long do they keep you for
that?"

"The return voyage counts as part of it. There's a week of
medical—"

"It might be a bit longer this time, don't you think? There are
rumors in Washington. I bet you know all about what's behind
them. No, you don't have to tell me. I don't want to know. I
already had the Secret Service on my ass."

"The Secret Service?"

"Sure. Why so surprised? They did a background check a little
while ago. Don't worry, it was nothing. The usual horseshit. You're
clean. Even though you're a limey, no, excuse me, a person of
Scottish descent, you're clean."

"I'm a citizen. And a government employee."

"Yeah, and you go off drumming with those people out in the
desert."

"It's more than—"

"Sure. Ecological consultant. That's what I told the Secret Service. You help people manage low-impact lifestyles, give them advice on recycling their shit. Just like the work you wanted to do
on the Moon."

Mariella smiles. "You actually said that?"

"I thought it wouldn't hurt. Anyway, there are rumors. I hear
them, but I hear a lot of things, and I don't necessarily believe
everything I hear. But now they want to send a team of microbiologists to Mars. What's not to believe any more?"

"What kind of rumors?"

"You don't tell me anything, I don't tell you. Okay? All I have to worry about is putting a good spin on this, and maybe think about beefing up the security a little. Don't worry. The press office will compose a statement they can send out on the wire, about how thrilled we are, et cetera. They'll set up a few interviews, too."

"Interviews?"

Joe Sandeval grins at her dismay. "Sure. Interviews. Local scientist goes to Mars, that kind of thing. Hey, don't worry, it'll be a boost for this place, and it makes me look good too. I was the one pushed to get you away from UCLA. Do good science, that's all I ask."

The last time Sandeval did any scientific work was five years ago, on a cruise around the Galapagos Islands. When he returned, he was as thrilled as a little boy who'd just been to Disney World, but the specimens he brought back are still unanalyzed, the paper unwritten.

Mariella says, "I'm not sure about interviews—"

"What's not to be sure of? Five minutes, a bit of personal background, something for the tail end of the local news. The press office'll brief you." Sandeval looks down at the ocean tank again. "I hate my office. I sit over in the far corner most of the time, anywhere else the fucking tourists can gawp up at me. But I have to be visible. It's part of the job. You have all that waiting for you."

When Mariella goes to the canteen for lunch, there is a dip in the usual din of clatter and chatter, then in widening circles people stand and applaud. Someone calls loudly for a speech. Mariella blushes and holds up her hands in surrender and shakes her head, but others take up the call and she says the first thing that comes into her head, "I didn't realize how far I had to go to get noticed around here," and to her relief people laugh and clap and resume their seats and their conversations.

Mariella grabs a sandwich and settles down in a corner, but almost immediately the press officer calls and begins to ask impertinent questions about her career. "It's just background material," he says when she bridles. "I have some of it on file, but it's best if I get it right for the press release."

"No interviews," Mariella says.

"Joe told me to set them up."

"How many?"

"One tomorrow, Dr. Anders, and two Friday. So far just the local TV stations."

"Okay. But no more."

"That isn't—"

Mariella cuts him off, asks the slate to process all calls through the agent it has modeled on her own personality, dumps her half-eaten lunch in the recycling bin, and goes off to find her research student.

Tony May takes the news with his usual equanimity. He is very tall and intensely serious, black hair caught in an untidy ponytail with rubber bands, an indoor pallor. He is more interested in showing her his latest work than the possibility that she might be going to Mars. She listens, makes some suggestions for which he seems grateful.

They are sitting at his metal-framed desk in a corner of the basement room that holds Hell Prime, a stainless steel bomb the size of an old-fashioned furnace which squats beneath a tangle of pipes and cables. Inside, turbines force water pressurized at two hundred atmospheres through mineral matrices heated to three hundred and fifty degrees Centigrade, simulating the cycling of seawater through a deep-sea hydrothermal vent. The green-painted walls of the basement sweat. Printouts of Little Iva cartoon strips (Little Iva Meets the Giant Squids! Little Iva and the Psychedelic Surfers vs. Dr. Sewage and his Effluent Torpedo) curl at the edges. The air-conditioned chill smells of seawater; every surface is damply gritty.

Visiting Hell Prime always makes Mariella a little nostalgic, for she started her research career working on one of the first artificial vent communities in another basement room, at the New Cavendish Institute in Cambridge.

Even before she arrived at Cambridge, Mariella knew that the majority of scientific advance was due to dogged accumulation of facts, to reducing problems to their component parts, rather than by sudden insight. She knew that flashes of inspiration were so rare that they acquired legendary status. And she knew that most scientists were as narrowly specialized as tropical beetles able to live only in one kind of rainforest vine. But it was frustrating to be confronted with this every day, and the research project she had been assigned was not especially intellectually engaging.

Although she was using molecular biological techniques to track genetic exchange in the microbial communities of hydrothermal vents, it was essentially a descriptive approach dating back to the era of gentlemen naturalists, butterfly nets, camphorated killing bottles, quill pens, and hand-colored illustrations. She soon realized that she should have expected this. Research students were not given groundbreaking work, but problems designed to confirm the cherished hypotheses of their supervisors. Mariella's was a time-honored apprenticeship, and she hated it. Anyone with sufficient training could churn out the results. Even when her thesis was completed, it might not lead to anything more exciting.

Mariella knew too that she lacked both the natural talent and the dogged application to perfect the necessary black arts of DNA extraction, gel running, Southern blots, electrophoresis, and all the rest. She trained herself to be competent, but she was soon spending much of her time wandering around the Institute, asking the other postgraduates about their research, helping to solve their problems and learning a battery of useful techniques in the process. It was not that she had a short attention span, but she did lack patience. If she couldn't crack a problem quickly, she'd put it in the back of her mind and move on to something else. Usually, the recalcitrant solution would present itself a little later, as if by courtesy of some calculating demon living in her head.

Her impatience and her refusal to specialize prompted her supervisor, David Davies, to suggest that perhaps she wasn't cut out for the painstaking benchwork required by biological research. Davies had spent fifteen years working out how to maintain a black smoker community in a pressure vessel; it had earned him his fellowship of the Royal Society, and his popular book on the subject had won him the Aventis prize and a seemingly endless series of media appearances, for he unwittingly fulfilled the popular image of a scientist. He was a perpetually untidy man, with dark eyes and shaggy eyebrows, his hair cut short to disguise incipient baldness, his jeans unpressed, his gaudy sweaters full of holes. There always seemed to be the whiff of sulphur around him, the anaerobic breath of his artificial hydrothermal vent, although administration and teaching duties meant that he had less and less time for laboratory work. He paid formal visits to the lab each Monday morning in a starched white coat, its collar endearingly askew and pens in a snaggled row in the top pocket, and found an hour each Friday to treat his students and postdocs to a pint in the Eagle. The very same pub into which Francis Crick had breathlessly burst one March day in 1953 to announce to his colleague, James Watson, that he had solved the last part of the problem on which they had been working. That they had discovered the structure of DNA. That they had cracked the secret of life. Despite a recent restoration, the Eagle was still the same network of dark, cozy cave-like rooms full of black, heavily varnished furniture; the ceiling of the Air Force bar still bore the numbers of squadrons traced in candlesmoke by Second World War aircrews. Mariella always sat at the edge of the group, usually distracted by someone else's research problem, sipping her vodka and tonic whenever she remembered it.

She was where she wanted to be. Her father had pulled strings to get her there. She had made it to the New Cavendish Institute, one of the last bastions of pure biological research in the country, where a replica of Watson and Crick's original model of DNA's double helix, endearingly lashed up from retort stands, wire, and cardboard, stood in a glass case in the foyer, where a clutch of Nobel laureates lurked like carp in a deep, still pond. Unlike most of the other science labs in Cambridge, the Institute was free of corporate logos and secure labs, although much of the research was commercially sponsored. David Davies's work on the biology of deep-sea hydrothermal vents was funded by several deep-sea mining companies, for instance, including the one for which Mariella's father worked.

And yet she was not happy. Her own research was not going well, and she found Cambridge to be a depressing place, especially in winter, with low clouds and cutting winds blowing straight from Siberia, and the gray, intricately carved fronts of the colleges hunkered against driving rain like so many fossilized reefs. Winter seemed to last even longer in Cambridge than in Scotland, and although it was only an hour's train ride from London, the small town seemed hundreds of kilometers from anywhere, its long history reduced to touristy quaintness, its provincialism stifling, its customs pointless, its narrow streets crowded with raucous, overfed arts and politics undergraduates who disdainfully labeled anyone who had anything to do with science a "Northern Chemist," the willfully ignorant heirs of leaders who had let Britain become in the twenty-first century a kind of heritage park peddling its own past, proud of its irrational bans on genetic engineering and AI, and the censorship laws that regulated Internet traffic. At night, in her attic room in college, alternately stuffily overheated (when the power was on) or freezing (when it wasn't), listening to the wind dashing rain against the window, Mariella could imagine that Cambridge was being driven across the flooded fens to meet the incoming sea, with the rest of civilization foundering far behind, as in the ecological-disaster soap opera that was currently so popular.

That first winter, she got her first piercings—a couple of rings in the rim of her left ear, a ring in her navel—and a tattoo of interlaced thorns around her ankle. The pain sanctified her unhappiness.

As well as the continuing disappointment of discovering that research wasn't as exciting or intellectually engaging as she had imagined it would be, she was beginning to learn that in science work was not enough. Pedigree was just as important. The whole course of your scientific career could be shaped by the work and reputation of your supervisor. Not only were you working on a problem he had defined for you, but you were expected to agree with his intellectual position; if his hypotheses turned out to be wrong, your own career would be seriously damaged. And even when you had won your Ph.D., he would be instrumental in obtaining your first postdoctoral position. Mariella had known something about this already—she'd known enough to push for the New Cavendish Institute when her father had wanted her to do something practical at Edinburgh or Glasgow—but she was beginning to realize how limited her father's influence was, that David Davies was a good scientist but not an exceptional one. His best work had been done years ago, and it was a technical rather than an intellectual achievement.

But she could hardly explain any of this to David Davies, and when, at the end of her first year, he asked her if she was happy, she shrugged and said sure, why not.

"Well, I suppose you've made adequate progress, despite the, let's call them diversions, shall we?"

Mariella smiled. She'd discovered that when you were a woman talking to a man, a smile was often enough to defuse any awkward questions. On the other side of the cluttered desk, Davies took a long drag on his cigarette. It was a Camel, a made-in-America Camel, the kind that didn't give you cancer, the kind that was illegal in Britain but which could be bought in most pubs if you knew who to ask (if talk of a complete ban on cigarettes in America was true, Davies would have to revert to carcinogenic Third World brands or give up). He kept the window of his room open. He was a considerate man. A cold wind was stripping yellow leaves from the sycamore outside. It blew through the open window and ruffled the stacks of reprints piled everywhere, weighted down with books or beach pebbles. Mariella waited patiently, thinking about a vector analysis problem on which one of the postdocs in the enzyme lab was stalled.

Davies exhaled a riffle of smoke, looked at it with satisfaction, and said, "You came here with a reputation, Mariella, of being something of a whiz kid. Frankly, I wouldn't have taken you on if your father hadn't assured me you were mature beyond your years."

"I'm used to being the youngest," Mariella said.

"Yes, but you're so much younger than anyone else here. I know that can be a strain. We're used to prodigies at Cambridge, although usually in math or computing. Great talents, of course, but sometimes, well, they need special attention. Biologists, on the other hand, usually take a while to mature, like good wines. There's no room for impatience in biology."

He was giving her a chance to confess, in his kindly roundabout fashion. He was giving her a way out.

She said, "Biology is what I like to do."

"As long as it doesn't bore you."

She smiled. She said, "I have plenty to do."

She could see the wiggle of the enzyme-reaction vectors in her head, like the thrashing tails of spermatozoa. As if she was down among the protein chains, watching as they grabbed one reactant and changed conformation so they could grab the other. A very slight change, but yes, with a lower potential energy than the resting state, which was why the reaction tended to go in *that* direction, a big mess of stuff going around this corner. Her fingers were drumming on the arms of her chair, tapping out rhythms that corresponded to the ratios of the most likely vectors. She saw that Davies was looking at her, and then realized what she was doing.

"Patience," Davies said, and forcefully stubbed out his cigarette in a scallop shell ashtray, the signal that the interview was at an end. "Cultivate patience, and the rest will come easily enough."

But that wasn't really it, because there wasn't enough time to find out everything she needed to know. Nature seemed bottomless. Mariella couldn't concentrate on her own little corner of it. She had to keep asking questions, driven by the same kind of pressing impatience she'd felt when trying to catalog all the beetles she'd caught in light traps in the garden of the house in Mexico.

She was bored by the research project she had been given, but there were plenty of other things to engage her. People came to her with intractable problems, and she helped to solve them and asked questions in turn. She was impatient with compartmentalization, which left people toiling away in self-created cells like so many worker larvae in the brood comb of a beehive.

She became known as the woman who fixed things. She explained her vector analysis to the enzymologist, translating her intuition into numbers. Mathematics formalized the way she grasped the physicality of the problem, but it was harder to explain how she got there because the process broke down if she looked too hard at it. Curious about how other minds worked, she read biographies of the most prominent twentieth-century scientists, and discovered that most of them used the same intuitive process. Einstein's best work was over once he could no longer visualize the problems and was reduced to pushing equations around; Feynman beat out rhythms, and even rolled around on the floor, his mind extending into his every muscle, literally wrestling with problems. After she read about Feynman, Mariella self-consciously cultivated her habit of drumming as a way of freeing up her thoughts.

Soon after her interview with David Davies, Mariella started to ask people what they thought were the fundamental unanswered questions in biology. She brought it up in conversation in the coffee room or in the canteen, buttonholed people in laboratories, in offices. One day, she got up her courage to ask the Institute's newest Nobel laureate, Professor Naval Roy.

"I thought you were the young lady who *answered* questions," he said, twinkling at her. He was a large man with a comfortable belly swelling the front of his white shirt, on which he now folded his hands. His ID was hung around his neck on a loop of red ribbon; it was a maximum-security day at the Institute. Guards armed with tasers were walking the corridors, a dozen police officers were at the gate, confronting a carnival group of protesters in chimeric animal costumes, and the garlicky tang of CS gas was in the air. Mariella had gotten into trouble at the gate. She had stopped to congratulate one of the protestors on the underlying truth of his costume, half seal, half penguin, for after all, didn't seals and penguins share almost eighty percent of their genes? The boy had thrust a leaflet toward her, but she had refused to take it, remembering the warnings about paper impregnated with topical hallucinogens or surfactant vomitants, and a moment later was bundled inside by an angry cop.

Naval Roy had come to Britain as a refugee from Idi Amin's Uganda. He had won the Nobel prize for medicine three years ago, for his work on protein folding, and seemed to fulfill the old and mostly untrue canard that creative life ended after the award ceremony. The fact was that for many laureates it had already ended long before the fame attendant with winning the prize began to make long inroads on the time and energy required for active research. Even before he had been awarded the prize, Roy had become sidetracked into computer modeling of the endless nested loops of ecological interactions, but had published very little. His office, no bigger than any other in the New Cavendish Institute, was spartan. No photographs or keepsakes, none of the clutter associated with active research, just a few books leaning against each other on otherwise empty shelves, and a computer with a huge flat-screen monitor, like a window onto an artificial grassland where a herd of things like aluminium-skinned balloons bobbed and weaved.

Mariella said, in the boldly blunt way she had cultivated, "I'm wondering what to do when I finish here."

"You're very young, and less than halfway through a Ph.D. You have a long career ahead of you. My advice is to work on the problem you have until you discover a new one. Since there are plenty of problems, there's a very high probability that you'll find one that engages your interest and your talent."

Mariella knew that she was being politely fobbed off. She said, "Why do they float?"

Roy glanced at the screen. "They have symbiotic bacteria that generate hydrogen from methane produced by cellulose digestion."

"I suppose it's a nice fantasy, but no real animals float."

"Many do. All bony fish, to begin with, have swim bladders."

"Land animals, I mean. Oh, I suppose except spiders, when they deploy parachute threads. But what I mean is that it isn't real, is it? It's a game."

"It is based on rules derived from the real world. And it has its own reality. It is a game that plays itself. These balloon creatures were not designed. They evolved."

"I don't think that artificial reality is very interesting," Mariella said, and opened her little notebook and clicked her pen as if to write something.

"Perhaps I might agree with you," Roy said, and smiled. "You are as tricky as your reputation. Sit down. Let me tell you something."

She sat down. They talked for half an hour. He told her that winning the Nobel prize had changed everything for him. All organisms are changed by experience, and the experience of becoming a Nobel laureate was a very great change indeed. People were no longer interested in his ideas; they were interested in him, or rather, in their idea of him.

The thing he tried to remember was that personality did not matter, only truth. The most wicked man in the world could create the purest, most powerful synthesis, and all his crimes and corruptions would not make it any less true. Nor was truth diminished if it contradicted the prevailing consensus, for truth was an absolute. The world was as it was, no more, no less. The fact that most people unquestioningly accepted a particular hypothesis did not make it correct, and science thrived only when ideas were vigorously debated and tested, when there were people willing to divert their careers into areas that might yield no reward. If your theory contradicted the ideas of ninety-nine percent of your colleagues, then there was only a small chance that it was correct, but that did not mean that it might not be correct.

Mariella listened. She said, "I think that could be modeled."

"It's a trivial algorithm in artificial ecological systems," Roy said. "It describes how certain top predators balance the requirement to chase prey and the need to conserve energy."

Mariella remembered a jaguar she had once seen on a Venezuelan riverbank. She smiled.

Roy said, "Do you still want me to answer your question?"

Mariella closed her notebook. She said, "I think you've given me a kind of meta answer."

She thought she saw a way in which her assigned work on mobile genes could be made not only interesting, but important. She should not try and solve the particular question it addressed, but the general class of questions of which it was a member. Within a month, she started to develop a new way of analyzing genetic diversity, applying it not only to her own problem, but to others in Davies's laboratory as well. Six months later, with five papers in press, she was awarded her Ph.D. and had won a NATO scholarship. She had been at the Institute for less than two years. She was just twenty. She was going to America.

She saw Naval Roy a few days before she returned to Aberdeen. They had become friends. She'd wanted to list him as a coauthor on her first paper, but he had politely demurred, saying that he had done nothing to deserve it (later, she realized just how polite he had been, and just how presumptuous she must have seemed, postgraduate trying to co-opt the imprimatur of a Nobel laureate, although the sentiment had been genuine). On the day she left, he said that he would answer her question now.

She had forgotten her survey, and blushed to be reminded of it.

"You once asked about fundamental questions that remain unanswered," Roy said. "I will give you a question that is one of the most fundamental in biology. One that can never be fully resolved, but one on which someone like you could perhaps make useful headway. It is this: what was the origin of life on Earth?"

It is a question that has settled into the center of Mariella's career. At the Arizona Biological Reserve she has come full circle. Tony May is analyzing the genomes of archaebacterial species that inhabit the hot, anaerobic waters of hydrothermal vents and deep rocks, looking for highly conserved genes that may have belonged to the universal ancestor of all life on Earth. So far he has discovered three strong candidates; it is almost time for him to write his first paper. They talk about this. For that little while, Mariella feels a reassuring normalcy.

But when at the end of the day she returns to her office, a woman gets up from the couch by the battered vending machine at the end of the corridor and calls her name.

"Dr. Anders? I hope you don't mind the imposition, but I have a few questions for you."

"Who are you? And why don't you have a badge?"

The woman sticks out a hand. She is short and dark complexioned, black bangs framing a plump, olive-skinned face, her clothes expensive but casual, a heavy canvas bag slung from one shoulder. Her smile deepens dimples on either side of her rosebud mouth, and she says, "Clarice Bushor." She has a throaty, downhome Southern accent. Mariella looks at her hand but doesn't take it. The woman drops it to the top of her bag and says, "From the Bushor Report."

"I don't know it. And you didn't answer my question. How did you get in here?"

"This is a government facility. Surely its research should be open to free and fair investigation."

"That depends on what you're investigating."

"You're going to Mars. What do you plan to do there?"

"Did the press office send you down?"

The woman's smile doesn't waver. The fingers of her be-ringed left hand are making shapes against her skirt. She says, "We're not part of the official media, Dr. Anders. We're interested in the truth behind the truth. For instance, what does Mars have to do with a secret research program in the Pacific Ocean?"

Mariella realizes that the woman's fingers are tapping out some kind of thumbcode. She says, "You're wired up. You're recording this right now." Looking for the camera drone, which is hanging beneath one of the light fixtures: a thistledown-light shell of blown epoxy like a palm-size black flying saucer, mostly a fan motor and a gyroscope.

Clarice Bushor says, "You don't deny there's a secret research program?"

Mariella sees the janitor wheel his cart out of the service elevator at the far end of the corridor. She calculates a vector and starts to walk.

Clarice Bushor has to trot to keep up, her heels clicking on red tiles. She says, "The Bushor Report investigates all aspects of environmental science. It's interested in why NASA suddenly feels it has to send a microbiologist to Mars. The implications—"

Mariella accelerates, suddenly outpacing the woman, wedges through the door of the service elevator just as it slides shut, and punches the bottommost button on the panel. Her heart rate is slightly accelerated and she is a little dizzy but otherwise she feels fine. More than fine even. Adrenal glands pumped up, capillaries dilated, slight carbon dioxide excess. And she is grinning like a loon. She takes a deep breath, another. Why did she flee? Because there was a threat she intuited at some nonverbal level? Or simply because Clarice Bushor was the last straw in a thoroughly exasperating day?

Mariella rides the elevator down to the subbasement, follows a long corridor to its end, slow robot trolleys and carts stopping and beeping and moving aside for her, and walks out into the public part of Gaia Two, mingling with the tourists who have come to visit what Penn Brown slightingly calls the zoo. Of course, the Biological Reserve is very much more than the plants and animals exhibited in the self-regulating biomes, but in truth it's these that the tourists mostly come to see, especially the re-creations of extinct species, pygmy mammoths, dodos and sway-necks, dire wolves and sabretooths, patched from DNA sequences taken from close relatives and fossilized material, raised to term in cow wombs, in ostrich and crocodile eggs.

Mariella has come out in the dark, humid tunnel alongside the tropical ocean biome, and threads her way through the tourists who clump at the brightly lit underwater windows. Couples, families, a high proportion of snowbirds, a noisy party of fifth-graders, only one little boy among all the little girls, tended by a couple of weary teachers. Tourists aim cameras through sweating glass at schools of brightly colored reef fish turning and turning above purple and brown pillows and shelves and fans, at foureye butterfly fish fastidiously working the crevices of the reef's pavement, the gaping mouth and cold eye of a moray lurking beneath an over-hang, a nurse shark patrolling the reef edge in the blue distance.

There are no red-jacketed guides about; the formal tours have ended for the day. Mariella is looking for a security phone when she hears her name called and sees Clarice Bushor pushing through knots of tourists with businesslike determination.

A service door recognizes Mariella's implanted chip and opens at her touch. She steps into hot light, salty humidity, and the roar of pumps and fans. The door locks behind her with a reassuring click. Stretching away beneath brilliant lamps simulating tropical sunlight are waist-high tables filled with shallow, pea-green water: the dense blooms of algae that act as the reef's kidneys, filtering out ammonia and other toxins, adding oxygen. Saltwater pours into a huge concrete tank, percolating through bacteria-rich sand at the bottom. Electric pumps vibrate the harshly bright air, their hum punctuated by the periodic thump of the tide surge simulator.

Mariella walks between the filter tables, opens another service door and comes out in the middle of the rainforest biome, between a tall fold of rock and the buttress roots of some soaring, liana-draped tree. She climbs a ladder to the plank-floored ropeway and a few minutes later is at the security desk beyond the Reserve's shop at the end of the tourist loop.

The security guard is very young and very overweight, with a maddeningly placid manner. Chewing, like a cow at cud, something green and liquidly rubbery. His ruddy complexion is enlivened by volcanoes and craters of ripe acne; a prodigious stomach strains the buttons of his sand-colored shirt. The nails of his pinkies are so long they have twisted into corkscrews, and are painted with something that keeps changing color. His name tag proclaims to anyone who cares that he is Ralph. A true twenty-first-century American, a myopic snack-fed creature of malls and TV's hypnagogic light.

Ralph doesn't seem to understand Mariella's problem, and is reluctant to leave his wraparound desk. His glance keeps straying to a bank of TV screens, and to one in particular, which is showing a soccer game. Mariella reaches over and switches it off and tells him again, "Someone got herself into the research building without a pass. She followed me into Gaia Two, and she's probably still in there. Why don't you use those cameras and look for her?"

"She was, what did you say? A reporter?"

"She said she was a reporter. A short woman, well dressed, black hair, olive skin. Maybe you could go look for her."

"I guess we can get the computer to do that," Ralph says, and pulls a keyboard onto his ample lap and looks at Mariella expectantly.

Mariella sighs and describes Clarice Bushor again. The young man hunts and pecks, breathing heavily through his mouth and angling his long-nailed little fingers out with a curious delicacy, like a dowager holding a cup of tea.

"Okay," he says, "anyone looks like that, the computer'll pick them out. But if she's in the walkways like you said, they'll be closing in twenty minutes."

"She found me again on the tropical ocean walkway, but before that she was in the research building. So my thought is that she could be anywhere. Aren't you supposed to keep a watch for intruders?"

"Well, I'll tell you, we don't get too many of those. Mainly folks who've somehow managed to get themselves lost. What do you want with this woman, anyhow?"

"I don't want anything to do with her, but I imagine your boss might want to ask her how she got into the research building without a pass. Ask the grown-up security guards to look for her, Ralph, and then you can escort me to my jeep. In case she's waiting for me in the parking lot."

The fat boy smiles slyly. "Well, I can't leave the desk, Professor. But I'll put in a call if you're worried, and someone will be over directly."

Mariella has to wait ten minutes until another rent-a-cop arrives, an older man who, when he comes through the sliding doors, takes off his billed cap to reveal a horseshoe of baldness pushing into his sandy hair. He looks as if he might know how to use the pistol holstered at his hip, although Mariella suspects that his air of amiable authority is not earned but has been borrowed from some movie, a Hollywood behavioral meme out of Eastwood Wayne. JIMMY DEAN is printed white on black on his name tag. Isn't that the name of another old movie star? As he walks Mariella to her jeep, he says that they lately haven't had much trouble with what he calls kooks.

"We got these new critters out along the perimeter. Look a bit like crabs, if crabs were made out of stone. They mostly sit tight, but they go like gangbusters if someone breaches the perimeter. They spray stickyfoam, fire taser threads, in a real bad situation gang up and release riot gas. About ten thousand of them out there, give any bad boys considerable pause for thought."

"That's fine, but this woman walked in like any tourist, and somehow got into the research building. Which is very definitely a restricted area."

"She was carrying a gun or a bomb or even a knife, the detectors would have shown it," Jimmy Dean says. "Everyone goes through the detectors, even you and me. Don't you think she might have been what she claimed to be, a reporter just a mite overeager about getting her job done?"

Mariella has to admit to herself that it may be true. The way she almost collapsed in girlish giggles in the service elevator suggests that she did not take Clarice Bushor as seriously then as she does now. Like many scientists in the public eye, she receives her share of mail from nuts who by algebraic juggling or startling leaps of associational logic claim to have proven (although their "proofs" aren't proofs based on the rigid doctrines of falsification of hypotheses by observation and experiment; they are irrefutable assertions) that *Homo sapiens* evolved not from a common ancestor shared with apes but from Venusians, or that the genetic code holds some cosmic truth or predicts the future or hides the instructions to create angels or demons or a race of supermen, or that the Earth was indeed created in 4004 B.C. as Bishop Usher calculated from biblical genealogy, and that evolution has been directed by God, slowing like a child's wagon after that initial divine push to its present state of inertia. Like the authors of these cris de coeur, the woman, Clarice Bushor, seemed to want to include Mariella in some hermetic conspiracy, and perhaps Jimmy Dean is right, perhaps the whole silly episode is no more significant than crank mail.

Jimmy Dean says, "This here's your pickup? You take care, Dr. Anders. Folks will be getting interested in you, I guess, all the way to Mars."

On the drive back to Oracle, Mariella realizes that she keeps checking the rearview mirror. It is getting dark, the lights of Tucson glimmering off to the south. Broken glass and crumpled cans flash in her headlights all along the shoulder of the road. Every stop sign at the intersections with unmade desert tracks is peppered with bullet holes. The skeletons of saguaro cacti spin past like imploring giants, knee-high in engineer grass. Mariella starts thinking about the implications of reduced planktonic emissions of dimethyl sulphide, and forgets about Clarice Bushor.

Mariella flies out to Hawaii on a commercial scramjet. Its suborbital lob outruns the sun; when she lands at Honolulu International Airport it is just before dawn. Maury Richards is waiting for her, a bear of a man in baggy shorts and a ragged T-shirt, standing like a stranded mariner amid the tide of businesspeople and tourists. White hair tangles around his weather-tanned, wrinkled face. The silver scar of an old shark bite circles his right thigh. He embraces Mariella, says with mock gruffness, "How you been, Anders?"

"Thanks for getting me here."

"You know why we're here? We're here because Cytex is trying to take over the whole operation and the Navy wants to assert its scientific credibility. Cytex wants a piece, NASA wants a piece, and the Navy wants a piece too. Besides, what's to thank? I've been after an eyeball of the slick ever since I got involved. Somehow, your name unbent Crystal Collingwood. My question is, what does this have to do with your trip to Mars?"

They are walking past the ticket desks, the shopping arcade. Departing tourists are checking piles of luggage and boxes of pineapples.

Mariella says, "You know I can't answer that, Maury."

"Come on, Anders. You can let slip a little hint."

"I don't like having secrets, but I also want to keep my place on the mission."

"I hope this doesn't hurt it."

"NASA doesn't know about it yet." Although she was careful to tell Senator Thornton. Or at least, leave a message with her chief of staff.

Maury Richards looks at her gravely. "You got balls, Anders."

She grins. It's hard not to be flirtatious with Maury. She says,

"I guess I'm supposed to take that as a compliment."

Maury has a card that opens a door into the service corridors, opens another which lets them out into hot wind and sun. Carts loaded with luggage follow yellow arrows toward scramjets which nuzzle up to the jetways of the terminal like immense patient animals at their stalls, venting white vapors as they are topped up from stainless steel tankers of hydrazine.

Maury pushes elflocks of white hair from a forehead scarred by the surgical removal of benign skin tumors, squints off across aprons of sun-whitened concrete and strips of seared brown grass. A Navy helicopter is coming in from the west. He points at it and says, "Here's our ride."

The helicopter takes them on a ten-minute hop over the blue waters of Pearl Harbor, where boats packed with Japanese tourists videoing grandpa's or great-grandpa's handiwork circle the gray skeletal tower of the sunken *Arizona*, to the Quonset hut hangars and runways of Barbers Point Naval Air Force Station. After Mariella's second breakfast of the day, she and Maury are fitted with bright-orange survival suits, and a gruff chief petty officer gives them a brief but graphic coaching session about what to do in case of what he calls a wet landing. And then they fly out in a big, long-range Sirocco helicopter to the site of the slick, a thousand kilometers southwest of the island chain.

The Sirocco is noisy and cold and its cabin is spartan, thinly padded seats facing backward and bolted to the steel plates of the floor. The toilet is a tall stainless-steel bucket behind a flimsy curtain which has been duct-taped to fretted struts as a courtesy to the two civilian passengers. Mariella huddles with Maury, poring over data on carbon exchange and the growth rate of the slick, trying to refine and simplify their model. They are still working when the pilot's voice comes over the intercom and says dryly, "There she blows."

Mariella and Maury squint through the port, bumping helmets like excited children at a keyhole. The helicopter is making a wide turn as it drops toward deep blue water that in early morning sunlight sparkles out to the horizon in every direction, and as it continues to turn they suddenly see the slick, an oil stain stretching out toward the joint of blue water and blue sky. Its boundary is irregular, bays and peninsulas and archipelagoes as fractal as any coastline. A kilometer beyond its eastern boundary the research ship, white against the blue ocean, rides beside a grid of orange containment ponds.

Mariella says, "Gosh. Look at it. It's bigger than I thought."

"And still growing," Maury says, his grin framed by his beard and his helmet. "About a hundred square kilometers now. Isn't this something?"

Maury wants the pilot to circle above the slick, but apparently overflights are strictly forbidden. When Maury presses the matter, the pilot says, "I'm sorry, sir, but we can't. If we went down, no one could come in to rescue us."

"Is the slick more dangerous than we've been told?"

"Standing orders, Dr. Richards. I guess because of the contamination factor."

"That thing is growing out in open air. There is already contamination."

Mariella touches Maury's shoulder and he switches off the intercom and leans close to hear what she shouts above the roar of the helicopter's turbines. "Do you think this is the only place it's growing!"

"Unlikely!"

"Yes! I think so too!"

The Sirocco beats down toward the research vessel's landing pad, lands with a single heavy bounce. When the turbines of the four tilt-rotors cut, Mariella realizes just how loud they were. Their roar has gone bone deep. It is with her all through the rest of the tour.

The day officer offers Mariella and Maury breakfast. They eat doughnuts and drink black, sweet coffee in the wardroom of the ship, and then are given a tour of the laboratory facilities by the chief scientist, Jenny Kaplan. The Cytex representative, Bob Eckart, tags along anxiously.

Jenny Kaplan is a small, energetic, deeply suntanned woman about Mariella's age, her vigorous sandy hair barely contained by her long-billed baseball cap. She has been on station for more than a month, and is eager to show off her team's work. She has a proud, proprietorial attitude toward the slick, as if it is in some way her own child, wayward and strange and menacing, yet also profoundly wonderful.

Well, it is all that and more, Mariella thinks, although her first close-up sight of it is disappointing. A Class Four Mobile Biological Containment Facility has been welded to the upper deck of the research ship, a white-painted steel pod ten meters long and three meters in diameter, the Cytex test tube-and-double helix logo blazoned in red down its length. There's a disinfectant shower outside its airlock. Workers in white body suits with umbilical cords connecting them to a central air supply can be dimly seen through its thick glass bulls-eye ports, like fish in an aquarium. Bob Eckart makes a big deal of the cost to Cytex of providing this facility; when he's finished, Jenny Kaplan leads them to a bank of TV monitors under an awning. She snaps one on with a flourish and says, "I think this is what you came here to see."

Maury says, "What is this? We can't go inside?"

"That would compromise lab integrity," Bob Eckart says. He's a young, neatly groomed man in a denim suit. A long thin pigtail braided with little colored ribbons is draped over one shoulder. His manner is smooth and plausible, and Mariella doesn't trust him at all.

"He means it's Cytex territory," Kaplan says with a brightness that's palpably brittle, "but we can at least take a look."

The monitor shows a glass crystallizing dish with what looks like dirty detergent bubbles clustered in it. Kaplan lifts up a handset and says, "Put it under the scope, Tony."

A gloved hand picks up the dish and the view switches to the stage of a low-power binocular microscope, suddenly occluded by the dish. The focus sharpens, shows bubbles slopping and swirling in the water, bright highlights gleaming. They look a little like colonial volvox algae, or soccer balls exquisitely fashioned out of blown glass and bits of diamond. The walls are mostly transparent. Internal strands and nodules glimmer with fugitive colors.

Maury says, "Is it all like this?"

Kaplan shakes her head vigorously. "Not at all. This is the most complex form, but there are plenty of others. Streamers, mats, plain old slicks. It's always changing."

"I wasn't told about that," Maury says, staring at the screen. "How many organisms are we dealing with here?"

"That's the beauty of it," Jenny Kaplan says, smiling brightly. "There isn't anything you can define as a single organism or species because it is always in flux. And it's all connected, a single cytoplasmic continuum. I don't like to make analogies because this is so different from anything else, but it's something like a primitive fungus. A single cytoplasmic mass spread through millions and millions of threads and bubbles."

Maury says, "So it's what? Colonial?"

Bob Eckart says, "I'm not sure if you should answer that, Jenny."

"I'm not asking for the sequencing data," Maury says. "I just want to know a little bit about the way it works."

"Hey now," Eckart says. "This compartmentalization isn't Cytex policy. We're doing contracted work, just like you guys. It's government policy. Navy policy. It's a matter of security."

"That's good," Maury says, "because we have clearance from the Navy oceanographic office to be here. You've been working on this for more than a month, Kaplan. I assume that you have established some basic facts about the organism. Perhaps you can enlighten us. Is it colonial?"

Jenny Kaplan says, "In a sense, yes. But that implies a division into cell types that really doesn't apply here. I'll show you. Tony, will you turn up the UV?"

"Hey now," Eckart says again, and switches off the TV monitor. He stands in front of it and smiles at them all and says, "Look, I'm sorry, but this isn't on the schedule."

Maury looms over him and says gruffly, "I didn't come out here for coffee and doughnuts."

Jenny Kaplan says, "I'll take you out to one of the ponds and show you how the slick behaves. That's the easiest way."

"I don't know if that's a good idea," Eckart says.

Jenny Kaplan says, "What's the problem, Bob? We go out every day for sampling."

Mariella says, "I must see it," and Maury, staring hard at Eckart, says, "Now that we're here, we should take a look at everything."

Eckart flinches under Maury's gaze. He tells Jenny Kaplan, "You cannot be serious about this. I'll have to talk with the captain."

Jenny Kaplan shrugs. "Go ahead. It won't make any difference. I'm in charge of the open sea experiments. Asshole," she adds, sotto voce, after Eckart stomps off.

Maury Richards says, "I didn't realize that Cytex had such a presence out here."

"They brought in the lab and their own people. They do all the biochemical work and the gene sequencing. And they don't like to share data."

Mariella says, "Do you know what they are doing with the organism?"

"I long ago stopped asking. Fuck them. You come out with me. I'll show you what the slick can do."

With the help of a couple of sailors, Mariella and Maury pull white, hooded containment coveralls over their orange survival suits, strap on filter masks and goggles.

"If anyone is prone to motion sickness, speak up now," Jenny Kaplan says, "and I'll have the medical orderly administer Dramamine. You can't throw up in the masks, and if you take off your mask near the organism you'll have to go into the isolation facility for a few days. No one? Good."

Jenny Kaplan makes sure that Mariella and Maury smear every bit of their exposed skin with sunblock, and then they all climb down into a Zodiac inflatable and zoom out across the open ocean.

The tropical sunlight strikes a fierce, salty white glare off the water. The day is hot and growing hotter. Within the casing of survival suit and overalls, Mariella feels sweat roll down her flanks. Her skin itches fiercely around the seal of the mask.

Jenny Kaplan shows Mariella and Maury how to polarize the plastic of their goggles, points to a ship shimmering about a kilometer off, says that it is a destroyer on picket duty.

"We have two of them at the moment, and they fly constant helicopter patrols. Luckily this isn't a fishing area, and most cargo vessel routes are to the south. The big worry is that one of the green campaigning groups will find out and pull some kind of stunt."

Mariella asks about the size of the slick, and tells Jenny Kaplan about her estimates of growth rates and biomass.

Kaplan nods. "That sounds about right. In fact, there's been a jump in the growth rate just recently. I think the slick is adapting."

"Are there any other places where it grows?"

"No, luckily enough."

"You seem very sure," Maury Richards says.

"We have its infrared fingerprint," Jenny Kaplan says, "and there has been a very intensive satellite survey with a resolution of less than a meter. This part of the ocean is a stable area between two opposing currents, rather like the Sargasso Sea. We think the slick has an absolute requirement for stable conditions."

Maury glances at Mariella and, behind his goggles, raises his eyebrows exaggeratedly. Mariella nods. Either Jenny Kaplan is not telling the whole truth, or there is something very strange about the way the slick grows.

The Zodiac draws up to the first of the experimental ponds. It is a ring of inflated yellow plastic about twenty meters across, with a weighted plastic skirt dropping down deep into the clear blue water. They all stand up and hold on to a line that loops around the skirt, leaning against taut plastic like drinkers bellying up to a bar.

Inside, crusts and greasy plates coat the surface of the water. Growths that look like fairy castles, glimmering with the black crystalline slickness of iodine, rise at the center.

"We gave this one a light dose of nutrients," Kaplan says. "No more than a doubling of ambient levels, but this is how it responded. It's extremely efficient at absorbing nutrients from the water, and it can fix gaseous nitrogen too. It's a closed ecosystem — primary producer, decomposer, the works. Carbon, nitrogen and all the micronutrients are tightly recycled. That's how it's able to grow so quickly. And of course nothing seems to eat it."

Mariella says, "So if it gets into a nutrient-rich upwelling, it will grow explosively."

"Without question," Jenny Kaplan says.

Maury says, "These structures have to be cellular. With such a high degree of differentiation, surely the cytoplasmic matrix can't be as continuous as you suggested."

"Well, it is," Jenny Kaplan says. "Look, this is a unique organism. For instance, there are no nuclei. The cytoplasm appears to have been derived from parasitized planktonic algae, but their nuclei have been either digested or expelled."

Maury says, "What about the algal photosynthetic systems? Have those been retained?"

"There's a whole bunch of photosynthetic systems in there. They seem to be in competition. The slick is protean, continually changing."

Maury asks about containment, and Jenny Kaplan says that the water is lousy with particles shed by the slick, down to at least five hundred meters. "We don't yet know how far down they go. We're waiting on a submersible to check that out."

"If you want my opinion," Mariella says, "you should destroy it now. Before it spreads. Before you lose control of it."

"Well, that's not my decision," Jenny Kaplan says. "We've done some experiments that show the slick is resistant to metabolic poisons, even methyl bromide and cyanide. They seem to work to begin with, but then the slick grows back, and the new growth has resistance to whatever toxin it has been treated with. The same with more complicated organic toxins. It's a tough little bugger," she says fondly. "We even tried basic poisons like silver and copper nitrates, but the slick altered its metabolism and excess metals were sequestered in vesicles."

Mariella says, "What about biological control?"

"Nothing we've tried will eat it, and no normal phytoplankton pathogens infect it. Cytex is supposed to be working on genetically modified pathogens, but that's classified. I know they haven't done any field trials yet."

Mariella says, "Surely they've sequenced all the different forms of the slick."

Jenny Kaplan starts the Zodiac's twin motors and says over the roar, "I guess, but if they have, they haven't told me."

The second pond contains a glossy black crust that sloshes heavily to and fro against the inflated plastic.

"This is what you mostly get on the surface out here," Jenny Kaplan says. "It doesn't look like much, does it? And it isn't. A basic soup of undifferentiated strands or threads, what we call the primary iteration. But take some of it and give it nutrients or isolate it from UV, and structure begins to assemble."

There are paddles clipped to the sides of the Zodiac, yellow plastic shafts, orange leaf-shaped blades. Mariella says, "Let's try something," and unfastens one, leans up against the warm plastic wall of the pond and holds it over the edge of the slick. Almost immediately, long fibrous structures begin to grow through the shaded portion, crystallizing out very quickly, like a speeded-up video of fungus spreading through oil.

"This is what we call the second iteration," Jenny Kaplan says. "Other forms grow out of it if you shade it long enough, but it'll take a few days. I can show you more of the ponds, but they're pretty much like this."

Maury wants to see the main body of the slick, and Jenny Kaplan takes the Zodiac in an arc past one long finger of it, keeping a safe distance. The slick mantles the ocean all the way out to the horizon. Low-amplitude waves roll sluggishly beneath its heavy film. Its growing edge is almost invisible, seen mostly by the way it fractures sunlight into spindrift rainbows. A terrible beauty, Mariella thinks, imagining all the world's oceans covered with the slick, the base of all oceanic food chains transformed into a single self-sufficient organism. And what if it can grow on land too?

Back at the ship, Bob Eckart is waiting for them at the rail of the boat deck, his slate raised like a phaser set on stun.

Washington, D.C.–Kennedy Space Center, Florida:
October 22–23, 2026

While Jenny Kaplan was giving her tour, Eckart started an alarm trail which led at last to Howard Smalls, who is considerably pissed off to find Mariella on the research ship at the edge of the slick in the middle of the Pacific. Mariella, sweating in her survival suit and containment coveralls, trembling with indignation, lets him rant, and then refers him to Senator Thornton.

But that's the end of her field trip. She and Maury Richards fly back and get drunk at a little restaurant Maury knows in Honolulu before taking separate flights to the mainland.

The day after Mariella returns to Tucson, she flies out to Washington at Senator Thornton's request, and over dinner in the same discreet Italian restaurant in Alexandria tells the senator everything she has learned about the slick.

"What's unusual is that it isn't completely alien. Its structure is very like that of a simple fungus. Its adaptivity is comparable to that of many populations of bacteria, which are very good at moving genes between individual cells, either on little rings of DNA— plasmids—or via phage viruses. That's how genes that confer resistance to antibiotics spread through a population of bacteria very quickly. The slick seems to spread favorable acquired characteristics through itself in much the same way."

"You've shown considerable resourcefulness," Senator Thornton says. "I should have expected it."

"I was wondering if perhaps I might not have had a little help in persuading Admiral Collingwood to allow me to go."

Senator Thornton's smile is as enigmatic as the Sphinx's. "I couldn't say, my dear."

"I need to know more. To begin with, I would very much like to know more about the mechanism by which the slick appropriates the genes of other organisms."

"No," Senator Thornton says firmly. "No, I don't think so."

"I thought that you would back me. You wanted me to be, what was it? An advocate for the truth."

"I got you onto the mission, my dear. It does not make you a free agent."

"I have to know more."

Senator Thornton's stare is frank and appraising. Mariella becomes aware of the clatter of cutlery elsewhere in the restaurant, the murmur of the conversations of the other diners. The senator says, "I appreciate that it must be frustrating. But if you press too hard, you will endanger your already delicate position."

"Because Cytex wants this for itself."

"It holds the license for research into the slick."

"And you won't help me try and get around that."

"I don't have that authority."

"I see."

"I hope you do, my dear."

"At least make sure that Maury Richards isn't hurt by this."

The senator promises that she will do her best. On the scramjet back to Tucson, Mariella tries to forget about the oppressive sense of a vast and invisible battle over her head. There's so much she needs to know about the slick, and even if she doesn't have access to primary data, there's plenty of work to be done. She and Maury have been emailing back and forth, refining their calculations on the slick's growth, speculating about its behavior, trying to work out why it has appeared in the middle of the Pacific. And there is also the training schedule which will keep her occupied between now and the launch date, set for January 6. Her blood quickens at the thought.

It is snowing lightly the next day when Mariella leaves Tucson for the Kennedy Space Center. She's going for the first fitting of her Martian excursion suit, and for a photo shoot. She's certain that Penn Brown will confront her about her trip, but she doesn't see him or the other crew members until the shoot late in the afternoon.

She spends the morning having every joint measured and a dummy suit adjusted to her body millimeter by millimeter, and then endures a stream of short, one-on-one interviews over an extended lunch, painless anodyne stuff, the type she gives whenever the press office at the Reserve thinks one of her papers is worth publicizing, or when some TV or Web program wants an expert to talk generalities about the origin of life, exotic bacteria, genetic modification or half a dozen other topics. She finds it easy to stick to the cover story. What will happen if the media gets hold of the real reason for why the expedition doesn't bear thinking about.

When the last interview is wrapped, she takes out her jewelry, puts on orange flight coveralls with her name stitched above her left breast and the mission patch on her shoulder, laces up heavy boots that are slightly too tight, and is driven out in a golf buggy by an assiduous PR flack to where the others are waiting on a blue carpet in windy sunlight beneath the exhaust bells of a Saturn V. Penn Brown and Anchee Ye, the other passengers, the flight crew. The photodocumentarist, Alex Dyachkov, photographs the photographers as they climb off a bus and set up their cameras.

Penn Brown stands next to Mariella and says quietly, "You're quite the operator, aren't you?"

"There's a lot I need to know."

"You won't find out much on joy-riding trips."

"I found that one very enlightening."

"I'm glad you think it's worth it. Because it could cost you more than you realize."

"Are you pissed off with me, Penn?"

"Al Paley is pissed off at you. Howard Smalls is pissed off at you. I'm amused. No, really. And I can offer you a way of finding out what you want to know. Cytex is willing to make you a consultant on their side of this project."

"Seriously?"

"Seriously."

"No. No, I don't think so."

"You'd get access to commercially sensitive material. You'd learn what you want to know."

"Thanks, but I'm already learning a lot."

"Senator Thornton can't protect you, Mariella."

"What does that mean?"

"Think about it. They'll be in touch."

Mariella doesn't need to think about it. Cytex wants her inside the tent pissing out. The price of being a consultant will be a gag clause in her contract.

After the photo shoot, she changes back into her own clothes and gets a limo ride to Orlando airport. She buys a vodka and tonic at the bar and sits at a table near the smoked-glass wall that looks out across the runways, opens her slate and checks her email. Sure enough, there's a long message from Cytex, from the company's secretary, no less, asking if she will consider becoming an environmental consultant with an unspecified brief. The terms are generous; the money would support a couple of postdocs. She sends a brief message of regret, is working through the rest of her mail when a young man sits across from her and says, "Dr. Anders, right?"

She glances at him and he stares back at her frankly. Great, one of those embarrassing one-sided encounters that are a minor but irritating side-effect of her media appearances. She says, "I'm rather busy."

"Well, this is kind of about your work," the young man says. He has a broad Texas drawl, with a closely trimmed crop of dirty-blond hair, washed-out blue eyes, a long freckled face. Gold loops sewn into the lobes of his ears, a suede jacket over a white, hairless chest, tight blue plastic pants and black boots with little mirrors stitched up the sides. Pure sex. He sees her looking at him and stretches out in the chair like a cat and says, "You know, we had trouble catching up with you again."

"I'm sorry. Have we met before?"

"Sure. Only a few days ago. But we couldn't make our case then. I hope you'll listen to it now. We have the same interests."

"Really?"

"We know you're a sympathizer."

Mariella says, "I really don't think I know you."

The man presses one hand to his chest, a curiously old-fashioned gesture. His fingernails are painted black. "We really did meet before, but I guess you don't realize it. I'm Clarice Bushor."

"What?"

His smile widens. "Clarice Bushor. Of the Bushor Report."

Mariella closes up her slate, ready to go. "Even if you are a journalist, which I very much doubt, I'm done with interviews for the day. If you want to talk with me, try the NASA press office."

Neither the Reserve's computer nor any of the security guards found the woman who ambushed Mariella. Video loops from security cameras showed her going through the gated door to the research building by dogging the heels of a couple of staff members, and another showed that she had waited for more than two hours outside Mariella's office, but after Mariella escaped her, she seemed to have vanished from the building without trace. Joe Sandeval said that she was probably just a nut, but promised to shake up security just in case. Mariella has forgotten about the incident until now.

The young man tells her, "We've been wanting to talk with you on a kind of unofficial basis. You got alarmed before, at your place of work, and we're sorry for it, but we can't talk with some PR person hovering. And maybe you don't know it, but your home is being watched. A public place like this is neutral territory."

"My home is being watched?"

"Well sure, by the Secret Service. They're compiling a dossier on you, too. Seems that someone believes you are a fellow traveler with environmental extremists."

"I see. And I should believe you."

"You could ask the agent on your case. Glory Dunn, I believe her name is."

"And how do you know this?"

"There are plenty of people sympathetic to our cause, Dr. Anders."

"You haven't told me your name."

"Clarice Bushor. You really should look at our web site. You'd see that we're interested in the same kind of things as you. Specifically, in whatever is going on out in the Pacific. Is that where you went, a couple of days ago?"

"Have you been following me?"

The young man's gaze is candid. "You went to Hawaii on a commercial flight, but we couldn't track you after that. You returned via Washington, D.C., and you've just now been at the Kennedy Space Center. We've heard rumors about something new and dangerous coming out of some skunk works in Shanghai. China has scrambled a second mission to Mars, and NASA is sending a bunch of microbiologists there, too. Even though it gave up on the search for life on Mars a while back, after the first Chinese expedition reported finding nothing. They lied, didn't they?"

"I can't talk to you," Mariella says, and shuts her slate and starts to get up.

The young man says quickly, "We think there's something

growing out in the Pacific. It originally came from Mars, and was modified by one of the Chinese biotech companies in Shanghai. The question is, how did it get all the way out in the Pacific? No way it could have got there on ocean currents."

Mariella is grudgingly impressed, because that is one of the questions she has been puzzling over. The young man grins at her and says, "NASA hasn't told you anything about that, I bet. And neither has Cytex."

Mariella sits down. "What's your interest in this?"

"We're a clearinghouse for information."

"You're activists. Radical greens."

The young man's smile is broad and white. "We're a broad church. We think you might be sympathetic."

"I give advice to local people who have chosen to live in sustainable communities. That hardly makes me a radical green. I'm from Scotland. I know all about green parties. They have the right sentiments, but they've gone too far in the wrong direction, especially after the Firstborn Crisis. The green parties in Europe grab votes by frightening people with imaginary consequences of biotechnology, not by telling them the whole truth."

"Science has a lot to answer for."

"It isn't science that has caused so much damage to this planet. It is too many people, and the misapplication of technology through ignorance or greed. There aren't any quick fixes for that, and calling for blanket bans on scientific research is worse than wishful thinking. It's an abrogation of responsibility. It excuses the need to think of the consequences of any action, because you can blame everything on the other guy. Am I making myself clear?"

"What about the stuff growing out there in the Pacific? It's some kind of GM organism, right?"

"You're fishing, Mr. . . . ."

"Clarice Bushor. We're looking for the truth, Dr. Anders. We were hoping we might have that in common. We live in the same world. A very small world, too. It's a case of can you trust us and can we trust you, isn't it? That's what I've been sent to establish."

"You're right about trust," Mariella says. "For instance, how do you know I won't just report you?"

"Go ahead. But you know there's more to this than just one

person. After all, this is the second time we've met, right?"

"Yes, and I still don't know what you want from me." She is curious, although she doesn't want to admit it, and a little scared, too. After all, he really could be a nut. And that would mean that the woman who ambushed her a few days ago is the same kind of nut. Maybe she's the focus of a conspiracy of nuts.

The young man smiles and pushes back from the table. "Someone as resourceful as you can find out about us easily enough, I think. Ask around. Plenty of people know Clarice Bushor." And then he is up and walking through the crowded bar toward the door.

Oracle, Arizona:
October 23–25, 2026

Mariella drives home from Tucson airport, once more checking her rearview mirror more than necessary. She stops at the gas station by the turn off on Highway 89 to top up her tank, and Rosa, the old woman who has run the station for more than thirty years, from back when it still served unleaded and diesel, says that she has heard that Mariella is going to Mars.

"Sure. Why not?"

"Then no wonder you are famous. It is an age of miracles." Rosa slaps the fat, insulated pipe pumping methane slurry into the tank of Mariella's pickup. "The gas company just now sends me a video. In three years I'll be selling gas thousands of millions of years old, older than life on Earth. From a rock they bring from the depths of space. Age we cannot comprehend, and people will burn it to go shopping. And now one of my customers goes to Mars. Yes, an age of miracles."

"Many people have been there now. I'm hardly the first. I'm not even the fiftieth."

Rosa shakes her head. She is rumored to be more than a hundred years old. Her skin is wrinkled and sun-blotched. Her white hair is braided in a thick rope that hangs halfway down the back of the dungarees she habitually wears. She says, "A thousand could go. A million. But still for me it would be a miracle. You are happy with this? You look happy."

Mariella smiles. "Don't I always look happy?"

"You work too hard and sometimes leave no time for happiness."

"I hope you are not going to tell me that I need a man."

"Of course not. Why would you need a man? Why would any woman?" Rosa steps closer and gives a little smile. She has been working up to this. She says, "But now, some men, they look for you."

Mariella thinks at once of Clarice Bushor. She says, "Did they say who they were?"

"They came by this afternoon. Two men in black suits like Mormons, in a big rental car. The driver was a big man, very muscular, did not speak at all. The other asked me if I knew where you lived. I told him I do not know. Don't worry. No one will tell them. We all live out here for a reason." Rosa jerks the hose, its nozzle drizzling heavy white vapor, from the pickup's tank, racks it on the pump, strips off her heavy gloves. "Twenty-five dollars. And please, you take good care of yourself."

As she drives the rest of the way home, Mariella thinks that perhaps the two men are nothing to do with Clarice Bushor. Perhaps they are from NASA, on some nonsensical bureaucratic errand. She supposes it is quite possible that they do not know where she lives. Even her colleagues know only that she lives in a trailer home somewhere in Oracle. It's not uncommon. In this age of universal phone numbers and electronic banking, you need reveal only your post-office-box number and the address in cyberspace you keep all your life.

Perhaps it means nothing, no more than a routine check, and she tries to get it out of her mind as she drives up the winding road to Oracle.

It is dusk. Mariella switches on the pickup's lights. And when she turns onto her property, she sees by the glare of the high beams that the door of her trailer is open. Her heart gives a little fluttering lurch, even though her first thought is that Lily, the daughter of her neighbors, has stopped by to feed and exercise Twink. But then she sees the black sedan parked down by the fence of the corral, and at the same moment a man steps out of the trailer onto the metal grid at the top of the steps, and looks directly at her as she sits frozen behind the wheel of the pickup.

She switches off the motor and climbs out, her legs a little shaky. She thinks of the ancient rifle in the stable, which she found with a rotting box of cartridges when clearing up the place after she moved in. Thinks of the .22 pistol she keeps in a drawer by her bedside, for dispatching the occasional trespassing rattlesnake. She says loudly, "Just what do you think you are doing on my property?"

"I'm pleased to meet you, Dr. Anders," the man says. He's young, white, and clean-cut, in a neat dark suit. He reaches into his jacket and pulls out a badge case and flips it open and holds it up. Someone else appears in the doorway behind him. A tall African-American woman. Glory Dunn.

The two agents, Glory Dunn and J. C. Dinkel, the local FBI field officer, sit side by side on Mariella's rug-covered couch and explain that there have been threats against the Mars astronauts.

"What kind of threats?"

"There's the usual kind," Glory Dunn says, "but they're nothing to worry about. But there's also the woman who penetrated security at your place of work."

"It is possible that you are in jeopardy," Dinkel, the FBI agent, says. "You might consider moving to another location. Agent Dunn here is staying at a Days Inn right in town. We can get you the room next to hers."

Mariella is perched on a stool at the breakfast bar, a mug of coffee cooling by her elbow. She says, "I heard about your background checks," and wonders how the young man at the airport knew about this.

Glory Dunn leans forward and says, "Really?"

Mariella thinks fast. "Someone saw you. Mistook you, actually, for a man. This is a small community, and we don't get much attention from the sheriff's office. Everyone knows everyone else and keeps an eye out for trouble, although they don't poke their noses into each others' business unless asked. And you want to take me away from here and put me in some motel where no one knows anyone, or cares about them either. You think I'd be safer there?"

"We can move you there under cover," Dinkel says. "No one will know about it except us."

"You'll go to Kennedy Space Center a little earlier than expected," Dunn says. "No big deal."

"I've just flown back from Florida," Mariella says. She thinks she knows what this is about now. This is payback for her trip out to the slick. They want to make sure that she doesn't pull any more stunts. She decides not to tell them about the man at the airport; it'll only give them more leverage. She says, "I have a lot of loose ends to tidy up. I'm not about to fly out again until I've finished. You said that I might be in jeopardy. Who's making these threats?"

"Well that's the thing," Dinkel says, after glancing at Glory Dunn.

"You say you don't know who they are but you want to move me. I need to know more than that before I do anything."

Dinkel says, "If you have work to do, I'm sure arrangements can be made to accommodate you."

"I *live* here," Mariella says. "I *work* here. Are you going to bring all this along?"

She bitterly resents this blunt intrusion into the one place where she can utterly relax into her own self, where she does not need to disguise what others call her eccentricity. For a moment, she sees it the way these two government agents must see it. The tiny kitchen with its ancient humming refrigerator, the greasy stove she has never used, except as a place to stack plates, the microwave and the pile of neatly folded cartons, the sink with a week's worth of washing up; the chipped woodgrain plastic paneling of the trailer's living area, still bearing the darker rectangles and squares where the previous owner hung pictures; the worn stained carpet and the thriftstore furniture, the sagging couch with its lapping armor of Navajo rugs, the Formica-topped table and the kitchen chair by the rear window where she works, the ancient CD player and the stack of CDs in their plastic jewel cases. *Sacred Steel. Angola Prisoner's Blues. Louisiana Blues.* Dock Boggs. Blind Boy Fuller. Frank Stokes. Music from America's raw heart, unforced and unaffected. Deadpan voices singing of death and love and exile—America's secret history. And everywhere strewn with paper, stacks of printed or photocopied reprints, dogeared journals, rough paper with scribbled calculations, a whole heap of torn and crumpled sheets of paper under the table. She had to move stacks of reprints from the couch so the two agents could sit down. This is the place where she does most of her work—here, or walking or riding in the desert. And they want to take her out of this, want to take control of her. They are exemplars of the same patriarchal system that has caused so many problems in science: overcontrol, overdeterminism, suppression of dissent from the orthodox paradigms.

She says, "I can't work anywhere else, and I need to finish my work before I leave."

Dinkel says, "I don't want to alarm you, Dr. Anders, but we may be talking about systematic stalking. It could escalate, to, well, something unfortunate."

"He means kidnapping, or even wet work," Glory Dunn says, with a big smile. She has a gold tooth in back that catches the light.

"Probably best not to talk about it here," Dinkel says. "This place isn't secured."

Glory Dunn says, "He means someone might be out there in the dark, bouncing a laser off one of your windows and picking up our conversation."

Dinkel says doggedly, "This is a very vulnerable spot, Dr. Anders. I have orders to protect you, and I don't want to do it here."

"And what will you do if I don't want to go? Handcuff me?"

Glory Dunn laughs.

"We expect you to cooperate," Dinkel says. He is sitting as straight as he can on the sagging couch, looking very uncomfortable.

Mariella takes a big swallow of her coffee. Instant, made with hot water from the tap; neither of the agents has touched it. She says, "What we have here is a cultural clash, a variation on the old imperialistic mindset. You expect me to adopt your culture, with its safe rooms and its guns and all the other boys' toys. Not because it's necessary, but because it is the only way you know how to operate. I appreciate your concern, but I won't be wrenched out of context. So you'll have to find a way to work around me. I'm not prepared to leave at a moment's notice because I have work to finish up here. NASA understands that, and you'll have to understand that too. Okay?"

Dinkel straightens his tie. He has a class ring on his index finger. He says, "We do have our orders. I hope you can appreciate that."

"Then perhaps I should talk to whoever gave your orders. I assume that you both work for Howard Smalls?"

"I work for the FBI," Dinkel said. "I'm here, officially, because you are a government employee who was harassed on government property."

Glory Dunn smiles. "You don't need to talk with Mr. Smalls. You don't want to bother him."

Mariella says, "Then perhaps I should speak with Senator Thornton."

Dunn's smile doesn't alter. "You'll find she has no influence on security matters. There's no need to worry, Dr. Anders. I'm here to do what I think is best for you."

"Then you'll have to adapt to what I need to do."

"We can be adaptable," Glory Dunn says.

Dinkel looks from one woman to the other, realizing that an agreement has been reached but not understanding how. He says, "We could be dealing with some very bad people."

"Oh, they're not front line," Dunn says. "You don't have to worry about any unpleasantness on your territory, Dinkel."

"That's exactly what I do have to worry about. How are we going to do this if we can't move over to the motel? Maybe I should check with Phoenix."

"You do that," Glory Dunn says, with sudden decisiveness. "Get them to roster a couple of extra bodies. We'll do shifts."

"One of you can sleep here," Mariella says, although it isn't what she wants at all.

"There'll always be someone outside," Glory Dunn says. "Awake and alert. And someone will be dogging you when you go to work or do whatever it is you have to do. Is that acceptable? You can organize the rotation," she tells Dinkel, "while I take first watch."

Mariella showers and goes outside to find Glory Dunn leaning against her black sedan, a tall shadow visible by moonlight and the yellow light spilling from the trailer's window. It is cold, the sky clear and full of stars.

Mariella says, "I thought you'd be hiding somewhere, not standing out in the open."

"If we can't move you to a place of safety, we have to let the bad people know that you have protection. Are you thinking of going somewhere, Dr. Anders?"

"I'm going to see to my horse and then visit my neighbors." Mariella points to the lights of the house beyond the windbreak of eucalyptus trees that marks the boundary of her property. She has changed into jeans and a plaid shirt—she has four pairs of each, so that she does not have to go to the trouble of deciding what to wear each day—and her fleece-lined denim jacket. "I have a flashlight," she adds, shining it briefly, "and a gun. If I get into trouble I'll call for help. Okay?"

"The Glock from by your bed? Ever used it?"

"On rattlesnakes. Though recently I haven't been bothered because a couple of king snakes have taken up residence under the trailer. King snakes eat rattlesnakes."

"Damn. I wish you hadn't told me that. I hate snakes."

"King snakes aren't poisonous."

"They're still snakes."

"This is the desert. There are scorpions, too."

"I don't mind anything I can squash," Glory Dunn says. "I don't think you'll need the gun, but if you know how to use it there's no harm in you taking it along. Do you have a carry permit?"

"Should I get one?"

"It won't be necessary. In fact, I'd rather you didn't drive around with it or take it to work. It could escalate any confrontation."

"If I drew it, it would be with the intent to use it."

"That goes without saying. But drawing a gun on a person means that you've given them the right to try and kill you, seeing as how you're threatening to kill them. I thought the English were squeamish about guns."

"I'm from Scotland. Half Scots, half Norwegian. And I live in the desert. You're not coming with me?"

"I've already talked to your neighbors. They didn't seem to care for me."

Twink hangs her long head over the stall when Mariella clicks on the light in the stable. She undoes the latch and goes inside and nuzzles the mare for a little while, breathing in the scent of horse and straw and saddle leather until she feels calmer. Lily has put oats in the feedbox and hung a bundle of hay over it, filled the zinc trough with water. And cleaned out the stall, and cleaned and dubbined the harness too.

"You'll be well looked after," Mariella tells Twink, who is snuffling at the pockets of her denim jacket. She feeds the mare the carrot she brought, and feels unexpected tears prick her eyes when Twink snuffles at her jacket again. "No more treats, you monster. I know it's only cupboard love."

Glory Dunn is still leaning against the car when Mariella crosses the sandy yard and goes down the slope and through the trees to her neighbors' house. She thanks Lily, gives her the NASA cap she bought at the Kennedy Space Center, talks to the girl about looking after Twink while she is away.

"I don't know when I'll be back," she says. "When training starts it'll pretty much take up all of my time."

"But you can email," Lily says. She is just thirteen. With a boy's skinny figure, cropped hair, Kim's slanted black eyes and Kathe's long-limbed figure, she is already a heartbreaker. She has just had her ears pierced, and keeps fiddling with the starter studs. She says, "I'll take pictures with Kim's camera and post the files. I have this fractal program that can compress them real small. And maybe you can send pictures back."

"I don't know. I'll have to check the bandwidth."

"We're going to do a project on you at school," Lily says, suddenly serious. "I have something to ask you, as a matter of fact."

"I'll come and give a talk, if that's what you want."

Lily grins. "Clean."

"I'll bring back pictures if I can't email them. Maybe even a postcard or two."

They talk a little longer, until Lily says abruptly that she has to do her homework because her favorite program is on in half an hour. Mariella sits with Kathe in the kitchen, sipping hazelnut-flavored coffee from one of Kathe's earthenware mugs and nibbling at a buttery, home-baked cookie. Kim is on shift work in the cocoon, teleoperating construction robots in a copper mine in Ellsworth Land, which at the moment is where most of the couple's money comes from. Kathe was a history professor at Arizona State University and is now a potter, and also helps run Oracle's bookstore, which sells old books on Arizona's history and flora and fauna. She is sixty this year, and beneath her New Age flakiness is one of the most serene and sensible people Mariella knows.

Kathe tells Mariella that the two government agents talked to her and Kim that afternoon. "Then they went over to your trailer. I told them they had no right, but they didn't pay any mind. Typical government people."

"They'll be around for a couple of weeks, until I go away."

"Are you in trouble, honey?"

"They think I might be. A couple of people have been bothering me."

"Journalists?"

"Not exactly. I'm not so famous I have to hide from the media."

"You live so much inside your head you can't see what other people think of you," Kathe says. "Of course you're famous. I read the piece that the Copperhead Hourly News Byte did on you."

"I bet it was buried among the announcements for concerts and art lessons."

"There was something on the local TV news yesterday, too. Lily was tickled pink."

"Well, I don't care what people think."

"Will they let you go to the moot?"

"I'll take them along. I'm sure they'll enjoy it."

"Lily will take good care of Twink. I'll keep an eye on her, but she's a sensible girl and the responsibility will do her good. Kim and I will keep an eye on the rest."

"If you see anyone on the property or if anyone comes asking about me, I don't want you to confront them. Here. Call this guy."

Kathe runs the ball of her thumb over the embossed seal on Agent Dinkel's card, and says, "Just what kind of trouble are you in?"

"None at all I hope."

Kathe purses her lips and says, "Anyone comes bothering us, they'll find out Kim and I put all our time at the range to good use."

"If anyone does bother you, just call this guy. Promise?"

Mariella talks with Kathe about the NASA training program. She hates herself for dissembling when Kathe asks her what she is going to do once she gets to Mars, but laughs when Kathe says that she doesn't want to be responsible for hearing any state secrets.

"You know I can't begin to understand what you do," Kathe says. "Not that I'm not interested. After all, Kim and I wouldn't have been able to have Lily without the cell fusion treatment."

When Mariella goes back to the trailer, Glory Dunn is still at her post. The next morning, she has been replaced by J. C. Dinkel, who takes the mug of coffee Mariella brings out and says that he'll drive her to work.

"I'm not going to work just yet," Mariella tells him.

He follows her into the stable and, when she lifts down the saddle, says, "What are you doing?"

"What does it look like? If you put down your coffee you can give me a hand."

"I don't think you can go riding."

"That's what this monster thinks too. Bloody hell, Twink, why do you always do this?" Because the horse as usual is holding her breath when Mariella tries to tighten the girth strap. "What is it, you want me to fall off a loose saddle? There we go," she says, when Twink lets out a long sigh, and she pulls the buckle tight.

"Really," Dinkel says, standing in the way as Mariella turns the horse around, "you can't do this."

Mariella swings up into the saddle, ducking the beams that hold up the sheetrock roof, and urges Twink through the doorway. Dinkel steps back so suddenly he spills coffee on his tie and says, "Damn it!" and follows her out of the stable, saying again, weakly, "You really can't do this."

Mariella checks Twink; the mare is eager to be off now she is in the open air. She says, "I'll be back in an hour or so. I'm going down the dry river there, past those eucalyptus trees, and then up along the ridge. Don't try and follow on foot—you won't be able to keep up. I'm not in any danger, Agent Dinkel. The only way someone can follow me is if they're also on horseback."

Dinkel is dabbing at his tie with a handkerchief. He says, "They could be."

"Then you should be too, but you're not. And if they are, they're one step ahead of you and I'll be no safer here than on the trail. See you in an hour," Mariella says, and gives Twink her head and leaves Dinkel in the dust. It is a rotten trick to play really, but she won't let the government run her life.

She takes one of her long circular routes through the desert, mostly thinking about what she discovered last night. The slate's librarian located more than two hundred living individuals by the name of Clarice Bushor, including one in Tucson, although she turned out to be a hundred-and-thirty-year-old great-grandmother. Mariella refined the search, looking for people affiliated with eco-logical campaigns. There were still several matches, but one had more than a hundred times the number of entries than any other, even though she is dead.

Or, it turns out, because she is dead. This particular Clarice Bushor died six years ago. She was the widow of a media wizard who was killed in a helicopter accident. Much of her dead hus-band's fortune was locked up in trust funds, but Clarice Bushor deeded a ranch in Montana to a group of conservationists who wanted to re-establish the old grasslands, sold an apartment in New York and her husband's collection of antique cars and movie mem-orabilia, including a mint Delorean which had featured in the

Back to the Future trilogy, and used the money to buy the deep-ocean trawler with which she and a small crew harassed fish-factory ships and clathrate mining rigs for several years. Until, on an action against an experimental fish farm sited over an artificial upwelling bringing nutrient-rich water to the surface, the Zodiac in which she was riding flipped and she drowned beneath it.

Clarice Bushor left all of her estate to her sister, Anna, who finally received it after several years of litigation by relatives of Clarice Bushor's dead husband. Mariella finds a small photograph of this sister embedded in an item from the *San Francisco Chronicle* about the case. It is the woman who ambushed her outside her office, the woman who calls herself Clarice Bushor.

The web site mentioned by the young man at the airport is closed. A little more research takes her to a discussion thread on a deep green site, where someone with the ename Treebeard has posted a message stating that the Bushor Report has been busted by the feds, but mirror sites have been set up *here* and *here*.

One address leads to a server in Green Libya; the other to a vast site in New Zealand that includes copious extracts from the Bushor Report site. The usual rad-green journalism, tracing links between politicians and companies, analyzing statistics, reporting scams and corruption and broken promises. It is impressively de-tailed—these people obviously have sources deep in a dozen governments—but none of the articles are recent, and there is nothing about the slick or Mars. Perhaps the mirror site in Green Libya has been updated more recently, but Mariella can't access it from the United States.

A group that has taken on the mantle of a martyr, particularly one led by the sister of that martyr, might very well be dangerous, but Mariella thinks that the Bushor Report is no more than it seems, a bunch of rad-green journalists running a site that is a cross between an ezine and a clearinghouse for clandestine information. Dinkel and Dunn are here to keep her in check rather than protect her from murderous green zealots.

On the way back, Mariella takes the last kilometer along the dry riverbed at a gallop, letting cold clean air drive every thought from her head. Dinkel is waiting at the edge of her property, and helps her give Twink a rubdown and a vigorous currying before letting the horse loose in the sandy lot behind the stable.

"I used to ride when I was a kid," he says.

"Maybe you should take it up again."

"If you're going to do this every day, maybe I will."

"You grew up around here?"

"Colorado. The agency likes to move us around. Tucson is my first field assignment. I've been here three years, mostly hunting down black biotech labs out in the desert, and chasing smugglers trying to move prohibited technology into Mexico. I can make some coffee if you like. Proper coffee, I mean."

"You don't like my coffee?"

"It's pretty horrible."

"We'll go to the diner. I work there sometimes."

Mariella sits in her usual booth, occasionally scribbling on her slate but mostly staring out of the plateglass window, across the roofs and trees of Oracle toward the wide desert basin beyond. The air is very clear. The peaks of the Bastamonte Mountains are hidden by clouds; it is snowing up there, above the tree line. Ordinarily, she would be thinking about going skiing at Mount Lemmon, but she has won one argument with Dinkel and doesn't want to get into another just yet.

She works for several hours. Dinkel restlessly rummages through the news, his sheet of epaper flickering as millions of microscopic balls, each one half white and half black, realign into new text and pictures. Mariella drinks several mugs of coffee and eats two corn dogs loaded with onions and chili sauce, followed by a packet of Twinkies. Dinkel picks at a sprout salad. Mariella learns that his parents were economic refugees from Los Angeles after the collapse of 2016, downsizing to an old silver-mining town refurbished as a tourist trap. His father runs hiking tours in the summer and ski tours in winter; his mother dabbles in painting and pottery, and tells fortunes with Tarot cards. Dinkel is married, with a son less than a year old. He shows Mariella a couple of animes. The kid looks like Dinkel: the same dark-eyed solemn gaze.

Mariella lets Dinkel drive her down to the Reserve so she can talk Tony May through his plans for the research he will carry out while she is away. In the afternoon, she visits one of the local green settlements to give advice on seeding its new sewage-recycling system. The place is up in the hills, just above the tree line, a split-log lodge and little cabins scattered among pines on either side of a deep gully crossed by several rope bridges.

The extended family who own it run classes in pottery and yoga and T'ai Chi in summer, and skiers lodge there in winter. They know that she is going to Mars. "I hope it's true," she says, confirms several times that no, it won't be for a while, that she will still be at the moot. When she has a moment alone with the eldest son, a fifteen-year-old who is something of a net wizard, she asks him if he knows anything about Clarice Bushor.

"There's a web site. Not great design, but they do pretty good work."

"It's closed down. I was wondering how to get in touch."

They're out on the porch of the lodge. It's cold up in the hills, cold enough to turn their breath into vapor. The kid is wearing insulated skinthins, silver with a black stripe, patched at elbows and knees. He leans on the rail and looks off through the pines to where Dinkel is waiting in the black sedan. He says, "Gee, I really wouldn't know."

Mariella sighs. "You made him for a fed at once."

"He's been here before. Asking about this and that."

"It's not my idea to have him drive me around."

"He's coming with you to the moot?" The kid laughs when Mariella nods. "That'll be interesting."

Dinkel drives her home, and another agent, a paunchy middle-aged man, takes over the watch. Mariella tries to work but makes little progress, and toward midnight goes out and finds Glory Dunn back on shift, enveloped in a long navy blue down-filled jacket with the FBI logo on the back.

"I must be boring you people rigid," Mariella says.

"This is the easy stuff," Glory Dunn says. "I get a lot of reading done while you're asleep."

"You don't sleep?"

"Not much when I'm pulling duty. I've a tweaked reticular

activating system. I can live on catnaps for weeks, catch up later. Maybe you have some of Dinkel's coffee left?"

Mariella makes a pot, and then tells Glory Dunn about the moot.

There's a moot every full moon, not because the full moon is significant to any particular faith (although the Wiccans always put on a good show), but because it is a calendar marker on which everyone can agree. It starts in the afternoon, the day cold and the sky covered in cloud, and is in full swing when Mariella, Glory Dunn and J. C. Dinkel arrive after dusk.

This month the moot is being held at the Garcia Memorial Motel, north of Tucson on I-10. The motel is owned by Jake Boyle, a seventy-year-old ex-Dead Head patriarch with four common-law wives. Yurts and teepees are scattered through a desert garden of lovingly tended cacti and yuccas and artfully arranged rocks. There is a drip fountain made of soft-drink cans collected from the shoulder of the highway, a spiral knot maze of cloned cholla, a UFO landing site marked out with colored sand and white pebbles.

Like all green settlements, the Garcia Memorial Motel aims to be as self-sufficient and environmentally neutral as possible. Its horseshoe of cabins have solar panels and a variety of exotic windmills on their flat roofs; solar stills supply potable water. Mariella helped design its shit cycling facility, basically a sand seep seeded with microorganisms that turn organics into carbon dioxide and ammonium; the water is used to irrigate small, Navajo-style fields of corn and squash. The increased rainfall caused by global warming has extended the growing season to ten months of the year in the Tucson valley, and there are now dozens of small self-sustaining green communities living in much the way the Pima Indians lived before Spanish explorers arrived. Most of the greens gather at the monthly moot to trade, to gossip, to dance or drum, and tourists and people from Tucson and nearby towns come too.

The parking lot is already full. Mariella and the two agents have to leave the sedan on the shoulder of the highway and walk back toward the motel, which is outlined by hundreds of strings of fairylights. Torches and bonfires flare beyond it. People surge along wide avenues between rows of stalls selling raw minerals and finished jewelry, woven hats and baskets, beads, blankets, quilts, vegetables, live quail, cultures of soil-improving microorganisms and seeds of native plants, joss sticks, software, handmade computers and data chips. The Chili King, an old man dressed in a red jumpsuit and a comically large sombrero, sits on a great gold-sprayed chair in the middle of his mounded baskets of peppers. There are stalls offering temporary or permanent tattoos, piercing and scarification; a whole row of food stalls, including a barbecue pit. A dozen styles of music blare from speakers.

Mariella sees Jake Boyle moving through the crowd, dressed all in black, as usual, his white beard tangled with black ribbons, an electric guitar slung on his back. She knows the old rogue well; she's a part-time drummer in his pickup band, and often joins in the free-form jams that traditionally end a moot held at the Garcia Memorial Motel. "I need to talk with you later," he shouts, and moves on before she can reply.

Every kind of green is gathered here, from serious techheads to khaki-clad survivalists. Children run and shriek with excitement. There are stilt-walkers, fire breathers and jugglers, a man with a talking crow that's either tweaked in some way Mariella hasn't heard of or is a clever simulacrum. Before she can ask, the man steps back to make way for a procession that suddenly divides the crowd: a naked woman, skin painted silver, face masked with a featureless white disc, goes by on a white horse, followed by a gaggle of white-robed acolytes whooping and beating on little drums and tambourines and sticks.

"Avatar of the Moon," Mariella tells the two agents, grinning as she taps out the acolytes' three-over-five beat against her thighs. "They'll be making a sacrifice later."

"Close your mouth, Dinkel," Glory Dunn says. "You're a married man."

The Secret Service agent seems to be enjoying the spectacle, looking this way and that with a quick eagerness, her long, quilted coat unzipped, flaring like the wings of a cloak as she walks along. Like Dinkel, she has a receiver plugged into her left ear and a mike patch on her throat. She has given Mariella a little field phone with a fractally folded two-hundred-meter aerial that can pick up a whisper from the Moon.

"I was wondering how she keeps warm," Dinkel says. "It feels like it's going to snow."

"Hell no," Dunn says, exhaling a huge plume of smoky breath. "It's way too cold for that."

"Aconite and hemlock in the body paint," Mariella says. "The traditional ointment used by witches in Europe before they went flying. She and her followers are members of a Wiccan cult. I hope you won't try and bust her, Dinkel."

"We know what goes on here, but it isn't a federal problem. People growing peyote and tweaked plants in desert plots for interstate commerce, or people smuggling stuff in and out of Mexico, they're another matter."

Mariella says, "Well, they're here too."

"You have some odd affiliations for a scientist," Glory Dunn says.

"I dislike irrationality in all its forms, from deliberate distortions of statistics to fortune-telling. No disrespect to your mother, Dinkel. But I'm human too, as human as the next woman. Don't you ever want to cut loose?"

Mariella comes to the moots for a session with her drumming school, and to get laid. There is usually no shortage of likely partners, but there's little chance she'll get lucky this time, with two obvious feds dogging her heels.

Glory Dunn says, "I don't lay waste to my body like some of these people, if that's what you mean."

"A lot of these people have jobs. Most of them, in fact. They telecommute, make handcrafts, paint and sculpt, write software, compile databases. Shake out any suburb and you'll find people doing exactly the same kind of work. But the people here generally aren't employed by large corporations or multinationals or the government, and they all try to make as close to zero impact on the environment as they can manage. A few are solos, but most of them live in self-sufficient communities. They take carbon taxes seriously, and recycling and conservation goes without saying. And while they're greens, most aren't anti-technology—in fact, they're probably more dependent on technology than most people. The desert is a hostile place. A good place to test models for space communities in fact, which is what I stressed the time I was turned down for a research trip to the Moon."

She realizes she is babbling. She smoked a couple of joints before setting out. To get her in the mood, and because she knew she wouldn't be able to hit up with the two agents at her back. The stuff was mellow and strong, and is working on her nicely now. Lights are getting smeary and starry, and she does a double take when a pack of wolfish youngsters goes past, half-naked and dressed in what look like animal skins and shirts woven from dried grass. No, they are real, ultra-rads who've undergone morphogenesis to toughen their skins, enhance their night vision and hearing and sense of smell, increase the lengths of their ulnas so they can scamper in a semiquadrupedal gait if they need to. Light glows green or gold on the tapeta at the backs of their eyes. One boy snarls at Glory Dunn as he lopes past, showing an impressive row of implanted teeth. Ultra-rads run in nomad packs out in the desert, living off the land by foraging or hunting. They believe in a return to nature by invisible use of technology: not only body modification, but planting genetically modified fruit trees and scattering corn and other wild crops to create a kind of prelapsarian garden. It is a movement growing among second-generation greens, its legal status ambiguous, its association with ecotage groups indisputable but rarely proved. The ultra-rads are waging a guerrilla war against ranchers, and there is wild and unsubstantiated talk of cattlemen bringing in hunters to clear them off the ranges.

Some members of the drumming school have already set up near the UFO landing site, and Mariella slowly makes her way toward them through the crowds, stopping to exchange words with people from the various communities she's advised. She refuses offers of tequila and beer and skin patches, even a fat reefer which a young man holds out while giving the two agents a big shit-eating grin.

Halfway there, Kathe and Kim wave to her from the other side of the crowded aisle. Both women are wearing only leather pants and boots and body paint; Lily trails a few paces behind them in her usual jeans and baggy sweater, looking slightly embarrassed by her exotic mothers. Kim pushes forward and hugs Mariella and shouts loudly, "Damn! I haven't seen you in an age!"

"I guess we've both been working."

Kim is staring at Glory Dunn and Agent Dinkel. She has shaved off all her hair again; her bare scalp gleams with oil. She smells of patchouli and wood smoke and sweat. Her black eyes are halved by tucks of skin, their pupils hugely dilated. She is flying on something. She says to Mariella, "And now you're going to Mars. I was there once, supervising this so-called autonomous rig. The lag is way bad."

"It's a long way away."

"When you're there, maybe I'll try and pull that slot again. Wouldn't that be wild?"

And Kim laughs and hugs Mariella again, slapping something against the back of her neck and saying, "Fly right, girl," before whirling away after her partner and her daughter.

Mariella peels off the patch at once, but she can already feel a slight dizziness and a fluttering at the edge of her vision, and a metallic taste is growing at the back of her throat.

Part of the crowd circles a group of bare-breasted women in long white skirts of pleated linen, like priestesses who have stepped down from an Egyptian mural. They are lighting dozens of torches, which have been thrust into the ground. The torches burn with crackling red or yellow flames and give off dense white smoke that smells of sage. Beyond is the makeshift stage, where, lit by a rack of red baby spots, half the drumming school is beating out a polyphonic clatter.

Mariella is suddenly gripped by a wild exultation and grins and shouts loudly, "Make way for the drummer! Drummer coming through!" and people laugh and clap, or hoot with mock derision, but get out of the way.

"I'll do an hour's set," Mariella says loudly to Glory Dunn. "Finish right after the sacrifice. Okay?"

"I don't know," Dinkel says. "All this is pretty exposed." He is looking this way and that, his hand resting at the lapel of his black coat.

Glory Dunn cups her hand over her left ear, listening to something transmitted by her plug, then says to Mariella, "What was in that patch your friend spiked you with?"

Mariella grins. Everything seems to stand out from everything else as if italicized, or like the quaint computer-rendered 3-D movie she once saw in an art house in Pasadena. She says, "I think just a little stimulant. Kim doesn't mean any harm. She gets hyper because she spends most of her time teleoperating."

"You can have thirty minutes," Glory Dunn says, and holds up three fingers in front of Mariella's face. "For once I agree with Dinkel. It's wide open."

All around them the crowd roars. The naked woman on the white horse is making her way toward her acolytes. On the stage, someone starts a low pulsing riff on a bass guitar; keyboards ornament the riff with scattershot trills, and two electric guitars pick out a broken counterpoint as the drumming settles behind the band.

Mariella whoops and claps her hands over her head, accentuating the offbeat, and starts toward the stage. Dunn and Dinkel are right behind her. Rockets shoot up and burst overhead in glittering drifts of falling silver stars. And out among the cabins and teepees and yurts of the motel there is a crackling and rapid stutter of red flashes.

"Shit," Glory Dunn says, "those aren't fireworks." She stops, looking this way and that, the crowd closing about her. A few paces in front of Mariella, Dinkel turns, reaching inside his coat. And then the pack of ultra-rads hits them.

They come from either side, very fast, tightly grouped. Thirty or forty of them, moving like a tide. Someone wallops Mariella in the side and she falls, catching a confused glimpse of Dinkel tumbling backward and Glory Dunn reaching out toward her. Then the ground and the black sky flip over and Mariella is in the middle of a dense wedge of nearly naked bodies. Hard hands grip her arms and legs. She is lifted up and borne away, her captors jinking left and right around stalls, running straight through racks of chili peppers tied in bunches, New Mexico style, the racks crashing down behind them as they run on into the packed parking lot.

Mariella tries to twist free but she is held too tightly. Nails or claws prick through her jeans and her flannel shirt. The side door of an ancient white Volkswagen van slides open and she is lifted and tossed through the air, lands with a breathless thump on a thin carpet laid over unforgiving ribbed steel. Wolfish faces leer at her and then the door slams shut.

Mariella gets to her knees as the van peels away. Fairylights come on, strung like electric spiderwebs around the cabin. She is crouching on white shag pile carpet under a ceiling from which at least a hundred dolls' heads hang on wires and springs, jostling and jouncing. Two people are sitting cross-legged on the carpet, their backs to the driver. One is Jake Boyle, his big hands moving tenderly over the body and neck of the electric guitar in his lap; the other is the woman who has named herself after her dead sister, the woman who calls herself Clarice Bushor.

Mariella tells Boyle that he has to be crazy, that he is in real trouble here, trouble so deep there will be no end to it, and Boyle tries to reassure her.

"Hey, Mariella, we're friends, right? Haven't we always been friends?"

"What is this, Jake? What have you gotten into here? Was that really gunfire?"

"Firecrackers, a few smokepots, maybe someone getting excited and taking a shot at the Moon. Nothing heavy and no one got hurt. We just wanted to talk with you, away from your bodyguards."

"Jesus, Jake. They're FBI, Secret Service—"

"I know Agent Dinkel. He's not a bad guy, for a fed. He won't take this to heart." Jake Boyle's smile is as sweetly enigmatic as Buddha's. He strokes faint tinny chords from the unplugged guitar and adds, "You've helped us, and now we want to help you."

"Just hear us out," the woman says. "We ask no more than that."

Mariella stares at her with the same cold revulsion and shock she felt when she once walked into her trailer and found a rattlesnake coiled on the worn rug. As before, the woman is expensively dressed, and she has a prim but determined expression, like a teacher about to try to persuade a recalcitrant child to do something against its will. Her hands are gripping her butter-soft black leather bag so tightly they are white at the knuckles.

Mariella says, "What should I call you? Anna, or Clarice?"

The woman smiles. "I hoped you would find out about that, Mariella. Now you know why the Bushor Report is so important."

Mariella feels a vibration over her breast: it is the little field phone. She takes it out and the woman says quickly, "Don't answer. They'll get a fix on us."

Mariella flips open the phone and puts her thumb on the YES button. She says, still dazed by Kim's drug and the shock of her abduction, "I know who you are."

"We told you who we are," the woman says. "They took down our web site but it won't stop us. The truth is too powerful to be suppressed. You have to listen to what we want to tell you."

"You really should listen," Jake Boyle says. "Put away the phone, why don't you? If you answer it we'll have to leave you. And you really do need to listen to this. Man, but it's a wild story."

Mariella looks past him, past the driver, but all that is visible through the van's dusty windshield is the center marker of some road endlessly rushing out of darkness.

The phone stops vibrating, starts up again.

The woman says, "Just take it off her."

"I don't think I can do that quickly enough," Jake Boyle says. "Let her keep it. It makes her feel safe."

Mariella says, "Where are you taking me?"

"We're just driving around," Jake Boyle says. "We don't have long. We'll drop you off somewhere you know, somewhere safe. But listen to my friend here first, okay?"

The pleading note in his voice seems sincere. Mariella says, "Five minutes. Any longer and I'll answer the phone."

The woman speaks quickly, and Mariella has trouble concentrating. Kim's drug, the electric jolt of adrenalin settling coldly in her guts. Overhead, the dolls' heads clatter against each other like castanets; there is a dry clicking, like the scratch of myriad cockroach claws, as their weighted eyelids open and close. The woman tells her that they know something is growing in the Pacific, some kind of GM organism, and launches into a complicated explication of half-guessed motives, of why commercial greed has let loose something devastating and allowed it to spread, of why the government doesn't want to make it public because it is involved too. Mariella starts giggling, and finds that she can't stop.

The woman loses her composure for a moment and says, "This is important!"

"She's wired on something," Jake Boyle says genially.

"I may be wired, but I still think you're both crazy," Mariella says, and with an immense act of will mashes her thumb down on the phone's YES button.

There is a tinny squawk which might be Dunn's voice, and then Jake Boyle reaches out and closes his big hand around Mariella's. "That's it," he says loudly, and the van suddenly lurches as it leaves the highway for an unmarked dirt road.

The woman who calls herself Clarice Bushor clutches the back of the driver's seat and says with tightly contained fury, "You people are idiots."

"We got her for you. The rest was up to you." Jake Boyle leans back and asks the driver, "How are we doing?"

The driver glances around. She is the youngest of Boyle's wives, Tammy Faye, her expression uncharacteristically grim. She says, "Two more minutes. We'll have to abandon the van."

"It's just a van," Jake Boyle says, and tells Mariella, "This is all real. This is all true. You understand?"

"You're as crazy as she is," Mariella says.

The woman says, "The two sides seem to struggle against each other but they are joined back to back by a web of deceit and lies and secret deals. The Chinese might have started this, but they are a side issue to what's going on in this country. Be very careful, Dr. Anders. We can't reach out to you once you are inside the system, but you can always reach out to us. We'll let you know how."

"I'm not going to tell you anything."

"We already know more than enough. That's why they closed

us down. If you don't believe me, ask them about the Florida reefs. And to prove how much we can help you, we've planned a little surprise for your friend Penn Brown."

"What do you mean?"

For the first time Mariella is truly afraid. But before the woman can answer, Tammy Faye shouts, "Time's up!" and the van slews to a halt. Tammy Faye jumps out, throws the side door open and pulls Mariella through it, dumping her on her ass on cold dirt.

"You'll see!" the woman shouts. "We fixed Penn Brown good!"

And then the van is speeding away from the cloud of dust it raised when it stopped. Mariella dropped the phone when she was pulled out, but she quickly finds it by the light of the full Moon. It starts to ring as soon as she picks it up; when she answers, Glory Dunn tells her to keep the line open so that she can get a fix.

Mariella, shivering with shock as much as cold, hunkers down and pulls her sheepskin-lined jacket around her. The dark, quiet desert stretches away on every side. Stars are sprinkled everywhere across the black sky. The Moon sits in a kind of cowl of its own light. The stuff Kim spiked her with has worn off. She's too tired to string thoughts together. Minutes pass unmarked, and at last the rasp of a car engine cuts through the quiet night. Mariella stands up. Headlights are coming toward her along the road.

Johnson Space Center, Houston– Kennedy Space Center, Florida: October 26, 2026–January 6, 2027

The day after the moot, Mariella flies with Glory Dunn to Houston, where she learns that there has been an attempt on Penn Brown's life. An explosion demolished his car as he walked toward it. He is pale but eloquently defiant, his left arm bandaged, two raw stitches in the corner of his left eyebrow.

Mariella feels a pang of guilt when she learns that the bomb went off five minutes after the ultra-rads abducted her, although she has already told Glory Dunn everything about the conversation in the van, and told her about the encounter at the airport with the man from the Bushor Report, too. The Secret Service agent took notes but didn't say how it would be followed up.

Penn Brown takes a grim satisfaction from the fact that none of the flight crew or the other passengers have been threatened. "They see that we're the key to this," he tells Mariella, a couple of days later. "That's good. It'll make our bargaining position so much stronger."

They are sitting in a booth of the bar in the lobby of the NASA hotel. It is late in the evening. They have spent all day listening to presentations by engineers from the flight control center at Goddard. Glory Dunn and Penn Brown's bodyguard are perched on tall stools at the polished iron crescent of the bar counter, watching everyone who comes and goes.

Mariella says, "I'm not here to bargain. I'm here to work."

"Don't bullshit me, Mariella. I know you won't work on any terms but your own. Come in with me. Together we can shape this into a real scientific expedition."

"I've already turned down Cytex's generous offer. As I'm sure you know."

"Perhaps it wasn't generous enough."

"What do you want with me, Penn? And why are you here? To do science or to turn a profit?"

"Both, of course."

"Because you can't do one without compromising the other."

Penn Brown smiles. He has a very thin but very flexible mouth, product of generations of Boston Yankee inbreeding. Mariella thinks that it lends a mean edge to his conventional, white-bread good looks: someone more charitable would say that it gives him character. She realizes that she knows nothing about his sex life except that he's unmarried. It's impossible for her to imagine him kissing anyone with those bloodless lips.

He says, "If the science isn't good, Mariella, then neither are the profits."

"You can't sell shares in the answers to fundamental questions about the origin and evolution of life."

"As a matter of fact, we have a little research unit working on evolutionary theory. It's run by an oddball character who's very bright and very focused, but a bit of an innocent. An English guy, a refugee from the anti-science atmosphere of the European Community, just like you. He's a biomathematician interested in intrinsic rhythms of evolution. We're applying his theories to the high-tech end of the stock market with some interesting results."

Mariella sighs. "That's just my point."

"We're the key players, Mariella. We're the ones our enemies fear. They didn't threaten Ye, they didn't threaten any of the crew, or any of the other scientists. Just us. We should be allies. We should put our differences aside."

"I'm not sure that you should base your conception of your importance on the fact that someone tried to kill you."

"They owe us, Mariella. They owe us and they know it. We'd be foolish not to take advantage of it. In the name of science."

"Yes, but it depends what you mean by science, doesn't it? And we've always had such different ideas about that. For instance, you measure the value of ideas in dollars, while I value their intrinsic worth."

"This isn't a debate, Mariella. This is real." With his right hand, Penn Brown squeezes his left forearm, where the sleeve of his suede cardigan is bulked out by a bandage. "Real pain, real blood. I could have been killed. So could you."

"They just wanted to talk with me."

Penn Brown shakes his head. "We're up against fanatics. It's our duty to make sure the risks we're taking are properly recognized, and to use that recognition as leverage to get a better deal on the science. NASA shouldn't be setting the agenda. We should. They know that, or they would not have asked us to do the work, and we have to make it clear that we will do it our way. Surely you see that you have to take my side on this."

"My God, yes, there must always be sides. Always divisions. That's the way men argue, isn't it? A versus B. Darwin versus Lamarck. Black or white. My country right or wrong. Well fuck that shit," Mariella says, her sudden fury rising so strongly that she feels it is larger than she is, like wings beating around her in the cramped space of the booth, with its silver-dyed leather banquettes and replicas of old mission badges fixed beneath the clear varnish of the laminate tabletop. "Fuck it," she says again, relishing Penn Brown's look of surprise. "The real world is so much more subtle, but you'll never see that because you're too busy drawing boundaries and battle lines. Too busy playing corporate power games instead of doing science. Well, play all you want. The truth is the truth. It doesn't go away, even when people like you choose to ignore it because it conflicts with the compromises you've made to get where you are."

When Mariella stands, she sees that the two Secret Service agents are watching her. Glory Dunn is leaning forward on her stool, one foot planted on the floor, as if ready to spring.

Penn Brown blinks up at Mariella. He says, "We'll talk about this again. When you're not so upset."

"Upset!"

"It's understandable —"

"Yes, because I'm a woman. Of course. That's why I get upset. And you can't deal with me when I'm upset because then I'm not acting like a man."

For a moment, she has the urge to throw her vodka and tonic in his face. To prove her point. To discharge the anger that boils in her like electricity in a thundercloud.

She says, "I have to work with you, and I'll do my best. But don't you dare ask me to play your games."

Mariella and Penn Brown don't mention this argument the next day, but it is always there between them. As ever, what they have in common is also what divides them.

For several weeks it does not matter. They have entered the training program. They have become part of a huge, impersonal process. They have stepped upon the conveyer belt of tests and checklists and examinations that leads inexorably toward the Mars Shuttle.

Mariella does her best to conform. She takes out her rings and studs and wires, has her hair cut in a neat bob. She suffers the extensive NASA medical and psychiatric evaluations without complaint. She gets with the program.

Although more than a hundred people have set foot on Mars, it is still no routine matter. Usually, training for a mission takes more than a year, and the science specialists have been steering their applications through a maze of peer review and NASA bureaucracy for even longer. Mariella and Penn Brown and Anchee Ye have been put on a fast-track program. They have a lot of catching up to do, a prodigious amount of technical information to absorb. Ye has the advantage here, of course, because she has already been on a mission. To her, this is simply a refresher course, and she takes turns with other members of the flight crew to act as instructor to Mariella and Penn Brown, something Brown takes badly.

Mariella, Penn Brown and Anchee Ye are lodged in the Space Center hotel in Houston, with Secret Service agents in adjacent rooms. Any trip off site requires many hours' notice, and even while out jogging they are followed ahead and behind by unmarked cars. Mariella chafes under the constant surveillance, but she grows to admire, if not actually like, Glory Dunn's dutiful and selfless vigilance. She tries to teach the agent some biology, and they fall into the habit of spending an hour or so together last thing at night, companionably watching TV.

Glory Dunn can't understand why the mission doesn't leave straightaway, so Mariella writes a little program that draws feasible flight paths between Earth and Mars.

"It's all very well," Glory says, after Mariella has run the program half a dozen times, "but why can't you just fly straight across from Earth to Mars right now? That way you beat the Chinese by months. I thought that was the point of the antimatter drive."

"Not exactly. Let me try another way of explaining it. Look here. This is one of the minimum energy paths, leaving Earth when Mars is in conjunction, at its maximum distance from Earth, on the other side of the Sun. That way, you see, you travel along an ellipse that's tangent to Earth's orbit at one end and to Mars's orbit at the other. Any deviation from this ideal uses more energy, and because the Mars Shuttle has only a finite capability for acceleration, there are limits to the kind of flight path it can use. That's what this shows. See?"

Mariella resets the relative positions of the planets and the program draws a recursive set of loops, like a lopsided sketch of half a chrysanthemum flower. She says, "I admit it's a difficult concept—"

Glory Dunn stares at the slate, and a little dent appears above her broad nose. "If that means I have to take your word for it, then fine. But it would make my job easier if you were on your way."

The instruction and simulation sessions are held in Houston, but final fittings for Mars excursion suits, microgravity practice in water tanks, and drills in a full-size mock-up of the Mars Shuttle, take place at the Kennedy Space Center. Usually, Mariella travels between Houston and Florida as copilot in a T-40 trainer jet flown by Anchee Ye; there is still a requirement that all astronauts possess at least minimal qualifications in jet flying. It's on these flights that she first gets to know the woman with whom she is going to look for life on Mars.

Like many astronauts, Ye has a public image of dedicated enthusiasm and open friendliness which is really a construct of NASA's insatiable public-relations operation. In private, she shields her true feelings with a frosty, functional politeness. Although reticent to the point of invisibility, she is possessed by ferociously concentrated ambition. It is evident in the set of her small, somewhat prim mouth, and in the steadiness of her gaze, which is as bold and candid as a child's. She drives herself hard, works punishing hours to catch up or overtake those who rely only on natural talent. She had a vile childhood in Kansas, her parents both members of some miserable hardscrabble millenarian cult that believed it was living in the End Times, with the Rapture close at hand. There is a rumor that Anchee and other children in the cult were brutalized by its leader, who was later shot dead during a botched bank robbery.

Anchee Ye used science as a way to climb out of this pit. In some ways she is like Penn Brown. To her, science is not a great cathedral, its pinnacles of pure unsullied thought soaring high above the base mud of mere facts, but a kind of corporate ladder with an intricate system of challenges and rewards. She has worked her way through the hierarchies of NASA with dogged determination, from technician to section leader in the Mars Sample Return Facility. She lives with her husband, Don, in a trim ranch-style house in Nassau Bay, a gated retro-community based on one of the original housing developments that grew up around the Space Center in the heady days of the Apollo program in the 1960s. Don is also an astronaut, mostly flying Lunar shuttles. For Anchee, marrying an astronaut was a way of penetrating NASA's rigid social strata, as a scullery maid might marry a gentleman's manservant in some great Victorian household, a savvy knight move that gave her access to the operation levels where missions and science projects are planned. She has learned the language of grants and the politics of grant-awarding committees. She has been ruthless in pursuing the advantages her ethnic-minority status provides. And by sheer hard work and tenacity she won the great prize: a place on the Mars Shuttle and three months of research along the fossil shores of Mars's ancient lakebeds.

Mariella finds a way through Anchee Ye's armor when she asks for a tour of the Mars Sample Return Facility. It is there, in the shadowless white light of the huge laboratory where Anchee is most at home, where she is an acknowledged aristocrat, that she begins to confide in Mariella.

The Mars Sample Return Facility is at the center of a series of elaborate precautions and barriers that protect the precious samples of Martian rock and soil from terrestrial contamination. Mariella and Anchee Ye have to strip and shower and scrub in water loaded with a pink, sickly sweet-smelling antibacterial agent, don sterile, electrically heated thermal undergarments and paper coveralls. They are helped into self-contained pressure suits equipped with big Perspex bubble helmets. They step into a huge airlock and withstand a brief but fierce shower that sprays them from all sides with more antibacterial agent, then a dense white vapor, and finally blasts of hot air, and pass through another airlock into the laboratory at the core of the MSRF.

Here, atmospheric composition and air pressure are kept as close to those of Mars as possible: ten millibars of bone-dry carbon dioxide at a temperature just above the freezing point of water. A central access hub links the laboratory to the underground bunkers in which the Martian rocks are stored; radiating from the hub, like the arms of a starfish, are chains of carrels in which people in pressure suits work on samples with the concentrated diligence of monks poring over illuminated manuscripts.

Anchee Ye takes Mariella through the analytical sequence: initial eyeball descriptions and X-ray and laser fluorometric analysis; analysis of trapped gases and of isotopic composition to determine age; sectioning and milling and polishing of samples for crystallography and transmission electron microscopy. Samples are flaked off and sputtered with gold and viewed at every angle by a scanning electron microscope; the scans are patched together into holographic views that are analyzed by an AI for any traces of fossilized life. Yet more samples are ground into fine powder and subjected to a series of extraction processes, and the resulting distillates are tested for organic molecules.

Anchee Ye is clearly known and liked here. Passersby give her salutes or handshakes or high fives, gestures deliberately exaggerated because it is hard to read expressions through the bubble helmets. "Nice to have you back," they say, and, "Bring us more conglomerates," and, "This time bring back a live one."

Mariella is amused to see how this attention makes Anchee Ye relax and grow expansive, like a daisy opening under the warmth and light of the sun. She is the local hero, parrying wisecracks, even giving clumsy bear hugs to one or two especially effusive people.

"We've learned a lot about aerology from samples processed here," she tells Mariella, "but right now the sample return program is mostly dedicated to searching for traces of life. That was always the underlying thrust of all the Mars missions, of course, but the discovery of fossil life means that it's pretty much all that's done here these days."

"I saw the display in the Space Park."

"Those are just clever replicas. The originals are too precious to be put on public display. Do you want to see them?"

They sit in a set of cabinets in a quiet room off a corner of the laboratory complex. Each stands on a Perspex plinth under spotlights activated by large red buttons. They are obdurate lumps of red or reddish brown or dark chocolate-colored stone. Those

collected directly from the surface are pitted with impact craters
or smooth deep holes eroded by windblown dust, but most are
sections of cores or carefully excavated and preserved layers of sedimentary material.

Mariella surprises Anchee Ye by being able to recite much of
their history. She speed-read the original research papers before
the visit, refreshing her memory of a conference she attended eight
years ago.

Here is the core of impacted and subtly banded sediment,
taken by the first manned Martian expedition from a three-billion-
year-old lake bed in a crater near the south pole, in which the first
unambiguous traces of life were found. Nothing more than a pre-
ponderance of left-handed amino acids and subtle variations in the
isotopic ratios of carbon and oxygen, but as clear to those who
know how to read it as a burglar's fingerprint.

Here is the unprepossessing lump of iron-stained layered rock
in which the first unambiguous microfossils were found, clusters
of spherical inclusions like microscopic bunches of grapes, including some frozen forever in the act of division. When Mariella read
the paper describing them, she was strongly reminded of the stiff
foam growing in the ponds in the middle of the Pacific. That
transformed Earth life mimics ancient Martian species might be a
coincidence of form following function, but she doubts it.

Here is the Stump, the first macrofossil to be found. It resembles with startling fidelity the ancient fossilized stromatolites found
in three-billion-year-old sedimentary rocks on Earth, which in turn
resemble living stromatolites found in certain shallow bays of the
Australian coast, low mounds or pillars formed, layer upon layer,
by sediment trapped and stabilized by mat-forming microorganisms, that each year grow over last year's layer because they require
light to live. On Earth, stromatolites are primarily formed by cyanobacteria, the first organisms to have developed the trick of
oxygen-evolving photosynthesis, and if in this case form does follow
function, then the Stump is evidence that photosynthesis of some
kind developed far earlier on Mars than on Earth; possibly even
before life began on Earth. For by then, life on Mars was already
retreating to its last redoubts beneath the icy skins of deep lakes

and around thermal springs. Only a billion years after Mars formed, the lakes and marshes that once covered most of the northern hemisphere had evaporated, water dissociating into hydrogen and oxygen under the onslaught of raw sunlight unfiltered by any ozone layer, hydrogen escaping Mars's light gravity, oxygen locking with iron in the surface, the dried lifeblood of the planet.

And yet the Chinese have discovered life that has persisted in the pores of rocks deep under the polar cap, where pressure liquifies water and the overlying ice prevents its evaporation. Life on Mars, the last redoubt of a brief period that ended three billion years ago. It is the unspoken, forbidden knowledge that hangs over both women as they contemplate the relics of ancient Martian life.

"I promised Don that we'll start a family when I get back," Anchee tells Mariella.

"Really?"

"I laid down a store of ova before my first Mars flight; it's standard procedure because of the possibility of radiation damage. What about you?"

Forrest had wanted children, and Mariella had wanted to give them to him.

"I'm an old broad wedded to science," she tells Anchee. "Finding life on Mars—that's enough for me."

The tempo of the training program increases. There does not seem to be enough time to learn everything they need to know, and peripheral matters eat into the timetable. A whole morning is wasted on an internal NASA ceremony in which the flight crew and science specialists hand out certificates and plaques to what seems like almost everyone in an audience of several hundred engineering and support personnel. There are press conferences at Houston and at the Kennedy Space Center, attended by the entire mission team, groomed and made up, wearing crisply pressed orange coveralls. The flight crew field most of the questions, because the press has long ago learned that the public is not particularly interested in science, but journalists representing specialist channels and zines ask some penetrating questions about the objectives of the three new members of the science team. Mariella and Anchee Ye stick closely to the agreed-upon NASA script, while Brown handles the trickier questions with aplomb, speaking in orotund, well-rounded sentences and minting the kind of aphorisms ("The discovery of life on Mars would justify the expense of the entire space program") that journalists love because it means they don't need to think about their own copy.

"He sure can shovel the shit," Anchee Ye whispers to Mariella, in the midst of one of Brown's flights of oratory.

Mariella, Anchee Ye and Penn Brown spend a week at the Kennedy Space Center, learning how to use the proton drill rig. First in a workshop, then while wearing Martian excursion suits in a hangar mocked up to resemble the Martian landscape, taking cores from blocks of basalt, fixing unexpected problems the instructors throw at them, then in the field, where on the first day Mariella and Anchee work by themselves because Penn Brown is off on Cytex business in Washington. Mariella surprises Anchee Ye by her deftness in handling the drill.

"You're a quick study," the geologist says, toward the end of the first day of fieldwork.

"My father was an engineer in the business. Oil, then methane clathrates. Mostly overseeing the construction of pipelines and cracking plants, but he took me out to the production platforms a couple of times. The technology is different but the principle is the same."

Usually, Martian fieldwork is practiced either in the dry valleys of Antarctica or on Devon Island in the Canadian Arctic, but there's no time for that, and they are working on a limestone ridge inside the Merritt Island Refuge. The support team lounge by the jeeps and trucks pulled up along the shoulder of the road below the ridge, in the shadow of tall straight pines. The Atlantic Barrier is a twinkling white line beyond the saltwater estuaries and brackish marshes to the east. It is the largest man-made construction on Earth. The level of the ocean has risen a meter in the last twenty years and, like embattled Holland, some of the Florida coast is now permanently below sea level.

Anchee Ye tells Mariella that people still surf off the Barrier.

Cocoa Beach, the traditional surfer's hangout, has been washed away, but a few stilt shacks and pontoons survive.

"It's like that old movie," Anchee says. "You know, the one where Kevin Costner saves the world."

"That's not much of a clue. He did it so many times. Him and Bruce Willis and that other guy, the one who tried to become a politician. What happened to all those tough boys?"

"They went out of fashion. The world became too complicated for them."

"Yes, but there's still plenty of macho bullshit around, even if men wear blusher and eye shadow now." Mariella finishes tightening the bolts of the tripod's cross-struts, sets down the heavy, meter-long wrench, and says, "I think this beast is ready to start work."

They have spent four hours assembling the tripod drill rig, the lubricant pump, and the pipe feed hopper, which is driven by a simple chain-and-ratchet assembly. Without ceremony, Anchee throws the knife switch on the battery box. The proton drill head makes a deep burring vibration as it drives into the rock, smashing apart atomic bonds. Fine, nearly monatomic dust spews from the top of the drill head, a cloud that rises a hundred meters into the air and drifts slowly westward. It is a cold, crisp day, the sky a pure unmarked blue: Mariella wishes she has her sheepskin jacket to wear over her orange coveralls.

Anchee Ye watches with a critical eye as the first length of pipe augers in after the drill. She says, "We had to study all those old movies on the farm. It was part of preparing for the Rapture."

It is the first time Anchee Ye has mentioned her childhood. It hangs between them for a moment; then Anchee Ye turns away and increases the flow of lubricant, suddenly brisk and businesslike again, explaining that you can tell from the pitch of the noise the pipe train makes if more grease is needed.

Penn Brown is still skirmishing with the mission planners, flying to Washington, D.C. once or twice a week to argue over control of the Martian side of the research program, and he keeps trying to persuade Mariella to take his side. A couple of days later, he corners her on the bus ride back from the drill site and once again presses his case.

"I don't have the influence you think I do," she tells him.

She's tired and she has the curse and a spot is erupting in one corner of her mouth. She's in no mood to play at micropolitics.

"That's bullshit, Mariella. You have your reputation and everyone knows you have Senator Thornton's ear. You just don't want to use it. Maybe you're scared they'll throw you off the mission. Believe me, that won't happen. They need you. They need me. We saved the world once, and we can do it again."

"A whole team of people did that."

"And you were up there at the top."

"Why are you so keen to do everything in the field? It's clearly better to process the samples once they have been brought back to Earth."

Penn Brown flushes up. Somehow, Mariella always seems to say the wrong thing to him. She is amazed that the NASA psychologists haven't picked up the hostility between them—or maybe they have, but can do nothing because NASA is committed to using them both. If that's the case, it gives her a certain freedom she doesn't want to cede to Brown's boneheaded ambition.

He says, "I can't believe you agree with the Mickey Mouse biological program."

"It should work. At least, if your company's promises hold up."

"We know the test kits will work. But there's so much more that can be done in the field. Not just finding the Martian organisms, but studying them in their native habitat. We'll want to know as much as possible about them as soon as possible, so that knowledge can be applied to controlling the slick."

Mariella looks at him for a moment, then says, "You mean eradicating the slick."

"Yes. Yes, of course. It can't be done quickly if we have to bring the Martian organisms all the way back to Earth before beginning to analyze them. I trust your ability, Mariella. I'm on your side. Much more than you realize in fact. Give a little back."

"If you want to grab most of the glory, go right ahead. I'm just happy to be going to Mars and doing the job I've been asked to do."

Penn Brown sighs. "You just don't get it, do you?"

"If this is something about Cytex making money from the mission, then no. No, I don't."

As well as practicing with the proton drill, they are learning techniques for isolating and identifying living Martian organisms. Mariella has to relearn lab skills she has not put to use for several years. She finds it more enjoyable than she expected, a confirmation of the messy intractability of life. Even the simplest procedure has something of the mystery of alchemy about it.

She learns how to extract organic material from rock samples, how to use a Wolf trap to detect metabolic activity in soil samples after incubation with radioactive nutrients, how to use the DNA assay developed by Cytex. Because the latter involves testing unknown DNA against putative Martian genes isolated from the slick, this part of the training is conducted in a high-security facility, and is closely supervised by Cytex technicians.

Mariella spends the Christmas holiday with Anchee Ye and her husband, and she and Anchee fly back to the Kennedy Space Center for the final time. Training is at an end. From now on, their time will be dominated by preparations for launch of the Dynawing that will take them up to the orbit of the Mars Shuttle. A maintenance crew is already aboard the shuttle, awakening and testing its systems. And then, three days after Christmas, everything unravels.

Mariella is awakened before dawn by a call from the press office, is told not to answer any calls from journalists, even those who have been given on-site accreditation. A quick trawl through news channels reveals the reason for the press office's panic. Someone has broken the story about the slick. Aerial shots of the research vessel and the ominously calm sea around it, satellite pictures, experts pontificating, even a blurred close-up of the slick's microscopic fairy castles.

An hour later, Howard Smalls arrives from Washington and

addresses the entire mission team. Rumpled from his red-eye flight, he tells them that an investigation is under way and they will all undergo routine interviews, but meanwhile they should concentrate on the job at hand. There is a press embargo and they must be sure to observe it, and for their own safety they are to be confined to base until launch.

"I hear the ghostly sound of stable doors closing," Bernie Thomas says to Gus Plafker, as they file out.

"Fucking A, dude."

Mariella's interview is conducted by Smalls himself. He runs through a list of questions about her contacts with journalists and colleagues, and then says, "We both know who it was."

"I have an idea."

"They haven't contacted you since the episode at the, the—"

"The moot? No. I would have told you if they had."

"I have to ask, Dr. Anders, because you didn't tell us immediately about the second contact, at the airport."

"I didn't think it was important at the time. And I told you everything about what happened at the moot."

"And you told them nothing about the slick."

"Of course not."

"You might have let something slip by accident. Something that could have provided a clue—"

"How many people are involved in research into the slick? Not just at the site, but in the Cytex laboratories that are carrying out the DNA sequencing. Any one of them could have leaked the information."

"We're investigating every possibility," Smalls says smoothly, and dismisses her.

Mariella is being driven over to the full-scale mock-up of the Mars Shuttle, where the others are practicing start-up procedures, when her slate rings.

It is Senator Thornton's chief of staff. He and Mariella spend a couple of minutes setting up an encrypted line, and then the Senator comes on and says without preamble, "It's Cytex."

"I thought it was the Bushor Report. I've just been talking to Smalls about it."

"The press release certainly purports to be from the Bushor Report," the Senator says, "but it was sent out from an anonymous server. Anyone could have written it. My people are having little luck tracing it back to its original source, but my instinct tells me that Cytex was responsible. They're already spinning this hard, emphasizing their selfless contribution to the mission, their commitment to research into this threat to the ecosystem. It's a clever move, designed to bolster their case for more on-site research. The publicity will ensure a good return on their investment while making the government look like it was trying to cover up the slick."

"My advice always was to be as open as possible, and in my opinion that's how everything should be handled from now on. Ask Cytex to release the genetic sequence of the slick to the scientific community. Call their bluff on their claim of commitment."

"I'll take that under consideration, Dr. Anders. Meanwhile, it's more important than ever that you keep me informed of Penn Brown's side of Cytex's campaign."

Putting her in her place, reminding her of the price she paid to get on the mission.

Mariella says, "And I'll take *that* under consideration."

"See that you do," the Senator says, and hangs up.

Mariella does not want to spend the last day of 2026—perhaps her last New Year, although it doesn't do to dwell on that—in the institutional Siberia of the accommodation block, nicknamed the Star City Motel, which is reserved for astronauts waiting for launch. She is tired of the intrusive security measures—the Christmas excursion to Anchee Ye's home required logistical planning worthy of a small military campaign—and takes pleasure in evading Glory Dunn and her minions. So it is with a sense of adventure, of entering into a dare, that she executes a plan that will allow her a little extracurricular R&R.

Apart from the space museum, the Kennedy Space Center is mostly off limits to tourists, but there is a bus tour that crosses the crawlerway along which Dynawings, X-2s and Big Lifters are transported from the Vehicle Assembly Building to the launch pads.

The bus loops past the VAB and one of the launch pads, and stops at the Saturn V rocket and a simulation of an Apollo countdown before returning to the museum.

Mariella obtains a timetable of the tour buses, and keeps a surreptitious watch on them whenever she can. If the VAB doors are open, the bus obligingly stops and disgorges its passengers so they can take pictures of what is still one of the world's largest structures; the security people suffer fits whenever Mariella or one of the other members of the mission team wanders into view.

On New Year's Eve, the VAB is open because the Dynawing that will take the mission team up to the Mars Shuttle is being readied for transport to the launch pad. Mariella asks to be taken on a tour of inspection in the afternoon. When the last tour bus of the day arrives, it is easy enough to slip away from the bored security man who has been detailed to look after her. She circles around and boards the bus with the tourists. It was only half full, and she has taken the precaution of wearing a quilted coat over her blue coveralls, even has a little camera around her wrist. She suffers the inane commentary of the rest of the tour, her pulse quickening when a jeep races past, its siren wailing and its light bar strobing in the dusky gloom.

No one thinks to check the bus. Mariella gets a transfer at the museum, rides another bus through the perimeter and over the bridge across the Intercoastal Waterway, gets off at the first of the hotels along Highway 1 and snags a taxi that drives her south and west to the Cocoa Beach section of the Barrier.

It is a popular destination. The strip of motels and bars and restaurants along the edge of the Barrier is busy, the parking lots full. Christmas lights are wound around the scaly trunks of palm trees along the edge of the highway; spotlights pick out colorful murals painted on the twenty-meter-high concrete slope of the Barrier. Tethered inflatables sway in the stiff sea breeze: Elvis in all his incarnations; Little Iva; a suffering Christ with bloody stigmata. People brown-bagging booze are jumping in and out of cars cruising for action along the strip. Music roars from the veranda of every restaurant. A steel band is making slow progress through the crowds, followed by a lively conga line.

Mariella joins a gaggle of brightly clothed tourists for a short, noisy airboat ride that skims past the half-submerged streets of Old Cocoa Beach out to the ramshackle pontoon city two kilometers offshore. As the neon glare of the shore recedes, more and more of the Barrier's long sweep becomes visible, a chain of lights stretching a hundred kilometers north and south: it is visible from the Moon. Oceanward, the sky is cloudless and black and full of stars. The lights of the pontoon city are like a nebula fallen into the sea. As the airboat bounces over the waves toward it, a cluster of rockets shoots up, and the tourists around Mariella *ooh* and *aah* as the fireworks burst overhead.

The pontoon city is built around two oil rigs that were towed around Florida's long spit from the exhausted Mississippi coastal fields by a wildcatter who bankrupted herself in the process. They sat there for several years, anchored to a gravel bank that grew up after the destruction of Cocoa Beach by superstorms and rising sea levels, passing through the hands of various receivers until a group of greens took them over and declared a pirate republic. A strange community has established itself on and around the rigs, half gambling houses and bars, half a utopian experiment in self-sufficiency.

Mariella climbs a steel ladder inside the hollow leg of one of the rigs, from the pontoon levels where, in barges lashed side-by-side, most of the floating city's permanent population lives, to what was once the production platform. The derrick has been transformed into a Christmas tree of lights and solar panels and windmills. Little cabins cling to it like wasps' nests, overhanging the geodesic dome that tents a bazaar-like maze of tiny bars and gambling joints.

Mariella trolls the perimeter, disappointed that most of the people in the noisy crowds seem to be tourists. The steel deck vibrates to the beat of a disco carved out of the old crew levels. The first bar she tries won't accept her card; she has to find a moneychanger in a cage of welded steel mesh and pay an appalling exchange rate for what the woman calls doubloons and octoroons—old nickels and dimes. She sits at the counter, fashioned from a couple of ancient surfboards, of a minuscule bar slung at the outer edge of the deck. Black waves surge thirty meters below its plate-glass floor. The bartender brings her a Tecate, a slice of lime wedged in the neck of the bottle. It costs two doubloons: twenty cents, or eighteen dollars. She drinks, says to the man next to her, "I'm an astronaut. Does that bother you?"

"Not yet it doesn't."

"Then let me buy you a drink."

She buys more beer, and a plate of gulf shrimp with chili dip. She tells her new friend that she is going to Mars.

"I know. I saw you on TV. You scared?"

"Sometimes I'm walking around and it hits me. That in four weeks I'll be strapped in above a huge explosion that'll shove me right into orbit. And I won't be coming down for a long time."

"I'd go in a New York minute if they'd let me. Places like this are just the first step. If there was some way of getting this whole thing up to Mars, we'd have us some great times. Even scientists like to cut loose now and then."

"Like me."

"Sure. Like you."

His name is Jed. He is about her age, perhaps a little older. His hair, dyed jet black, is cropped close to his bumpy skull, closer than the whiskers on his chin. He wears leather pants, a horrible red vinyl vest over a black T-shirt. He has eight rings through his left eyebrow, a diamond nose stud, a barbell in his tongue. A Celtic knot tattoo is wrapped around the biceps of his right arm. A crusty red patch in one eyebrow might be an incipient carcinoma; his nose and cheeks are speckled with half a dozen little knotted scars where precancerous polyps have been removed.

Anywhere else he'd look like an unshaven, sunburned drifter. Here, he's a pirate. In his time he's been in a rock band (his soft, hoarse voice is the result of shouting over too much bad guitar), in jail ("Both times for vagrancy. The second time was in L.A. They put me in a work camp for the winter"), has worked on the Barrier ("Mostly driving a crane; cleanest I've ever been in my life, thanks to the judas chip they put in me.") and then helped build the pontoon city. He is mostly an electrician now, and also plays in pickup bands and takes tourists out fishing, although he says that the fishing has been going all to hell.

"The last of the coral died out twenty years ago, but the government put in these artificial reefs for fish? Mostly old tires, concrete from wrecked condos. That worked pretty well, until just lately. Either no fish or what you catch is real unhealthy. I once found a whole patch of ballyhoo floating on the surface. And now the federal government has put the whole area off-limits. More pollution I bet. Some new thing, or bad shit washing out from something some scumbag contractor dumped."

They have moved on to another bar by now. It's somewhere beneath the production platform's deck, and as narrow as a cinema aisle. If someone wants to get from one end to the other, everyone in the bar has to stand up to let them squeeze by. The walls are tiled in battered hubcaps; fairylights loop from the ceiling; bad C&W is playing on an ancient jukebox.

Mariella drains her beer and says, "That's a sad story. You want to fuck?"

Jed has a room in one of the barges, a tiny space partitioned by raw fiberglass. A hammock slung from two ceiling hooks takes up most of it. They fall out twice, Jed giggling from the laced joint he's smoked. Mariella had to pass, mindful of NASA's strict medical screening. Jed has a Prince Albert through the head of his cock. She likes to hold it in her mouth; he likes it too. It is hot and close. They fall asleep in each other's arms.

And are awakened by bright lights in their faces, and people behind the lights. Glory Dunn, the security guy Mariella had ditched. And Penn Brown.

After the debriefing, Penn Brown comes in and says he'll lay it down straight, that he will help her if she helps him.

"Who I fuck is no one's business but mine."

"You compromised security, Mariella, with only six days before launch."

"I wanted a break. No harm done."

It is four in the morning. Mariella is very tired, headachy from the bleary flicker of the fluorescent light of the windowless office, her mouth dry from too much coffee.

Brown sits down so he's knee to knee with her, and says, "Agent Dunn doesn't think so. If this starts going up the chain of

command, Mariella, then you could be pulled from the mission.
You put yourself in danger."

"I keep up with my shots."

"You know what I mean. If we could track you from use of
your credit card, so could they."

"They?"

"The people who tried to kill me."

"Oh. Them."

"They could have killed or kidnapped you, Mariella. I really
don't think you realize what's at stake here."

"Well, Glory Dunn found me and they didn't. I've been over
this with her a dozen times. I'm back. I've had my wrist slapped.
End of story."

"Unfortunately not, unless I intercede on your behalf. Al Paley
is on your side, and I can be on your side too. As long, of course,
that you to do the right thing by me."

Penn Brown takes a piece of paper from the inside pocket of
his jacket and smooths it out on the table beside them. Mariella
reads it upside down, and feels ice mantling her heart.

"You're a bastard. Of the old-fashioned school."

"This is a legitimate contract. You know it's the right thing to
do, Mariella. I'm acting against my own interests. I could easily
allow you to be pulled, allow someone else take your place."

"Smalls wouldn't dare pull me from the mission so soon before
the launch."

"Smalls has never trusted you, and not just because of your
connection with Senator Thornton. That's why he has someone
ready and waiting to replace you."

"I don't believe you."

"I know the man. He's not quite up to speed with training for
the mission, but he knows the science. Believe me, Mariella, if
this gets to Howard Smalls, he'll use it as an excuse to get rid of
you. I'm your last chance."

"I see. This replacement, he's another Cytex affiliate, isn't he?"

Penn Brown doesn't deny it.

Mariella says, "But you don't want anyone else from Cytex to
be in on this. Because any chance of making some money of your
own would be lost."

Penn Brown doesn't deny this, either.

Mariella says, "All this secrecy and security is so much bullshit. It gets in the way of the science. I'm pretty sure a daughter slick is growing right off the Florida coast. No, you're not surprised, are you? You knew. How far has it spread?"

"That's a matter of national security."

"Off the record, did Cytex leak news of the Pacific slick to the Bushor Report?"

"No one needed to leak anything. The slick is spreading, and no security measures could keep it secret forever."

But he doesn't quite meet her gaze when he says this, and she knows then that Senator Mae Thornton was right. She says, "What about Jed?"

"I'm sorry?"

"The guy I was fucking. Glory Dunn says he's being held on some bullshit charge. Drug possession, as if the police don't know about what goes on out there. I want him released."

"I'm not sure you can bargain—"

"Let him go and I'll do what you want."

She does it. She hates herself, but she has no choice. She signs the contract. She flies to Washington two days later, sits in front of the members of the ad hoc subcommittee, and tells them of her concerns about the biological rationale of the mission. The arguments Penn Brown has told her to use taste bad in her mouth. Senator Thornton listens to her with ill-disguised amazement and contempt. Afterward, Mariella throws up in a washroom, and then has to wait interminably while Penn Brown takes his turn. He is smiling when he comes out. He has won. He is in charge.

Mariella spends the next few days with the Cytex biophysics instrumentation team, helping with the final tests of the hastily redesigned biological experiment packages, keeping away from Anchee Ye. Whenever the two women are thrown together, at a press conference or a briefing or during the dress rehearsal for the Dynawing launch and transfer onto the Mars Shuttle, Mariella flushes with shame and her hatred of Penn Brown tightens a notch.

And so it goes, until the launch of the Mars Shuttle out of Earth orbit toward Mars.

PART TWO

LIFE ON MARS

Earth Orbit–Mars Orbit:
January 6–February 23, 2027

"In the beginning was the planetary disc, spinning out flat around the central flare of the new-born sun. It was a violent and chaotic place, but gradually, by a kind of sedimentation process, dust grains settled through the turbulent gases and formed wide concentric rings in the plane of rotation.

"In the outer part of the disc, where water ice was too cold to sublime in vacuum, the large planets accreted quickly. Jupiter in only a million years; Saturn a million years later. But the inner dust rings were orbiting faster than the outer rings and so were much hotter, driving off water and other volatiles. The tiny grains of iron and anhydrous silicates that remained slowly drew together into loose, fluffy balls that collided and coalesced into hundreds of billions of irregular planetisimals a few kilometers in diameter. These collided with each other in turn, and since they were all rotating in the same direction, the collisions were gentle. The planetesimals clung together, growing by aggregation into rocky protoplanets.

"As these protoplanets swept out their orbits, they grew larger still, colliding and recolliding until at last they had swept up most of the smaller bodies around them, and had stabilized their orbits. After forty million years, there were only five major bodies in the inner zone of the Solar System.

"One of them would eventually become the Earth.

"This was the Hadean epoch. The proto-Earth was about half its present size, and still drawing in planetoids and comets that crossed its orbit. The tremendous energies liberated by these impacts heated and melted its crust. The whole surface was covered in liquid lava. Its heat propagated outward in the form of violent volcanic explosions and geysers of molten rock, and slowly propagated inward, melting inner layers of metallic iron and silicates. The molten iron settled at the core of the planet and, like slag in a blast furnace, the lighter silicates floated to the surface.

"As the proto-Earth differentiated, its outer layers began to cool, but it was to suffer one final cataclysm. A protoplanet about a third its size swung around the sun in a dangerously similar orbit. Fifty million years after the beginning of planetary formation, it finally collided with the proto-Earth. The first impact was only glancing, shattering the crust of the smaller body and deforming it into an elongated ovoid, but on the next orbit, the two bodies struck each other squarely. The protoplanet's heavy iron core sank into the Earth and its mantle of molten rock arced away into orbit, quickly coalescing into what would become the Moon. The heat pulse of the impact remelted the proto-Earth's outer layers and drove off all water and gases. If any life had evolved prior to the impact, it would have been completely destroyed.

"The Earth was now about two-thirds its present size, closely orbited by a two-thirds-size Moon. Cometary bombardment and a constant rain of ultramicroscopic dust added to the bulk of both Earth and Moon, and the Earth's gravity allowed it to retain much of the comets' inventory of gases and water.

"Beneath a dense atmosphere consisting mostly of carbon dioxide, the planet was covered with a steaming sea interrupted only by a few lava ridges. Although the young sun was much redder and cooler, incessant vulcanism and the greenhouse effect of the dense, carbon dioxide atmosphere kept the Earth's surface at a temperature above eighty degrees Centigrade. Its day was very short, and the Moon orbited much closer than now, raising huge tides that sloshed around the watery globe. Cataclysmic cometary impacts blasted craters the size of Texas, generating huge hurricanes of live steam and ejecting vast amounts of gas and water into space.

"And somewhere in this cauldron, something happened that would forever change the face of the planet. Life began."

This is the preamble to one of the talks Mariella gives as the

Mars Shuttle, the *Beagle*, accelerates on a long ellipse away from the Earth toward Mars. The members of the scientific team take turns to give informal presentations on their specialities; Mariella's are based on the early part of the legendary undergraduate course she gave at UCLA, before the Firstborn Crisis.

She started her life as a legal alien in Los Angeles a few weeks after the formal interview in Cambridge at which she was granted her doctorate. At the beginning of his career, David Davies had worked for two years in Steve Zwerek's laboratory in UCLA's Biology Department, funded by a NATO exchange program intended to strengthen the alliance between the United States and Western European countries at a scientific level. And now Mariella, his best graduate student, was following in his footsteps.

Steve Zwerek was a dryly humorous, avuncular New York Jew with a gravelly voice and salt-and-pepper hair combed back in stiff waves from his lofty, creased forehead. Mariella knew him from conferences and the sabbatical visit he had made to Davies's lab, where, like any new graduate student, he had learned from first principles how to grow microbial cultures in the high-pressure, high-temperature containment vessel. He had five kids from three marriages, a house in an old, leafy neighborhood south of Westwood, an antique Datsun Z80, and a pilot's license. On weekends he liked to hire a small plane and fly to Taho or Carmel or Sedona. He was a senior figure in the Biology Department, had just finished an obligatory year as department chairman, and was eager to get back into research.

In her first few months at UCLA, as in Cambridge, Mariella built a reputation as a whiz kid who could solve intractable problems on the spot. The postgraduates and postdocs in Zwerek's lab were all much older than Mariella—she was in fact younger than most of UCLA's senior-year undergraduates—but she was used to being the youngest and it did not faze her.

She quickly adapted to life in Los Angeles. She rented a studio apartment in Santa Monica, a converted garage at the end of the garden of an old woman who was once a costume designer at Universal Studios, and who kept rare ornamental ducks in a conservatory attached to her house. After her early-morning run, Mariella ate a quick breakfast at a local diner and commuted into work on one of the old blue-and-white Santa Monica buses.

The red brick Life Sciences Building was at the Westwood Village end of the big campus. African lilies flowered under the mature cedars and pines in front of it; its staff and students ate lunch in the nearby Bombshelter cafeteria, at tiled tables under coral trees in the warm winter sunshine. There was a row of tall glass-and-steel lab complexes, monuments to the boom in biotechnology, the shabby engineering building that had once housed, amazingly, a nuclear reactor, older buildings in Spanish-colonial style, including a huge shopping center, brick-paved plazas, fountains, rolling lawns, the football stadium, a theater and a cinema complex, fraternities on the north side and sororities on the south.

Mariella bought a second-hand electric car, small and battered but with enough pep to zip around the freeways that knitted together the four ecologies (Surfurbia, Foothills, The Plains of Id, Autopia) and the two dozen suburbs in search of a center. She discovered that in Los Angeles distance converted to time, and time was defined by routes. By this standard, the gardens of the Huntingdon Museum, over in the Valley were, on Sundays, as close as Venice Beach.

Like the rest of the States, Los Angeles was enjoying a booming economy that pundits were beginning to compare to the Eisenhower fifties. There had been a bad El Niño in the previous year—winter rainstorms had washed out roads and homes along the coast, and the L.A. basin had been fogged out every summer morning—but in the year Mariella arrived, the city's famously balmy climate made a brief return. It rained most of February, and when it was not raining the snow-capped peaks of the San Gabriel Mountains showed clear and sharp at the skyline. And then it stopped raining and every day unfolded under perfect blue skies, each a little warmer than the one before.

Mariella saw in real life places she'd seen a thousand times in movies. She saw movies being made on the streets, like dreams recreating themselves. On Sundays, she took tea on the lawn with her landlady, who entertained her with stories of old Hollywood, before digital actors and CGI. Steve Zwerek flew her to Catalina

Island, where they ate bison burgers at the primitive airport before flying straight back, a silly, extravagant gesture that perfectly encapsulated the American ethos. Anything that could be done should be done, a perpetually widening horizon of possibilities. She went skiing at Mammoth with a bunch of Australian postgraduates, had a brief fling with a husky chap who taught her how to surf in the surprisingly chilly water off Zuma Beach. Her parents visited after two months, a diversion on a business trip to Mexico, where her father's company was assessing the potential of a new methane clathrate field. They were amused to discover that their daughter had acquired an American accent; Mariella had cultivated it because she had grown bored with explaining to bank tellers and store clerks that, yes, her cute way of talking was real English, and that, no, she was from Scotland, not New Zealand or Canada.

Most of all, she worked.

She had come to Los Angeles to work on Zwerek's pet obsession, the origin of life on Earth, and in particular the origin of the deal struck between the two great polymer languages of nucleic acids and proteins. As Mariella said later, a throwaway line in an interview for a TV documentary that would haunt her career, with DNA life entered the information age. Work on this problem would establish her at the forefront of her generation of biologists, a generation that would, with the Firstborn Crisis, be united in an urgent and world-changing enterprise. But that was five years in the future. In the beginning, in Steve Zwerek's lab, Mariella worked on the structure of primitive RNAs.

RNA molecules transfer information from DNA to the cellular machinery that assembles proteins. Both RNA and DNA encode the recipe for life, but while double-stranded DNA always coils in the famous double helix, single-stranded RNA molecules are more versatile and can cross-link with themselves, forming shapes like so many bent paperclips. Some of these configurations are self-replicating; others can act like simple enzymes. While life based on DNA always requires the partnership of proteins, it is possible that very early life could have been based entirely on RNA.

Within a year, Mariella and Steve Zwerek had defined all the possible structural configurations of RNAs able to function both as information carriers and enzymes — instruction manuals that could not only print copies of themselves but also carry out the limited functions they encoded. For the first time, the ecology of the hypothetical prebiotic RNA world was clearly delimited. Mariella and Zwerek published three papers, and Mariella gave a ten-minute presentation at the annual conference of the American Society of Cell and Molecular Biologists.

A week after the conference, Mariella was in the library, which in those days was still located in the first floor and basement of the UCLA teaching hospital — you followed a third-floor corridor that suddenly became a closed bridge over the service road that separated the hospital and the Life Sciences Building, or went through the foyer of the John Wayne Cancer Clinic, past a gnarled bronze statue of the actor. (Mariella's landlady told her that Wayne had been exposed to the fallout of a nuclear test in Nevada, while shooting *The Conqueror*.) Mariella was writing up the paper she had presented at the meeting, and had the habit, learned from David Davies, of looking up relevant research papers in the original printed form. Editors of scientific journals often bundled distantly related papers together, but serendipitous discovery of these connections was possible only if you gave up the convenience of electronic recall and actually went down into the stacks and cracked the volumes.

While Mariella was working, a young man, dark-complexioned and burly, came over and asked if he could buy her a coffee. She accepted, partly because she had never before been addressed as ma'am. His name was Forrest Oramas. He was from Florida, a biomathematician specializing in application of chaos theory to the spread of pandemics. Mariella agreed to his suggestion of a hiking trip in the San Gabriel Mountains, and was thrilled to find an entire wilderness tucked away half an hour's drive east of the city center. They talked about their research as they hiked steep slopes between pine trees in cool, clean air. They talked about departmental gossip, about movies, about the weird and wonderful city in which they were both strangers, amazed and happy at their ease with each other.

They moved in together six months later; two months after that they were married in Las Vegas by an Elvis impersonator. And four years later, after Mariella had become an American citizen and a tenure-track associate professor at UCLA, in the middle of the beginning of what would come to be known as the Firstborn Crisis, Forrest was killed.

The informal scientific talks are held in the *Beagle*'s radiation storm shelter, at the center of mass of the accommodation module. It is a circular chamber three meters in diameter, wrapped in a double-skinned water reservoir intended to absorb most of the radiation should the sun throw off a flare while the *Beagle* is in transit.

Mariella sits cross-legged with one foot hooked around a rung as she addresses the others, who lie flat on the white, ribbed rubber that covers the chamber, or hang vertically in the air around her, bobbing slowly this way and that in the cross-drafts of the ventilators. By common courtesy, everyone keeps to the same orientation. Most of the crew suffered from some degree of nausea while adapting to microgravity, and those especially affected, such as Ali Tillman and Alex Dyachkov, are still prone to attacks if they spin around too quickly, or if they find themselves without an absolute reference point.

Penn Brown lounges against what has by consensus become the back wall of the spherical chamber, his attention fully focused on Mariella as she explains how life arose on Earth. He shaved his head just before launch, and the square shape of his skull is more prominent than ever, a box of bone with a helmet of black bristles.

Mariella is acutely aware of his unwavering, inquisitorial gaze as she tells her audience about the steady rain of organic material delivered to the Earth by comets and by interstellar dust, silicate grains, the size of smoke particles, which are blown off the banked furnaces of old stars. As specks of dust form the seeds of raindrops or snowflakes on Earth, so in space these tiny grains accumulate frozen ammonia, methane, water and carbon monoxide, and when they drift near another star and are bathed in its raw light, complex molecules are generated from these precursors. This is the raw stuff of the outer edge of the primordial planetary disc, preserved still in comets; samples snatched by probes have revealed the presence of vesicles containing complex organic molecules. The precursors of life could have been delivered from space into the early Earth's hot oceans.

Now Mariella asks her audience to take another step, and to imagine two kinds of replicating systems. The first is a series of autocatalytic chemical reactions concentrated within tiny vesicles whose skins are self-organizing lipid bilayers. They accumulate chemicals from the surrounding medium, grow, and cleave into daughter vesicles. Competition for resources drives the evolution of ever-more-efficient metabolic pathways. In particular, those vesicles that have developed the ability to synthesize simple proteins that stabilize their delicate lipid bilayer membranes will be more likely to survive than those that have not.

The second replicating system has no real metabolism; it is based on a nonorganic template, most likely crystalline arrays in montmorillonitic clays, which catalyze formation of chains of nucleotide bases. This is Cech's RNA world, in which, from a huge and random variety, emerge some forms capable of making copies of themselves.

Now Mariella asks her audience to imagine metabolically active liposomes electrostatically adhering to clay templates rich in RNA chains. When the two systems combine, two kinds of RNA molecule quickly evolve, one a template encoding the amino acid sequences of the simple proteins that stabilize the liposome membranes, the other able to read that sequence and bond appropriate amino acids together. The first step on the road to life has been made.

Mariella's work on the problem of how the code of life evolved cemented her reputation as one of the best biologists of her generation. She stayed on at UCLA when her fellowship ended, at first supported by a grant she wrote with Zwerek, then as a tenure-track associate professor, one of two junior positions created when Zwerek retired. Research funding had been badly affected by the sudden collapse of the economic boom, but Mariella managed to do some theoretical work in the little time left by her lecturing and assessment duties.

She found that, unexpectedly, she enjoyed teaching. She worked hard on the freshman biology course she had been assigned, taking apart everything she knew and reassembling it to reveal the fundamental questions and principles too often obscured by thickets of trivial facts. She titled it *From Hydrogen to Human,* and it later become part of the cultural mythos of UCLA, circulating in samizdat copies assembled from notes taken by various hands (Mariella famously did not use lecture notes herself) and later published as the *UCLA Red Book.*

Mariella began her first lecture from a cosmological viewpoint, asking why the basic building blocks of life, hydrogen and carbon and oxygen, are so universally abundant, using this question to explore fundamentals of fusion processes in stars, the strong and weak anthropic principles, and the principle of mediocrity. She followed this with six lectures on the origin of the Solar System and of life on Earth, including chunks of work she had not yet published. She spent another six lectures on the ways by which organisms capture energy, blithely sketched the evolution of animals and plants in a single lecture, then looped back to use various incidents—the Precambrian explosion in animal body form; the Permian extinction; the great meteorite impact at the end of the Cretaceous era; the last great Ice Age—to illustrate how evolution is driven by chance and contingency.

An odd thing began to happen. Although fewer and fewer undergraduates turned up, intimidated by the intellectual challenge, attendance numbers did not fall. Postgraduates and postdocs and even some of Mariella's colleagues sat and listened as day by day she outlined the evolutionary pressures that drove life to spread into every available niche and to utilize every possible biochemical repertoire to process energy, concluding with an examination of the horizontal spread of genes across species barriers caused by biotechnological manipulations, and the reconceptualization of nature this had caused.

When the departmental committee met to review her status, there was little dissent. Mariella had turned away graduate students who wanted to work with her, her research grant record was mediocre, she was not considered a team player by her male colleagues, and she was appallingly bad at keeping up with the flood of bureaucratic documents that all academic institutions ceaselessly generate. But in only two years she had published nine papers in high-ranking journals, had been invited to speak at more than a dozen international conferences, had been the subject of articles in *Science* and *Scientific American*, and had just published what was widely considered to be a seminal critical review on theories of the origin of the genetic code. She was granted tenure at once.

Mariella and Forrest had been married for almost exactly three years. They had the little house in Silverlake, with its cactus garden and its terraced slope of orange and lemon trees. Forrest wanted children, but they agreed that there was still plenty of time for that. They were young, with hectic careers. They spent a lot of time apart — Forrest's work on epidemiology meant that he had to commute between Los Angeles, Atlanta and Washington, D.C. — but they made up for the periods of separation with scuba-diving holidays in Hawaii and the Caribbean and Brazil, or long skiing weekends in Colorado or New Mexico. They redecorated their house, created a vegetable plot where they cultivated bell peppers and chili peppers and tomatoes, held informal dinner parties in the cactus garden. They were so very happy.

But then Forrest volunteered to go into the field to study a puzzling downturn in live male births in Central America. No one knew it then, but it was the beginning of the Firstborn Crisis, in which Mariella would make her reputation, and lose her husband.

Mariella was still working on the origin of life. Steve Zwerek had retained an office and half a lab after retirement, and they were exploring possible ways by which the genetic code might have evolved in their hypothetical RNA world. This work is what Mariella tries to explain to her little audience in the *Beagle*'s radiation storm shelter.

The genetic code of DNA is written in an alphabet of four letters, A, T, C and G, standing for the nucleotide bases adenine, thymine, cytosine and guanine. These four bases are able to code for the twenty amino acids that form proteins because they are organized into triplet codons. Three consecutive bases form a single codon that corresponds to a particular amino acid. Since there are sixty-four possible combinations, most amino acids are specified by more than one codon, and there are tantalizing hints of patterns and repetitions that suggest the origin of the code.

Generally, the first two bases in each codon are more important than the third. Carl Woese proposed that since the codon assignments and the translation mechanism must have evolved together, both were initially messy, with perhaps fewer than twenty amino acids involved. Mariella took this further, suggesting that at the beginning of the evolution of life, it may have mattered only if the amino acids were polar or nonpolar: whether they were soluble in water or in lipid. Short chains of amino acids with alternating domains of polar and nonpolar amino acids could have stabilized the lipid membranes of prebiotic vesicles, and projected beyond them to snag and internalize chemicals required for the vesicles' primitive metabolisms.

With Forrest away, Mariella worked hard and long on this hypothesis, her initial insight steadily complicated by the need for actual proof. She missed her husband more than she would admit. They kept in touch by e-mail. Forrest wrote vivid and funny and touching descriptions of the places he travelled through. He confided to her that it was clear that something fundamental had happened to the ratio of male to female births. The sex ratio of embryos at conception was as expected, roughly 1:1, but almost half of all male fetuses spontaneously aborted when two months old. It was almost certainly due to a sex-linked factor.

Work was a way of not thinking about how much she missed him. She made endless computer simulations to prove that it was possible to construct functional proteins organized by simple, nonspecific domains of polar and nonpolar amino acids. And by applying esoteric mathematical techniques such as symmetry breaking and continuous transforms, she was able to identify the bases that had coded for different functional types of amino acid in the first self-replicating RNA-based metabolic systems: uracil (which in RNA substitutes for thymine) or cytosine for nonpolar amino acids; guanine or adenine for polar amino acids. Doubling the size of these single-letter codons permitted more specific amino acid determination; addition of a third base gave even more specificity, and gave rise to sequences that terminated synthesis of proteins, so that a single RNA molecule could code for more than one protein. With this modification, it was possible to string RNA genes together, but as only relatively short lengths of single-stranded RNA are stable, these primitive chromosomes could contain only a few genes. And so information was transferred to a highly stable double-stranded molecule closely related to RNA. To DNA. The first species differentiated out of the amorphous soup of liposomes. Life on Earth truly began.

At this point in Mariella's talk, Penn Brown can keep quiet no longer. He says loudly, "But all this is pure speculation! You talk about two hypothetical structures, and jam them together and call it a proof. It's like blending an orange and a banana to make lemon juice. And even when you use proven facts, you select just what you need to shore up your hypothesis. By that method anyone else could select another equally valid set of facts. It is fantasy science. No, not even that, because it is not testable by experiment. It is not falsifiable. So we are left only with fantasy."

This outburst stirs even the flight crew. Everyone had turned to look at Penn Brown when he spoke; now they turn back to Mariella, who takes a deep breath and says, "I don't deny that someone else could come up with a different hypothesis. In fact, I have frequently challenged people to do so, but no one has. Yes, it is impossible to know the exact prebiotic conditions in Earth's early history, because those conditions have long ago vanished. But it is possible to imagine it with considerable rigor. We know that certain things are possible, and certain things are not. Unlike God, we do not start from nothing."

"Of course not," Penn Brown says. "But even if I grant your set of initial conditions—and there are many unknown variables—there are still an infinite number of paths between that set of conditions and the actual conditions we're familiar with today. So why choose one path over the others?"

Mariella allows herself a smile. She knows now that his critical assault is not based on any rigorous analysis of her work, but on simple prejudice. He does not believe in any of it because he does not believe that she can be right. His challenge is not against the hypothesis; it is against her.

She says, "As a matter of fact, the number of pathways is not infinite. A moment's thought shows that there are a finite number of components, and that many pathways must be invalid because they do not agree with known facts. And there is another winnowing mechanism. Instead of breaking the pathways into their component links, A to B, B to C, and so on, it is better to think of the problem as a whole, to imagine its shape and then to discover which links can nest within that space."

Brown's eyes darken. He says, "Holism. How I loathe that word. It demeans the hundreds of years of human intellectual effort devoted to identifying the forms and functions of the fundamental components of life. It's the intellectual equivalent of oatmeal."

"The particular branch of mathematics to which I refer is hardly as shapeless as oatmeal, dry or boiled. I believe it is used by NASA to analyze complex systems and identify potential weaknesses."

Bernie Thomas, the flight engineer, says, "You're talking about province mapping? Well, that can be pretty crafty stuff, but it's hardly magical. I didn't know you could apply it to this kind of thing, though."

Mariella smiles at him. It is difficult to dislike Bernie. He's the youngest of the flight crew, amiable and easygoing, taller and broader than most astronauts, a college and then state football hero with a Ph.D. in the esoteric mathematics of the eighteen-dimensional space in which gravity operates. He habitually wears a baseball cap turned sideways, spends more time exercising than any other two people, and chews gum with machine-gun intensity, which is what he is doing now as he returns Mariella's smile.

"Of course," she says. "Province mapping not only finds the areas where linkage is problematical, it also by default highlights those areas where it is not problematical."

"You mean, if it ain't broke, don't fix it," Bernie Thomas says, and laughs.

"Damn right, bubba," Gus Plafker growls. He is the constant

cynical foil to Bernie Thomas's sunny good humor. The two men are inseparable, and during simulations of potential emergencies fall into a private language packed with codes and allusions.

"A fantasy is still a fantasy," Penn Brown says, but there is a note of appeal in his voice now. He knows that he is losing his audience.

Anchee Ye says, "I do not understand what you object to, Penn. Is it to the hypothesis itself? If so, the only valid objections must surely be based on opposing hypotheses. But you do not propose one. Is it the facts that make up the hypothesis? Almost all of them have been thoroughly established by research, or are backed by mathematical derivation."

"I'll tell you exactly what I object to," Penn Brown says. "Mariella's little holistic theory is not science, but storytelling. Science is about the actual world. It is about stripping away mystery to get at the heart of the matter. Once you understand the fundamental rules, the whole world becomes transparent."

Mariella says, "A flower is still a flower, even when you have sequenced the genes that control its development."

"AM/FM," Bernie Thomas says. "Actual machines versus fucking magic."

"Fucking A," Gus Plafker growls, and both men crack up.

Martin McCord says, "I do believe we have a live mike, gentlemen."

"Hell, Martin," Bernie Thomas says amiably, "who listens to this stuff but a couple of techs at the Goddard FCC? And they're probably passing the time by reading some really thick manual."

"Mister Dyachkov is recording it," McCord says, reminding them all of the little semiautonomous camera that squats on Alex Dyachkov's shoulder like a cybernetic parrot.

"I've said far worse than that in front of him," Bernie Thomas says.

"Fuckin' A."

"NASA will edit out the swearing," Alex Dyachkov says.

"Even so," McCord says. He is a humorless team player with a seamed face and perpetual five o'clock shadow. Bernie Thomas and Gus Plafker have nicknamed him the Ice Commander, but nevertheless show him great respect. He is of the old school of astronauts, a Navy aviator who won two field promotions while flying recon missions in the "firefighting" actions that secured the USA's hegemony over the Mexican border cities in the revolution after the Firstborn Crisis, a veteran of two textbook Mars Shuttle missions and numerous Earth orbit and Earth-Moon flights, one of the few mission commanders without a Ph.D. Perhaps that accounts for his brusqueness when dealing with the science team. He clears his throat and says, "Well, I think I speak for everyone when I say it was a really good talk. Stirred up some debate and, the main thing, kept most of us awake most of the time."

Alex Dyachkov says, "Is this the kind of thing you guys hope to prove when you get to Mars?"

Mariella says, "It's certainly possible that any Martian microbes may have remained in a more primitive state than their terrestrial counterparts." Looking at Penn Brown, who has refused, despite her new status as a scientific consultant contracted to Cytex, to divulge any of the results of the DNA sequencing and biochemical analysis of the slick.

Bernie Thomas says, "By the time we get there, we'll find a bunch of Chinese restaurants selling Martian chicken, heavy on the red chili, lightly sprinkled with superoxide dust, kind of dry. And served deep frozen."

"We don't know where they intend to land," McCord says.

"Oh sure," Bernie Thomas says. "As if it isn't where they went before. The north pole icecap. I'm happy to take any bets against it."

"The icecap is a big place," Ali Tillman says.

Bernie Thomas says, "But we all know the rumors. The first Chinese expedition found themselves some Martians, and these guys are going to check it out. Except they have to wait until the Chinese clear the plate before they get their turn to bat." He winks at Mariella. "Am I right or am I right?"

"If there is life on Mars, it will have evolved far from initial conditions," Penn Brown says doggedly. "This fantasy construct of Dr. Anders will always remain just that."

"That's true," Betsy Sharp says. Like Penn Brown, she cut her hair short prior to the mission's start, an even centimeter of gray hair crowning the narrow blade of her face. She is a careful, unimaginative scientist, the kind who does well via a combination of hard work and adroit, tireless politicking. Her dislike of Mariella is palpable. To her, science is a serious, sacred business, and Mariella is altogether too casual about it. She says, "It isn't my field, but surely the Martian fossil record shows a wealth of diversity."

Mariella says, "I'll leave you with a final thought. We have strong evidence from Martian fossils that life arose on Mars before it arose on Earth. That's not surprising, because Mars is a smaller planet, and it cooled more quickly. And we know now that life on Mars and life on Earth share the same genetic code, and so must have a common origin. It is possible that life originated elsewhere and infected both Mars and Earth, but it is more likely that some form of early life could have been carried from Mars to Earth on a rock ejected by a big impact. So in a sense we could be going to Mars to rediscover our origins, because we could all be Martians."

"Another pretty fantasy, half fact and half wild speculation," Penn Brown says. "We don't have any firm evidence that the slick has any connection with the life the Chinese supposedly found on Mars."

He stares hard at Mariella, as if daring her to say more, to risk breaking the confidentiality clause of the contract she signed, and smiles when she does not reply.

Anchee Ye says, "If you don't know if the slick has a Martian origin, why is Cytex risking so much of its money on this mission?"

"We're a risk-taking enterprise," Penn Brown says, and spins neatly in midair and swims through the exit hatch.

When Mariella thanks Anchee Ye for her support, the geologist says, "Perhaps I may be permitted a question of my own. Why do you take Cytex's coin when Dr. Brown so clearly dislikes you?"

The door of the barge's cabin banging open. Trying to untangle her legs from Jed's, naked to the rush of cold air and the sudden light. Mariella can feel herself blushing, and hates herself for it. How to explain the human heart? She says, knowing it sounds feeble, "They're on the inside track."

"Yes, because the government took it away from NASA and gave it to them. I think Penn is an intellectually weak man. He attacks you to hide that."

"Like it or not, he's in charge."

Anchee Ye says solemnly, "On Mars it will be different. Everything is different on Mars."

Mariella imagined that the voyage out would be no more than a transition. Forty-eight days of empty time lent meaning only by routine. And yet even within the first few days, everything is changed. The Earth and the Moon shrink with surprising rapidity to a double star of merely ordinary brightness that is soon lost in the sun's glare; the only world left is that of the spacecraft, a busy little island falling through profound emptiness. Mariella finds that she must make a conscious effort to remember the void. The human mind, with its amazing capacity for adaptation, quickly accommodates to what can be measured by the senses.

The Mars Shuttle, the *Beagle*, is an asymmetric dumbbell one hundred and twenty-three meters long. Most of that is taken up by the Ion Compressed Antimatter Nuclear propulsion system. The engine itself, with its intricate arrangement of pusher plates and shock-absorber baffles, is thirty-six meters long, separated from the accommodation module by a seventy-two meter stalk with storage rings for antiprotons, target uranium slugs, electrical generators, and a collar of dense shielding against the ICAN's neutron emission. The accommodation module is a mere fifteen meters long, the lander-SSTO ascent vehicle capping it beneath a gold foil shroud. In total, the *Beagle* resembles nothing so much as a spermatozoon configured back-to-front, its tail swollen by the motor that, through a constant series of fusion explosions as antiprotons guided by magnetic field lines strike uranium targets and generate showers of fast neutrons, accelerates the spacecraft to a hundred and twenty kilometers per second, out of Earth's fecund orbit toward the dry ovum of Mars.

Mariella once visited the University of Kansas's lovely old-fashioned natural history museum, on a break from a dull, single-track conference on extremophile archaebacteria. In a corner of one of the glass cases was a cross-section through a pack rat's nest, a neat ball of woven grass decorated with bottle tops and scraps of foil and brightly colored paper. The *Beagle*'s accommodation module is like the nest of a family of pack rats with a bad jones for technology. It is a maze of small cluttered spaces linked by tunnels, where nine people, their life-support system, and several tons of electronics and cargo are packed into the volume of a large truck. There are little nooks that, with gimballed racks of equipment, can be transformed into laboratories, a cubbyhole dedicated to the various mapping and survey projects that will occupy the two crew members left behind in orbit; a tiny space like an ultra-high-tech kitchen where material science experiments are performed as part of the defrayment of commercial sponsorship, the control module with its three acceleration couches amid panels filled with dedicated switches and rainbows of indicator lights (although impressive, this is a backup system, since most of the control functions have been subsumed by virtual reality), passages lined with white, ridged rubber grubby with fingerprints; panels that can be pulled out to reveal rats' nests of wires, optical cables, and color-coded tubing. The longest line of sight, down the central axis tunnel from one of the storm shelter's hatches to the inner hatch dogging the airlock of the lander, is no more than four meters. The air is either too hot and moist or too cold; one of the unending housekeeping tasks is to wipe every surface with cloths impregnated with biocides to prevent fungal growth. And the entire module is perpetually filled with the noise of fans pushing air around, the hum of electric motors, the tick-tick-tick of heat stress as the shuttle slowly rotates in barbecue mode to even out temperature differences, and there's always the sound of people working somewhere, conversation, the percussive thuds of someone scooting along a passageway, Bernie Thomas's Country and Western music or Ali Tillman's bangra-beat.

Each of the crew has a privacy module not much bigger than a vertical coffin. They sleep strapped in silvery bags, fans whispering a few centimeters from their faces so that they will not suffocate in a cloud of rebreathed air. Despite an eye mask and ear plugs,

Mariella's sleep is always disturbed, with horrible dreams of falling. Most of the crew take refuge in VR during their R&R periods; headsets give the illusion of a panorama three meters wide hung beyond the walls. Mariella, who has never had any time for TV, takes refuge in work, and the routine of housekeeping and exercise.

Everyone has to exercise in the little gymnasium for at least two hours a day, wired up for heartbeat, breath rate, muscle tension and skin temperature. They are all suffering from the effects of microgravity. Fluid redistribution causes head congestion and puffing of facial tissues; for the whole voyage, Mariella feels that she is suffering from a bad, sinusy head cold. Microgravity also shrinks muscle mass in the lower body, reduces blood plasma volume, and increases kidney filtration rates. They all have to measure their fluid intake, and smart toilets monitor their output. Mariella's rib cage and chest muscles have relaxed and expanded, and unless she remembers to keep her abdominal muscles tight she can feel her guts float up and press against her diaphragm. Luckily, unlike more than half the crew, she does not suffer from motion sickness; Ali Tillman spent the first few days with a plastic bag sealed more or less permanently to her face, until a medical officer on the ground prescribed something that has left her dopey but functional.

Other effects of the voyage are more insidious. Cosmic rays and other particles sleeting through the spacecraft increase the risk of cancer by just over one percent: a hot proton striking a cell nucleus can cause dozens of breaks in the intricate coils of DNA. And despite shielding, the neutron flux of the ICAN motor, summed over the entire mission, is almost half a billion neutrons per square centimeter, a dose of about thirty rem, two hundred times the normal dose due to natural background radiation at sea level on Earth. This is not insignificant, although in most cases natural cellular repair mechanisms and anti-cancer treatments can cope with it.

And day by day their weight-bearing bones lose calcium and their muscle tone deteriorates, and so they must all exercise; and Bernie Thomas and Gus Plafker must exercise the most because they will stay in orbit while the others descend to Mars. They will be in microgravity for more than one hundred and twenty days, far less than records set by Russian cosmonauts on the old Mir space station, but still a significant risk to long-term health. They will travel to Mars but never land there, and will not be allowed to take part in another extended mission. They face lowered life expectancy, an increased risk of arthritis, heart trouble and strokes. So it is not unusual to scull into the little gymnasium and find one or both of them grimly working on the tethered treadmill or on the exercise bicycle or against spring-loaded weights in a muggy halo of sweat and male pheromones, wearing nothing but flimsy nylon shorts and sensor pads (but neither Gus Plafker, with his dense swirls of black hair across the fish-white skin of his chest and back, nor Bernie Thomas's well-defined muscles under smooth brown skin, do anything for Mariella).

The three flight crew are kept busy running simulations, checking and rechecking the AIs that nurse the spacecraft's intricate systems, using radar and telescopes to add to the inventory of minor bodies in the vastness between the orbits of Earth and Mars, running experiments on materials technology and biomedical cell cultures.

The scientists have less to do. They will not start their real work until they reach Mars. They stay in contact with colleagues on Earth via email, for face-to-face conversations are soon made impossible by the pauses as radio signals crawl at the speed of light across the growing gulf between Earth and the *Beagle*. Longer messages, mission updates from Earth and one-sided press conferences (the crew responding to prepared questions) are broadcast in compressed squirts. Not that anyone, aside from a few science journalists and space freaks, is much interested in the mission now that it is under way. The flurry of excitement about the origin of the slick has blown itself out. The media has moved on to the next scandal, like a caravan to the next oasis. Still, Alex Dyachkov dutifully files a selection of video clips every day, and seems to spend most of his time looking over people's shoulders or interviewing them, presumably practicing for his work with Barbara Lopez, the Old Woman of Mars, the red planet's first permanent inhabitant.

Mariella likes Alex. He is obsessively neat and somewhat vain, the only man on the spacecraft to go to the trouble of maintaining a neatly trimmed beard. Every three days, he spends an hour working on it with little scissors and a vacuum line, and in an idle moment is usually to be found buffing his nails with an orange stick. Most of the crew have broken and dirty fingernails because they use their hands to haul themselves about, but Alex's are manicure-perfect. Although he is usually very quiet, the quietness of a trained observer, he has a driven intensity that emerges at unexpected moments. When he gets too excited he starts to stutter and has to take several deep breaths to calm himself. "Oh man," he says, "I shouldn't get carried away."

He performed badly on most of the training exercises, and Mariella and Anchee Ye helped him whenever he got into real difficulties. One evening, a couple of weeks before the start of the mission, he took them to a Russian restaurant to thank them, and they all got smashed on a variety of flavored vodkas under the stern, disapproving gaze of their minders.

Alex's father had been a filmmaker too. His family, third-generation Russian immigrants, owned a restaurant in the Hollywood Hills, and Alex's father was expected to take over the business. Instead, he worked his way through UCLA film school and after graduation directed TV commercials, a series of acclaimed short features for MTV, and a couple of slick but forgettable caper movies. Then he went to Russia to shoot, from his own script, a comedy about a Russian hit man, but the production was fatally derailed by the chaos after the assassination of the President. The shadowy entrepreneur who put up most of the front money vanished, and Alex's father fled the country ahead of death threats from creditors who, if not actually Mafiosi, definitely had acquaintances who were. Alex's father was bankrupted and his career was poisoned; no one returned his calls; his family disowned him. He wrecked his health with alcohol and a bad cocaine habit, died of a heart attack in the middle of a porno shoot in a cabin outside the Mammoth ski resort.

"The cartoon, Little Iva, has a great truth in it," Alex told Mariella and Anchee Ye on that night in the Russian restaurant.

He spoke with the grave correctness of the very drunk. "You know that guy is from Russia? His family came to the States after the communists fell. He sees very clearly how strange his adopted country is. I'm a fourth-generation American, a Hollywood brat through and through, but I feel that strangeness too. I think that's why I became a historian. I wanted to understand where I found myself."

Alex has been to Russia several times, researching the history of cooperation between NASA and the Russian Space Agency and gathering material for a biography of Sergei Korolyov, the Great Engineer of Russia's early space program, the man who designed the rockets that put Sputnik and Gagarin into orbit, whose designs were the basis of the big Energia Three boosters still used as the workhorses of the space construction industry. Alex is going to Mars partly because the permanent station is ten years old, and NASA wants footage for TV and web programs, but more importantly because he is going to make a documentary about Barbara Lopez, the only survivor of the landing party of the second manned mission to Mars.

Of all the people on the *Beagle*, Alex is the one with whom Mariella might have performed personal experiments in human biology in microgravity, but he is married and in the close quarters of the spacecraft there is no way of screwing someone and not having everyone else know. Ali Tillman and Bernie Thomas have been practicing what Gus Plafker calls face-to-face docking maneuvers whenever their free times coincide, and although they make a pretense that nothing is happening, everyone knows anyway, and talks about it with everyone except the happy couple.

Mariella doesn't want that kind of complication, and most especially doesn't want Penn Brown to gain even more of a hold over her. So while she spends a lot of time with Alex, she does it in public, playing endless games of speed chess while they talk, and mostly beating him. Otherwise, she works, answering her email, trying to get a paper assembled from Tony May's work so he will have something to present at the Florida conference, and helping Penn Brown maintain the little greenhouse bolted onto the *Beagle*'s life-support system.

The greenhouse is a tunnel not much bigger than a couple of coffins stacked on top of each other, lined with chrome racks of plants, sunlamps, and the loops of plastic tubing of bioreactors through which dense suspensions of single-celled algae are pumped. Although it contributes only fractional amounts to the food and oxygen supplies of the spacecraft, the greenhouse is important for morale, a literal oasis. Everyone contrives to pass through it at least once every day, lingering in the purple-tinted glow of the lamps, gently brushing the fresh green leaves of the plants, breathing in newly minted oxygen. Martin McCord spends a surprising amount of his free time there, tending his own rack of fast-growing dwarf strains of carrot, lettuce, radish, and kohlrabi, which he doles out with the grave courtesy of a maiden aunt bestowing sweets on favored nephews and nieces. And Penn Brown endlessly tinkers with the bioreactors, trying to edge their cycles closer to the ideal of a completely closed system.

Their simple design is more than fifty years old, but growth of the algal suspensions is subject to unpredictable and sudden fluctuations. Owners of commercial bioreactors avoid the problem by shutting them down at intervals, cleaning them out, and restarting them with fresh cultures, but Penn Brown claims that it has a technological fix, that by constant manipulation of growth conditions, bioreactors can continuously recycle sewage water, turn carbon dioxide to oxygen, and supply most of the food in a closed system like a long-range spacecraft or a small habitat.

His first large-scale attempt to demonstrate this in a closed-cycle habitat, at the Moon's Copernicus Station, was a spectacular failure. A change in pH precipitated phosphate from the system and the reactors crashed overnight, releasing sulphurated decay products that overloaded filters and made the air unbreathable. He was running a new version when he bulled his way onto the Mars mission.

Now, he drafts Mariella as stoop labor to help him make improvements to the *Beagle*'s bioreactors. She has to admit he has an instinctive feel for the intricate intellectual puzzle of balancing nutrient inputs with carbon dioxide flux and the growth rates of different strains of algae, but she thinks that he is missing the point.

Any small, high-energy system that relies on multiple inputs cycling through different species or biochemical pathways at different velocities is inherently unstable. Bioreactors will always crash, no matter how much they are tinkered with, but Penn Brown has closed his mind to this obvious fact. It is the worst violation of scientific method, and yet it is not only a common sin, but one that paradoxically strengthens science. It is all too human to reject data that conflict with a cherished hypothesis, and older scientists, often the most influential, are notable for their fierce defense of outmoded paradigms. Thus, the proof required before a new paradigm is accepted must be very strong indeed; old, rigid minds are the Darwinian selection gates through which scientific hypotheses are filtered.

Mindful of her contract with Cytex, Mariella keeps her peace, and works quietly under Penn Brown's instruction, allowing him to flex his boss muscles, finding it oddly companionable to be working silently side by side with her rival in the greenhouse tunnel, in the green odor of growing plants, in brilliant light that's tinted purple with UV, so that they have to wear goggles. Excess algae harvested from the bioreactors is compressed and served with ceremony at breakfast as crisped-up little cakes; a GM strain of *Chlorella pyrenoidosa*, with a high sugar and fat yield, tastes particularly good.

There are two landmarks during the voyage. The first is turnover. The *Beagle* accelerates for more than thirty days, adding to the speed at which the Earth swings around the sun, thirty-three kilometers per second, until it is climbing outward at almost four times that velocity. But Mars is traveling at only twenty-four kilometers per second, and the spacecraft has to shed its excess velocity before it can enter Martian orbit. Some is traded for potential energy, just as a flung ball slows as it climbs toward the top of its arc. The rest is lost by turning the *Beagle* around at day thirty-four, pointing the motor counter to the direction of travel, and lighting it up for a short, fierce deceleration burn.

The second landmark is the distant encounter with Murchison-8, on day forty. It is two days after they receive news that the Chinese have landed at the edge of the north pole's ice cap, less than three kilometers from the base camp of their first mission, putting an end to speculation about their objective.

Murchison-8 is a fragment of a small carbonaceous chondrite asteroid, probably the nucleus of a captured comet, with an eccentric orbit that crosses that of Earth and takes it out past Mars. Two years earlier, funded by a consortium of U.S. and Pacific Rim companies, a team of engineers blew the asteroid apart along its axis of rotation with carefully planted low-yield hydrogen bombs. The fragments were shaped and equipped with reaction drives, each controlled by an AI. Once they have entered their parking orbits around the Moon and processing has started, they will provide a yield two orders of magnitude larger than that of the North Sea oil fields. It will put an end to the need for methane and oil mining on Earth, and completely realign political maps drawn by the scarcity of hydrocarbons. Those oil-producing countries not savvy enough to have contributed to the cost of the project will be ruined. Already, political commentators are predicting social chaos and war across the Middle East, although the first fragment is not due to reach its parking orbit for another two years.

It is the biggest engineering project ever known. Those engaged on it were, briefly, inhabitants of the most far-flung human outpost, but the engineers and astronauts have returned home, leaving robots and AIs to guide the bounty toward Earth.

Murchison-8 has just completed a slingshot maneuver around Mars to accelerate it toward the inner Solar System. Even at its closest approach to the *Beagle*, it is not visible to the naked eye, for it passes more than fifty thousand kilometers away—a distance four times greater than the diameter of the Earth. And even when viewed through one of the *Beagle*'s telescopes, it is no more than a dark battered brick only occasionally relieved by the sparkle of its reaction drive as one of the ice pellets mined and shaped by robots is flung backward. This will ultimately consume about one percent of the fragment's mass.

Everyone takes a look at Murchison-8 as it grows closer, as sailors on a long voyage might once have crowded the rails of a sailing ship to glimpse an island in an otherwise empty ocean, and everyone feels a little diminished as it dwindles away into the vasty black of space.

And hour by hour, Mars swells astern, growing from a star to a globe to a brick-orange landscape, the place where most of them will soon walk.

Chryse Planitia, 19°N, 34°W:
February 24–March 3, 2027

Mariella comes down the ladder unsteadily, clumsy in her three-layered excursion suit. After a month and a half in microgravity, she feels heavier now than she did on Earth. Her first step on Mars is an ungainly backward hop onto blackened concrete. The landing apron stretches away for hundreds of meters in every direction, scorched and scored and cracked, spattered with sooty blast rings. Rippled sheets or little hummocks of red dust lie here and there. The lander touched down at noon, and the sun is still high in the sky, distinctly shrunken but still too bright to look at directly, swimming in a kind of fused mingling of gold and bruise-dark purple. The cloudless dark sky is not as pink as Mariella expected it to be, shading to dark blue at the close, level horizon.

"Here I come!" Ali Tillman says loudly and cheerfully over the common channel, and Mariella steps away from the ladder as the climatologist clambers down.

The others have already moved away from the lander. They are as clumsy as toddlers dressed by an overprotective mother, bulked out by helmets and excursion suits, their quilted overgarments tinted violet by an artificial photosynthetic pigment that supplements the suits' batteries, their helmets different colors. Mariella's is blue, Ali Tillman's green.

A plume of dust boils up to the west, raised by a truck-size vehicle speeding toward them. Something twinkles in the sky beyond it, something streamlined and silver that flashes as one of its edges catches the sunlight. For an absurd moment, Mariella thinks that it must be a huge craft moving with tremendous speed at the horizon; then, with a sudden reversal of perspective, she realizes that it is one of the hundreds of camera drones that roam the Martian skies. It has come to watch their arrival.

Now she sees other drones. A little wheeled platform, like a turtle coated with photoelectric cells, perches on a scalloped ridge of ocher sand a hundred meters away. A camera array hung beneath a cluster of tubular balloons slowly revolves as it drifts from north to south across the landing field.

The truck slows to a halt in the shadow of the lander and its banner of dust washes over everyone, fine-grained dust that clings like talc to their oversuits and helmet visors. Mariella wipes her visor with the back of her glove and follows the others onto the load-bed behind the spherical, pressurized driving cabin. They find places on the big padded bench that runs down the middle, and the truck makes a long arc away from the lander, doubling back on its tracks. Mariella feels a touch of dizzy nausea: the otoliths in her ears, redundant for so long in the *Beagle*'s microgravity, are now oversensitive to sudden changes in position. Perhaps Ali Tillman feels it too, because she says in a small, subdued voice, "Isn't this kind of dangerous?"

"Quickest way to get us inside," Anchee Ye says.

The truck bounces over the edge of the concrete landing apron onto rock-strewn, red-brown dirt, swings past a junkyard collection of robot supply rockets. Most have been stripped of their paneling and tanks, leaving only skeletons of fretted alloy beams. Beyond, Lowell Experimental Station extends to the horizon. It looks like a Siberian chemical factory. Junked equipment is scattered everywhere. Tanks raised on struts above the frozen ground cluster around the tall stainless steel towers of the atmosphere plant, where hydrogen is split from water and combined with cracked atmospheric carbon dioxide to make methane, propane and oxygen. A huge field of black solar panels stretches eastward. Power lines on poles march in straight lines across fields of red boulders. To the south, the three long trenches of the bioplant, where sewage is treated by a Swedish closed-loop system, are like diamond and emerald bracelets laid on red sand. Tubular greenhouses radiate from the chunky cube of tan concrete that encloses the nuclear reactor, and beyond these are the huts and domes and tanks of the science park, and the soil-covered hummocks of the station itself.

Everywhere, raised like flags on poles, hung from the struts of the power lines, emblazoned on the sides of tanks and huts, are the logos of the companies that have supplied equipment, machinery and construction material.

The road dips down and the truck drives into a big, low-roofed underground garage, where a man in a white-helmeted excursion suit is waiting for them. He shakes their hands as they clamber down from the load-bed, saying over and over on the common channel, "Welcome to Mars, welcome to Mars." A turtle-size drone tracks them from a respectful distance as they follow their guide into a brightly lit airlock chamber. They shuck their dusty overboots and drop them in a big waste-bin, stand on electrostatic pads and brush dust from one another like a bunch of grooming monkeys (the silky carbon-fiber brushes and pads also go into the bin), step over the sill of a hatch into another chamber. A hiss of air as the chamber pressurizes, a brief pounding spray of water that drains through the grid in the floor, buffeting blasts of air.

It reminds Mariella of the Mars Sample Return Facility—but here terrestrial organisms are protected from the Martian environment. The thought fills her with a dizzy, stomach-hollowing elation.

She is on Mars.

At last they can take off their helmets and shuck their gloves. The air is cold and dry, and there's a salty ozone tang that tickles Mariella's nostrils. It is the odor of the minute traces of dust, loaded with superoxides, that still cling to their suits. Anchee Ye sneezes three times, knuckles watery eyes.

Their guide's homely, creased face, framed by his snoopy hat, is cracked by a toothy white grin. "Welcome to Mars," he says again, shaking hands all around before he opens the inner hatch.

They follow him into a bare, brick-lined vault like the undercroft of a church. Sunlight piped through recessed shafts falls in glossy patches on the red tiles of the floor. There is a big sign on

the wall opposite the exit. THE UNITED STATES OF AMERICA WEL-
COMES YOU TO MARS. Flanking it are the flags of the eighteen
Martian Treaty nations. Half a dozen people are waiting to meet
them, all of them in blue paper coveralls over waffle-weave-heated
undergarments. The NASA Executive Officer and Science Director, Donald Poole, steps forward. Martin McCord, his helmet
tucked in the crook of his elbow as a ghost might carry its own
head, salutes him, shakes his hand. Alex Dyachkov dances about,
taking photographs with a palm-size camera. Behind Mariella
there is a discreet choking sound, Ali Tillman being sick.

Welcome to Mars.

Penn Brown sequesters himself with Donald Poole while the others inspect their room assignments. The standard module of the
Station's accommodation and laboratory wings is a double-skinned
extruded steel tube buried in a cut-and-cover trench, a service corridor connecting it to its neighbors at one end, its own emergency
exit to the surface at the other. There are three modules in the
accommodation wing, each named after a writer associated with
Mars. Mariella's small room, three by one-and-a-half meters, is in
the Edgar Rice Burroughs dormitory.

Most of the scientists are away in the field, and the station has
the air of an out-of-season resort hotel, full of the poignant ghosts
of the living. But when Mariella, hair still wet from a long shower
(aboard the *Beagle*, in microgravity, you took your sixty-second
scrub in a clinging plastic tube, wearing an air mask), wanders into
the canteen, she finds a small party in progress.

The canteen takes up an entire module, a steel-walled tube
twenty meters long and four wide, red tiles on the floor, a sus-
pended ceiling of plastic gridwork diffusing intense white light.
Half a dozen people are talking animatedly with the *Beagle*'s crew.
Glasses and plates of food are set out on the steel serving counter.
Plastic flasks of vodka distilled from freeze-dried potatoes are cooling in polystyrene chests brimful with ice and fuming lumps of
carbon dioxide; smaller flasks contain a sticky sweet liqueur made
from strawberries. Mariella samples both. The vodka is made from

a recipe left by a visiting Russian atmosphere chemist; the strawberry liqueur is a new invention.

"Just about everything else dies, but the strawberries go crazy," a friendly bear of a man says. He is Joe Skulski, a tractor driver whenever he gets the chance, but otherwise a glip.

"Glip?"

"GLP. General Labor Pool. Here, try these."

He rattles a plastic sample bag half-full of green flakes under her nose.

"What are they?"

"Chlorella, mostly," a woman says. "He's the only one around here likes them. I'm Sue Sabee, another glip. We're mostly glips here right now, everyone else is in the field finishing off their work before they're rotated back. Welcome to Mars. How do you like the strawberry crap?"

"It's a bit sweet."

Sue Sabee's scrubbed face and severe crew cut make her look older than she is, like a blond, all-American cheerleader inducted into the Marines. "Yes!" she says. "Yes, that's just what I tell Bill. Too much sugar left over from fermentation. You have to mix it with the vodka. One to three over crushed ice. It's kind of not bad then."

Mariella drinks more. It takes the edge off her fine-grained tiredness. Her joints ache. The gravity is lighter than Earth's and she exercised assiduously on the *Beagle*, but her body has been weakened by forty-eight days of microgravity and she did not sleep much in the last twenty-four hours, anticipating the stress of the descent, although in truth the jolting of the aerobraking maneuver and the solid shock as the parachutes opened and the retrorockets fired were less brutal than in simulations. But this isn't a time to be sleeping. She is on Mars.

She meets the others from the station. Bob Neft, the man who escorted them through the airlock. Joni DeSanto, Tyler Madigan. She asks Sue Sabee if anyone has gone out to the pole. "Since the news about what the Chinese really found, I mean."

"No. Not at all."

"Really? It's what I would have done."

"The old man is serious about sticking to regs and standing orders. And he's fanatical about the airship's flight plans."

"You could have driven there."

"Well, I guess it's possible," Sue Sabee says, in a way that suggests she doesn't think it possible at all.

"But no one did. I mean, off the books."

"You haven't been on Mars long. You'll soon realize there's no 'off the books.' See up in the corner?"

A camera lens.

"Takes pictures for our web site," Sue Sabee says, flashing the camera a two-hundred-watt heartbreaker of a smile. "They're refreshed every thirty seconds. NASA thinks it's good for public relations. It probably is, too."

"People watch you eat?"

"And drink. Here, have another."

Mariella drinks more strawberry-flavored potato vodka. Everyone is drinking, even Martin McCord, who for once has dropped his Ice Commander act. They all join in a conga line that, with Joe Skulski banging a tray at its head, winds through two modules, down a flight of brick stairs, along a brick-lined corridor, and up more stairs into sunlight.

It is one of the greenhouses. While the others dance along aisles between long rectangular plots of potatoes and peanut vines and tomatoes growing in orange dirt, Mariella stares out through layers of transparent plastic at the sun setting beyond the towers and tanks of the atmosphere plant. A machine digging a trench in the middle distance sends up a plume of dust that drifts a long way before it begins to sift out of the air. A drone crawls up a lip of crusty earth on the other side of the greenhouse's laminated plastic and turns a camera lens toward her.

"You get used to them," someone says behind her.

A tall man, with a lean, runner's frame and a weather-beaten face, gold-rimmed data spex and a bristly crewcut. The sleeves of his flannel shirt are rolled above his elbows; his chino cuffs puddle over bare feet with long, almost prehensile toes. He shakes Mariella's hand, tells her that he's Bill Glass, the agronomist.

Mariella asks him who uses the drones.

"Anyone who wants to. You can rent them by the hour, back on Earth. You never did that?"

"No," Mariella says, and remembers something her neighbor, Kim, once said.

"They're all over the place, but at least they aren't allowed in the station. One of the companies that run the system sued for access a couple of years ago, but they lost. There are the web cams, of course, but pretty soon you don't notice them. Wow, look at that."

They watch the tiny disc of the sun swiftly drop to the sharp-edged horizon. It shows none of the oblateness or reddening of a terrestrial sunset because the atmosphere is too thin. The sky darkens through every shade of blue to a deep purple. Strings of brilliant lights come on, hung from the scaffold arches that frame the greenhouse. Cytex's double-helix-and-test-tube logo is set at the top of every arch.

"I never get tired of that," Bill Glass says, with a boyish grin. "Red sky by day, blue at sunset. You want I should show you around?"

"I'd like that."

They talk about the problem of generating viable soil from the salty, oxidizing Martian caliche. Bill Glass explains how he bakes and chemically treats it to remove oxidizing materials and excess iron, sulphate and chloride salts.

"But it's still real cloddy," he says, hunkering down and sifting a handful through his long fingers. "Most of the surface rocks are volcanic basalts—amphiboles, pyroxenes, olivines. This stuff is mostly smectite clays and zeolites derived by weathering and modified by acidic leaching by periodic input of volcanic volatiles, and it's loaded with grains of shocked glass from meteor impacts. So it's very free-draining and poor at retaining nutrients, and to get anything to grow you have to add plenty of organic matter. I get most of that from the station's sewage system."

"We have similar problems in Arizona."

Light fills the lenses of Bill Glass's data spex when he looks up at her, his face intent and serious. "Yes, I heard you have something to do with the green communities there."

"There are many shades of green. The people I advise are at the moderate end of the spectrum. Techheads or urban refugees into self-sufficiency. They could certainly tell you a thing or two about living off hostile land."

"I'd like to talk to you about that," Bill Glass says. He straightens up, dusting his hands on his chinos, drinks from a plastic bottle, and hands it to Mariella. As she sips, he grins and says, "Careful. That's the good stuff from my reserves."

"Wow." Mariella blinks tears from her eyes, hands the bottle back.

"It's not so bad, huh?" Bill Glass is very drunk, Mariella realizes, but his grave, intense love of his work burns through. They talk about the cocktails of microorganisms he uses to condition the soil, and he tells her about his dream project.

"All you need to do is pressurize a nice flat piece of ground and warm it up and seed it with the right bugs. The best solution would be to flood the soil and use a cocktail of halophyte sulphur-reducing bacteria to dissolve the iron and sulphur before draining out the water. After that, you pump carbon dioxide enriched with methane and nitrogen from Sabatier reactors through the soil, and inject cocktails of cyanobacteria, especially capsule-forming species, nitrogen-fixing bacteria and a variety of decomposers. The cyanobacteria would fix carbon dioxide into organic material and release oxygen; the nitrogen-fixers would turn nitrogen gas into biologically useful ammonia and nitrate; the decomposers would begin to cycle organic material. Anyone could live here if they worked hard at it.

"Now these greenhouses, they aren't part of any self-sufficiency project. They're testing beds for GM crops. The companies write off the costs, get good publicity. Maybe the data is even useful. But it's too small scale and energy intensive to support long-term habitation. We should think big, tent over a large crater, a hundred square kilometers or more, use robots to till and chemically condition the soil, add as many species of bacteria and soil macrofauna as possible and see what falls out."

"That's possible? Tenting over a crater?"

Bill Glass nods slowly. "Sure. There's an extensive literature on doming craters. Forty years ago, someone even proposed doming most of the Northern Hemisphere."

"Seriously?"

"Seriously. It's possible. And with modern materials like construction diamond and foamed rock it really would be a trivial engineering problem to dome a relatively new, relatively small crater. Something two or three kilometers across, with an uneroded rim wall, could be enclosed for less than a couple of billion dollars. The dome would be floated above the rimwall, with cantilevered suspension towers set inside the crater. Foamed rock sealing the gap between rimwall and dome would support an internal pressure of four hundred millibars. Mostly carbon dioxide to begin with, which would contribute to a greenhouse effect that would be more than adequate to warm the interior above the freezing point of water. The pressure differential would also lighten the load on the suspension towers. You'd get water from the atmosphere and from burning rock. The main problem is conditioning the soil."

"You've really thought hard about this."

They have walked all the way to the end of the long greenhouse, and are now walking back. Someone has set up a music box: a Brazilian voice floating soulfully above a samba beat.

Bill Glass says, "People have been thinking about it for fifty years. All of us here are serious about a permanent settlement."

"The discovery of life may change that."

"Yeah. The conservationists are already making noise. I'm torn between wanting it to be true, and hoping the Chinese were telling the truth when they said they didn't find anything. If there's life on Mars, it'll put an end to the terra-forming lobby, at least for a while."

"And you're part of the terra-forming lobby."

"Sure. We can't stay stuck on one planet forever. And you can't support a significant population by doming over a few craters." Bill Glass is staring at her earnestly. He says, "Wouldn't you like to walk out there wearing just an air mask?"

"It's a utopian notion."

"Well, of course."

"I mean utopian in the root sense. Impossibly idealistic, especially given what I've seen. The station is an underground refuge from a surface so hostile even a short stroll requires a mission plan and strict safety procedures. And I understand that most of the outlying facilities are linked to the central station by tunnels, so that no one goes out onto the surface unless they have to. It's hardly the behavior of rugged pioneers."

"Well, the tunnels came about because of the robots we were sent. They cut trenches and line them with bricks made from the overburden. Once you set them running, they just keep going in a straight line until told to stop."

"I saw one, lying junked out by the garage. It seems to me that this place is like a high-tech cargo cult, completely dependent upon constant resupply for its existence. If something breaks you don't bother to try and fix it; you just throw it away and wait until a replacement arrives from Earth. And the supply line is too fragile to sustain anything other than a small scientific community."

"Not at all," Bill Glass says. "Right now there are two ICAN shuttles, just like the *Beagle*, waiting in mothballs."

"Yes, but NASA doesn't have the funds to run them."

"And in a couple of years," Bill Glass says stubbornly, "when the first Murchison fragment goes into lunar orbit, there'll be a virtually unlimited supply of conventional fuel outside of Earth's gravity well. It'll be cheaper to send a cargo rocket to Mars than to fly a scramjet around the world. The Old Woman relies entirely on cargo rockets for resupply, and she has survived with much more primitive technology than we have at Lowell. We have a lot to learn from her."

"Perhaps. But can you extrapolate an entire world from a unique case?"

Bill Glass takes a slug from his plastic bottle, but this time doesn't hand it over. He says, "You haven't been on Mars long, Dr. Anders. I'm surprised that you're so quick to judge us."

"I suppose I do have a tendency to speak my mind," Mariella admits. "But I'm disappointed with what I've seen, and while I don't want to belittle your plans, they seem impossibly idealistic."

"The station might not seem like much, but I think it's amazing that it's here at all. When you've been on Mars as long as I have, perhaps you'll understand that it isn't such a big step between what we have and what we want. You'll have to excuse me now; I need to go check the other greenhouses."

Sprinklers come on as Bill Glass walks away. People clap and cheer. Rain on Mars, under the darkening Martian sky. Ali Tillman and Tyler Madigan are dancing arm in arm in slow circles beneath a fantail spray. Joe Skulski offers his bag of chlorella flakes to Joni DeSanto, who says, "No thanks, man. I'm trying to give them up." And Penn Brown is standing at the top of the stairwell, looking right at Mariella.

Penn Brown is in a fury over obstructions the NASA executive officer, Donald Poole, has put in his way. He tells Mariella that he wants to change the plan, go straight to the borehole the Chinese expedition has already drilled and left behind. "But the paper-pusher in charge here won't allow it. We have to wait. We have to take our turn. Unbelievable."

"What's wrong with the original schedule?"

"What's wrong? Have you forgotten that the Chinese tried to kill me?"

"That was some ultra-rad green group."

"Yes, yes," Penn Brown says impatiently, "but who funds them?"

Mariella is too startled by this bit of paranoid logic to think of a suitable reply. They are talking at the bottom of the stairs to the greenhouse, away from the others and out of the gaze of the cameras. Laughter, loud conversation and music echo from above.

Penn Brown says, "The Chinese have something to hide. Perhaps they are in the process of hiding it right now. They've already drilled one borehole, they're working on another, and we have to wait right here while they do as they please."

Mariella, exhausted by his stubborn indefatigability, says, "I promised to help you get to be in charge, but I didn't say I'd do anything more than that."

"Yes, well, I didn't expect you to understand."

"We can do the science. That's the important thing."

"Fuck science!" He turns away for a moment, turns back. "I'm sorry. I'm tired. But you have to understand that this isn't about science. It's about resources. Without resources we can't even begin to do the science. And the Chinese control the resources."

"Meanwhile, we have our own work to do, and they will have to leave before we do."

"Yes, but they have the sweet spot right there in the Chasma Boreale, at the edge of the icecap. Do you think they'll leave us anything to find?" Penn Brown rubs his eyes with the heels of his palms and says, "I hoped you might understand."

"Maybe you should relax a little. You can't keep this up. You'll burn out before the job's done."

"Someone has to keep pushing. Howard did his best, but NASA won't budge on this."

"You talked with Smalls?"

"With Howard and Al Paley, while Poole stood over me and offered patronizing suggestions. That's what took so long. All the delay in the messages back and forth. Christ. I told Paley from the first he can't run this from Houston. That we're right here on the ground, that we should decide what to do. We're playing for high stakes, but I can't get anyone to understand. I want you to back me up on this."

Mariella feels an unexpected pang of sympathy for Penn Brown. He has won what he wanted, but it is not what he expected it to be. She says, "Did I say I wouldn't?"

"You didn't say you would."

"I signed that contract, Penn. I didn't want to but I did, and I'll do the right thing by it. But not tonight. I'm tired and I've drunk more than I meant to. Tomorrow. I promise that I'll help you with this tomorrow. You'll have to trust me."

"Yes," he says. "I suppose I will."

He has a strange look that's both tender and calculating. For a moment, Mariella is afraid that he might lean in and try to kiss her, but then there's a noise from above and they pull away from each other and turn toward the intruder. It's Ali Tillman. She stumbles down the stairs, says with the solemnity of someone profoundly drunk, "You'll have to excuse me," and throws up in a corner.

Mariella sleeps uneasily on the pallet bed in her little room. Her bones ache in unaccustomed gravity; wrinkles in the spidersilk sheets make her toss and turn. When Donald Poole ambushes her in the canteen early the next morning, she is still half asleep, flicking through the station's operational manuals on her slate and hoping that strong black coffee will ease her bleary headache. At the other end of the long table, Alex Dyachkov is talking with Ali Tillman and Tyler Madigan. From the way Ali sits hip to hip with Tyler, it is clear that with Bernie Thomas left in orbit she hopes to make another conquest before she goes into the field. Mariella is half amused, half envious.

Tyler is a two-year veteran who will be shipping out on the *Beagle*'s return flight. He is trying to persuade Alex that he should go along with Ali to the south pole. He speaks quickly and force-fully, jabbing forkfuls of grits into his mouth at the end of every sentence. "It's awesome down there. Long swirling ridges and val-leys like a mandala centered on the pole itself. Like this," Tyler says, turning his fork in his grits to illustrate. His skin is the color of milky coffee; his shaved, oiled scalp gleams in the bright light of the canteen. "Right now there's carbon dioxide spread hun-dreds of kilometers all the way around the pole, but it'll be spring in the southern hemisphere soon and then most of the carbon dioxide will sublime. That's why the laminated deposits are very accessible there, much more so than in the north. You should go down there, Alex. It's like nothing on Earth."

Ali has recovered from her motion sickness. She looks very young, very happy. "Alex isn't here to make that kind of docu-mentary, Tyler."

Tyler scrapes up the last of his grits and says around the mouth-ful, "I know you're going to see the Old Woman, but aren't you interested in how the planet got the way it is? Right now the north-ern ice cap is dominated by water ice and the southern icecap is dominated by carbon dioxide, but every fifty-one thousand years

the position reverses. Once we know what drives the climatic fluctuations on Mars, we can figure out how to terraform it. The Old
Woman is old news."

Alex laughs. He says, "That's the point. It's been ten years.
NASA thinks it's about time someone told her story."

Tyler says, "I saw that movie about her. Although—" he
crunches his dark eyebrows together "—the truth is stranger than
fiction."

"*Stranded*," Ali says. "It's one reason I came here."

"It wasn't very good," Tyler says.

Ali shrugs. "I was just a kid when it came out. It made a big
impression on me then."

"There was a Japanese movie, too," Alex says. "But I'm not
interested in that kind of story. I'm interested in how she lives
now."

"In a cavern in a canyon," Tyler says, "excavating for a mine.
She doesn't talk much to people. Ask the paleontology crew. Except they're down in Candor Chasma right now."

"She'll talk with me," Alex says. "We've been exchanging
email for more than a year."

"Yeah," Tyler says, with the affectless cynicism of the young,
"she does have plenty of online fans."

That's when Donald Poole sits down next to Mariella. Tyler
and Ali begin to gather up their cutlery and trays, and Poole says
with a benign smile, "Don't leave on my account, Tyler. And your
friend, Ali Tillman, I believe."

Ali says, "Tyler is going to give us our field certification training."

"I'm going along, too," Alex says. "See you later, Mariella."

When they have gone, Poole says to Mariella, "One of the
problems of having authority is that no one likes to be around it.
Here, have a granola bar. It's a real one, all the way from Earth."

Mariella takes it and puts it on the table in front of her. She
closes her slate and says, "We're causing you a lot of trouble."

Poole is a craggy, sandy-haired man in his fifties, with dry,
freckled skin and nests of hair in his ears and the nostrils of his
hooked, large-pored nose. His blue paper coveralls are creased and

wrinkled, and he affects a vague, avuncular air, although Mariella is sure that he's far more dangerous than he seems.

He says, "I suppose that Dr. Brown is quite angry with me, but I'm sure that it will blow over. On a happier note, I'm pleased to have such a distinguished visitor. I must say it's about time. I supported your grant application of several years ago, and was very disappointed when it was turned down."

Mariella says, "I can't take your side on this. Dr. Brown is in charge of the investigation, and if there's even the smallest chance that he's right about what the Chinese are planning to do, then something should be done to speed us on our way."

There is an uncomfortable pause. Betsy Sharp is at the far end of the other table, talking with Bob Neft and Bill Glass. A TV flickering above their heads says: "It's the tailored beans that give Coffiest its zing."

Poole says, "Will you come to my office? I'd like to explain something to you."

There is a touch of flint in his smile. No, he is definitely not the affable old buffer he pretends to be.

"Dr. Brown—"

"I know that you have to take Dr. Brown's side, but I do want to help you understand the situation."

Poole's office is spartan. A tidy desk, a couple of plastic chairs like those in the canteen, a flagstaff in one corner, with NASA's blue flag and the Stars and Stripes entwined. A signed portrait of the President and photographs of fighter planes taking off or landing on aircraft carriers on one wall, a map of Mars on another. The map is two meters long. Black and yellow pins mark the sites of scientific surveys. Most are strung along the equator.

"My children," Poole says, when he sees Mariella looking at the map. "Did Dr. Brown explain to you exactly why I wouldn't jump through his hoops?"

"The point is that we need to get up there as quickly as we can."

"And so you shall. But we only have two long-range rovers at the station, and one of those is stripped for repair. The rest are out in the field. Two per expedition." Poole taps the map. "Spread widely, as you can see. However, NASA diverted the latest robot supply rocket, which carries two new rovers. It touched down a few hundred kilometers east of the Chinese landing site. I can assure you that the airship will get you there in good time. Dr. Brown wants to make a dash for the pole using the station's only operational rover. But it won't save more than five or six days, and it is quite contrary to operational rules. Better to wait for the airship."

"And where is the airship?"

Poole taps the map again. "Currently on its way from Noctis Labyrinthus, the end of a resupply trip that has taken it all the way around the planet. It has to make two more stopovers, and then turnaround at Lowell will take three days. So you see there is no faster way of doing it."

"Unless it comes straight here."

"I'm not prepared to disrupt the important work of other scientists at Dr. Brown's whim. They need resupply, or they'll have to cut their research short, and that means NASA will be in breach of contract. NASA backs me up on this, but it wouldn't really matter if it didn't. I have the last word here, but Dr. Brown doesn't seem to understand that."

Mariella says, "And you want me to explain it to him."

"Perhaps you can calm him down. He doesn't understand how important it is to maintain an even strain here."

Mariella resents being caught up in this silly pissing contest. She says, "You know what? We're here for something so important that it takes priority over your routines and schedules and your even strain. You seem to want my opinion on this, so I'll tell you what I recommend. You can cancel the rest of the airship's scheduled drops and have it come straight here. And turnaround should only take a day, not three. That cuts three to four days off the waiting time right there."

"Three days really is the minimum time for turnaround. The airship has been out for a long time and has flown all the way around the planet—"

"I'm sure you can organize it. You might not like it, but it's your job."

"Really, I don't think you should—"

"Be telling you what to do? Well, someone should. You've got what, two more years here? Then you retire. I know you don't want to fuck up before that, but maintaining an even strain and sticking to routine is just what will fuck up our mission. And that will certainly fuck you up, too."

"I see," Poole says, all flint now. "I'll take that under advisement, Dr. Anders, but it's clear you don't understand the reality of life on Mars."

"I understand the manuals. I was just reading in them. The people out in the field have plenty of margin. They can easily wait an extra week or so for their supplies. And as for turnaround, the airship is much less high-tech than a scramjet, and they're turned around in a couple of hours. In fact, I seem to remember that the airship can be refuelled and checked out in more or less the same time. We could look it up in the manual, but I'm sure I'm right."

"I don't think we need to start discussing operational procedure, Dr. Anders."

"No, because I'm right, aren't I? That's what I'll tell Penn Brown, and I'll leave you two boys to work it out. I have to get ready for my own work."

After that, Mariella tries to stay out of the way of Donald Poole. She runs long circuits around one of the empty greenhouses, checks and rechecks the equipment that has been unloaded from the lander, carefully repacks it. Under Penn Brown's watchful eye, she and Anchee Ye practice using the test kits and the Wolf traps. Although Brown is grudgingly pleased about the way she trumped Donald Poole, wounded male pride makes him acerbically critical of her performance.

Mariella asks him, "Would you really have driven to the pole?"

"If I had to. And you would have come."

"Yes, I suppose I would."

"Because we both know how important this is."

"If it's so important, why didn't anyone from the station go months ago?" He looks at her. She says, "I heard about the standing order forbidding it."

"To prevent contamination by untrained personnel."

"Come off it. These people know how to take a core."

"They don't have a proton drill."

"They could have reopened the boreholes the Chinese made."

They are loading samples into the DNA readers. For a while, Penn Brown concentrates on using his pipette to spot microliter droplets into the wells. At last, he says, "There were also commercial considerations."

"Yes, I thought that might be the case. NASA wanted to send people to the pole as soon as the origin of the slick was discovered, but Cytex used its political muscle to prevent it. And that's why NASA is dragging its heels now. How did Cytex get such a hold on this?"

"We're smart, hungry and aggressive. We put a lot of money into this project, and we expect a commensurate reward."

Which isn't any kind of answer at all, but Mariella knows better than to press the matter. It touches on the tangled triangle of affiliations between Cytex, Penn Brown and Howard Smalls. Penn Brown wants to use this to get better leverage in Cytex's internal politics, and she's sure that Smalls is Cytex's man on the ad hoc subcommittee, in it for either money or power. Maybe it even goes up to the President; Cytex made large contributions to the Democratic Party coffers at the last election. And now Cytex is using that leverage to make sure that it can get hold of the Martian organisms and mine them for commercially important genes. It must know something about the potential value of the Martian genome already, from its analysis of the slick. And where did the slick come from? The Chinese took Martian genes and added them to terrestrial species of phytoplankton, that much seems certain. But how did the resulting chimera get to the Pacific?

She discusses these questions with Anchee Ye, on her first walk on the surface. At the Cape, they practiced helping each other suit up, then practiced doing it alone, then did it all over, in darkness or in strobing red light with a loud siren shrieking operatically. They took apart and reassembled every valve and pump in their backpacks, practiced linking suits to share air, learned to set transmission frequencies by touch, learned how to prevent expansion bruises with pump patches in case any part of the pressure overalls should fail, and practiced walking across a mockup of the Martian surface while strapped into harness rigs that simulated the lower Martian gravity.

So when Mariella walks out of the big garage into sunlight, stepping for the first time onto actual Martian soil, she has to force herself to react. I am standing under a pink sky on the surface of Mars, the red planet. All around me, just over the horizon, are landscapes where no one has ever walked, which no human eye has ever seen.

But they have to walk a long way to leave behind the junkyard clutter of the station. Past the berms of rubble that cover the interlinked modules of the station's living quarters and laboratories, like two combs set at right angles, past the clutter of the science park. The ground is everywhere marked with cleated footprints and the tracks of vehicles. Pallets, plastic and metal packing cases and plastic drums are stacked in several haphazard piles. The stripped frames of two trucks have been dumped beside the road; beyond them is a stack of junked air-conditioning units. A big machine stands at the end of a half-completed trench, its central processor and servomotors removed, its green paint etched by dust storms.

Mariella and Anchee follow a road out to the east, a wide track between rocks that have been bulldozed aside to form rough curbs. A level plain stretches away on either side. Rocks of all sizes and colors: black, brown, yellow, bright red, scattered over soil the color of day-old dried blood. There is hardly a piece of ground a meter square that does not have a rock on it. The rocks are mostly rounded and pitted. A few show grainy strata, or are split along fracture planes. Most have sunken part way into the surface; the largest have tails of granular dust in their lees. Flatter rocks have yellowish dust on their tops. It is like an endless beach from which the sea has permanently withdrawn. Most of the surface of Mars is like this. A beach waiting for its lost sea, littered with the debris of three or four billion-year-old meteorite impacts and volcanic eruptions.

Anchee leads Mariella toward a low ridge in the middle distance. Rounded hills stand at the horizon, a broken chain extending from west to east. They mark the edge of Burton crater, an ancient infilled impact site whose rim has been degraded and partly buried. Anchee Ye forges ahead as they near the ridge, a small blue figure bounding eagerly across the stony red landscape.

The ridge rises abruptly from the plain: a low, fractured cliff of dull red rock. There is a narrow path between two bluffs, with steps cut into the rock and metal staples for handholds. Seventy meters to the top, where fracture planes make irregular platforms and ledges among pitted boulders.

Mariella jams herself between two rounded rocks, feeling their coldness through the layers of her suit. Even in early summer, at noon, it is as cold as the inside of an ordinary domestic freezer. Looking westward, across the gentle terraced slope, she can make out lighter scour marks that cut across the brown-red land like ripples on a beach, and, at the very edge of the horizon, a flat mesa that must be the rim of Haskin crater. For the first time she can see nothing of the works of man, and with a sudden rush it comes to her that she is here, now, on Mars, and she laughs to remember how she rode out on that frosty night in Arizona and pretended to grasp the entire planet in her hand.

She says into her radio mike, "Can we go on?"

"I find that I always want to know what's over the next horizon too," Anchee Ye says, as she works her way around the red rocks to Mariella. "But we have done enough for your certification, and we have reached the limit of our file plan. This isn't a great view, but it gives you some idea of what happened here. At least one of the flood episodes washed over this bench terrace. See the ripple marks, and the longitudinal grooving?"

"I see them."

"I'm happy that I'm back. If it was possible, I would never leave."

It's easier to talk of things that have nothing to do with the knot at the center of the mission.

"What does Don think of that?"

"We've talked about it. He would be happy to come here with me. Many of the station staff feel the same way. That's why they stay on instead of rotating back to Earth. I think we'll see more and more of that. People want to make a life here."

"Like the Old Woman."

"Well, she's an extreme case, but yes."

"Or Bill Glass."

"He's still pissed at you."

"It seems to be a talent I have."

Anchee holds out a patch cord and Mariella plugs it in. Now they can talk about Penn Brown and the mission without anyone overhearing. Anchee has been thinking about Cytex's involvement too, but says that she has no more answers than Mariella. Maybe NASA really is out of the loop. If it isn't, Mariella doesn't ever want to play poker with Anchee Ye. But Anchee does tell her that she knew about Penn Brown's plans to change the mission profile. "He put it to me just before we came down. He wanted me to back him up."

"But you didn't."

"And you did."

Mariella had to back him up; she gave her word that she would when she signed the contract, so that she could stay on the mission. But she hasn't been able to explain to Anchee Ye why she owes Penn Brown and why she hates him for it, and so she feels an undertow of wounded pride, of shame, whenever she talks with the woman. Bullies prey on human weaknesses, and Penn Brown has a bully's knack for uncovering them.

Anchee Ye says, "We've a job to do here. We have to work as a team. You have to be alert every moment you are out in the field. It isn't like the Moon. You're in a landscape that looks a little like a desert on Earth. There are clouds in the sky, wind is blowing dust around. And something in your brain relaxes. You forget yourself."

"And Penn Brown has only been to the Moon."

"Right. He doesn't have the experience to lead the mission. He also said, when he told me about the changes he wants to make in the mission profile, that you didn't count. That you had no influence with NASA or the congressional subcommittee."

"He's right."

"But you did a number on Don Poole. So I think he's wrong."

This clumsy attempt to flatter amuses Mariella. She says,

"Don't you want to get out there as quickly as possible?"

"You know NASA didn't want anyone to go, originally? They didn't want to get involved in international politics and fuck up any future collaborations with the Chinese. Al Paley turned them around. He's in it for the right reasons, and I think I am, and I think you are, too. But Penn Brown sees it as a way of promoting his reputation and making money for Cytex, and I can't understand why you're going along with him."

"You should teach me what you know about Mars," Mariella says.

Anchee Ye thinks about this. She says, "Maybe that would be a start. Look, I don't want to know what happened between you and Brown, and I don't much care. I just don't want this fucked up."

"No, neither do I. And, I'm not defending him here, but neither does Penn Brown. So maybe things will work out."

"I think it's time we went back," Anchee Ye says, and unplugs the patch cord and starts down the rough stairway.

They walk back in silence, Anchee Ye loping along a hundred meters in front of Mariella. The hell with her, Mariella thinks. The hell with Penn Brown. What matters is the science. What is important is what they might find. Strange life in a refuge deep beneath the polar ice, and yet life that must be rooted in the same origins as life on Earth. Our distant ancestors or our long-sundered children, as Penn Brown put it in one of his diary pieces, borrowing heavily from Mariella's "pretty fantasy." There is no doubt that the man can coin a pithy phrase, even though it isn't strictly accurate. Whatever they find will not resemble any universal ancestor, but will have followed a different evolutionary path to that of life on Earth, shaped by the contingencies of the ancient Martian environment. The truth is always larger than the compass of pop-sci slogans.

Mariella muses on these notions as she tries to match Anchee Ye's easy stride. Gravity is weaker than the Earth's, and although Mariella has practiced many times in NASA's harness simulator, she is inhibited by the idea that one false step can kill her. Fall and shatter her faceplate—*ffffpp!* Game over. Even a small rip in her excursion suit would cause bad pressure bruising and frostbite.

She thinks that she has hit upon the right gait, a sort of extended canter, when she finds that she is going too fast. She tries to slow down, and her boots lose traction and slide out from under her, and she rolls over in a huge cloud of dust.

She fetches up on her back, the frame of the backpack digging into her shoulders, laughing because she is alive and unhurt. Anchee Ye has turned and is coming toward her. And there is a bright star in the pinkish-yellow sky behind her.

Mariella presses her gloved hands against the freezing ground and rolls over and pushes up to her knees. Dust hangs in the air all around her; she is coated in it. She wipes her helmet visor and stares at the star. At first she thinks that it must be one of the two moons, but it is too low in the sky. And it cannot be the Earth, for with the two planets just past opposition it is close to the sun, an evening star seen only for a few minutes after sunset.

Besides, the star is moving, drifting from south to north. Mariella thinks that it is one of the balloon drones, but then it drifts behind the towers of the atmosphere plant and she sees that it is far larger than any drone. And then she understands. Of course. It is the airship.

Chryse Planitia, 19°N, 34°W–
Deuteronilus Mensae, 46°N, 336°W:
March 3–4, 2027

The airship rises straight up for two hundred meters before it begins to make its turn toward the northeast. Because there is no need for streamlining in Mars's thin atmosphere, the airship's body consists of six fifty-meter-long tubes quilted with cells of hydrogen and bundled around a central spine like an air mattress rolled up lengthwise, with the pressure cabin and the cargo pods hung beneath. I-beam struts extend either side of the center of gravity, each bearing four turboprop motors.

The airship's four passengers are crowded into the little viewing platform, a double-walled bubble of flawless construction diamond hanging like a dewdrop at the nose of the tubular pressure cabin. All of them in half dress, waffle-weave thermal suits under yellow, smart-plastic pressure garments that mold to the body to produce an even pressure of half an atmosphere, big bunny boots on their feet and white snoopy hats on their heads.

As more and more land comes into view, Anchee Ye points out the great dry meanders of the flood channel to the west, a delta more than two hundred kilometers wide, its far edge well below the horizon.

"Tremendous," Alex Dyachkov says, turning his little camera this way and that.

"Yes," Anchee says, "and this is only one of the flood channels that extend beyond the mouth of Ares Vallis. They were cut by a succession of catastrophic outbursts of water and ice from immense underground reservoirs capped by several kilometers of rock. There are vast areas of chaotic terrain in the highlands to the south, scablands where land shattered and sank as the underlying water drained from the reservoirs, but they aren't big enough to have contained all the water needed to create the entire system. It didn't happen all at once, but probably extended by headward growth as more and more terrain collapsed, until it reached the highlands. This channel runs for two thousand kilometers across the lowland plains, mingling with the channels of Shalbatanu Vallis, Simud Vallis and Tiu Vallis. And all that water drained into the Great Sink to the northwest. An ocean's worth of water just pouring out across the land."

"And it all vanished."

"Some of it's locked up in the polar caps," Anchee says, "but we don't know where the rest went. There are theories — that it was lost during the catastrophic vulcanism that built the Tharsis bulge and resurfaced huge areas of the planet, or that over more than three billion years it simply dissociated into oxygen and hydrogen. The oxygen became locked up in rocks, hydrogen was lost into space. It is possible that there are still some deeply buried reservoirs of ice, but no one knows. I'm pretty sure we'll find some.

There were floods released by volcanic activity as recently as two hundred and fifty million years ago. There's good evidence that there may be reservoirs of water under the big volcanic shields."

"Yes," Alex says, "I haven't forgotten your cover story."

"There might be life there too," Anchee says blithely, "but it will be buried very deeply."

As the airship continues to rise, the curve of the horizon becomes evident: this is a much smaller planet than the Earth. The station is a scattering of Tinkertoys on red sand beside the scarred white circle of the landing field. The lander is a golden bead centered on a splash of black char.

A drone slung under a cigar-shaped balloon ten meters in length hangs beyond the viewing platform, looking backward as it races the airship, the blur of its props slicing rainbows from the sunlit air. Penn Brown calls the pilot, Rudy Wildt, on the intercom, and asks who's running it.

"It's just an AP feed, Dr. Brown. You'll have to get used to them."

Mariella says, "Worried it'll upstage your diary?"

Penn Brown refuses to rise to the bait. "Not at all," he says. "It's a security risk."

The broad embayment of the bench terrace slopes away to the west of the station, ten kilometers of mostly level rocky ground that abruptly drops down to the flood channel itself. Anchee Ye leans beside Alex, and he sights along her arm as she points to a flat apron of rock with scour holes worn in it by rocks rotating in whirlpool currents. Each hole still contains the rock that carved it, she says. There are fossilized longitudinal grooves, long ridges running parallel south to north like corrugations in cardboard or the grain in a piece of wood. A teardrop-shaped shoal of sediment extends beyond a knob of rock.

Alex takes panoramic shots, moving his camera in slow, wide sweeps, zooming in on particular features. He says, "It's hard to believe that water could ever have existed on the surface. What's the temperature now? Well below freezing, for sure."

"Minus twenty-eight at the surface," Anchee says. "Pretty warm for Mars, but it's summer and we're more than a kilometer below the datum point, so the atmospheric pressure is relatively high.

When the flood channels were formed, the atmosphere was thicker and Mars was warmer, and there was certainly ice close to the surface. There's no doubt that this channel was carved by a lot of water that was moving very quickly, probably at close to two or three hundred kilometers per hour. And even if the surface of that flood quickly froze, water could still flow beneath the ice — that's partly what caused the benching and terracing of the sides."

Anchee keeps up a running commentary and Alex keeps taking pictures as the airship reaches cruising height and begins its turn to the east, the ripsaw howl of the turboprop motors rising in pitch as their big, carbon-fiber blades bite into the thin air at supersonic speed. The plan is to fly north and east across the plains of Oxia Palus and Ismenius Lacus before turning over the fretted table-lands of Deuteronilus Mensae toward the Vastitas Borealis. They will leave Alex with the Old Woman, and fly on, more or less directly north, to rendezvous with the supply rocket at Kison Tho-lus. And then their mission will at last begin.

Mariella feels no apprehension about the possible dangers, ei-ther from the raw landscape or from the Chinese, but instead is filled with a bubbling excitement now that they are finally under way, flying at a steady seventy kilometers per hour over a wide orange and tan plain under a pink sky.

A million shadows cast by rocks tangle across the gently un-dulating plain; the shadow of the airship flickers through them like a cursor moving over a slate. This land is relatively young by Mar-tian standards, and has not been heavily reworked by wind erosion or cosmic bombardment. And yet there are rocks everywhere, thrown from impact craters and volcanoes near and far. Small dunes combed among the rock fields catch sunlight on their west-ern slopes, glimmering like tarnished mirrors.

Mariella thinks that, yes, it is very like the badlands of Arizona, except that it is quite without life, and pockmarked every two or three kilometers by a crater. Some fresh, with sharp rims and little hills in their centers; some with slumped walls; some merely ridges, circles or half circles, eroded or half-buried in windblown sand. Craters overlapping one another, craters within craters: an infinite variety.

And this is nothing compared to the ancient landscapes of the southern hemisphere, which retain the marks of the massive bombardment by material left over from planetary formation. The southern hemisphere contains the really big impact craters: debris from the impact that created the two-thousand-kilometer wide, ten-kilometer deep Hellas basin was scattered several thousand kilometers across the planet's surface, a ring of material that could cover the United States in a layer two kilometers thick. And many areologists believe that the lowlands of the Vastitas Borealis are the remnants of an even bigger collision, one that remodeled the entire northern hemisphere; the southern highlands are perhaps built of debris flung halfway around the world. If the Vastitas Borealis is an impact basin, it is the largest in the Solar System.

Amazing that life managed to get started here at all, or that it persisted for as long as it did. Perhaps it is everywhere, if you know where to look. No one apart from the Chinese has managed to drill more than 1.2 kilometers into the crust; it is possible that there is residual heat further down, pockets of magma like that which pushed up the crust and eventually burst out to create the Tharsis volcanoes. And where there is magma, there are likely to be seeps of hydrogen and sulphur dioxide, gases that microorganisms can use as reducing agents to fix carbon. On the Earth, the biomass of microorganisms living in pores in deep rocks outweighs that of life on the surface.

Yes, it is possible that there is life everywhere deep in the Martian crust, not just in a single precarious reservoir beneath the polar ice. But that is the only life known on Mars, the life the Chinese found, and lied about finding. Unforgivable, especially as the cover-up was motivated by commercial greed, by companies that want to keep the Martian organisms a secret so they can sequence and copyright them. And now Mariella is bound by the same repugnant ethos.

As evening falls, the airship skirts to the west of McLaughlin crater, whose rampart rises steeply from the land like a mesa, catching the light of the setting sun and burning like a bar of red-hot iron against the darkening sky, and crosses crater Mu, a lake of inky shadow thirty kilometers across, contained within sharply defined rimwalls. The land has risen more than a kilometer, and continues to rise gently ahead. The sun sinks through thin bands of yellow and pink cloud and vanishes with a flash of blue light that seems for a moment to embrace the gently curving horizon. A double star hangs above the sun's residual glow: Earth and Venus. And all around, the land is as dark as an untraveled ocean.

They eat from hotpacks, slouched in the padded green tube of the pressurized cabin like hobos camping out in a boxcar. Sue Sabee, who has come along as copilot and general dogsbody, shows them how to polarize the little round windows and sling their hammocks across the narrow space.

Mariella falls asleep quickly, but wakes in thrumming dimness from a dream of falling. There are two types of Martian clock: one freezes its hands at midnight and restarts thirty-seven minutes later, a brief grace note at the end of each day; the other continues to mark time through a wedge of red thrust between the day's twelve-hour halves. Mariella's wrist-strap watch is the second kind, and tells her that it is twelve minutes between midnight. Everyone but Penn Brown is asleep. He sits in one of the big chairs at the far end of the cabin, his intent face underlit by the blue glow of his slate.

The next morning, the airship passes over more densely cratered land and then crosses the wide, winding canyon of Mamers Vallis. The canyon floor is littered with lineated fill, frost-shattered from its walls and graded by water or ice flows. And then the fretted tablelands of Deuteronilus Mensae are ahead, long flat-topped mesas like ships stranded by low tide, separated by valleys ten or twenty kilometers wide, their sides stepping down in a series of bench terraces to a floor still marked in concentric whitened ripples by the retreat of paleolakes, as if preserving imprints of God's thumb in the fundamental clay of the world.

The whole region along the scarp between the uplands and the low northern basin is like this, fretted by interlocked massifs and plateaus and hills, all slowly eroding by mass-wasting, the debris filling the valleys between them to leave outlying mesas or knobs of more resistant rock, often the eroded rims of craters. Three-and-a-half billion years ago, this area was littered with lakes, all slowly shrinking as Mars cooled and most of the carbon dioxide in its primordial atmosphere was fixed in carbonates. Liquid water persisted beneath thick ice for several million years after it vanished elsewhere. It was the last refuge of life on the surface of Mars.

Penn Brown has monopolized the viewing platform to make the latest of his diary segments, and Alex and Anchee have gone forward to the cockpit. Mariella is alone in the cabin's long padded tube, sitting crossed-legged with sunlight streaming in through a round window beside her, the Smithsonian's recording of Muddy Waters's country blues playing through her earphones as she works at her slate.

She's been amassing data about the spread of the slick ever since the *Beagle* left Earth's orbit. Now she's thinking about the latest news, about a big drop in fish catches off Hawaii. There's no solid evidence that it was caused by the slick, but it is suggestive. Zooplankton can't eat the slick, and as it spreads fish starve or move elsewhere. The daughter slick could have been carried to Hawaii by currents, or more likely by a Navy destroyer returning to base after a spell of picket duty, but Mariella can't find out anything about the movements of Navy ships. She's pretty sure that it reached the reefs off Florida via a cruise liner; an established route from Australia, through the Panama canal and on to Miami, passes a few hundred kilometers west of the site of the original slick. Perhaps the liner pumped up some Pacific Ocean water to adjust her trim in the middle of her voyage, then discharged it off the Florida coast.

Cruise liners, cargo clippers, ocean trawlers, currents, sea birds, whales: there are so many ways the slick can spread. So far, with the help of Maury Richards, Mariella has logged the sites of more than twenty possible daughter slicks, mostly in an arc along the Pacific coast of the American continent. Her models are very tentative—no one will answer her questions and she doesn't like extrapolating from scanty data—but they all yield the same bad news. Within a year, there will be daughter slicks in every ocean. How can you clean up an entire planet?

She's still working when the intercom crackles and Rudy Wildt sings out over the howl of the turboprops and the bass thrum of the air conditioning. "There she blows!"

Mariella climbs the spiral staircase into the crowded little cockpit. Rudy Wildt grins at her and leans forward in his big chair, pointing through the curving windshield toward the horizon, a few degrees starboard of their course.

"Right there," he says.

"She must be using explosives to widen her latest borehole," Sue Sabee says.

Anchee Ye, leaning on the back of Sue Sabee's chair, says, almost fondly, "I told her she was crazy to be working alone with high explosives."

"Well, she is crazy," Rudy says. He is a big, ruddy-faced man, the owner of one of the only two beards on Mars, the other being Alex Dyachkov's. Rudy's is black and bushy, with little glass beads braided into it. "Not too late to change your mind, Alex, if you want to bail out."

"There it goes again," Sue Sabee says. "The whole area must be like a piece of Swiss cheese."

The airship is flying along a wide valley, parallel to a terraced cliff that rises to a flat-topped mesa. The valley stretches away to the west, interrupted by smaller mesas that may once have been islands or reefs in a deep lake. Its floor is marked by long, gently curving ridges like ripples expanding out from a dropped stone, each succeeding ridge younger than the one before, each a fossil shoreline. Windblown sand has polished the tops of the ridges, and they glisten like salt in the raw sunlight.

At the horizon, a yellow geyser of dust shoots up into the pink sky, rising very high before it begins to feather away in the constant west wind.

Mariella feels her heart pump faster. They are approaching the lair of the Old Woman, the first Martian citizen of a country of one.

*   *   *

The Old Woman of Mars, Barbara Lopez, was a member of the ill-fated second manned mission to Mars. It touched down at Deuteronilus Mensae in 2017 and successfully completed all of its objectives, including locating and identifying formations that resembled fossilized stromatolites, but when the landing party attempted to return to orbit, the motor of the ascent stage flamed out a few seconds after liftoff. One of the three members of the landing party was killed in the crash; Barbara Lopez's leg was broken. She and the other survivor, Owen Tibbets, took four days to cross twenty-five kilometers to the habitat they'd left behind, and there they stayed, conserving their dwindling supplies and waiting for a robot relief rocket, until Tibbets died.

Only Barbara Lopez knows the true story. She claims that Tibbets sacrificed himself just as Oates had sacrificed himself in the doomed British expedition to the south pole a hundred years before, leaving the habitat while she was sleeping, walking until the air supply of his excursion suit gave out. But there are rumors. That they drew lots, and Tibbets lost. Or that he won, and Barbara Lopez killed him. Or that she became pregnant and killed Tibbets when they argued about abortion. No one can know for sure, because Barbara Lopez chopped up his body and used the biomass for fertilizer in the little garden she established after the relief rocket finally arrived.

The third mission arrived two years after the disaster, but Barbara Lopez refused to return with them or move to the permanent base they established at Chryse Planitia. Unlike Crusoe, she had not been separated from humanity by her shipwreck. She sold the rights to her story to Time Warner, obtained sponsorship from half a dozen companies, and retained a legal team that is still pursuing a tangled suit against NASA, the government, and the thirty-eight engineering and aerospace companies that contributed to construction of the ascent stage's motor.

All this has made her millions of dollars, which she has used to maintain and expand her little habitat. It is the only private research station on Mars, and Barbara Lopez, the Old Woman of

Mars, is its only inhabitant. She is not, in fact, really that old—fifty-five—but she is the oldest person on Mars, and holds the record for living on another planet: ten years.

Her research station is at the fossil shoreline of an ancient lake. The stumpy cylinder of the original hablab module has been covered in reddish soil, like the burial mound of a technopagan prince; only its small airlock shows. The trenches that provided the soil are raw scars nearby. A dust-stained satellite dish tilts toward the sky beside a small geodesic dome full of plants. There is an air factory; there are four rows of black solar panels. And all around are junked machines and litter and vast numbers of footprints and tire tracks.

The drill site is out in the bed of the paleolake, a short tower with a long plume of darker material laid across the ground to the southeast. "There she is," Sue Sabee says as the airship drifts above the tower, and Mariella follows the line of her finger and sees a small figure standing by a rover vigorously semaphoring its arms.

The airship makes a ponderous turn above the station and Rudy fires the anchors, two from the tail and one from the nose, which haul the airship toward the ground like a remora settling against a whale's flank.

As they climb down the ladder and begin to walk away from the airship's shadow, Barbara Lopez speeds up in her rover. It bounces recklessly over the crest of the arctuate ridge that marks the ancient shore, accelerates at a slant down the thirty-degree slope, and swerves to a halt in a cloud of red dust and small stones. Barbara Lopez strides out of the settling dust, shouting cheerfully over the common band that she hadn't expected a fucking picnic party to be dumped in her lap. A small drone with six fat balloon tires scoots after her, and Alex has his own camera out.

Barbara Lopez is only a meter and a half tall—all the astronauts on the first three expeditions were of slight stature, to save space and conserve consumables—but her excursion suit is wrapped in layers of tattered cloth that lend her an imposing bulk. Behind her scratched visor, her gaze is shrewd and appraising.

"I've heard of you," she tells Mariella, and says to Anchee Ye, "I told you you'd be back, girl."

She shakes Alex's hand last, and holds on to it and says, "I hope you know how to work hard. I could do with some help around here. Now, where's your stuff? And have you guys brought me everything I ordered?"

It takes them more than an hour to winch down the appropriate cargo pod, unpack it, and haul it back up. Another drone joins the first, a low-slung turtle that keeps getting underfoot, until at last Rudy picks it up and sets it on a flat-topped boulder. Barbara Lopez inspects everything thoroughly, muttering to herself, and says that everything she ordered seems to be here and maybe they'd give her a hand hauling it to the station.

"We don't have time," Penn Brown says firmly.

"Of course you do," Barbara Lopez says. "It's only neighborly. I haven't seen anyone for three months. You stay and talk a while. You can tell me about this proton drill you're carrying. It sounds like something I could use."

"We're already several days behind schedule," Penn Brown says.

"It won't take long," Sue Sabee says.

"Those Chinese aren't going anywhere for a while," Barbara Lopez says. "And if you quit bitching and pitch in with everyone else, it'll go more quickly."

When the work is done, Mariella slips away and climbs the low ridge of the ancient shoreline so she can look out across the fossil bed of the paleolake, which slopes away toward the close horizon, overlain by orange soil and gray rocks, a cliff swinging around to enclose it to the east. The ridge is made of some kind of conglomerate, a badly weathered limestone matrix cementing what had once been a pebble beach. Mariella manages to work a pebble from its socket. It is black basalt, worn smooth by water, heavy and very cold, numbing her fingertips through her gloves. It would be unremarkable on any beach on Earth.

Anchee Ye crabs up the slope, holds up four fingers to indicate the channel on which they can talk. "He's pretty pissed off," she says.

Mariella drops the pebble between her dust-coated boots. "The work will calm him down."

"I hope so. Isn't this place amazing?"

Anchee points at the cliff to the east and counts off the terraces that record changes in the lake's level. Mariella tries to recreate it in her mind. Four billion years ago, the waves of a long, deep lake broke on a shoreline of polished black pebbles. The atmosphere was a thick blanket of carbon dioxide leavened with a little nitrogen and methane, much like the primordial reducing atmosphere of Earth. The inner planets were still being bombarded by debris left over from their formation; on Mars, these impacts, and precipitation of carbonates, slowly stripped away the atmosphere. The little world cooled. The lake iced over, protecting the life teeming in it. There were domical and flat-laminated stromatolites almost identical to those on Earth but an order of magnitude bigger. There were plant-like sheets or ribbons one cell thick, sponge-like baskets fixed to the lake floor and cabbage-like floaters, all preserved in fine sheets of silt.

But Mars continued to cool and lose its atmosphere, and like all open bodies of water the lake began to shrink. Its waters became saltier and saltier. The species living in it died out one by one, until all that remained were dense blooms of iron-fixing microorganisms, which left huge deposits of iron oxides and organic carbon in the sediments. And at last these blooms also died, unable to tolerate the increasing salinity, and the lake finally evaporated, leaving a thumbprint texture of beach ridges and bars, and the fossilized remnants of the life it once harbored.

Anchee tells Mariella that, at the site of another paleolake five hundred kilometers to the west, there's evidence that hydrothermal vents kept the water liquid under ice for perhaps a hundred thousand years after life died out here. Until now that was believed to have been the last refuge of life on Mars.

"And that dried up two-point-seven billion years ago," Anchee says.

"Yet life persisted."

"Yes. Amazing that it survived for so long after the surface became uninhabitable."

"What's amazing is that no life has been discovered elsewhere on Mars."

"People looked. They even kept looking after the Chinese lied about their discovery at the pole."

"They were looking in the wrong place. As I told NASA some years ago."

"It must be comforting to be proved right," Anchee Ye says evenly.

Penn Brown hails them over the common frequency. He is toiling across the rocky ground behind the ridge, his shadow thrown toward them by the level light of the setting sun.

"Christ," he says, climbing up toward them, "now that woman wants us to eat with her, and those two glips say that's just what they're going to do."

"Well," Anchee Ye says, "it's a tradition."

"We shouldn't have come here in the first place," Penn Brown says.

"But here we are," Mariella tells him. "Isn't it magnificent?"

Penn Brown slowly turns through three hundred sixty degrees. He says, "Very nice, if you like that sort of thing. What are those stars, there?"

There are three points of light at the horizon, winking as they drift slowly from north to south.

"Balloon cameras," Anchee Ye says.

"We're going to have to do something about that when we get to the pole."

"Barbara has cameras all over the station," Anchee Ye says. "Uploading pictures twenty-four-and-a-half hours a day."

"All the more reason to get this done," Penn Brown says, with the sudden briskness that means he's come to a decision. "Otherwise the glips will want to stay overnight, and we'll lose another day. Things are tight enough as it is."

They hike back to the station. Before taking her turn to climb through the tiny airlock, Mariella inspects part of Barbara Lopez's fossil collection. Flat sheaves of sandstone are laid out across a neatly raked area of sand, each split to show the faint black imprints of organisms that have been pressed between layers of sediment like flowers in a book.

"An appalling waste," Penn Brown says. "Any one of these

would be worth tens of thousands of dollars in a museum on Earth, and here they're left to erode. This site is unique, and she won't let anyone else work it."

"She does a good job," Anchee Ye says.

"That's not the point. She should share her discoveries."

"Shit," Barbara Lopez says, breaking into the common channel. "Those are just my discards. You take one if you want, Dr. Brown. Go ahead. I keep the good stuff under nitrogen. And I get a lot more than tens of thousands of dollars for each one."

"I appreciate the sentiment. Thank you, but no."

Mariella says, "Perhaps on the way back. Maybe I'll have time to look at your greenhouse then."

"Maybe. If the Chinese don't get you first." Barbara Lopez laughs, and adds, "Now get inside and have something to eat."

The six people and their excursion suits make a crowd in the dome's single room. The walls are covered with swags of blue and green spidersilk — parachute material — and the same fabric covers slabs of foam on which they all sit, eating from hotpacks, drinking strong, sweet coffee from Pyrex beakers. A hammock is slung between aluminum poles, with boxes of rations piled beneath it. An air-conditioner mutters and hums in one corner; a dehumidifier in another.

Mariella has seen this room on the web, a fish-eye view from the camera hung above a workbench cluttered with leaves of sandstone and cores with neatly labelled horizons, a binocular microscope with a big stage and tentacle-like fiber-optic lights, airbrushes, picks, flasks of acid, resin kits and other implements of the geologist's trade. It's strange to be part of this familiar scene, like walking onto the set of a soap opera or one of those VR recreations of old movie sets. Penn Brown objects to the camera, of course, but Barbara Lopez tells him sharply that it stays on.

"You're in my house now. There are no secrets here. Eat. Drink. And don't worry, I'm not going to ask you about the Chinese."

In fact, she spends most of the time exchanging gossip with Sue Sabee and Rudy Wildt, absentmindedly stroking the white rat that scampered up onto her shoulder as soon as she sat down.

When the meal is over, Alex gives all of them bear hugs and says that he'll see them in twenty days. Barbara Lopez shakes hands all around, saying quietly to Mariella, "Clarice Bushor sends her best wishes." Before Mariella can ask her what she means, she has turned away and is checking the seals of Sue Sabee's excursion suit.

"About time," Penn Brown says, when they are outside. The sun has set, and they trudge toward the tethered whale of the airship in the glare of arc lights raised on tall poles above rock-strewn sand.

It is time to go.

Vastitas Borealis:
March 4–8, 2027

The rest of the flight takes just under two days. The airship flies north above a gently rolling landscape of smooth sediment in which ancient craters are visible as broken arcs of highly weathered knob-like hills, like the arthritic knuckles of buried giants. Apart from the hills and a few fresh craters, it is one of the flattest land-scapes in the Solar System, even flatter than the Bonneville salt flats or the salars of South America. Rudy Wildt comments that it is like the biggest pool table in the Solar System—you could drive across it blindfolded for hundreds of kilometers. From the way he says it, Mariella guesses that he's probably tried it once upon a time.

Marshland and huge shallow lakes once covered much of the northern hemisphere. To the east and west, their sediments have been covered by more recent lava flows from the Tharsis volcanoes and the massive outflows from Syrtis Major. Here, they have been modified only by the slow polishing of windblown dust. Parts of the terrain are pitted and etched, like vast limestone pavements, but mostly it is a flat, aching desolation over which the airship's shadow flows hour by hour without a flicker.

Gradually, the land rises toward the polar plateau of Planum Boreum. On the second night after they leave the Old Woman's station, the sun barely sets, merely dipping below the western horizon for a couple of hours; it is early summer, and they are above the Martian arctic circle. And the next day, just before noon, at 73°N, 358°W, they reach the edge of the lava fields of Kison Tholus, and follow the guidance beacon to the supply rocket.

The rocket is a fat white cone on five skeletal legs, standing on a flat lobe of black lava. The Stars and Stripes, the NASA badge and the Rocketdyne logo are emblazoned around its nose. Its huge blue parachute is still attached and covers one side like a cloak, stirring weakly in a westerly breeze that also kicks up little whirls of dust. Tall cliffs rise to the north, where the lava fields have been uplifted, and beyond them the domical summit of Kison Tholus itself is silhouetted against a salmon sky. To the east are several cinder cones, and the beginning of a huge trough whose rumpled floor is covered in dark material, lava and ash from a volcano field further to the east.

The airship ponderously circles the rocket, then descends and fires its anchors. Everyone suits up and goes out. Radio-controlled explosive bolts release panels that hinge down from the flanks of the rocket, and Sue Sabee and Rudy Wildt climb up these ramps and drive the two rovers straight out. Unloading of the rest of the rocket's cargo and the equipment carried by the airship, sorting it, and loading up the rovers take several hours. The sun circles around the close horizon, dipping toward the west; Mariella looks at her watch and is amazed to see that it is almost midnight.

They all wearily climb back into the airship's pressurized cabin, eat from hotpacks, and fall asleep, waking at six in the morning and depolarizing the windows to bright sunlight. Coffee, an attempt at breakfast. Mariella finds it difficult to choke down her cinnamon roll; her mouth is dry and her stomach suddenly queasy. Anchee Ye is scratching her scalp and complaining about the dust that has entered the cabin.

They suit up again and climb down the airship's ladder. Boxed and bagged supplies are scattered across a field of rough, ridged lava. Sue Sabee and Rudy Wildt will have to load the stuff into one of the airship's cargo pods before they can depart. They shake hands all around and the three scientists climb into the rovers: Penn Brown in the first, Mariella and Anchee in the second.

The rovers are blocky vehicles twelve meters long and two wide, not much bigger than the average mobile home of Arizona snowbirds. With bubble canopies of construction diamond at the leading edge of their flared cabins, six big, independently driven woven-wire wheels, and black photosynthetic paint, they look a little like the cybernetic beetle Mariella assembled from a kit when she was eight.

At first, the going is smooth, with only a few deviations to follow troughs back to their origin or to find places where their sides slump so that the rovers can cross them. Penn Brown keeps up a good speed, between forty and fifty kilometers per hour. Behind them, the tethered airship soon disappears over the close horizon.

The ground is rougher toward the edge of the lava fields. Billions of years of dust-laden winds have etched it into a channel-and-ridge system. Here and there, lava mixing with groundwater caused irruptions of piles of blocky tephra, which have weathered into fantastically tortured shapes, like sculpture gardens based on Dali paintings.

They leave the lava fields behind, head east over smooth rolling ground, then climb a shallow slope onto a wide meandering ridge of dark mantle material that winds northward for a hundred kilometers, rising toward the polar plateau. Penn Brown keeps up a steady, relentless pace. Behind him, Mariella and Anchee Ye take turns to drive their rover. In the wraparound driver's seat, in the transparent bubble of the cockpit, Mariella feels that she is skimming over the smooth dark ground as effortlessly as in a dream.

Penn Brown is determined to reach the icecap as quickly as possible, and presses on until late in the evening. The sun, a shrunken knot of glare low in the hard, purple sky, throws the insectile shadows of the two rovers a long away across the dark ground. At last, the ridge they have been following broadens into a gently rolling plain, and Penn Brown calls for a halt.

"Eight hours and we'll start again," he says. "The edge of the ice is only a hundred and fifty kilometers away, and with luck we'll reach the entrance of one of the chasmata by noon tomorrow."

Mariella eats lukewarm tamales from a hotpack and studies a map she has called up on her slate. In summer, the residual icecap of the north pole makes an off-center swirl mostly within the eighty-degree latitude, fretted by arctuate chasmata that curve inward in a clockwise direction and are echoed by swirling ridges on the ice itself. The Chinese are moving along the largest of these dry valleys, Chasma Boreale, which ends at crater Zw, nicknamed the Plughole.

The next morning, the two rovers drive at an unvarying speed across the monotonous plain, like two black boats crossing a calm sea. Around noon, they climb a steep slope and dip down into a smooth trough more than two kilometers across. Shaded hollows are luminous with frost. The sharply steep scarp that tops the ridge on the far side reveals that the underlying ground is stratified in alternating bright red and darker layers; they have crossed onto the layered deposits that two to three kilometers thick, underlie the entire polar plateau.

Anchee Ye, who is driving, tells Mariella that the darker material is from the dune seas around the polar plateau, mostly fines of volcanic origin; the bright material is a mixture of the wind-blown volcanic material and the red dust that is distributed and redistributed across the planet by the great storms. Both are cemented by ice, which tends to ablate more quickly on the south-facing slopes of the troughs. Dust-laden winds gradually weather the southern slopes into deflated, striped terrain while depositing new layers on their north-facing slopes so that, as they age, the troughs gradually move inward toward the pole.

"That's why we get the swirl effect all the way around the icecap."

"But what causes the layering?"

"No one really knows. One theory is that really big dust storms occur every ten thousand years or so. They might last a hundred years, and completely redistribute bright fines across the planet. Fines that land at the polar regions are trapped in the ice, and in the long periods between the superstorms are covered with ordinary darker material from the dunes around the icecap. No one really knows what might cause the superstorms, but because it doesn't have a big moon to act as a stabilizer, Mars's orbit is subject to oscillations in obliquity—the angle at which the poles are tipped relative to orbital plane? That might be important in driving major climatic changes on Mars."

"Because it changes the amount of solar radiation that Mars receives," Mariella says, thinking of something Tyler Madigan told Alex Dyachkov.

"Right. At maximum insolation, the atmosphere might thicken to almost twenty millibars, greatly increasing its ability to carry dust. But so far no one's come up with a model that reconciles changes in Mars's obliquity and the cycles of deposition preserved in the laminated terrain. Of course, we could be reading that record wrongly. You certainly can't tell much from exposed layers—erosional creep toward the pole keeps overturning them, like shuffling a deck of cards."

"And that's what Betsy Sharp and Ali Tillman are going to study."

"At the south pole, sure," Anchee says, perhaps a little too quickly. "The south pole is also underlain by layered material, but because the polar cap is carbon dioxide snow instead of water ice, more of the underlying material is exposed in summer."

Penn Brown's rover turns to follow the floor of the trough; over the radio, he says that it will eventually lead into one of the chasmata. It is like following one of the grooves in one of the old vinyl long-playing records Mariella's father occasionally and with great ceremony played on his hi-fi. The trough's floor is very flat, stripped by winds blowing perpendicular to its walls, only occasionally interrupted by small barchan dunes curved as sharply like boomerangs, with their arms and steep slip slopes pointing away from the pole.

And then there is ice blink shining sharply at the eastern horizon, and a wall of ice perhaps five hundred meters high slowly comes into view. As the trough swings around to meet it, ice appears low to the west as well. The ground becomes harder and more hummocky; less and less dust is thrown up by the wheels of the two rovers.

They drive for several hours along benches of exposed laminated material between slopes beveled at thirty degrees. Penn Brown is searching for a way onto the ice, but the cliffs that loom above them, although terraced, rise up from the floor of the chasma in setbacks fifty meters high. The dirty, yellow-white ice is seamed and pocked with wind-carved holes and flutings. Here and there it swells in convex lenses, like the belly of Buddha. They pass an arch which, eon by eon, has been carved from a weak seam in a slumped lobe of ice by dust-laden wind a hundred times less dense than that of Earth.

They drive on, ever deeper into the chasma, heading roughly east. Shadows deepen as the sun dips down in the west, and the glitter of the ice cliff standing at the eastern horizon begins to dim. Both rovers drive with headlights and the racks of lights above their diamond bubbles blazing.

Anchee Ye opens a radio channel and tells Penn Brown, "We should turn back and try and find the beginning of one of these lobes. They come right down to the basement and you can pick a way up the terraces."

"No. That will take us many hours out of our way. I'm heading toward a big slump that's clearly visible on the satellite pictures. We're only about thirty kilometers from it now."

"It's getting pretty dark, Penn."

"We have lights. We have radar. And it won't stay dark for long."

"Yes, and you've been driving twelve hours without a break."

"No problem. Another hour and we'll be there."

"It really would be safer—"

"It's all under control. Just follow my lead."

They drive on. And, in the last light, a great extrusion of ice appears at the horizon. They drive parallel to it for several kilometers, and at last stop. Mariella heats a beaker of tea in the microwave in the tiny galley, drinking it black because she hates the powdered non-dairy creamer. Penn Brown climbs out of his rover and fossicks around in the distilled glare of its lights, then opens a channel and says, "You should really come out and see this! Be quick!"

He is insistent and urgent. The two women pull on their excursion suits and one after the other cycle through the rover's cramped airlock.

"Look up," Penn Brown says. "Look up!"

They look up.

To the west, a luminous band of spectral blue defines the margin between the black terraces of ice and the plum sky. After a moment, Mariella figures it out: it is the light of the sun, refracted through the topmost layer of ice.

"Magnificent," Penn Brown says, with proprietorial satisfaction, as if he has arranged this for their benefit. "Magnificent sight."

Then he is all business again, bustling them off to examine the smooth twenty-degree slope of the ice extrusion. "It runs back all the way to the top," he says. "You see that I was right. Everything is under control."

For the first time since they landed at Lowell he is in a genuinely good mood. He visits Mariella and Anchee's rover, shares a meal of chicken and rice followed by cookies and, that staple of astronauts everywhere, dried apricots. One of the polar satellites is over the horizon, and he sends news of their progress. They talk over their plans, crowded together like conspirators in the little cabin. Their excursion suits, hung on a rack by the airlock like prisoners in a cartoon dungeon, radiate a chill the rover's air-conditioning is slow to dispel. Red fines have already stained the legs to the thighs, the arms to the elbows.

Anchee Ye brought back a lump of ice in an insulated container; now she lifts it out with nylon tongs and sets it on the little drop-down table. It fumes instantly, shrouding itself in vapor, and out of the vapor snow falls like grainy talc.

"You see how cold it is," she says. "The cold will cause a lot of problems out on the ice."

"We'll be doing nothing we haven't practiced a hundred times," Penn Brown says, pushing around melting ice grains with a forefinger. "And I've worked hard on this reconfiguration. Smalls backs me up all the way."

"And Cytex," Anchee Ye says sweetly, "is also happy?"

"If I'm happy, they're happy. And I am happy."

But Mariella notes that Anchee shakes her head very slightly. She does not share Penn's ebullient optimism. She has been here before. On the table between them, the fuming ice cracks open. Anchee puts the pieces in one of the food trays. By morning, it has completely melted and the melt water has evaporated, leaving concentric rings of salts stained with red fines.

The Polar Icecap:
March 9–March 15, 2027

The two rovers drive straight up the tongue of ice, their woven-wire wheels crunching through sublimation lace and gripping the hard ice that lies beneath, a gentle white ascent that seems to run all the way up to the sky. They reach the top in only two hours and drive on with ice stretching all around them, sloping away to the south and west and rising to the east, although these gradations are perceptible only to radar. They have entered a land of white light beneath a sun that glares like a crazy diamond in a purple sky. They drive northwest, parallel to swirling troughs in the ice which are gently contoured extensions of the chasma. Crater Zw and the end of Chasma Boreale are only three hundred and fifty kilometers away. A twelve-hour drive. And then another twelve hours to the latest Chinese camp. But that must wait. Right now, they have work to do on the ice.

For thirty years, there has been speculation that the weight of overlying ice at the north pole of Mars, more than two kilometers thick in places, might liquefy and trap water and create a haven for life. But radar surveys have been inconclusive, and two attempts by American expeditions to drill down to the rock beneath the icecap failed. And then the first Chinese mission to Mars claimed to have drilled into water-bearing rock in the deep trough of Chasma Boreale, and to have found no signs of life. They published extensive data sets. They released samples for testing by independent laboratories throughout the world. They fabricated an elaborate lie.

Chasma Boreale is now under occupation by the second Chinese expedition, which must depart within ten days to catch the launch window for return to the Earth. They have finished with their third borehole, have moved some hundred kilometers north, and are now working on a fourth. Meanwhile, according to the plan on which Penn Brown and Al Paley have finally settled, the American expedition will head across the polar icecap toward the inner end of Chasma Boreale, sinking boreholes as they go, hoping to reach the subsurface water table discovered by the Chinese while making sure that they always remain within striking distance of the Chinese camp. As soon as the Chinese have departed, the Americans will drive down the ice-choked ramparts of Chasma Boreale and take samples from their boreholes.

Well, Mariella thinks, at least it looks easy on the map.

They set the routine on the first day. Drive to one of the predesignated sites, using the global positioning system to pinpoint a place on the ice apparently no different from any other, stop, suit up, unlatch and spread out the solar panels that power the rovers' air makers, and unload and assemble and start the drill. The drill head is a scaffold tripod five meters high, with automatic feeds for the pipe train and the power cable, a diamond-wrapped superconducting thread not much thicker than a human hair. The proton drill, when it starts its first cut, makes a burring whine that sets Mariella's teeth on edge, but as it bores through the ice the whine is quickly muffled and soon cannot be heard at all. It goes very quickly. The main limitation to its cutting speed is the rate at which the automatic feeder can lay pipe in the bore train, and they soon learn that they have to keep an eye on the feeder all the time. The intense cold causes metal to weld to metal and the whole thing can quickly jam unless the magnesium alloy pipe elements are rolled back and forth in their racks.

It is hard work. Mariella is either too cold or too hot. The heating elements in her thermal undergarment are turned up full to compensate for the chill in her extremities, leading to overheating elsewhere. Sweat pools at her back, but her hands quickly go numb because, of necessity, the gloves are the thinnest part of her excursion suit. When she draws on thick clumsy mittens for relief, she feels intense pain in her fingertips as her blood warms, corpuscle by cold corpuscle.

The hard smooth blue ice of the cap is overlain by a few centimeters of fragile lace that crunchily gives way underfoot, or by deeper layers of dusty ice crystals. The crystals grow a few tens of microns each summer, accreting scant water vapor from the atmosphere after the overlying carbon dioxide snow is lost and the temperature rises above minus seventy degrees Centigrade. It is so cold that they do not bind together except under intense pressure. They form fluffy drifts of talcum-like powder, or particles as gritty as beach sand, or small delicate spicules that splinter sunlight into millions of tiny interlocking rainbows, a dazzling skin of transcendent light. Big grains of black dust are mixed at every level or sit right on the surface. On Earth they would melt little sinkholes, but it is too cold here, and in any case the atmospheric pressure is too low. Water does not melt, but sublimes into vapor. Every ice grain has formed around a speck of dust, and here and there are patches of ice stained yellow or red or black by dust deposited by one of the local storms that blow up around the edges of the pole in spring, mantlings of color so fine that they can only be seen at a distance, downsun.

Mariella sinks up to her ankles, to her knees, in drifts of fine, freezing-cold ice dust. Despite her insulated bunny boots and the electric heat of her thermal undergarment, the cold nips her toes. There is no respite from it except to climb back into the rover for a break. And the procedure of divesting herself of an excursion suit so cold it can weld to her bare skin, and of suiting up again and checking air supply connections and helmet and glove seals before going back out, is so cumbersome and exhausting that she prefers to stay outside and freeze and work.

But she does not mind the cold and the bone-deep exhaustion and aching muscles and sores from wrinkles in the pressure garment. None of this matters because she is engaged in the thrill of the chase. At any moment the hours of mechanical routine could pay off. There is no better way of living.

The drill sends clouds of white vapor shooting high into the air. The clouds drift westward, sparkling in the raw sunlight and falling out of the dark sky as snow—the first snow to touch this land in billions of years, because the air is too cold and too dry for snow to fall naturally here. Every hundred meters they stop and reset the drill and send down a core sleeve, and then pull the core up through the pipe. Always ice, white with pressure fractures and laminated by horizons of bright or dark dust, falling apart into discs of different lengths, like vertebrae.

On the second day, Anchee Ye and Penn Brown have a furious argument over documentation of these cores. He says that there is no time for the photography and measurements she wants to make, and she says she will work on her own time. "This is valuable data. We must not throw it away."

"It's not what we are looking for," Penn Brown says. "I won't have you exhausting yourself and endangering the mission objective."

"What are you going to do? Maroon me? Jesus Christ." Anchee Ye waves her arms angrily and turns around and walks off to calm down, her blue excursion suit vivid against the white glare.

Penn Brown stares at Mariella, his face ghostly behind the heavily polarized visor of his helmet. Mariella says, "You're thinking that you should have brought a couple of glips along instead of us. Maybe you're right."

"We have to stay focused," he says. "While we're fooling around here the Chinese are drilling all around that sweet spot."

"We can hardly go in and move them out. We'll get our turn."

"And meanwhile we have to complete our own series of boreholes."

"Well, you're right about that. I want to find this thing as much as you do."

Mariella wonders if Anchee is listening in to their conversation. She doesn't have much sympathy for the geologist's position. Like most ordinary scientists, Anchee has a fanatically curatorial attitude toward data. To her, all data is precious, for even the most insignificant measurement contributes to the great treasure-store of collective thought two centuries of scientific work has built. Mariella thinks it foolish. Most work is buried in the journals and never looked at again, so that any bit of its data is exchangeable with any other bit, and thus assumes the characteristic of noise, for it carries no information. The importance of trivial or repetitive data cannot be inflated by any amount of intellectual labor. What is important is not work for the sake of work, but selection of the correct problem on which to work. No, Penn Brown is right. The overriding priority of the mission is to exploit the area around the boreholes drilled by the Chinese; any data that can be obtained from the ice cores would be at best low grade.

Mariella thinks this through in a flash, and she also realizes that she doesn't want to piss off Anchee. Any three-cornered relationship is inherently unstable, but in a changing environment instability is to be preferred over an alliance that freezes it in a stable but inconvenient configuration. So she says carefully, "Anchee just wants to be thorough. It's in her nature. She can't help it. So try not to be so hard on her."

Penn Brown's mouth hardens and he might have, been about to make a cutting retort, but just then the automatic pipe feeder makes a sudden, clanking burr. It has jammed again.

They drill down a kilometer and a half on the first day, two kilometers the next, a little over two kilometers on the third day. Breaking the official U.S. record for a borehole on Mars three times over, although they are drilling through ice rather than rock. And presumably the Chinese have drilled as deep, if not deeper.

Each bore takes a whole day to make and then dismantle, and they find nothing but laminated ice and then laminated dust bound by ice. No free water and no traces of life, no matter how hard they look.

Working alongside Anchee Ye, Mariella uses a tiny diamond-edged knife to chip slivers from the iron-hard cores brought up at the end of each run. Each sliver is placed in a sterile Eppendorf tube preloaded with five milliliters of eighty percent ethanol, which in the cold becomes sludgy ice. In the rover, the samples are gently warmed in a heating block and extracts are taken and tested for the presence of amino acids and DNA. Every tenth sample is also analyzed for the isotopic composition of its oxygen and carbon content: metabolic activity preferentially selects the lighter carbon and oxygen isotopes, and these skewed ratios provide a clear fingerprint in any residues life might leave behind. But they find no sign of life with any of their tests. Mariella keeps back a few samples from the extraction process and seeds them in broth-filled microchambers in the little Wolf trap apparatus, but there is no uptake of radioactive nutrients.

Nothing grows.

No life.

Still, despite the headachy haze of exhaustion after a hard day on the ice, it is enjoyable to tinker with wet biochemistry again, to work out strategies to minimize differences between experimental runs. Enjoyable even though they obtain only negative results.

And of course every day they are treading where no human has ever trod before. That is not insignificant.

Sometimes, when Mariella takes a moment to gaze at the panorama of ice and sunglare all around her, she sees the silvery flash of a balloon drone in the bleached sky. Most drift from west to east, very high up. Penn Brown complains about them to Al Paley, but is told that nothing can be done. The camera balloons were released by commercial rockets, and time on them, shared or exclusive, is rented by hundreds of thousands of people, including NASA's own researchers. It is impossible to shut the system down. The balloons are very cheap, no more than tubular, hydrogen-filled envelopes of foil two or three meters tall, with a little camera platform and transmitter hanging below. Most simply drift on the prevailing winds; some, plated with photosynthetic polymer, can vary their buoyancy by heating and cooling the hydrogen, and so can change course by rising or falling into winds blowing in different directions. A few even synthesize propellant from the Martian atmosphere. And more and more seem to be drifting across the pole, like natives curious about the activities of clumsy intruders.

On the third evening on the ice, Mariella receives an email from Kim.

Hey neighbor. Small world. Saw you out working today. Told you I'd try and drop by.

Mariella emails back, asks if anyone has been using the camera balloons to see what the Chinese are doing.

Plenty try. It's the most popular site on Mars right now. But those people don't like to be watched. They shoot down balloons and satellite relay cover is patchy. Hard to snoop on them. This is the only clear pic. Snatched from a kilometer up.

The image is blurred by extreme magnification, but Mariella can make out the green dome of a pressure tent in the shadow of an ice cliff, what might be a vehicle or perhaps just a rectangular rock nearby.

She shows it to Penn Brown, but he says he has better pictures from satellites.

"It's a pity you don't share them with us."

"You don't need to know."

He stares right at Mariella, and she looks away and feels a hot flush of shame and anger.

He adds, "I'm going to have to insist that the whole drone system is shut down. It shouldn't be impossible to fake a problem with the relay satellite."

Anchee Ye says, "The Chinese don't need to hack into the drone system to know where we are. Their spacecraft comes over the pole at least once a day. It might be unmanned, but you can bet it has surveillance cameras. And then there's your video diary."

She is tired and drawn. There are sores in her scalp and along her hairline which she scratches when she thinks no one is looking, and she has developed a dry cough that often wakes Mariella at night. She stubbornly refuses to report this to the medical team at Goddard Flight Control Center, self-medicating with a steroid salve and insisting that it is no real problem.

"This isn't about the Chinese," Penn Brown says. "As long as they see us drilling they know that we haven't found what we're looking for. In fact, it's important that they know we're looking. It'll make them edgy."

Anchee says stubbornly, "Except they've already found what we're looking for. They already know everything about what we're trying to find."

"Not everything," Mariella says. "If they knew everything, they wouldn't have needed to come back. And if they'd shared what they found, if they hadn't lied about it in the first place, then we wouldn't have to follow in their footsteps. We could have solved this problem together. As it is, we can't know what they know and what they don't know. We might even find out what they want to know," she says, "and not know it."

"This isn't about the Chinese," Penn Brown says again. "This is about information control."

"Yes," Anchee says. "So that Cytex can be sure of its profits, while pretending to save the world."

"NASA will get credit too." Penn Brown turns his slate around. It displays a topographic map of the western half of the pole. "This is where we're going tomorrow," he says, tapping a spot close to the edge of crater Zw. "It will certainly give our friends something to think about."

Anchee says, "Isn't that too close to their latest camp? They could come right up the Chasma Boreale and be on us before we know it."

"They could have done that already," Penn Brown says. "But they haven't."

"Perhaps because they know we're no threat as long as we stay on the icecap," Anchee says. "I've been going over the radar pictures again, and I've come to the conclusion that they're even fuzzier than we first thought. What might be a lens of water could just as easily be reflectance from a thicker-than-normal layer of dust. The bright dust layers are pretty reflective anyway, because they're so iron-rich, and an unusually thick layer could give the same kind of signal as a water lens. I can show you the data—"

Penn Brown says, "Is there a way of distinguishing a real signal from a false signal?"

"Not with the data we have. A seismic survey might help, although the overlying ice is so thick it's bound to attenuate signals. We shouldn't expect much free liquid water anyway, because pressure will close up any cavity and force the water into the rocks."

"Which doesn't matter for microorganisms," Mariella says. "Water-filled pores in rocks are just as good a habitat as open water or water bound in clathrates."

"This is just speculation," Penn Brown says. "We can't know if there is water down there unless we look, and that's what we're doing. Unless of course there's something wrong with the analytical techniques."

"If you helped us with those you'd know that there isn't," Anchee Ye says.

Mariella adds, "The blind control sets we process alongside the samples always give the right pattern of positives and negatives. And all the positive results are well within one percent of error. Don't try and fault the analyses, Penn. We're getting to be fucking good at them."

Penn Brown holds up his hands. "No need to jump on me. I was only suggesting a possible source of error."

Anchee Ye coughs into her fist, then says, "If I had been allowed to look at the lamination sequences in the cores, it might have helped to resolve the ambiguity in the radar survey. But you didn't allow it, so we're stuck."

She glares at Penn Brown with such trembling defiance that Mariella thinks she might be about to burst into tears.

Penn Brown doesn't seem to notice. He says, as if to a particularly dense small child, "If we drill at a site close to the Chinese then we might have more success. And that's what we will do."

"Yes, as long as they don't come after us."

"They are scientists," Penn Brown says, with the same acid patience. "I met one of them five years ago, at a conference on human resources in space. He was a highly enthusiastic and very competent advocate for his company, but he certainly wasn't a crazed fanatic. Anyway, I've cleared it with NASA."

Mariella says, "So it's a done deal. When did this happen?"

"Just yesterday. You can see the emails if you like. I had very little sleep because it took a great deal of persuasion to get it past the usual NASA obfuscation. But don't worry, I don't expect thanks for it."

Anchee Ye says, "And what's that supposed to mean? My God, you make changes that might put us all in danger without consulting us, and then you expect us to be grateful?"

"It was conditional on today's core coming up empty. Which it has. Someone has to be responsible for the success of this expedition, and it has fallen to me. As you knew," he says, looking at Mariella, "before we left Earth."

Anchee says, "And suppose we don't want to go along with it?"

Penn Brown shrugs, affecting indifference. "We have two rovers. You could take one if you want to try and make it back to base alone. However, I would think it would be more dangerous to travel solo across several thousand kilometers of Martian terrain than to advance the schedule of the mission by a few days, and it would certainly compromise the mission's objectives. But I suppose that I could find some excuse for you."

Anchee takes a breath and says, "Yes, you'd like that. Don't worry. I'm not going to run out on you. Even if you are wrong."

"Well, that's your opinion. How about you, Mariella? Are you with me or not?"

"Don't try and make this an issue of personalities," Mariella says.

Anchee Ye laughs. "That's what he has to do. He can't help it."

"Someone has to take charge," Penn Brown says again. He runs one hand over his head. His hair has grown out a centimeter, and makes a crisp sound under his palm. For a moment, he looks very tired. He is driving himself hard. He says, "This is not the kind of thing that can be run as a democracy. And in any case, NASA has the final word, not me. I am merely an advocate."

"Perhaps I should talk to mission control," Anchee Ye says.

"If you can persuade one of the section heads or team leaders to be your advocate, I'm sure Smalls will listen to what you have to say. But I think you'll find that he is already convinced about this. Now, if you'll excuse me, ladies, we have all had a long day. I'll see you in the morning."

After Penn Brown has climbed into his excursion suit and cycled out through the airlock, Mariella polarizes the windows of the rover against the sunlight that at this late hour slants at a low angle across the ice, and starts to pack away the little galley to make space for their hammocks. Anchee Ye sits at the fold-down table and watches her, and eventually says, "It's as if the last fifty years never happened for that guy. Men are in charge, and women are supposed to accept it."

"Well, he is in charge, even if he also happens to be a man."

"It's because he's a man that he has to be in charge. My God. The Firstborn Crisis was a terrible thing, but I thought it made us all realize that men can be more vulnerable than women."

Mariella sits down on the other side of the little table and says, "There's no use trying to use logic on him, Anchee. He's the kind of man who is unable to discuss anything rationally because he has taken a position before the argument even started. And he'll defend it to the death even if he knows it isn't logically tenable, because he thinks that if he admits he's wrong he'll lose more than the argument. He'll lose his dignity."

Anchee Ye drinks a measure of water. Her lips are cracked and dry, and leave a smudge of blood on the rim of the plastic beaker. She says, "Meanwhile, we're just a couple of glips, following his orders."

"Look at it this way. If the expedition fails, all the blame will rest on Penn Brown's shoulders. But if it succeeds, then we all win."

"I know. He's staked his career on this."

"Before this blew up, he was on the Moon trying to prove that Cytex could build a sustainable closed ecosystem. He knew that it was impossible on the kind of scale NASA could afford, but he'd staked his reputation on it and he had to see it through. He wouldn't give up even though he knew that he was destroying his career. Getting on this expedition was a knight's move that got him out of that bind. It was a brilliant stroke. He's not a great scientist, but he is very good at tickling NASA's science board and cozying up to Washington politicians. I don't approve of that kind of behavior because it means that mediocre scientists like him are able to take advantage of the system without doing proper work, but I do find myself admiring him."

"He has the kind of attitude that got Scott of the Antarctic killed," Anchee Ye says. "And his companions, too."

They are awakened early in the morning by the insistent bleep of the radio. It is Penn Brown. "Something's happened at the Chinese camp," he says. "We have to move on at once."

Anchee swings around in her hammock and plants her feet on

the ribbed rubber floor. She says to the air, "We have to move? What's happened?"

"There's a message in your e-mail box. Take a look while you're getting ready. I want to leave in fifteen minutes."

The e-mail is a brief video clip from Howard Smalls. Although he is wearing a suit and tie, Smalls looks as rumpled as Mariella feels. He recorded the clip thirty minutes ago, in the early hours of the morning in Washington.

"We have pictures that show the Chinese moving out of their camp," he says. "They put something down their last borehole yesterday, and now they're driving straight out of Chasma Boreale toward their lander. They have left a lot of equipment behind—I understand that NASA technicians are trying to enhance the pictures so they can make an inventory. NASA has picked up some radio traffic from the Chinese, too, although it's deeply encrypted and we don't have a handle on it yet. I want you to move in and find out what's going on. More to follow when we know more, and meanwhile, good luck."

There are only three pictures, snatched by one of the polar satellites. Mariella tries to make sense of them as Anchee fires up the rover's motors and begins to follow Penn Brown at speed over the flat icescape. The pictures have not been processed or enhanced by any image-correction program, and the contrast between the bright western edge of the chasma and the dark shadows of the floor is so high that most detail is lost, but someone in the flight control center has circled the small dot that is the Chinese rover, and successive shots clearly show that it is moving away from the site of the camp. From the interval between the time-stamped photographs and a rough estimate of scale, Mariella figures that it is moving at about sixty kph. Recklessly fast. As if fleeing.

She gets on the radio and asks Penn Brown, "What did they drop down the borehole?"

Penn Brown says, "Some kind of cylinder, perhaps a meter high, fifty or sixty centimeters across. Most likely a bomb. They want to destroy the evidence, just as I predicted. I bet they emplaced bombs at the other sites, too."

"It could be a probe," Mariella says, and pulls out her slate and puts on her goggles and gloves and begins to type.

Anchee says, "It has to be nuclear. My God."

"We don't know that it's nuclear," Mariella says. "We don't even know that it's a bomb."

"We don't know that it isn't," Anchee Ye says, "and we're headed straight for it."

She has slowed down, and Penn Brown's rover has begun to pull ahead.

Penn Brown says, "You're drifting back. Not chicken, I hope."

Anchee Ye switches off the radio and says to Mariella, "What do you think?"

"He's going anyway."

"That's what I think." Anchee Ye eases the stick forward again and their rover begins to gain on Penn Brown's. "Who are you emailing?"

"A friend of mine. She's into remote sensing. Maybe she can give us a better picture of what the Chinese are doing."

"Christ," Anchee says, "you're as bad as him."

"We both want to know the truth, although I hope my motives are purer than his."

Penn Brown pushes his rover hard. Its six wheels throw up big roostertails of ice crystals. Anchee Ye follows off to one side. They drive hour after hour across a glaring white landscape that undulates in broad, frozen waves which are about two kilometers wide, but have a crest height of only a few meters. Much of the polar ice is tremendously smooth, with elevations that vary by less than a meter along profiles many kilometers long. It is another example of the tremendous age of Martian features. Although superficially like the Antarctic icecap, the polar ice formed far more slowly over a much greater time span. Most irregularities have been smoothed away by wind and sublimation, and by seasonal smothering beneath a meter-thick blanket of carbon dioxide snow. The ice is stable and does not creep. There are no sastruga fields, no snow humps, no crevasses or glaciers, no ice streams flowing through the sheet to calve bergs. The icecap sits like a patch of frost on a red beach ball in a freezer, accumulating and losing an imperceptible layer as the seasons slowly yield to one another.

And so they drive across a vast flat whiteness under a sky that is black at the horizon and shades to plum at zenith, each rover the tip of a cloud of ice that plumes backward and falls to either side of tracks cut straight across the ice plain, tracks that will take centuries to erase. The only sign of their progress is the slow downward creep of the altimeter. They are descending the long shallow slope of the icecap now, approximately four meters for every kilometer.

While Anchee drives, Mariella rummages through the rover's library. She plays the "Romance" and the "Troika" from Prokofiev's *Lieutenant Kijé*. She plays the sabre dance and then the icy adagio from Khachaturian's *Gayane Suite*. She plays the delicate yet ominous allegretto of Shostakovich's Seventh Symphony.

"All Russian," Anchee Ye points out.

"I suppose they have ice in their bones. There's always Vaughan Williams's *Sinfonia Antarctica*."

"Brr. Put something else on. Not that mournful death blues of yours. Something cheerful. Jazz. I like jazz. Old show tunes, something like that."

So they are singing along to Louis Armstrong's outrageous vamping of "I Wanna Be Like You" when Penn Brown's rover disappears.

It vanishes in a sudden explosive thickening of its icy plume. For a moment, Mariella thinks it must have hit a hummock in the layer of loose ice crystals, but then they pass through the slowly settling cloud and see nothing. Only the ice plain stretching all around to the razor-sharp junction of white ice and black sky, and the slow drift eastward of a thinning cloud of ice crystals.

"Shit," Anchee Ye says.

She brakes hard and the rover slews, throwing Mariella sideways against her harness. Anchee cuts the music and switches on the radio and says, "Penn. Penn, what the fuck did you do?"

Mariella switches on the radar, points to the signal, and says, "He's right there."

"I don't see him," Anchee says, leaning forward in her harness, anxiously scanning the level whiteness beyond the diamond canopy. "Christ, Penn," she says into her mike, "come in, okay? Over." She says to Mariella, "Do you think it was the Chinese? A laser pulse from orbit maybe? We're sitting right here on the ice —"

Mariella hits the release of her harness. "I think he drove into something. A crevasse."

"No. There aren't any at this elevation. Sublimation crevasses along the south-facing edges of the Chasma Boreale, that's all."

Anchee tries the radio again, and Mariella says, "He might be knocked out."

Anchee holds up a hand. "Quiet. Yes, I think I hear him breathing. What are you doing?"

Mariella has started to pull the outer layers of her excursion suit over her thermal undergarment. "We're going to get him out."

They make their way step by step toward the place where Penn Brown's rover disappeared. Mariella probes the lacy ice with a long aluminum pole before each step, fearful that they could be standing on an ice bridge that at any moment might give way and drop them into unknown depths.

But it is not a crevasse. It is a crater.

It is small and recent, perhaps only a few thousand years old. The meteorite that made it struck at a shallow angle, leaving a shallow elliptical gouge in the ice that's just over a hundred meters long and thirty meters across at its widest point. The upturned layers of ice at the edge of the crater have been worn down by sublimation into a smooth, annular hummock, like the rampart of a Stone Age earthwork. It encloses a wide shallow dish that has over the millennia filled with slow-growing ice crystals until it is brimful with soft white powder.

When Penn Brown's rover struck the crater's low rampart, it was launched into the air like a stunt rider's motorcycle. It almost cleared the crater, smashed nose-down in the deep pool of dusty ice, and settled so that only its boxy rear remains uncovered, tilted at a steep angle.

Mariella and Anchee Ye look down at the inside of the crater from the top of the rampart. Dust has accumulated on the surface of the ice, and ice thrown up by the rover's crash has made white rays across the crater's pink oval, centered on the black wedge of the rover's rear end. They can't see into the rover, and Penn Brown still isn't responding.

"I can jump across," Anchee Ye says.

"Don't be stupid."

"It's only ten meters. Maybe less. An easy jump in this gravity."

"We don't know how deep the ice is."

"In this suit I'm not going to drown if I miss the rover, and I'll be fairly buoyant."

"We should call mission control."

"No. They'll spend hours working on simulations and meanwhile he could be bleeding to death from internal hemorrhaging. And if the canopy didn't crack, a seam might have split in a slow leak. Look, I can do this. Let's get the cable reel."

They make a kind of harness from the hair-thin, diamond-tough superconducting cable, padding Anchee Ye's excursion suit with diamond mesh where the cable loops around her waist and shoulders. Mariella keeps on the diamond-mesh over-gauntlets they used for handling the cable. If Anchee falls, Mariella is supposed to haul her out.

Anchee makes several practice jumps, all of which fall short of what is needed, then says, "Fuck. If I don't do it I'll never do it."

And runs straight at the gentle slope of the rampart, yelling like a banshee. She takes off, legs pedaling in the air, and lands with a percussive thump and an explosion of ice crystals right beside the rover's tipped rear.

"I'm okay," she says, "I'm okay, I'm okay," her breath sounding loud over the radio link. "It's very cold though. I can feel the cold right through my suit. There's a kind of ledge here. I think the impact rammed the ice — oops."

She suddenly drops down to her shoulders in loose ice crystals. Mariella's heart thumps, but Anchee has already caught the staples beside the airlock at the rear of the rover and is pulling herself up. A minute later, she has cycled inside, and a minute after that says over the radio, "Well, the canopy held and the stupid fucker's alive. Wake up, Penn. Come on, you've got to wake up and help me."

There is the small but distinct sound of a slap.

"Wake up," Anchee says. "Come on now."

"Check his pupils."

"I did. Not fixed, not dilated. He's wearing his harness. I think he banged his head is all. Wait a minute. . . ."

Mariella stands alone and impotent at the edge of the crater in the middle of a glaring white plain under a dark sky, the alien landscape accentuated by the homeliness of the sounds coming over the radio, mysterious rustles and chinks as Anchee Ye rummages around. Then there is a brittle snap and a thrashing noise and muffled swearing.

"Ammonium chloride from the gas chromatography standards," Anchee Ye says cheerfully. "What do you say, Penn? Looks like I saved your life here."

Penn Brown is still groggy when they drag him across the bowl of the crater, lying prone on the outspread blue sheet of the dome tent like an ice hunter's trophy. Once he is safely at the crater's rim he shakes off their attempts to help him, laboriously gets to his feet, and plods toward the other rover.

Anchee Ye follows him through the airlock—she has not recovered from her immersion in the ice and is now shivering visibly—and when Mariella comes through into the crowded little cabin she finds Anchee sitting hunched in a corner under the tiny lab module. She has managed to strip off her helmet and gloves and padded oversuit, and is shaking tremendously, her arms wrapped around her knees. Penn Brown sits in the driver's seat, still in his excursion suit, but with the helmet and gloves off. He has switched on the rover's spare slate, and is typing with painstaking slowness.

Mariella dumps her backpack and says, "What do you think you're doing, Penn?"

"I'm okay. Have to report. What happened? I was driving along and then I was in the air."

"You did an Evel Knievel, and pancaked in a crater full of ice crystals."

"It wasn't on the map," he says. "That's what I'm telling them. It wasn't on the map."

"You hadn't engaged the navigation system," Anchee Ye says wearily. "You overrode it so you could drive faster than the safety limits allowed."

"No," Penn Brown says. "It was on. It was on, but it didn't show anything."

"It was off when I found you," Anchee Ye says.

Mariella says to her, "Are you okay?"

Anchee Ye clenches her teeth and says with effort, "Coffee would be good. A hot bath would be better."

"It was on," Penn Brown says stubbornly. "I didn't hear it give a warning."

He continues to insist on this, giving Mariella and Anchee Ye a flat recalcitrant stare as he repeats his story. "I was driving along and suddenly I was in the air. The navigator was on. I didn't hear a warning. I was driving at a fast but acceptable speed across perfectly level terrain, and then I was in the air."

The email beeps. His message has crawled to Earth and the reply has crawled back. He turns and reads the screen and starts to type again, one hand cupped over the big bruise ripening on his forehead.

Meanwhile, Mariella, still in her excursion suit, turns up the heat inside the rover, microwaves a cup of coffee, and hands it to Anchee Ye, who is shivering in brief, intense spasms now.

Penn Brown says, "We need to know the status of the rover."

"It's fucked," Anchee says, and drinks from the waxed paper cup of coffee she holds in both hands.

"We don't know that. We could haul it out—"

"I had a good view of both of the rear-wheel drive units when I climbed in," Anchee says. "Both bearings were cracked and leaking lubricant. They must have smacked into the rampart when you took off. And God knows what the front end is like. You're lucky you didn't pop the canopy."

Penn Brown looks exhausted and unhappy. He keeps touching the edge of the big bruise on his forehead. He says, "It's a tough machine. And it has to be done, NASA says, or we'll have to wait here for pickup. There's no safety margin with only one rover."

"Look," Anchee Ye says. "Your rover is nose down in several meters of loose ice crystals. Even if it was okay and we were all okay, we'd still have a hell of a time hauling it out. And in the process we might fuck the one functioning rover we have. You screwed the pooch, is what happened. Face up to it."

"There was no warning," Penn Brown says grimly. "I was driving along and there was no warning."

Anchee says, "There was a warning and you didn't hear it, or there was no warning?"

"The navigator was engaged, okay? And it didn't give any warning."

Again that dark and furious stare, searching their faces for any trace of denial. Mariella realizes that this is the story he has worked out for himself. He has done nothing wrong. The rover's navigation system screwed up, not him.

He says, "Perhaps the crater isn't even marked."

Anchee Ye says, "Every square meter of Mars has been mapped by laser altimetry. Those ramparts are on average three meters above the surrounding ice. They would show up clearly."

"Maybe they were buried when the maps were made, and were excavated in the storm last fall."

"You want me to check?"

Mariella says, "What's happened has happened. Now isn't the time to apportion the blame. We can't get the other rover out. Mission control doesn't want us to go on with only one. So what should we do?"

Anchee says, "We can accept that we're screwed, and wait for the airship to pick us up."

The aftereffects of an adrenalin spike and the shock of the cold have left her sullen and moribund, but at least she has stopped shivering.

Mariella says, "If I remember, the airship is taking Betsy Sharp and Ali Tillman to their research site. It must be most of the way to the south pole by now. How long will it take to reach us, even if it turns around and flies straight here? Six days? Seven?"

Penn Brown says, "Longer, if that asshole Poole has anything to do with it."

Anchee says, "What's your point?"

Mariella says, "That from the point of view of our rescuers one place on the pole is as good as another. We have an intact rover certified to carry four people for thirty days, and perhaps we can salvage material from the other one. The Chinese camp is only a couple of days away. There's plenty of margin. We just have to convince mission control."

It takes several hours to firm up the plan via email, with maddening delays between messages. They talk to the rover design team at mission control in Houston. They talk to Al Paley and Howard Smalls. There is a long delay while the section heads of mission control convene a conference. Mariella hands out hotpacks and drinks too much black tea. Anchee Ye hunches into herself and refuses to strip off the rest of her excursion suit; Penn Brown works at the rover's spare slate, writing up his report on the incident. He is still groggy. He was bruised badly by his harness, and his forehead is blackened and pulpy with blood, but there are no signs of any internal injuries, concussion or subdural bleeding.

At last the email beeps. It is a video clip from Howard Smalls. The three of them crowd around Penn Brown's slate as it decompresses and begins to run.

"Before I give you your status, I have some more news about the Chinese," Smalls says. "About twelve hours ago, just after the Chinese left, there was an explosion deep underground at their campsite, and simultaneous explosions at the other sites where they've drilled. Lowell Station picked up a very weak trace on its seismograph, and got a correlation from one of the field expeditions. NASA has only just now finished processing the data. The results are fuzzy, but it is clear that the Chinese placed charges at the bottom of their boreholes and set them off. The yields were pretty small, almost certainly nonnuclear, but so far we have no visual confirmation of that.

"That's the first bit of news. The second is that the Chinese rover has stopped about thirty kilometers short of their lander. It has not moved in the past six hours. Currently, NASA is trying to nudge the orbit of one of the relay satellites so we can obtain a better look at what's going on there. You'll know as soon as anything definite is discovered."

Smalls pauses, squares his hands on the top of his desk. He is wearing a gray jacket of soft suede, the wide collar of a canary-yellow shirt spread over its lapels. Behind him, a window overlooks a snowy lawn backed by a stand of conifers. Strange to see their vibrant green after so long on the *Beagle* and the red rock and white ice landscapes of Mars.

Smalls says, "I have obtained clearance from higher levels that you can go forward with your mission. Officially, we're claiming that you are on a rescue mission after the Chinese expedition got itself into trouble. That may in fact turn out to be the case. Privately, you'll press on and try and fulfill your primary mission objective. Good luck."

It is late in the afternoon. Mariella and Anchee Ye veto any further travel that day. Penn Brown agrees without much of a fight, but when he realizes that Mariella and Anchee are going to try to salvage what they can from the crashed rover, he becomes agitated and says he has to go out too. He tries to stand, but becomes dizzy and disorientated and falls back into his chair. Anchee is right behind him, and stabs a Syrette in his neck. He protests feebly, and falls asleep while brushing at the spot.

"Jesus fuck," Mariella says. She feels breathless, amazed and a little frightened by Anchee's ruthlessness.

Anchee shoots her a hard look. "Give me a hand," she says, and together they lift Penn Brown from the chair and lay him on his side on the floor. He is snoring loudly. Mariella puts a cushion under his head and says, "What did you give him?"

"Ten milligrams of Scolapine," Anchee says.

It is a powerful sedative, for use in case one of them gets cabin fever. "Wow," Mariella says. "Well, I guess he won't be a problem for a while, but he's going to be really pissed off when he comes around."

Anchee is quite unrepentant. "I've had enough of his shit. Let's get this job done."

The two women use heavy-duty electric cable and the drill's tripod scaffolding to construct a ropeway from the crater rampart to the half-buried rover. It is easy enough in the low gravity to swing across hand-to-hand and winch material back. They take the proton drill, the backup probe and as much pipe as possible, and then

Mariella goes down inside the rover. She salvages Penn Brown's slate and the rest of his personal kit, but leaves everything else. They have enough food to last well beyond the scheduled pickup, and water is all around them. The tilted rover is already cooling, its structure creaking as the stresses work through its frame. Frost has bloomed thickly across the walls. The canopy glows with an eerie blue radiance. A pipe in the galley has broken; spilled water has frozen in a wedge in the tilted cockpit. Mariella opens both doors of the airlock and switches off the batteries and leaves the wreck for later generations of Martians to salvage.

When they have stowed away their loot, they walk all the way around the crater. Anchee Ye takes pictures of the crashed rover from every angle, and Mariella videos it. She is very tired, and has trouble keeping the lightweight camera steady. She wonders briefly how Alex Dyachkov is doing, out there on the shore of the ancient lake with spooky Barbara Lopez.

"Let me show you something," Anchee Ye says.

They tramp north for three kilometers across virgin ice, until their rover is a distant black chip against the white landscape. It is very late in the evening. The sun has circled around to the west, sits just above the horizon. Stars show bright and stark against the purple sky. Every bump in the ice paints a long shadow across the white glare of the land, and every hollow is filled with the same blue radiance that leaked through the buried canopy of the crashed rover. Ahead is a slight rise, the edge of a second crater. It's perhaps twice the size of the first, its rampart higher at the northern end.

Anchee Ye patches a cord to Mariella's suit, so they can talk in privacy.

"Just where it should be," she says with grim satisfaction. "You see, the meteorite came in at a shallow angle and actually skipped over the ice, shedding velocity as it went. The crater Penn crashed into was the final point of impact; if we could dig down we might even find the remains of the bolide."

"You looked up the map."

"Of course I did. There's a chain of impact craters stitched across the ice. They were mapped more than twenty years ago.

This is crater Zwe. He hit Zwf. Look, it's impossible to run the navigational system and disable the alarm. And if he had the navigational system switched on, as he claimed, it would have warned him five kilometers before he reached the crater. Plenty of time to turn aside. So either he ignored the warning or he had turned the system off."

"I don't think he would have deliberately run over the crater."

"I wish I could be so sure. Maybe he thought he could get away with it. Maybe he wasn't paying attention. Maybe he was too tired to think straight, and switched off the alarm by reflex. Actually, it doesn't matter why he screwed up. The thing is that he did. He was careless, and out here a moment of carelessness can kill you."

"Well, in a way he did get away with it."

"We can't count on luck," Anchee says. "We'll have to watch him, or he could kill us all. As it is, we're still in deep shit. We no longer have a backup, and the airship is days away."

"Actually, I'm more worried about the Chinese."

"Right. What do you think the explosions were?"

"I don't know."

"I suppose it could have been worse."

"You mean they might have used nuclear weapons? Surely no one would be so crazy."

"Why not? The Chinese have clearly decided to ignore all international treaties. They found something valuable and they don't want anyone else to have it."

Mariella admits, "Penn Brown thinks that it is commercially valuable."

"Ah. So he talked to you about patents too."

"It's a sorry pass, isn't it, when we discover the first life on another planet and can talk only of how much it might be worth. We'd better go back. He's hurt, and we shouldn't have left him alone."

"Yes," Anchee Ye says, just before she unplugs the cord, "even when he is not here we must always think of what he needs."

*   *   *

With three people in it, the rover seems very cramped. Mariella lies on an aerogel mattress, and all night, dozing and waking to Penn Brown's sedated snoring and dozing again, feels the coldness of the rubber-floored deck beneath her.

Penn Brown is still groggy in the morning. He picks at his breakfast with dull inattention while Anchee and Mariella wipe condensation from every surface and run system checks. When Anchee settles into the driver's seat and starts the motor, he looks up and says, "We should salvage stuff."

"We already did that, Penn," Mariella says.

"There's a box," he says. "Box one hundred fourteen. It's important. I should go out."

The number places it in one of the crashed rover's forward stowage bins, buried deep in the ice. Mariella says, "We got what we could."

Penn Brown thinks about it, then says, "They left, didn't they?"

"The Chinese? Yes, yes they did." Mariella is worried that he might have been more badly hurt than he seems. Maybe it's an aftereffect of the Scolapine. She says, "What do you remember about yesterday?"

"Maybe it doesn't matter. If they left, I mean."

"What doesn't matter? The box? What was in it?"

Anchee guns the motors. The rover lurches up from the depression its waste heat has hollowed in the ice, starts to smoothly accelerate away from the crater.

Penn Brown cups a hand over his bruised forehead. "I have a really bad headache," he says. "Give me a couple of aspirin. And no more sedative, okay?"

He slowly perks up, even makes a joke about taking a spell at the wheel, but there's a tense atmosphere in the rover's cabin. Still, Mariella feels a measure of hope that things might go more easily now. His authority has been seriously, perhaps fatally, damaged, and that might allow her rather more freedom than she had counted on. And they are still on track, still in the race. It doesn't matter what the Chinese have found or what they have done as long as she can see with her own eyes living Martian organisms.

Anchee Ye, quiet and grim, drives at a steady thirty kilometers per hour. The ice slopes down, giving terrific views to the west. They cross more and more stretches tinted pink with dust, and at last Anchee turns south and they begin to descend a wide long ramp of ice with an ice cliff rising to the east. It is the first of the terraced benches at the edge of the great wind-carved valley of Chasma Boreale. They turn north and then south again, following a fairly even thirty-degree slope, and at last the floor of the chasma appears to the west, a light-tan plain mottled with black and ocher patches, the iceblink of the western wall flashing at the horizon more than twenty kilometers away.

Chasma Boreale:
March 15–19, 2027

They leave the ice as the sun dips below the western ice wall. Anchee drives on through deepening twilight, all the lights of the rover blazing. She has been driving for most of the day, with Mariella spelling her for only a couple of hours. She is trying to prove something. To herself, to Penn Brown, to Mariella. She is trying by force of will to stamp her own authority on the expedition.

She drives the rover down the gentle headslope of a little cirque some sixty kilometers south of crater Zw, continues straight out onto the main floor of the valley. The eastern ice wall looms behind them, rising out of a sea of shadows at its base. Ahead, at the horizon, the top of the western wall glows blue with the refracted light of the sun, which has briefly set beyond it.

After an hour Anchee at last stops the rover for the night. They eat in silence. Anchee and Mariella turn in straightaway, but Penn Brown stays up to record and transmit his diary. Mariella falls asleep to the rat-claw patter of his fingers on his slate's antique keyboard.

They start again early the next morning, after a quick breakfast of coffee, oatcakes and reconstituted scrambled eggs. Six a.m., the sun low in the sky and shining almost directly down the wide valley, casting the rover's shadow ahead as Anchee drives it south, still maintaining a steady thirty kilometers per hour. The ground is darkened by basaltic fines eroded from exposed mantle material to the south of the permanent icecap, and it is shaped by the permafrost that underlies it, a thermokarst terrain cracked into broad polygons hundreds of meters across with their edges raised into steep-sided dykes, interrupted by the low mounds of pingos, which are uniformly darker on their southern sides, and by alases, depressed areas like shallow dry lakes where ice has sublimed and caused the overlying soil to collapse. Here and there are small craters with slumped rims surrounded by lobate aprons of debris, clear evidence of impacts that temporarily melted the ice-saturated ground. It is easy to believe that all of Mars was once like this, before the water drained into deep undetectable sinks, or was locked up in mineral deposits, or was blown free of the planet, along with most of the early atmosphere, by massive meteoritic impacts. No one knows where most of the ancient water has gone, but there is still water here.

And in the pores of deep rock strata, compressed by the immense tonnage of the icecap and warmed by trapped heat, is a reservoir of liquid water. And in that water is the life they are looking for. So close now.

Mariella sits in the passenger seat and watches the somber landscape flow by. The Chinese camp is three hundred kilometers away, right under the western ice wall. If all goes well, they will reach it early in the evening. Already, anticipation of what might lie ahead is knotting her stomach. Perhaps the others feel the same; silence thickens in the cabin of the rover as Anchee Ye drives it south and the low sun swings around so that, despite fifty percent polarization of the diamond canopy, they all have to put on sunglasses against the flood of light.

They pass from the darkened thermokarst terrain onto linear dunes of tan-colored sand as hard and crunchy as clinker, eroded from layered deposits along the sides of the chasma. The dunes, with prominent slip faces and much gentler upwind slopes, form a rolling landscape with crest-to-crest spacings of about half a kilometer, and the rover pitches straight up and down them. In places, the sand is mingled with red dust and takes on the uncanny color of Caucasian flesh, as if they are driving over the wrinkled skin of a sleeping giant.

Mariella drives for a little while, and then Anchee Ye takes over again, turning the rover southwest. The eastern ice wall vanishes below the horizon as they leave the vast dune fields behind and drive up the wide benches and twenty-degree slopes of a laminated terrain. Ice cliffs a kilometer high take up more and more of the sky ahead, and then are rising on either side. They have entered an embayment several kilometers wide and more than ten kilometers deep, eroded into the western ice wall by wind and sublimation.

And then, less than three kilometers from the site of the Chinese camp, at 83°N, 55°W, as the rover enters the long shadow at the base of the first layback of the terraced ice wall, the intense red point of a signal laser glitters dead ahead. And at the same time the email chimes.

It is a brief video message from Al Paley. He tells them that the Chinese government has issued a warning that a hazardous microorganism has been released into the immediate environment of the camp, and that it is dangerous for anyone to approach it.

"They claim that one of their crew was infected and had to be left behind," Paley says. "We don't know the status of the other two, but their rover is still sitting in the same position, about two hundred and fifty kilometers south of you. We're trying to obtain more information from the Chinese, but at this time we suggest that you do not approach any closer. We'll try and draw up a contingency plan and we'll keep you advised."

Penn Brown immediately says that it is a bluff. "They're desperate to keep us away and so they'll make up any old bullshit to do it."

"Someone aimed that beacon at us," Anchee Ye says.

It is still glittering in the dark distance, like a star fallen to the surface of the world.

"Almost certainly automatic."

"Even so, I think we should wait," Anchee Ye says. She is sort of half-hunched around in the big driving chair, and will not look at Penn Brown. "We can't take the risk of exposing ourselves to a dangerous biological agent. Who knows what they pulled up this time?"

"In the first place," Penn Brown says with acid patience, "even if you accept that Martian and terrestrial life have the same common ancestor, the Martian organisms have a history of more than four billion years of completely divergent evolution. We'd be more likely to catch a cold from a tree than become infected with anything that lives here. In the second place, anything released into the atmosphere would instantly die. It would be frozen out of the air and fall to the ground, and its organic components would be destroyed by the ubiquitous superoxides in the soil. In the third place, we'll be wearing our excursion suits when we go outside. So even if, by some highly unlikely circumstance, something living has been released, and even if it is infectious, we'll still be protected. But there's nothing there anyway, because the Chinese are bluffing."

Anchee Ye says defiantly, "I don't care. I still don't want to take the risk. If there's something out there and we go wandering around, we'll pick it up on our excursion suits and bring it inside. Al said we should stay put and that's just what we should do. We're only the field operatives. There's a whole team working with us. Sometimes I think you forget that."

"Not at all. But they are on Earth and we are here. NASA is a lumbering bureaucracy with a history of overcaution, and Paley is covering his ass." Penn Brown pinches the bridge of his nose between finger and thumb. He looks tired and drawn. The crash has taken more out of him than he has admitted. He says, "Paley said that he *suggested* we stay put. That's not an order. And as for contamination, I think it's a chimera, but if one of us went for a recon the others could set up and pressurize the tent. We have salt and bleach, and that should be enough for an antiseptic scrub. Mariella, you're the microbiologist. Would that be acceptable?"

"We don't have enough pipe to make our own borehole," Mariella says. Penn Brown stares at her, and she adds, "After the accident, we lost half of our pipe."

"You didn't think to salvage it?" Penn Brown says.

"There was no *room*," Anchee Ye says. "We have the spare probe and the drill head, but we had to leave most of the pipe behind because there was no room on the rover for it. Okay?"

Mariella says, "So we can only lay about a kilometer of pipe. I don't think it will be enough."

Anchee Ye says, "If we can't drill deep enough, there's no point going in."

"No," Mariella says. "It means that we'll have to go in, and use the borehole the Chinese established."

"But they blew it up," Anchee says. "They blew up all of their boreholes."

"I'm not so sure. My father was in the oil business. There's a common trick that was used to maximize crude extraction. You didn't simply drill a hole and pump crude up; you'd leave a lot behind. So you pumped a mixture of viscous gum and sand down the well, then set off explosives to fracture the surrounding rock and force the mixture into the crevices formed by the explosion. The gum helped the sand disperse into the cracks and the sand propped open the crevices. Then the gum dissolved because you'd added enzymes to the mixture before you pumped it down. Perhaps the Chinese used that technique, in which case the borehole will still be there."

"All very interesting," Penn Brown says. "But why would they also blow charges at the other boreholes, where they've finished drilling?"

"Perhaps they intended to go back to those boreholes. Perhaps this time they wanted to maximize extraction, make sure they were sampling a wider range."

Anchee Ye says stubbornly, "Or they could have simply blown up the boreholes to destroy what they found."

"Of course," Mariella says. "But we don't have enough evidence to be sure."

"Which is why we have to go look," Penn Brown says. "I take it you're with me on this, Mariella."

"I don't think we should turn around and go back. That's not why I came here. But I don't think we should just walk in there, either."

Penn Brown says sharply, "There's no middle position."

Mariella says, "It's getting dark, and we've been driving all day. We should rest and wait for light. Then we'll drive closer and try and see what's there."

Penn Brown pinches the bridge of his nose again, says, "I suppose that it's a plan."

"I'll take that as high praise indeed."

Anchee Ye says, "As long as we don't plan on doing any EVA, I don't have a problem with that."

Penn Brown says, "Of course we'll be doing EVA. With or without you. I'm in charge here, not Paley and his group of pallid geeks."

"Yes," Anchee says, "and you were in charge when you drove your rover right into a well-mapped crater."

"Maybe I should have a word with Howard Smalls," Penn Brown says, "and explain to him just how you and NASA are conspiring to fuck up the mission."

Anchee says bitterly, "Just who is in charge here, Penn? You or Smalls?"

Mariella says quickly, "Anchee, you speak Chinese. Maybe you can use the radio to talk to whoever has been left behind."

"No one has been left behind," Penn Brown says. "They're bluffing."

Anchee ignores him. She tells Mariella, "I speak a little Cantonese."

Penn Brown says, "You'll be talking to an empty channel."

"We're not going anywhere until daylight," Anchee tells him. "It can't hurt to try."

But there is no response, although the signal laser continues to glitter out there in the darkness at the base of the ice cliff. Penn Brown spends a long time emailing back and forth with Al Paley and Howard Smalls, and at last says that although the people at mission control are a bunch of cowards scared of losing their good-conduct medals, he has persuaded them that the risk of entering the Chinese camp is minimal.

"Smalls is on our side," he says, giving Anchee a hard look. "He wants to see this through. He pushed Paley hard, and Paley gave way. We'll go in at first light."

"You make it sound like we're at war," Anchee says.

Penn Brown smiles. "If it is a war, the Chinese have already lost."

He is more cheerful. He thinks that he has won, that he has regained control of the mission. Mariella doesn't disabuse him. As long as she can do her own work, she doesn't much care what other people think.

She is woken by Anchee Ye.

"He's gone," the geologist says, sitting back on her heels. Her face, framed by black hair, is pale and drawn. Behind her, weak sunlight slants through the diamond bubble of the rover's canopy. "The stupid fucker knocked us out and took off."

Mariella sits up, squinting at Anchee through a blinding headache. Her mouth is very dry. She says, "Did he use Scolapine too?"

"He increased the carbon dioxide partial pressure. I only woke up because I fell out of the hammock. He could have killed us!"

"He would have blown the airlock if he wanted to do that. I think he wants to play the lone hero, going into enemy territory while the women are left behind in the homestead. Shit. I didn't think he would be so stupid."

It is the refrain of all women wronged by the selfishness of men.

They email mission control, summarizing the situation. To cover their backs, because they agree there's no time to wait for a reply. Then Anchee starts up the rover, driving slowly as she follows Penn Brown's footprints across a gentle rise in the land. They show clearly: the surface is lightly dusted with red fines, and the prints of his cleated boots have exposed the darker material beneath. Reflected sunlight shines from the icewall that looms ahead like a vast curtain, pleated by spurs and gullies. The whine of the rover's motors increases in pitch as Anchee steers it straight up the thirty-degree slope of a bench terrace, wire wheels biting crisply into duricrust. The ground levels out, and the low mound of a tent, its bright green contrasting sharply with the tan ground, is suddenly visible, less than half a kilometer away. Anchee brakes sharply; a faint cloud of dust puffs past the diamond canopy. There is no sign of Penn Brown, and the ground is so scuffed and churned by footprints and vehicle tracks that it's impossible to follow his trail any further.

Mariella says, "Try the radio."

As Anchee reaches for the headset, there's a chunky metallic thump. Glass shatters somewhere behind them and a high-pitched whistle starts up. Something strikes the diamond canopy only a few centimeters from Mariella's face; even as she flinches there is another thump, and the whistle increases in pitch.

"We're holed!" Anchee says in astonishment.

A fourth shot pierces the rover's triple-layered hull and the whistle becomes a scream. The air-conditioning is at full blast, trying to compensate for the sudden loss of pressure.

Mariella and Anchee drop to the floor, scrambling for their excursion suits. There are two more shots. One is deflected by the diamond canopy; the other punches through the hull and smacks into the rubber-cleated deck half a meter from Anchee's feet. When they are suited up, Mariella switches off the air-conditioning—otherwise the entire air supply would bleed out—and they tumble through the airlock and crouch in the lee of the rover.

Mariella is breathless and her heart is thumping quickly. Like Anchee, she sits in a half-crouch with her ass about half a meter above freezing dust and her life-support backpack wedged against the flank of the rover. She is very aware of the gap between the rover's undercarriage and the ground. It is possible that her legs could be shot out from beneath her at any moment, but there is no other cover, and this is better than waiting to be slaughtered like teenagers in some bad slasher movie, Spam in a can. She takes the end of the patch cord Anchee passes to her and plugs it in and says, "We should have thought of this. My friend told me they were shooting down balloon drones."

"What about Penn?"

"I don't know. The rover is much bigger than a man. You can't miss it."

Then they are both laughing, because it is a ridiculous situation. Anchee draws a breath and says soberly, "We might be wearing these suits a long time."

Something flashes in the corner of Mariella's vision, something drifting high above in the dark sky. The most popular site on Mars. Right.

Mariella says, "We can patch the holes in the rover's hull. But first we have to contact our lone gunman. Try the radio. He has to be outside and suited up to be able to shoot at us."

"I'll bet his radio isn't switched on," Anchee says, but starts to scan the fifty channels.

Mariella looks all around. The sky seems empty. Perhaps it was only passing by, tugged away by the strong westerly winds. It doesn't matter anyway, because there are no satellites above the horizon. Or not yet.

Now that adrenalin is dissolving out of her blood, she is beginning to feel afraid. A stone in her gut, her whole skin flinching in anticipation of a bullet's fatal punch. The gunman might be anywhere, working his way around to get a clear shot at them. And the rover is the only cover they have. The rocks strewn across most of Mars are buried here by deep layers of frozen dust, and the bench terrace is very flat.

There's an extensible mirror in the utility pocket on the left sleeve of her suit, in case she needs to make adjustments to her backpack. She runs it out to full length and angles it around the side of the rover. It must have flashed sunlight at the sniper, because dust kicks up several meters away. Mariella borrows Anchee's mirror and sets it in the ground so it gives her a view toward the green dome of the Chinese tent, wiggles the other mirror around. Dust kicks up again, a little closer this time, and she catches a glimpse of the muzzle-flash in Anchee's mirror.

"He's near a spoil heap to the left of the tent," she says.

"Well, he isn't talking."

"Keep trying. Work back up. He might be trying to contact us, and if you're both going the same way through the channels you could miss each other."

Mariella tries the trick with the mirror again, but this time the sniper isn't tempted. Or he's worked out what she is trying to do. A couple of minutes later, Anchee says, "Got him! Channel thirty-eight."

"Hello?" Mariella says. "Hello? Who am I talking to?"

A man's voice says, "You are Dr. Anders."

"Yes. Yes, I am."

"In other circumstances it would be an honor. An honor to meet with you." The man's voice has a liquid quality to it, as if his words are bubbling through pitch. Mariella can hear the harsh rasp of his breath. He says, "I am Dr. Wu."

"Why are you trying to kill us, Dr. Wu?"

Anchee Ye draws the edge of her gloved hand across the neck seal of her helmet, a request for silence, and says, "We would like to meet in better circumstances."

Dr. Wu says, "Yes. Yes, I regret these circumstances too."

"They are very regrettable circumstances."

"Unfortunately, you have come too close."

"We've been very foolish," Anchee says.

"You are the Chinese-American. You try to play the face game. In other circumstances we would share a drink together. We could talk science. But not here."

Anchee points at Mariella, who says, "Your English is very good."

"I study one year in America. In Lawrence, Kansas."

"I've been there. A nice city."

"Yes, very typical American town. Old part very quaint, like an old movie. Very hot in summer. Many thunderstorms."

"I remember some interesting gingerbread houses."

"Carpenter Gothic, yes. But I think the main highway was more typically American. Big barns dedicated to commerce, a wonderful disregard of space. In China we have many malls, but not your strip development."

Over the patch cord, Anchee says, "Perhaps the Chinese weren't bluffing about contamination. He sounds awful. He sounds like he's dying."

"Yes, but he still has a rifle," Mariella says, and tells Dr. Wu, "It is very likely that your companions are dead. Their rover has stopped some way down the chasma."

"Yes, I thought that might be the case."

Anchee Ye says, "We might be able to help each other."

"I appreciate your sentiments, but I regret it is not possible."

"Well," Mariella says, "what are we going to do about this?"

"I think you will keep talking to me, to distract me from what your companion might try to do. I do not mind. I thought I would die alone in this awful place. It is better that we die together."

So Penn Brown is alive.

Mariella says, "If there's a problem, then perhaps we can fix it together."

Dr. Wu laughs, a horrible liquid gurgling that breaks off in a spasm of coughing or retching. He pants for breath, and at last says, "You must excuse me. I am ill. As you will be, except that I will shoot you first. Perhaps if you came closer it would be easier. I promise it will be a clean death for both of you."

Mariella says, "You're a pretty good shot."

"I learned in Siberia, during field training. We must carry rifles against polar bears."

"It was the same in Canada," Anchee says. "We had a bear dog as well as rifles. He would bark like crazy if a polar bear came within a kilometer of the camp."

"I am not as excellent a shot as my colleagues, but I know I have hit your vehicle. I saw the condensation of your atmosphere as it leaked out."

"Well," Mariella says, "I guess the rover's a bit bigger than a polar bear."

"I think I can hit you, too. I practice now."

Three tall puffs of dark dust twist up one after the other, like tiny meteorite impacts. The nearest is less than ten meters from the rover's rear wheel.

"You see," Dr. Wu says. His breath is labored. "I have a sufficiency of ammunition."

"What can we do about this?"

"You are not American, Dr. Anders, but like all Westerners you have absorbed the post–cold war imperialism of America. America tells itself that only it can fix the world's problems, that it is the last superpower, the world's policeman. But it has no moral authority except that which it awards itself. Many countries do not recognize that authority. My country does not. Not on Earth, not on this world. After the unfortunate accident, my company tried to negotiate with yours, but they would not listen. They still thought only of exploiting what they had stolen, and so they sent you on your fool's errand. But it does not matter. We have fixed the problem. We do not need your help."

Mariella says, "Do you mean the problem here? Or do you mean the accidental release of microorganisms containing Martian gene sequences into the Pacific Ocean?"

"That was regrettable, but it was your company which tried to steal the Chi."

"The Chi?"

"The basic organism, yes? It must have taken phytoplankton genes into itself, but you will know more about that than I."

Mariella thinks fast. Dr. Wu believes that she knows more than she does. Well, she can guess now how the slick started, and why Cytex is so closely involved. She feels a peculiar clarity, as if all her hunches are a moment away from crystallizing into certainty.

Dr. Wu says, "I know, and you know too, that this is not about scientific research. It is about resources. My country and your country both want to grasp the possibilities represented by the Chi. My country succeeded where yours failed. Now yours wants to steal our prize. Too late. We fix the problem."

"Is that how you were hurt?"

"It was an accident. A blowback. Pressure vented liquid water full of infective agent over the site. My companions were outside, protected by their excursion suits, but I was inside. The pressure of the spray must have forced an aerosol of ice particles through the Kevlar. Perhaps through a seam. Certainly afterward there were a number of slow leaks. I became sick. To my shame, I infected my companions when they tried to help me. And you will become sick too, except I will show you mercy."

Mariella says to Anchee, over the patch cord, "Do you think he is under orders to do this?"

"The others tried to get back to the lander. He must have chosen to stay. Or perhaps there was a disagreement over what to do, and they ran away."

"What are we going to do? We can't sit here and wait for him to die."

"We have to find out what happened. He may be mistaken or lying about the contamination, but we can't take the chance. We must contact Al Paley. Perhaps he can get Wu's company to talk him out of this. The satellite will be over the horizon soon. I'll get my slate, set up the email."

"Where do you think Penn is?"

"Probably thinking of something stupid to try," Anchee says. "Talk to Wu, but don't let him lose face. Make out that this is our fault. Ask for his help. Shit."

Dust spurts up close by.

Mariella says, "He wants to get our attention. He wants to talk."

"You talk. I'll get my slate."

"Good. Get mine too."

As Anchee clambers back into the airlock, Mariella switches back to Dr. Wu's channel and says, "Did the blowback happen when you blew open the seams in your well, or afterward?"

"You plan something, don't you? Perhaps I come over and visit."

"There's an idea."

"Or get close enough to shoot at you from beneath your vehicle. The angle here is all wrong. I am a little way downhill from you."

Mariella says, "I don't think you can walk very far, Dr. Wu. You had better stay there and conserve your strength. Exertion is probably what killed your companions."

"They used much of the medical kit while trying to treat me. Then they became sick, and I persuaded them to try and reach the lander."

"Tell me about the Martian organisms."

"I think not."

"It'll pass the time while you figure out how to kill us."

Anchee Ye scrambles out of the airlock and hands Mariella her slate. Mariella opens it, activates the infrared port and selects a channel so she can talk to it.

Dr. Wu says, "You are a very rude person, Dr. Anders. I am disappointed."

Mariella switches channels, dictates a message and tells the slate to send it as soon as possible, switches back. "You're trying to kill me, Dr. Wu. That's pretty high up on my personal scale of rudeness. You could at least let me know what I'm going to die for."

The slate tells her that the satellite isn't over the horizon yet.

Dr. Wu says, "You are too long in America, I think. I admire the British. I was born in Hong Kong. I remember the celebrations of the handover. I was only a small child, but I remember very well how dignified it was. British imperialism was very different from the American kind. Americans want everyone to be American. The British never tried to make the Chinese British. Of course, they thought they understood us, and of course they were wrong. But their stupidity was no more than misguided benevolence."

"I thought most people in Hong Kong were against the handover."

"It's true, some foolish people were infected with notions of democracy. But democracy is an ideal that does not work well in the real world. It is like Marxist communism, or the horizon. Always it recedes as you try and approach it. Our communism is pragmatic. It flexes like a reed."

"Which company do you work for? We know that three more or less run the Chinese government."

The slate tells her that it is still trying to send the email message. When does that satellite clear the horizon?

Dr. Wu says, "It is a symbiotic partnership."

"Even in true mutualistic symbioses it's often difficult to determine that both partners obtain equal net benefit."

"As long as both host and symbiont survive and pass on their genes, does it matter?"

The slate beeps; at the same time Anchee Ye makes an exaggerated thumbs-up sign. The satellite is above the horizon. They can talk with Houston and Goddard now, although the exchange of messages will be painfully slow as transmissions crawl across space from Mars to Earth and back again.

Mariella tells Dr. Wu, "You'd like our partner, I think. He's a greedy reductionist too."

Mariella wonders where Penn Brown is. Like Anchee Ye, she does not trust him not to do something foolish.

Dr. Wu breathes heavily and liquidly in her ear. She says, "You cleverly changed the subject. We were talking about the Martians."

"Have you read *The War of the Worlds*, Dr. Anders?"

"A long time ago. At school."

When her father was working in Mexico. They lived in a sprawling single-story house in a secure compound patrolled by guards on loan from the army. It was not unusual to see soldiers roughly searching housemaids or gardeners held at gunpoint by the big steel gates. The few children who lived there were tutored in a room in the leisure complex by the eight-hole golf course. Mariella remembers the hum of the computers in the cool, tile-floored room, the fans turning slowly overhead beneath the white rafters of the roof, the noise green parrots made as they chased through the flowering bushes outside.

Dr. Wu says in his strangulated, straining gargle, "Perhaps you remember that Wells's Martians came to conquer the Earth, but were destroyed by a humble bacterium. He got it right, except his image was the inverse of the truth. Of course, our expectations of Martians have much dwindled. At the beginning of the century we hoped for ancient civilizations. As we learned more and more about Mars, we settled for humble lichens, and then could only hope for a few hardy bacteria."

"Is that what you found? My guess is that they are something like archaebacteria — that is, if life on Earth and life on Mars share the same universal ancestor. And they do, don't they? Otherwise the Chi could not have taken genes from phytoplankton."

Dr. Wu says liquidly, "Life on Mars and life on Earth share certain basic qualities. But evolution on Mars followed a different path from that on the Earth."

It does not seem strange to be engaged in this discussion while squatting behind a rover on the Martian surface, talking to someone she has never seen or met, someone who wants very much to kill her. Never before has Mariella had such a strong sense that her long apprenticeship has created another self, one that operates on a nonhuman level. Science is an artificial way of thinking, a collaborative dissection of the Universe using a powerful but completely abstract philosophical process. Mariella is part of that great collaboration; so is Dr. Wu. And so they can disagree about everything else — everything about their human situation — and yet still engage in a dialogue.

She says, "I can accept that Martian organisms evolved in completely different conditions from life on Earth. That despite a common ancestor, the two kinds of life took divergent paths. But surely there would have been little evolution after Mars cooled. In a very restricted habitat there would be no evolutionary motor to drive changes because there would be no new environments to exploit. Just as in the case of extremophile archaebacteria on Earth. They evaded competition by colonizing habitats like the hot, salty water in pores of deep rock strata, where conditions were similar to those of the early post-Hadean period. Other organisms evolved away from those conditions and can't return to the original state."

Dr. Wu makes a throaty noise which could be meant as a chuckle.

Mariella thinks hard. On Earth, early microbial life split into eubacteria and archaebacteria, and all multicellular organisms arose from the archaebacterial lineage. The Martian organisms must be something else again, as different from the eubacteria and archaebacteria as those two great lineages are from each other. But if she can make guesses about them that are close to the truth, perhaps she can provoke Dr. Wu into letting slip a vital clue.

She says, "The early Martian genome must have had much in common with the early Terrestrial genome, but that isn't surprising. After all, we share much of our genome with eubacteria, even though the evolutionary divergence between the eubacteria and archaebacteria occurred very soon after the origin of life on Earth."

She has a sudden insight, and for a moment all the world goes away. She taps her gloved fingers on the edge of the slate in a five over eight beat, says slowly, "It's possible, isn't it, that these Martian organisms have some property that drove the split between eubacteria and archaebacteria. In that era there were plenty of massive impacts on both planets, knocking rocks into outer space. And some of those rocks carried viable microbial spores from Mars to Earth. It's silly to posit just one instance of interchange—a single Martian survivor of an impact landing on Earth and becoming the universal ancestor—because that would mean that the origin of life on Earth depended upon a contingency so improbable it is unacceptable. No, Earth was seeded with life from Mars through many such impacts, and although life on Mars and life on Earth began to take different evolutionary paths, the exchanges between the two planets didn't stop. Perhaps the arrival of an advanced form of Martian life on Earth caused some kind of evolutionary pressure that initiated the split between eubacteria and archaebacteria. It would have been as fundamentally catastrophic as the major extinctions at the ends of the Permian and Cretaceous eras."

There is a long silence. Mariella listens to Dr. Wu's agonized breathing. At last he says, "You live up to your reputation, Dr. Anders. But this is no movie where I give up the secret because of an overdeveloped ego."

"I thought we were speaking as scientists."

Dr. Wu coughs, loud and long. It sounds as if he is trying to give birth to his lungs. He says, "So we are. But I am also loyal to my employers. As you are to yours. That is why we are here."

"I'm not here to exploit what you've found. Only to try to understand it."

The slate beeps again. The message is from someone she doesn't know, a Robin Schulz in Plevna, Montana. *I see you.* Mariella looks up at the sky above the ice ridge, but sees nothing. The balloon drone must be high up, hanging in still air above the winds that, driven by the temperature difference between the bright, cold ice and the warmer dark sands around it, blow off the polar cap.

Dr. Wu says, "Forgive me for being as blunt as you. But you are either lying or being very naive."

"I think I'd prefer naive. I've seen the effects of the release of your Chi. I can make some educated guesses about its properties."

Again that horribly liquid chuckle. "Yes, but you cannot truly know it, for it had already changed."

"Originally, I thought that the Chi had been given phytoplankton genes. I see now that it infected phytoplankton after it was released. It combined the genetic repertoire of many different organisms into something new, creating the slick. It is like a genetic parasite, incorporating useful genes from other species into its own genome. It operates at a kind of Lamarckian level; it does not evolve inheritable characteristics, but acquires and recombines genes already evolved by other organisms. That's why your employers are so anxious to keep this secret, because it allows massively parallel genetic engineering, very fast, very powerful. How am I doing, Dr. Wu?"

For a moment, there is only the sound of the man's horribly labored breathing. And then Mariella hears a faint, rapid staccato that she realizes must be the sound of his rifle firing on full automatic. She ducks instinctively, and Anchee Ye shouts, "The idiot!"

Penn Brown is running straight toward them, leaping like a ballet dancer in the light gravity, his blue helmet and the violet overgarment of his excursion suit vivid against the yellow ground. He runs as if pursued by the cloud of dust that springs up in his footsteps, its gauzy billows stitched with denser spurts and geysers. He dodges this way and that with huge balletic leaps, and then he is suddenly upon them, crashing into Mariella and knocking her to the ground. The rover briefly shakes—a deadly tattoo. Anchee Ye yelps and throws herself to the ground, and they all lie there as fine dust settles around them.

Anchee Ye slowly gets to her knees, looks down at Penn Brown's prone figure, and says, "Are you trying to kill all of us?"

Penn Brown is lying on his back, grinning up at her behind the tinted visor of his helmet. He says, "I got to the borehole! It's still there!"

Mariella sits up and brushes dust from the screen of her slate, hoping it hasn't penetrated the seals. The ground is very cold against her buttocks and thighs. There are more than a dozen emails waiting to be read, but she guesses that they'll all be much the same as Robin Schulz's message, and tells the slate to switch channels and stay quiet.

Dr. Wu's liquid voice says in her ear, "Now you are all together it is perhaps easier for me."

Penn Brown rolls onto his belly and looks through the gap

between the ground and the rover's undercarriage. He says, "I heard you talking with him. There's no point. He's a fanatic. Shit. He's pretty much shot up the rover."

"I have the honor of being loyal to my company," Dr. Wu says.

Anchee Ye holds out patch cords and she and Mariella and Penn Brown plug themselves into a private triangle of talk. Anchee says furiously, "Of *course* we've been talking with him. How else are we going to get out of this?"

"Well, it won't do any good," Penn Brown says. "I tried talking to him after he shot at me. The son of a bitch is in bad shape, but he can still shoot. He's right there, behind that little ridge of dirt by the tent. Lying on a foam mattress, but even so the cold must be getting to him, and sooner or later his air will run out. His field of fire is limited, too. After I got to the other side of the tent I could pretty much move about the site in safety. I made it all the way to the borehole. I need more air, that's why I came over. That, and I have an idea about getting rid of him. Of course, it would be even easier if you hadn't knocked me out after the crash. I would have made sure you salvaged what we need."

Anchee says, "What was in box one hundred fourteen, Penn? The inventory said miscellaneous spare parts for the proton drill, but that was a lie, wasn't it?"

Penn Brown ignores her. He says, "There was a blowback at their drill site. There's a spray of debris all across the ground past the tent. And the borehole itself is buried under a thick flow of ice. We'll have to clear that if we want to use it, but it isn't much of a problem. We'll get what we want."

Anchee says, "You brought guns along. Contrary to every international treaty. And you still think you can order us around?"

Mariella says, "Anchee, did you send off that email?"

"Yes, and I have an acknowledgment. Nothing else yet. They're probably brainstorming a solution right now. We have plenty of time. The satellite will be above the horizon for several hours."

Mariella tells Penn Brown, "That's why we were keeping him talking. We're sure that we can fix this."

"As one of your Brit prime ministers said, jaw-jaw not war-war, eh? Except it is war. That guy is dying out there, but he's doing it slowly and we can't wait him out."

"We're dealing with the situation," Anchee says.

"If lying here in the dirt is dealing with anything," Penn Brown says scornfully.

"Yes," Anchee says, "and what did you plan to do with those guns, Penn? Shoot your way into the Chinese camp? Murder them? Is that why you were so keen to get here before they left?"

"My tank is rattling. Help me with a new one, okay?" Penn Brown switches to his reserve bottle and, as Mariella helps him take off his backpack, says, "I know you both mean well, but we have to deal with this decisively. Consulting NASA might be proper protocol, but this is not a glitch in some piece of software. This is a lunatic raving with fever and armed with, my guess is, a Kalashnikov T53. High-velocity rounds, laser target acquisition, very rapid rate of fire. He had a mind to, he could shred the rover pretty thoroughly. He almost shredded me, but I managed to keep moving fast enough so that his rifle couldn't lock onto me. I kicked up a lot of dust too. I think it confused his rifle's computer."

Anchee Ye says, "You should have stayed where you were while we talked him out of it. You're as crazy as he is, both of you playing war games like little boys. He could shred the rover? Well, all he did was put a couple of holes in it, until you came barreling in like one of those old action heroes. *Then* he shredded it."

"We don't need the rover to get out of here. Pass me out a new pack. Okay, thanks. Mariella, can you? Good."

Mariella helps Penn Brown refasten his backpack. He checks the snap connectors of his two airlines, briefly vents them to test the flow, and switches from reserve to main.

"You have stopped talking to me, Dr. Anders," Dr. Wu says.

Mariella switches channels and says, "I haven't forgotten you. We were talking about what you found. Was I close to the truth?"

"I cannot tell if you were guessing or pretending to guess."

She confesses, "I don't know too much about what we found in the Pacific. I mean, I saw it, but the research into it was off limits."

"Ah. They keep you in the dark."

Penn Brown is making an urgent throat-cutting gesture. Mariella stares at him and says to Dr. Wu, "It's what we call a need-to-know basis. There are commercial considerations. It isn't the best way to do science." She switches to the patch-cord link and tells Penn Brown, "I *know*, you son-of-a-bitch. Cytex tried to steal what the Chinese had, but it didn't reach the States."

"Not just Cytex, Mariella. We found a Chinese scientist who could help us, but we needed help getting the sample out of China."

"How did it get into the Pacific? By boat or plane?"

"Scramjet. A commercial flight. The sample was in a diplomatic pouch, so the Chinese took out the plane."

"Which came down in the Pacific. No wonder Cytex is so closely involved. This isn't a research mission, is it? It's a damage-limitation exercise."

"You don't know the half of it," Penn Brown says.

Mariella realizes that he's relishing this chance to prove himself. She says, "You want it all, don't you?"

"We can both make a lot of money, Mariella, even if we have to share it with NASA."

"You're fucking your own company."

"I wouldn't say that. I just want to renegotiate the terms of my contract."

"You were a founder member of Cytex, but you couldn't contribute much cash, and that's reflected in your share allocation. One-point-five percent, isn't it?"

"Why, Mariella, you've been researching me."

"And you want more."

"It's business, that's all."

Anchee Ye says, "This isn't a private expedition. It's for the public good, not private profit."

"Don't be naive. More than half the cost of the mission came from Cytex, and neither Mariella nor myself is a NASA employee."

Mariella switches back to Dr. Wu and says, "I'm sorry. A little local difficulty."

"We do not live in an ideal world," Dr. Wu says. "Were you really guessing?"

"More or less."

"Let me say that if it was a guess, it was a very good one. The Martian organisms are indeed very different from anything we could imagine, but that is only to be expected. Life is wonderful because although its beauty is accidental, nevertheless it is still beautiful."

"I would like very much to see this beauty for myself."

"I regret it is not possible."

Penn Brown makes the throat-cutting gesture again, and Mariella says, "I'll have to come back to you, Dr. Wu. Be patient." She switches to the patch-cord link and says furiously, "I'm getting so close. Don't fuck this up."

"He's playing head games with you," Penn Brown says. "He can't get anything other than a stalemate, and that's what you're allowing him to do. You're moving back and forth but going nowhere."

Anchee Ye is bent over her slate. She says, "Al Paley's office has contacted the boards of the three Chinese companies. He says we must do nothing until he has a reply." She angles the slate toward Penn Brown. "Here. Read it."

Penn Brown pushes the slate away. "I have a better idea."

"It's a direct order," Anchee says. "I don't care what you say about Cytex. This mission is run by NASA."

"If they were in the foxhole with us I might take notice." Penn Brown stands up, and begins to unlatch the rover's port-side stowage bin. "We're not entirely helpless, as you'll see."

"We're being watched by at least one balloon drone," Mariella says. "Don't do anything stupid, Penn."

"We're being watched by the NASA satellite too. But this is our game, right?"

Mariella tells Anchee, "Send another email. Tell Al Paley that we know what the Martian organisms are. And tell him that we know about the commercial considerations."

Penn Brown pulls out a red plastic crate and says, "Don't be naive, Mariella. You have no evidence."

"For the second time, I admit that I was naive. But no more. What are you doing, Penn?"

The box contains charges designed for opening a recalcitrant borehole. Little brushed aluminum cylinders printed with garish red warnings, each containing thirty grams of plastic explosive.

Penn Brown holds one of the little cylinders close to his visor, and uses a stylus to poke at microswitches inside it. He says, "What I'm doing is ending this situation. With their fuses reprogrammed these make handy grenades. Now, I want you to create a diversion."

Anchee Ye says, "Wait a few minutes. Wait until we get a reply from Al."

"It'll be over by then. Take my emergency flares, Mariella. Use yours, too. You'll be the diversion. Aim them toward him, make him put his head down. I'll do the rest. Look, don't worry. There's no risk to you. Let them off from under the rover if you like. As low to the ground as possible. Don't give me that look. I'm going to do this with or without your help, and if you don't help you can be sure it'll go down badly in the debriefing. *Don't worry*. He's a sad, sick little fuck who can't even make his smart rifle shoot straight. On my count. Five—"

"Just a few minutes," Anchee Ye says.

"—three—"

Mariella says, "Penn, don't—"

Penn does. He pushes off in a great leap and starts to run in a zigzag course toward the tent, covering a tremendous distance with each stride. Mariella shouts to Dr. Wu, "I'm sorry!" and leans around the corner of the rover and fires off Penn Brown's flares one after the other.

One goes high, whizzing above the tent and exploding in a tremendous flash of white light; the other two bounce along the ground like errant fireworks, spitting white smoke. When Mariella tries to pull out her own flares, Anchee Ye grabs her gloved hand and says, "It doesn't matter."

Penn Brown is on the ground. He almost made it. In front of the tent, a figure in a bright red excursion suit gets to its feet. Mariella says, "Please, Dr. Wu. Please don't."

There is only the sound of Dr. Wu's labored breathing, each breath punctuated by a gurgling rattle. He leans on his rifle with each step, but moves with a crablike quickness.

Anchee Ye's grip on Mariella's hand tightens. Fear loosens

Mariella's thoughts. She tries to speak but her mouth is dry. She licks her lips and tries again. "There's no need for this, Dr. Wu. Let's talk. Please. Please stop."

No reply. Just that horrible stertorous breathing. The red-suited figure has reached Penn Brown's prone figure. It swings its rifle around and there is a tremendous flash of light, as if a meteorite has struck. Mariella tries to blink away bright afterimages as stuff patters down like hard rain on her helmet, on Anchee Ye, all around. There is only the hiss of the carrier wave in her ears, underscoring a terrible silence.

It takes Mariella and Anchee Ye several hours to bury the bodies. Two balloon drones drift down, adjusting their positions with puffs of gas. According to an email from Kim, more than four billion people are watching.

The ground is very hard. Here is the truth of that old carol Mariella loved to sing as a child. Earth as hard as iron. Water like a stone. They use the last of the explosive charges to loosen the permafrost that lies beneath the friable few centimeters of duri-crust, then chip out a rectangular hole and lay Dr. Wu and Penn Brown together at the bottom. Their bodies are not badly damaged; the excursion suits absorbed much of the blast, although it blew off most of Penn Brown's right hand. Dr. Wu's helmet is still intact. His eyes, behind the tinted glass of its slitlike visor, look beyond Mariella into infinity as Anchee Ye solemnly recites the prayer for the dead. He seems very young.

Mariella hopes that he will forgive her violation of his body.

The women cover the two dead men with clods of frozen dust, and mark the cairn with a GPS beeper. Let someone else retrieve the bodies, or let them remain here, preserved for millions of years in Mars's deep freeze.

Now Mariella and Anchee Ye have to consider the immediate problem of survival in an area contaminated with a deadly micro-organism, and the question of how they will be able to return to Lowell before the launch window for the shuttle closes.

The rover is out of commission. The holes Dr. Wu shot in its pressure hull could be patched easily enough, but the motors that drive four of the six wheels have been damaged, and a ricochet inside the cabin took out the computer that coordinated the motors' microprocessors. Techs at Goddard FCC think they can upload into one of the slates a program that will substitute for the damaged computer, but Mariella tells them not to bother. Even if she and Anchee redistribute the two working motors to the front wheels, the rover will be able to make no more than five kilometers per hour. Better that the airship comes and picks them up.

Except that the airship is at the south pole.

"I'm very much afraid it's your own fault," Donald Poole tells them, over a bad video link. "Your insistence on commandeering the airship caused all kinds of problems with the resupply schedules. It took more than a week to sort things out with established expeditions before I could release it for the south pole mission. That's where it is now, but I'll get it to you as soon as possible. You're in no immediate danger, although you may have a few days' discomfort."

The bad link keeps bleeding color from the picture and pulls the left side up, as if in a funhouse mirror, but despite this distortion, Poole's smile is very obviously insincere.

"Unfortunately, even if the airship leaves at once, it will be four days returning from the south pole, and then it must make a stopover for maintenance and refueling. So it will be at least ten days before it can reach you, and it will take a further four days to bring you back. By then, alas, the launch window for the shuttle will have passed. But we can always use more hands at the base, especially *experienced* hands."

Mariella says, "Can't the *Beagle* wait for us?"

Something terrible is happening to Poole's face. It is expanding like a picture projected on an inflating balloon, his eyes sliding apart and his smile growing as wide as a shark's beneath the swelling prominence of his nose. His voice, though, is suddenly very clear. "It isn't possible to reconfigure the return orbit—"

"Bullshit," Mariella says, but she knows that it's probably true. Earth has moved beyond opposition now. Every day it draws a little more ahead of Mars, and every day the delta vee needed to return is increasing. Soon it will exceed the Mars shuttle's capacity, and it doesn't have the shielding to survive a Venus flyby. And then she realizes that she doesn't need the *Beagle*.

Poole says, "You'll have plenty of work to do, Dr. Anders. That is, as long as you can recover viable Martian organisms. . . ."

The picture breaks up into a snow of gray and white pixels and Poole's voice fades, but the sound has not entirely gone. For a moment, another voice rises above the hiss of the carrier wave, a faint but exuberant shout.

"Don't worry about a thing! I'm on my way!"

Then only hiss and snow. The satellite that has been relaying the call has gone over the horizon. For a few hours, Mariella and Anchee are on their own. Already the drones that have been watching them are drifting higher as their autonomic programs take over.

Mariella says, "Was that who I thought it was?"

"The foolish woman! Even if she makes it here, she can't come near us."

"I don't think it's as bad as that."

"It was killing Wu. And it killed the rest of his team."

"Given the conditions here, I'm certain it can't affect us. But if you want to be sure, we could deploy the tent on the far side of this ridge."

"Don't you want to look at the borehole?"

"It can wait. I'd like to get the tent up as soon as possible. We're both tired and I've been in this suit for six hours and, frankly, I need to take a dump."

"Do it in your pants. Then you'll be a real brown-ass astronaut. I think we should stay in our suits until we get some advice."

"Anchee, you have to trust me. We're quite safe."

"I'd rather wait and see what the experts at Goddard and Houston have to say on the matter," Anchee Ye says stubbornly.

"The satellite won't be overhead for hours. How badly compromised is the mission?"

"NASA has control. That's all I care about. There may have been commercial contracts, but that doesn't matter now. You should be pleased. You will be able to work on the Martian organisms at Lowell, without interference from Cytex."

"I'm beginning to see why Poole was so keen to delay this mission. Did NASA plan to strand me here all along? No, don't bother to answer. I know it did. Al Paley is cannier than either Penn or Howard Smalls believed."

"You always think things are more complicated than they are," Anchee Ye says blithely. "We should take a look at the borehole. Two men died over it, and I want to see if we can complete this mission successfully."

The borehole is less than a kilometer beyond the Chinese tent. The ground rises toward the ice cliff, an irregular wave of earth broken by eons of frost heave. Slabs of dirty ice lie everywhere, some as big as houses, sculpted into fantastic shapes by wind and sublimation, and half-buried in dust. Mariella and Anchee Ye follow a well-used track to a ragged rift or embayment that cuts into the ice cliff. The borehole is a twenty-meter tower of aluminum scaffolding propped at a forty-five degree slant just inside the embayment's wide mouth. Beyond, terraced ice slants steeply upward, like a giant's staircase. The sun, only a few degrees above the top, shines directly down it.

The initial release of pressure shot water a long way, spraying a wide cone of spattered puddles and glittering bits of fresh ice that points directly at the distant green dot of the tent's dome. A thick, glassy skin of ice caps the borehole itself, like a half-melted candle stub. Despite her exhaustion, Mariella feels both awe and exhilaration. After all, this is the first water to have flowed on the surface of Mars for millions of years.

Anchee Ye walks around and around the borehole, and says at last, "There's no sign of any pipe."

"Maybe it's still down there."

"Or maybe they took it with them. Either way we're fucked. The borehole must be full of ice, and God knows what the explosion did to it."

"If we can blow off the well head, then perhaps we can get a live sample. It'll be frozen a long way down the pipe, but there must be a lot of pressure behind the blockage. I don't think we'll find much, though. Wu's team saw to that."

Anchee Ye is on the other side of the slanted scaffold tower, looking at the tent's green dome, which the walls of the embay-ment frame like a gunsight. She says, "They didn't come here just to take more samples, did they?"

"You figured it out too. Good."

"It wasn't hard. Wu wanted us to know. He couldn't tell us directly, but he did say that the problem had been fixed."

"Penn was right about one thing. Wu was playing games with us."

"What do you think it was?"

"Certainly a biological agent. Probably a virus. The Chinese have done what we were planning to do. They located some kind of vulnerability in the complete native sequence, and used it to construct a biological agent that could enter and multiply within the Martian organism without being absorbed. My guess is that those explosions were the self-destruction of suicide probes loaded with anti-Martian agent. The Chinese wanted to destroy all trace of biological activity under the ice cap, to make sure their com-mercial rivals couldn't copy their work. Like napalming a rainforest after extracting all the useful gene sequences from its plants and animals. What fucking arrogance! If we're lucky, some of the Mar-tian organism will be deep-frozen at the top of the borehole, but I want to try and get a live sample of the anti-Martian agent too."

"It killed the Chinese, and it could infect us as soon as we take off our suits. We should get back to the rover. The satellite will be back above the horizon soon. Mission control will have some advice about decontamination."

"I have my own idea about that," Mariella says, "but I suppose it won't hurt to run it past mission control."

By the time Anchee Ye and a team of NASA biologists have agreed to Mariella's proposal, it is after midnight, and the sun has set behind the ice cliff. Working in the glare of the rover's headlights, Mariella and Anchee put up the tent and rig a decontamination chamber. They use gaffer-taped pipe to make a frame, and spray construction foam into a mold dug in the hard, frozen ground to make rough slab walls. They rip a fan motor and tubing from the rover's air-conditioning system, shovel Martian topsoil into a hopper, bury one end of the tubing in it, crowd into the crude little chamber, and switch on the fan. Dust bursts out of the open end of the tubing and fills the chamber with a dense red fog.

After five minutes, Mariella lets go of the dead man's switch and smears dry dust from her faceplate. She and Anchee are both covered in dust loaded with highly reactive superoxides that can tear apart any organic molecule.

In Mariella's opinion, it's a needless precaution. She is certain that any infectious agent that escaped from the borehole would have been destroyed by the UV-rich sunlight and contact with the Martian soil; Dr. Wu was infected only because he was inside the tent when it was penetrated by liquid water sprayed by the initial pressure surge, and his companions were infected when they tried to treat him, not by contamination on their excursion suits. But Anchee Ye is still not entirely convinced that they are safe; there's a chance that spores or cells quick-frozen inside ice droplets might revive when the ice melts. When at last the two women crawl inside the tent and strip down to their thermal underwear, scratching themselves all over like hyperactive monkeys, Anchee immediately puts on an air mask, and diligently vacuums dust from their suits.

Mariella deals with her stinky comfort pad, cleans herself with wipes. The cold air in the tent is filled with a strong, acrid smell, like a compound of bleach and the heads of old-fashioned matches. It stings Mariella's eyes and nostrils. When Anchee strips off her mask, she immediately begins to cough, a deep racking cough that goes on and on until, tears streaking her dusty face, she opens the medicine pack, scrabbles for a Syrette, and jabs it in her thigh.

"Christ, Anchee," Mariella says.

"I'm okay," Anchee says in a small voice, and takes a deep breath that rattles with fluid, wipes the tears from her face with the back of her hand. Her face is mottled red and white; her eyes are puffed up.

"What was in the Syrette?"

"Adrenalin."

"That's not the first time you've needed to do that."

"It's the dust," Anchee confesses. "I've been taking antihistamines against it."

"The dust?"

"I must have become sensitized on my first mission. I had an episode at Lowell, after a solo walk."

"And you didn't tell anyone."

"Would you, in my place?"

"No, I suppose not."

"I started a course of antihistamines and was always super-careful when I cleaned up my suit after every EVA. And I knew I'd be okay on the icecap, because there's hardly any dust on the ice. And I *was* okay."

"But we brought in huge amounts of dust this time."

"I'll be all right at Lowell, as long as I don't go outside."

"We'll have to go through this again tomorrow," Mariella says, "after we open the borehole."

"I'll be all right," Anchee says stubbornly. "It's no worse than any other allergy. And if the adrenalin doesn't hack it, I'll stay in my suit until the airship picks us up. Don't worry."

Which was what Penn Brown said just before he got himself killed, Mariella thinks. But she's too tired to argue, and besides, there's really no point.

They sit cross-legged on airgel pads, eat from hotpacks and drink weak sugary coffee. The sun has risen again; its light burns through the tent's blue ripstop Kevlar. This, and the fierce cold radiated by the poorly insulated floor, keep Mariella in an uneasy state between sleep and waking for most of the night, despite her utter exhaustion.

In her troubled sleep, she sees again Dr. Wu's blood-red figure making its way toward Penn Brown. Sometimes she runs out and wrestles the rifle away from him. Sometimes she starts to run and he shoots her. Sometimes she is lying prone, pinned by tremendous gravity, as he looms above her. Again and again she half-wakes to find herself in a little tent full of blue sun-glow, Anchee Ye lying a meter away with an arm flung over her eyes and breath rattling in her chest, and then sleep claims her again.

*   *   *

The next day, watched by a single balloon drone that hovers at the mouth of the embayment, Mariella and Anchee open the Chinese borehole. They haul in equipment on a crude travois constructed from pipe and the spare tent, laboriously chip away the frozen gush of ice around the top of the shaft, then set up the proton drill and use it to cut through the ice that plugs the shaft itself. It has frozen more than three hundred meters down, but at last a thin slick of water spills out of the bore, bubbling and steaming as it evaporates into the thin dry atmosphere.

Anchee sits down, utterly exhausted, while Mariella takes samples that may well be useless. The Chinese biological agent, tailored to destroy Martian life, has probably killed everything at the bottom of the boreholes, and even now will be spreading through the rock beneath the icecap like ink staining a glass of water.

In time, it could destroy all life on Mars, and there is nothing they can do about it.

Once the samples have been frozen down, Mariella and Anchee return to their camp, take a dust bath, and retire to the tent. Although they spend two hours vacuuming up dust before cracking their suits, Anchee has another coughing fit, but it passes without the need for an adrenalin shot.

They sleep twelve hours straight. Mariella checks her email, suits up and walks past the green dome of the Chinese tent and the shallow mound of the grave. She climbs a little round hill, a frost-heaved pingo, treading where no one has ever trod before, and looks south. It is late in the morning and the sun shines straight down the chasma. The iceblink of the eastern ice wall glitters at the horizon. And there at last, as promised, its dust plume casting a long shadow ahead of it, is the rover. Mariella jumps up and down and semaphores with her arms, then remembers to open a radio channel.

Barbara Lopez answers at once. "Don't you worry about a thing. We'll be with you in less than an hour."

And Alex Dyachkov says, "Hey, I see you! I see you. This is going to make for some wonderful pictures."

"We've already been on TV. We're on TV right now."

"I know, but the quality's lousy. Real amateur-hour shots. I'm here to make you look good."

Barbara Lopez and Alex Dyachkov set off as soon as they heard that the mission had lost a rover. They drove more or less continuously for four days across the plains of Vastitas Borealis, skirting the scarp of the big Lomonsov crater and navigating the rolling dune sea to the mouth of Chasma Boreale. Along the way, Barbara Lopez sold the rights to her rescue mission to TV networks in more than forty countries, enormously adding to her fame, but Mariella suspects that she would have done it anyway, just to spite Donald Poole. If the airship meets them halfway back to Lowell they will have just enough time to make the *Beagle*'s launch window.

But Mariella has other plans.

She walks Alex around the site, showing him the borehole ice-lake, the spattered ice around the green tent, the grave of Penn Brown and Dr. Wu, the decontamination rig. Alex videos everything, taking closeups of the bullet holes in the hull of the rover, panning from the brand-new shallow crater where Penn Brown met his enemy in a final embrace to the empty sky above the ice wall. Mariella shows him the samples she has taken and, speaking straight to his camera, explains their significance in three different ways.

By now, it is late in the evening. Dust in the atmosphere scatters the sun's light; it sits at the horizon in the midst of shells of yellow and orange and red that shade imperceptibly into the dark purple of the sky, where sharp bright stars are pricking through. Alex and Mariella help the other two finish transferring supplies, and then they take dust baths in the decontamination chamber and climb inside the rover.

Anchee is the last to come through the airlock. Alex and Mariella vacuum her suit from helmet to boots, but she starts to cough as soon as she unlatches her helmet and lifts it from her head. She can't stop coughing, and squats down on the floor. Each hiccupping intake of breath seems to be forced through a narrowing space; her eyes roll as in a panic she tries to open the ring valve around her neck.

Mariella pulls a medicine pack from beneath a pile of hot-packs, scrabbles through it for an adrenalin Syrette, flips the orange cover from the needle with her thumbnail and jabs it into the soft skin behind the angle of Anchee's jaw. The woman rears up with unexpected strength, knocking Mariella backward and then col-lapsing across her. Alex Dyachkov and Barbara Lopez pull Anchee away, cursing as the cold of her excursion suit burns their hands. There is bloody froth at her nostrils and mouth and she seems to have stopped breathing. Alex probes in her mouth with two fingers, then finds a scalpel among the scattered medical supplies, snaps off its blade protector and leans over Anchee, pulling the skin of her throat taut.

"I've only ever practiced this," he says, and slices open her windpipe.

Blood and bloody froth leak out. Barbara Lopez breaks off the barrel of the empty Syrette and hands it to Alex. He pushes it into the bloody slit in Anchee's throat: air whistles through it as she breathes in.

Alex secures the barrel with adhesive tape and Mariella helps him strip off Anchee's excursion suit. Her face is puffy and her arms and legs are mottled with blisters that leak clear, sticky fluid. She has a high fever and Mariella can hear fluid rattling in her lungs with each breath.

Barbara Lopez has a medical wizard in the rover's computer. It confirms Anchee's self-diagnosis and suggests a high dose of an-tihistamines and a sedative. Once they have administered these and secured Anchee in a hammock, Mariella and Barbara Lopez and Alex sit on the floor and eat from hotpacks, and Mariella explains what she wants to do.

"You can't be serious," Alex says.

"I'm absolutely serious. I'll work on my own terms or not at all. I'll divide up the samples, and you, Alex, can take half of them back to Lowell."

"Surely they're all the property of NASA."

"I think Cytex might have something to say about that."

"Cytex is out of the picture."

"No. I'm still under contract with them, and I intend to honor that."

"The contract will run out—"

"Exactly."

Barbara Lopez says, "I think it's a great idea. I'll be proud to take you there."

Alex says, "Can you really do it?"

Mariella says, "With a lot of help, yes. Yes, I think I can. You have contacts, don't you, Barbara? The Bushor Report, for instance."

"Oh, I have plenty of friends. And many of them will be interested in a technical problem like this."

The anaphylactic swelling in Anchee's throat has subsided. Guided by the wizard, Alex patches up the emergency tracheotomy, tapes a mask over her face and feeds her filtered air from her suit's backpack. Then Barbara Lopez fires up her rover, and they pull away from the Chinese camp.

They take turns to drive through the brief night. By midmorning they have reached the Chinese rover, squat as a black bug in the shadow of the slip face of one of the swarm of barchan dunes blown along the eastern side of the Chasma Boreale. Barbara Lopez and Mariella suit up and go out. Barbara Lopez carries Dr. Wu's rifle. Mariella follows her rag-wrapped figure, tramping across hard, tan sand which wind has winnowed into a lattice of small, scallop-shaped hollows.

They walk all the way around the Chinese rover, and with surprising agility Barbara Lopez swarms up a ladder and leans out so that she can peer into one of its windows.

"Well," she says, "they're dead."

Alex says over the radio, "Are you sure?"

"We're going in," Barbara Lopez says.

She fries the chip of the airlock's safety mechanism with a brief overvoltage and opens both hatches. Mariella follows her inside, trying not to look at the two bodies. One is slumped in the driver's seat; the other is on the floor in a fetal huddle. Blackened skin, bloody froth dried around their mouths. A freezer chest is open, and sample containers are scattered on the floor. Half a dozen containers are stacked in the microwave, which is still running.

Mariella switches it off and says, "The poor fools."

Alex says, "What's going on?"

Barbara Lopez is rummaging among the scattered containers. "Looks like they fried their samples. They knew they weren't going to make it, so they destroyed everything they had. If nothing else, you have to admire the rigor of their thinking."

Mariella picks up a container. Capped and sealed microfuge tubes are racked inside, each neatly labeled, each containing about a milliliter of fluid grainy with sediment. The sterility seals have all turned black.

She pulls out a patch cord and, when Barbara Lopez has plugged in, says, "I have a little work to do here. Could you leave me alone for a few minutes?"

Barbara Lopez's expression is unreadable behind her scratched visor. "If you're going to do what I think you're going to do, it would be less suspicious if I stayed here. I couldn't care less about the profits of some company."

"It will hurt NASA, too."

"Fuck NASA. You know how much premium I have to pay them for my supplies?"

Mariella breaks out the pack of tubes she brought with her, half of the samples she and Anchee took from the Chinese borehole. It takes a good deal more than ten minutes to melt the ice inside them, using the lowest setting of the microwave, and to add a small amount of caustic dust to each. Bubbles fizz inside the tubes as superoxides react with organic material. Mariella wraps fresh sterility seals over the caps of the tubes, fits them back inside the sample box and adds a selection of the samples microwaved by the Chinese.

Barbara Lopez says, "You're sure that will work?"

"Not entirely. Boiling the samples would be better, but it would leave a big clue in the form of coagulated proteins. This is my best shot."

She and Barbara Lopez walk back, take a dust bath, and climb into the rover. Alex says, "You left their airlock open."

Barbara Lopez says, "They were beginning to puff up. Bacteria in their guts and on their skin would have rotted them down, so I thought the best thing was to let out the air."

"And let out whatever killed them," Alex says.

"The cold and UV will destroy it if the dust doesn't," Mariella says as she stows the sample box in the freezer. "How is Anchee?"

"Still sleeping, still feverish, still needing high oh two. While you were outside, the wizard told me to give her another dose of sedative."

"She's a sick bunny," Barbara Lopez says, "but I don't think she'll die. Anyone want to say a prayer for those two poor guys? No? Then we roll."

They drive on through the dune field, heading roughly southeast. The dunes are of a darker material than the floor, like a fleet of black-sailed ships on a wine-dark sea. Although some are more than a kilometer wide, it is easy enough to steer a course between them.

"I wish I'd come up here before," Barbara Lopez says. "I've been digging up fossils for far too long. It took this to make me realize that I'm the first and only true Martian citizen, and I've the right to go where I want to."

Alex said, "It was exciting all right. We broke down twice."

"And both times I fixed the old bus right up, didn't I? Anyway, I'm going to die on Mars some day, and I'd rather do it on the slopes of Olympus Mons or deep in the Valles Marineris than in my burrow. Maybe I should move my station out here. What do you think? With the right sponsorship and that proton drill of yours I can drill any number of holes. Whatever the Chinese injected into the water table under the icecap surely won't spread too fast. If I drill a few hundred klicks east or west I'm sure to find something."

"I wish I could be sure," Mariella says. "But if it's anything like the slick, Martian life is colonial, a single organism massing thousands of tons. Anything tailored to kill it could spread very quickly, and because it has existed as essentially a single organism for billions of years, it almost certainly has no resistance to infection. The slick is very tough, but it can draw on the resistance mechanisms coded in the genomes of the thousands of planktonic species it has absorbed."

"Well hell," Barbara Lopez says, "it's still worth a try. Or maybe I should move south. I hear that NASA has an interesting project down there."

She has raised the big wraparound driving seat to its maximum height, so that she can reach the controls. Her thermal garment is ragged and none too clean, and her long gray hair is tangled and greasy, but sunlight shines on her face like the aura of a saint. Religious medals, garish crucifixes and laminated 3-D postcards showing Leonardo's last supper or Christ holding out his bleeding heart are fixed among the indicator lights and digital readouts of the dash. All are gifts sent in supply rockets by her fans; the set of rosary beads wrapped around her left wrist has been blessed by the Pope.

Mariella says, "Where did you hear about this interesting project?"

"Oh, someone who took those two wetback scientists down there told someone else about the drilling equipment they had, and that someone else told me."

Alex says, "Why would they look for life at the south pole? The cap is so much smaller, and is mostly carbon dioxide."

"The poles change around every fifty-one thousand years," Mariella says. "That's why there is layered terrain around both the north and south poles. And considering that's just what Betsy Sharp and Ali Tillman are studying, I would say it's a pretty firm assumption that NASA would want them to look for spores or resistant capsules that might be deep-frozen under the carbon dioxide snow, waiting for the water icecap to grow again. I worked this out a while ago, Alex. It's a clever way of getting around the commercial restrictions the government has used to hogtie NASA." She laughs. "Penn should have realized that NASA would have a backup plan. It's in the nature of the beast."

They do not have far to drive. Barbara Lopez has locked on to the transponder of the Chinese lander, and it appears over the horizon after less than an hour, a squat cone resting on four splayed legs in the middle of a flat, rock-littered plain.

"I should come with you," Alex says to Mariella.

"I appreciate the gesture, but it would violate my agreement with Al Paley. And you have to get your half of the samples to Lowell."

Mariella feels a pang of conscience about making Alex the innocent dupe in her switch, but suppresses it. Besides, she doesn't yet know if any of the samples contain life. Her whole scheme might turn out to have been in vain.

Alex says, "You realize you'll be branded a pirate. If you land in Chinese territory, you'll be executed on the spot."

"It's salvage," Mariella says.

Barbara Lopez says, "Alex is right. I don't think the Chinese will agree with you. And the law is pretty ambiguous about salvage of spacecraft. Believe me, I should know. I went through half a dozen lawsuits against NASA until they finally gave up trying to take my station away from me. You're going to spend a lot of the rest of your life in court."

"I've got to get home first."

"With my help, honey, that'll be the least of your worries."

Barbara Lopez parks the rover at the lip of the shallow crater excavated by the blast of the lander's motor, and they swarm aboard. With the help of Barbara Lopez's contacts on Earth, it doesn't take long to prep it for liftoff. A group in Baltimore analyzes screen grabs from Alex's camera and provides translations for all the command lines in the virtual controls. A woman in San Francisco uploads a translation patch, and Mariella spends a couple of hours searching through the lander's help facilities and printing out all the operational pages. She is still making notes when the launch window begins to close.

"What's the problem?" Barbara Lopez says. "It's just a rocket. You light the fuse and up you go."

"That's fine," Mariella says, "as long as nothing goes wrong with the guidance computers. And with all this extraneous code your hackers have inserted, something's bound to conflict."

"Then email someone and ask for help," Barbara Lopez says. "Hell, ask the Chinese if you have to. If you're going to do this, you have to do it now. The launch window for return to Earth is closing fast. There's one more thing. You're taking Dr. Ye with you."

"You're kidding."

"She's stabilized now, but as long as she's exposed to dust she could undergo a seizure at any time. I don't have a full medical kit and it's going to take five or six days to get her back to Lowell. You'll be aboard the Chinese spacecraft in a few hours, away from the dust and with full medical facilities."

"But what if the launch kills her? Or if she has a seizure in the middle of it?"

Barbara Lopez gives her a flinty stare. "You don't like it, I can strip out all the help programs and leave you on your own."

"I suppose Alex agrees."

"That's why he went back to the rover. He's getting her into her suit right now. It's a done deal, lady."

It takes all three of them to seal Anchee into her excursion suit, carry her across to the lander, and strap her in one of the acceleration couches. Barbara Lopez fixes what she says is her second-best rosary above the pilot's couch. Alex gives Mariella a bear hug and says he'll do his best to tell their story when he gets back.

"The government may try and suppress it," Mariella says.

"Maybe, but the story is already out there. If they try and censor me they'll look pretty dumb."

"Enough talk," Barbara Lopez says. "We have only thirty minutes to get clear. You come back and visit me, Mariella. I still want to show off my greenhouse."

Mariella checks Anchee and tries to settle as best she can into an acceleration couch whose contours are molded for a man now dead. The guidance program marks the minutes and then the final seconds.

The roar of the motor suddenly fills the tiny cabin. It shudders and heaves, and acceleration pushes Mariella deep into the couch, pressing her bones against unexpected corners in the padding and wrinkles in her excursion suit. The roar grows louder and louder; the pressure increases. It feels like two people are sitting on her chest, and there's a terrific amount of vibration, an uncontrollable blurring jitter in her sight. But it is not too bad, no worse than the liftoff of the Dynawing that took her up to the *Beagle*. All she has to do is lie back and take it. She clamps her teeth so hard her jaw muscles ache, and concentrates on her breathing, taking fast little sips to top up the air already in her lungs.

There is a little mirror above her couch, almost exactly like the rearview mirror of a car. It is angled so that she can see out of one of the little triangular ports of the lander. Because of the tremendous vibration she finds it hard to focus on what the mirror shows, a broad ocher-and-tan crescent, splotched with white at the bottom and darkening toward the top, that seems to slowly draw itself tighter and tighter, like a bow aimed at the black sky.

It is Mars. The planet Mars, falling away beneath her.

PART THREE

FUGITIVE LIFE

The Chinese spacecraft takes four hundred and twenty-eight days to fall from Mars to Earth. It is a crude, multistage affair, fueled by chemical propellants, its thrust feeble compared to the ICAN motor of the *Beagle*—so feeble that return to Earth requires the gravity assist of a Venus flyby—but the extended transit time suits Mariella's plans.

Even so, four hundred and twenty-eight days, a year and change, is not enough time to do everything she wants, and in the first weeks her work is compromised by her attempts to cope with a flood of email. There are so many messages that the ship's overloaded intranet crashes two or three times a day: from network researchers offering exclusive interviews with world-famous news anchors and chat-show hosts; from schoolchildren who want details of life aboard the spacecraft for their class projects; from agents offering multimedia deals; from apocalypse junkies threatening to blow the spacecraft and its cargo of "degenerate spawn" out of orbit. Hackers, some of them almost certainly employed by the Chinese government, try to upload viruses designed to pry open files or gain control of the spacecraft's systems. And it seems that every scientist on Earth wants to know what was found at the Chinese borehole, and whether it can provide clues to how the slicks can be destroyed.

News about the spread of the slicks is patchy—it has become amazingly difficult to get access to remote-sensing data from U.S. satellites—but Maury Richards sends everything he can find to Mariella. It is thought that a reduction in release of methyl sulphide by phytoplankton is the cause of a serious drought along the

Pacific seaboard of the American continent, and Maury is trying to collate falls in phytoplankton productivity across the Pacific with low-resolution pictures from European, Australian and Russian weather satellites and reports from cargo ships of sightings of strange dark patches in the Pacific Ocean. Maury sends video clips culled from foreign news reports and web sites, too. Thousands of dead fish floating among iridescent swirls. Aerial shots of a slick staining the sea along the dead reefs of Australia's east coast. A fisherman in a pirogue in Papua New Guinea, jeweled strands dripping from his hands.

Mariella returns to one web site again and again. It seems to be engaged in an elaborate skirmish with something that is trying to shut it down, because it keeps changing its address and spawning mirror sites, and links are often abruptly cut. A group calling itself the Tipairu Liberation Front has set up a multicam system in a slick growing in some tropical lagoon. Beneath a silver, sunstruck ceiling that flexes and heaves a meter or so overhead, a floor of white sand stretches away into the blue distance of very clear water. Stuff grows on and through the sand like the work of some mad, obsessive confectioner: golden towers and fantastically ornamented globes and minarets, thorny cables and threads intricately woven into asymmetrical baskets. Little drones, like crabs armored in black resin, scuttle here and there. If Mariella is lucky, she can grab control of one of the crab-drones when she logs on to the site and send it to investigate the fairy-castle growths, pop the video magnification to 50X and glimpse the syncytial threads that have woven the fantastical forms. The site lasts six weeks, and then one day Mariella finds nothing but broken links and error messages. She imagines soldiers in biowar suits wading the blue lagoon in a long line, scooping up struggling crab-drones and raking the slick's frothy confections from the sand, although probably all that really happened was that some government or corporate hacker got around to setting a military-grade cancelbot on the site's trail.

Maury sends clips of news programs about her, too. She finds them by turns amusing and infuriating. The unsympathetic majority portray her as a reckless scientist willing to risk anything to fulfill a godless craving for knowledge; the minority opinion is that

she is a cunning operator who'll either parlay her knight's move into a fortune or spend the rest of her life in court or jail. The docusoaps are the most painful. Here is a snippet, culled from a BBC interview the day after the discovery of the cause of the First-born Crisis was announced, of her mother in the living room of her Aberdeen bungalow. Here is a brief excerpt from a home video of Mariella and Forrest walking arm in arm along Santa Monica Beach at sunset, the lights of the pier and its funfair, rebuilt for the third time, twinkling in the distance. She can't remember anything about that evening, but the date stamp in the corner of the video sequence tells her that it was shot September 12, 2010, three weeks before Forrest left for Central America, five weeks before he was killed.

Any reminder of his death still stings. Not because of what they had—their love, their marriage, their little house with its citrus trees and cactus garden—but because of what they can never have. Their careers growing around each other like two sturdy briars, children, companionable old age . . . all their lost futures, all the stillborn unbudded possibilities, erased in a single moment of casual brutality.

"You won't tell anyone anything," Cornish Brittany tells Mariella, in one of her video messages.

Cornish Brittany is the Cytex VP in charge of Mariella's "project." She introduced herself after Mariella tried to get in touch with the only two founding members of Cytex still on the board (of the others, one was assassinated while trying to make a deal with the government of Mali for rights to their gene bank; another is in cryogenic storage after a lupus infection caused massive damage to his nervous system; the third has been circling the globe in a self-sufficient boat for the last six years). She's a Californian babe of indeterminate age, part Barbie doll, part praying mantis, her blond hair swept back in elaborate frozen waves, her face so sculpted by cosmetic surgery that she looks like an alien trying to pass as human.

She says, "Security is the first and last rule. No messages to news agencies to tell your side of the story, no letters to papers or to scientific journals. The networks have to fill their news channels with something, and it's better they use anodyne stock than actual information. That clip with your husband? Pure gold. It shows you as vulnerable, human. The spin wizards in publicity can put a peachy gloss on that."

Mariella emails her at once. *Did your wizards leak the video? Where did they get it?*

That infuriating lag, as light crawls down to Earth, crawls back.

There are probably a hundred AIs trawling the data vaults right now, looking for usable footage. Just be glad they don't have anything about your recent adventures.

I hope that's not a threat.

We're on your side, Mariella. I wish you'd understand that.

Cornish Brittany is so indefatigably persistent that Mariella begins to suspect that she might be a computer-generated expert system. She bombards Mariella with suggestions about backup specialists who could help with her research, proposes roundtable discussions, asks for raw data and progress reports. Mariella refuses everything, sticking to the argument that she doesn't want to compromise security by transmitting sensitive data on an open line. Cornish Brittany counters by offering an unbreakable encryption system; Mariella parries by expressing concern about its effect on the ship's already overloaded intranet. She doesn't tell the woman that one of Barbara Lopez's friends has already uploaded a filter that has turned the flood of email to a trickle.

With all this distraction, it takes Mariella several weeks to set up a sterile glove-box cabinet and to learn how to use the little laboratory of the Chinese spacecraft, and several weeks more to develop a medium for isolation and growth of the infective agent in the samples of sputum, blood and lung fluid she took from Dr. Wu's body, samples she kept to herself because she believes they contain the key to the whole problem.

Everything seems to take about twice as long as it should. She tries to make cultures of cells isolated from scrapings taken from the inside of her mouth, but this simple procedure is complicated by microgravity. The cells do not form neat, single-layer sheets, but tend to clump up and then die off suddenly when the clumps get too big to be fed by simple diffusion. Pride and caution prevent

Mariella from asking Cornish Brittany's experts for help. She sifts through hundreds of research papers and performs dozens of painstaking empirical experiments to establish which stirring method is best at keeping small clumps of cells in suspension without damaging them, and the optimal balance of the several dozen nutrients in the growth medium. Only when she can reliably and repeatedly grow the cell cultures does she finally expose them to microliter aliquots of Dr. Wu's body fluids.

By this time, the *Beagle* has returned to Earth. Mariella is certain that Cytex will be attempting to process the samples she gave Alex Dyachkov. She questions both Cornish Brittany and Howard Smalls, but their replies are blandly vague and disturbingly similar. The crew and passengers of the *Beagle* are undergoing quarantine procedures at the Cape. In view of the nature of the events at the pole, processing and analysis of samples will be slowed by stringent application of sample return protocols. Yeah, right. And while Brittany and Smalls are stalling her with carefully scripted bullshit, a cadre of molecular biologists is attempting to extract and sequence every molecule of DNA from the Martian ice. She is pretty certain that the superoxide-laden dust she added to their set of samples will have shredded any DNA beyond all possibility of reconstruction, but she can't know for sure. It gives an exquisite edge to her frustration with the slow progress of her own work.

At first, Anchee Ye shows little interest in Mariella's research, except to nag her about precautions. "Look," Mariella says in exasperation, after having exhaustively detailed the seals of the glove box, its three-stage lock for passing material inward, the 0.22 micron filters and all the rest for about the tenth time, "do you really think I want to infect us?"

"I am only thinking of the sample return protocol," Anchee Ye says, with the cold, distant composure she now habitually displays. Anchee Ye: human robot. An icy exterior mantling a core of molten anger at what she calls her abduction. Alex's hasty surgery damaged her throat, reducing her voice to a husky whisper.

Mariella says, "The flight plan means that by the time we reach Earth we'll have been in quarantine far longer than the San

Diego protocols demand. That's the plan, remember?"

"It's your plan," Anchee says. "My job is to see that I get you back safely."

"Then worry about that. And I'll worry about keeping the infectious agent inside the glove box."

"It should be sequenced on Earth," Anchee says stubbornly.

"That's just what Cytex would like, of course."

"You mean NASA."

"I mean Cytex."

"Who are licensed by NASA to process the samples."

"You know that it matters who does the sequencing first. Especially if the research is to be buried under a blanket of commercial confidentiality."

Anchee says in her hoarse whisper, "You're doing this because you can't bear to think that someone will beat you to the sequence. You accuse Cytex and NASA of secret plans because all the time you want to be in charge of everything. You can't bear not to be: it's in your nature."

"Absolutely. But I didn't keep all of the samples from the borehole, Anchee. Think about that."

It is only a small lie—a lie by omission, made for the best possible reason—but Mariella's conscience still pricks her and, in her lowest moments, she thinks that Anchee may be right. She could be home now, part of a Cytex team, unraveling the DNA sequences of the Chi, locating its weaknesses, applying that knowledge to control the slicks. A project as urgent and as important as the Firstborn Crisis. More glory, more fame. But it is more likely that, had she returned in the *Beagle*, Cytex would have frozen her out, that commercial considerations would have swallowed the truth, that the cash-strapped government would have suppressed publication of the data in exchange for a percentage of the profits from exploitation of the Chi. Controlled evolution, with Cytex's thumb on the fast-forward button. A revolution in biotechnology as profound as the discovery of the structure of DNA, and the government and its commercial collaborators are willing to risk the Earth for it. Or worse, their arrogant greed blinds them to the risk.

Although their living quarters are cramped, Mariella and An-chee avoid each other as much as possible in the first months of the voyage. Every attempt to discuss what happened on Mars ends in a furious row. Sometimes more than a week will pass before they can bring themselves to speak to each other again. Mariella tries not to mind. She always has her work. But she knows that she will need Anchee Ye's cooperation when the spacecraft finally inserts itself into Earth orbit—and besides, the proud, recalcitrant woman is the only human being for several million kilometers in any direction.

With the lander abandoned in Mars orbit, and the stage that accelerated the spacecraft out of orbit jettisoned after its long burn, only a small motor stage, the cramped crew module, and the de-scent capsule are left. The crew module is divided into three com-partments, each two meters across and three meters long, their curved walls packed with equipment lockers and storage modules. As with NASA, commercial sponsorship was a significant part of the funding of the Chinese mission. The logos and slogans of equipment suppliers are plastered everywhere; there are even ads embedded in the control programs. Digital readouts and status reports are headlined by company slogans; activation of each con-trol procedure triggers a stentorian product announcement in Mandarin, Cantonese, Korean and English, or a clip of lively teen-age actresses singing a company song, or a rapid-fire shoutline. The ads are efficiently insidious memes evolved in the Darwinian pres-sure cooker of the marketplace; quite often, Mariella will find her-self humming one of the perky jingles in the middle of an experiment. She thinks that it would be easy enough to strip out the ads, but Anchee refuses to touch the source code.

Anchee spends most of her waking hours in the command compartment of the crew module, where, aided by a team of NASA engineers, she is learning to master the spacecraft's guid-ance, communications and navigational control systems. The cen-tral compartment, where Mariella works, is the science bay; the third compartment is the crew area. There are three privacy mod-ules, much like those on the *Beagle*, with sleeping bags that smell of the men, now dead, who used them; a microgravity toilet that

Mariella and Anchee have jury-rigged so they can use it (they have had to improvise tampons from bandages and cotton wipes too); a small galley stuffed with garishly packaged varieties of noodle soups; a pharmacy with an eclectic collection of branded medicines; and gym equipment, plastered with decals, which Mariella uses assiduously. Unless she is careful, four hundred and twenty-eight days in microgravity is going to do some serious damage to her muscles and bones. Anchee Ye is less scrupulous, often going for days without exercising at all. They have arguments about that too.

Anchee Ye is not well. Her persistent cough has deepened, and it has gained a worryingly liquid quality. Her face is puffy, and sores in her scalp have caused her hair to fall out in patches, while what remains is dry and lusterless. A butterfly rash spreads its wings across her eyes and nose. NASA doctors prescribe a short course of steroids—the dispenser sings a sprightly little tune every time Anchee opens it—but the sores do not clear up and the rash returns as soon as the treatment ends.

When she is not studying the ship's systems, Anchee is writing long, self-justifying position papers and reports, or is engaged in tedious conferences with teams of NASA lawyers. As Barbara Lopez predicted, the Chinese government has claimed that Mariella and Anchee committed an act of piracy by taking their spacecraft, and want them to be extradited upon their return. The spacecraft is registered in China and, under the 2013 extension of maritime law, is part of Chinese national territory, regulated by Chinese laws. NASA argues the case in the United Nations and then in the International Court in the Hague. No one has ever hijacked a spacecraft before, and the case is sure to go into the legal textbooks. It attracts lawyers as a wounded whale attracts sharks, and the feeding frenzy spins off several dozen subsidiary cases. Mariella and Anchee are being sued by the families of the Chinese crew for the "undue belligerence" that caused the deaths of the three men. They are also being sued by the three corporations that underwrote the Chinese mission: for risking the safety of the spacecraft; for theft of corporate material; for potential breach of intellectual rights regarding isolation of Martian organisms and sequencing of their genes.

This last, Cornish Brittany points out, means that the Chinese have admitted for the first time that they have already done research on indigenous Martian life, and that by implication they lied about what their first mission discovered.

We can use it to smash them flat in court. Isn't it wonderful?

The truth is the truth, Mariella replies. *It is what it is, and it can't be changed by a legal judgment.*

In her opinion, most of the legal flak is a smoke screen for maneuvering by Cytex and the Chinese companies over control of the Chi. She is certain that they will eventually settle their differences in private rather than risk having their business stratagems exposed in the International Court. Meanwhile, the trick is to avoid becoming caught up in the gears of the juggernaut machinery of legal processes that will, in the end, be proven irrelevant.

The truth is the truth.

While Mariella has her research, there is less and less for Anchee Ye to do. She has read all the manuals uploaded by Houston and Goddard FCC, run every one of their simulations dozens of times. The interconnected legal cases have a momentum of their own. Apart from maintaining the intricate life-support system, the spacecraft needs little attention as it falls on its long arc sunward. Anchee begins to spend more time watching Mariella work, until at last Mariella tells her that she might as well lend a hand, and teaches her how to grow and maintain the cells in which the infective agent is cultured.

For a while, there is something like companionship between them, although they talk about nothing but the work at hand.

The first thing Mariella wants to understand is why it is possible to culture in human cells an infective agent modified to invade and kill the Martian Chi. As she expected, it shows the classic pattern of viral reproduction. It injects its genetic material into the cells, leaving behind protective protein capsids. At first, it is nonvirulent; its DNA inserts itself into host-cell chromosomes and is replicated along with the host genome each time the host cell divides. During this lysogenic stage of infection, only one of the infective agent's genes is active, producing a repressor protein that inhibits transcription of genes responsible for virulence. But when the host cells are mildly stressed, the lysogenic truce breaks down, production of the repressor protein halts, and the entire suite of infective-agent genes is transcribed independently of the host cell's genome, making so many millions of copies of DNA and protein capsids that at last the host cell bursts open. It is unlikely that the Chinese gene engineers produced by design something that could infect both human and Martian cells, yet here it is. Something has gone wrong, but what?

Part of the answer comes when Mariella sequences the infective agent's DNA and compares it to a library of viral genomes. The closest match is to a strain of paramyxovirus that causes mild fever in pigs; it is also similar to viruses that cause atypical pneumonia in humans. That isn't surprising. Because pigs and humans are quite closely related, so are the viruses that infect them; in fact, pigs are part of the chain by which reservoirs of influenza viruses harbored in duck or chicken populations ultimately infect humans. The library comparison also tells her that the virus contains several highly unusual sequences, and she suspects that these were derived from the Chi. Perhaps they allow the virus to latch onto the cell membrane of the Chi and to insert its DNA.

Presumably, the scientists who engineered this virus used something familiar and off-the-shelf to speed the process, a convenience that turned out to be a fatal mistake for the Chinese astronauts. Given that Dr. Wu more or less admitted that the Chi is similar to terrestrial bacteria, it is odd that a mammalian paramyxovirus rather than a bacteriophage was chosen, but Mariella dismisses it as a minor mystery, is more concerned with proving her hypothesis that, after infection, the Chi altered the virus.

This part of her research takes far longer than isolating and identifying the infective agent from Dr. Wu's body fluids, and she has to work alone on these experiments because Anchee Ye is preoccupied with preparing the spacecraft for the Venus flyby.

As the spacecraft falls sunward, its internal temperature climbs by a degree every ten days, and although rotating in barbecue mode evens out temperature differences, it begins to gain heat faster than it can lose it. At last, Anchee deploys a huge monomolecular film, a circular parasol silvered like a mirror. Although it masses less than twenty kilograms, it spreads out to a final diameter of fifty kilometers, and reflects more than eighty percent of the sun's radiant energy. The internal temperature of the ship stabilizes at thirty-four degrees Centigrade.

Venus swells ahead, an increasingly bright star aligned in the central hole of the parasol like a target in the crosshairs of a sniper's rifle. Then, on the day of closest approach, it suddenly resolves into a crescent, a blindingly white bow drawn across half the sky.

Mariella watches the transit on a TV screen in the command section, where she and Anchee Ye lie side by side on acceleration couches. By visible light, the smoggy clouds that wrap the planet's entire surface seem uniformly white, but filters reveal bright and dark features caused by absorbence of ultraviolet light by sulphur-rich particles in the tops of the clouds, seventy kilometers above the planet's surface: broad luminous swirls at the poles degrade to broken bands and streaks toward the equator, where V- and Y-shaped arrowheads are shaped by jet-stream winds moving at a hundred meters a second. As on Mars, most of the atmosphere is carbon dioxide, but on Venus a runaway greenhouse effect baked the total inventory of volatiles from the crust, smothering the planet in a shroud ninety times denser than Earth's atmosphere, keeping the surface at an infernal four hundred seventy degrees Centigrade, hot enough to melt lead.

And yet, four billion years ago, when the sun was much cooler, before the runaway greenhouse effect began, Venus was much like Earth and Mars. Life may have briefly flourished there—perhaps life derived from material flung from the surface of Mars or Earth by meteor impacts. But on Venus there is no longer any refuge for life, and any physical evidence of a biological past will not have survived the episodes of catastrophic vulcanism that periodically resurfaces the entire surface. The planet is as sterile as the simmering cauldron of a blast furnace.

Anchee Ye does not once glance at the pictures relayed by external cameras. She is too busy monitoring the parameters of the transit. Greasy globules of sweat hang like a halo about her face as, gloved and masked, she uses the virtual-reality system to check and recheck the spacecraft's angle of attack as it whips around Venus. Even a tiny deviation from the flight plan will be disastrous.

At its closest approach, the spacecraft passes less than a thousand kilometers above the cloud tops, gaining a vanishingly minute fraction of the planet's momentum and accelerating away toward Earth.

The stress almost breaks Anchee. She spends the next few days mostly asleep. Even before the transit, she gave up almost all forms of exercise; after it, she does none at all, and any physical effort quickly exhausts her. She retreats into herself, spending more and more time in the descent capsule, while Mariella works on, with less than a hundred days left.

Mariella has already confirmed the presence of DNA in samples taken from the borehole. Now she uses the virus she has isolated from Dr. Wu's body fluids to make two sets of complimentary traps on DNA chips, runs DNA isolated from the borehole samples through polymerase chain reactions to make thousands of random copies, and passes aliquots across the chips.

Most of the DNA sequences bind to trap sequences derived from the genome of the paramyxovirus, but a few bind to traps derived from the putative Martian genes. So it is possible that there is Martian DNA present in the ice, although Mariella does not yet know if there is anything viable.

She sequences random samples of viral DNA from the borehole samples. It is as she thought. All are from the same virus; but many show subtle variations. The virus successfully infected the Chi, but was subjected to a high-speed recombination process while reproducing, producing thousands or perhaps even millions of variants. And at least one of those proved to be infective in humans.

"They didn't think it through," Mariella tells Anchee Ye, once all the evidence is in.

"But we can't know that the Chi caused the mutations," Anchee says. "And after what the Chinese did, there won't be anything left alive beneath the icecap, so we can't repeat the experiment."

"I wonder about that. No doubt the virus worked perfectly well in the laboratory, but compared to what happens in the field, laboratory experiments use relatively small amounts of material over relatively short periods of time. It's possible that the Chi managed to adapt to the virus after all. If we return to Mars in ten years, we may find it back where it was, seemingly unchanged. Except that it will have included the virus in its genetic repertoire.

"It reminds me of one of those early attempts at biological control. Rabbits escaped into the Australian bush and multiplied uncontrollably, destroying the grazing on the cattle ranges. The Australians released cats in an attempt to control the rabbit population, and it worked for a while, but the rabbits multiplied faster than the cats' appetites. Eventually, the cats turned to other prey, and were found living side by side with the rabbits in their burrows. It's just the same with the Chi. No biological control will work on it because it simply incorporates anything that attacks it. It raises all kinds of fundamental questions about the evolution of early life. Once something evolves the ability to incorporate the genetic repertoire of other organisms, it should absorb or destroy everything else. Presumably that's what happened on Mars, yet it certainly didn't happen on Earth. Perhaps because of different evolutionary pressures. Or perhaps the Chi did evolve on Earth, but continued to evolve into something else, so that the Martian organism is a frozen accident."

She is rapping more for herself than for Anchee, trying to crystallize notions as slippery and as vaguely glimpsed as carp in a murky pond. She does rather like the idea of the Chi as a frozen evolutionary accident—a self-referential attractor of such density that nothing can escape its horizon, a biological black hole that turns all information into its own self.

She says, "Once I have it pinned down, it will make a nice little paper."

"It will have to go to review through NASA," Anchee says stubbornly.

"NASA will be acknowledged."

"I don't think it will be as easy as that. And that Cytex woman won't allow it anyway."

"Oh, she's irrelevant. My contract expired before we reached Venus."

"You've thought of everything," Anchee says bitterly.

"I've tried to. This is horribly important."

"But I think you'll run into some serious opposition to your plans for a nice little paper."

Anchee is right. Neither *Nature* nor *Science* will even send the paper out for review. Other journals resist her overtures with varying degrees of politeness. A friendly editor tells her that no one wants to touch it because there are doubts about the provenance of the research. Translation: Cytex is threatening to sue, because it wants to keep the information out of the public eye.

Cornish Brittany sends a video clip. "I've heard about the problems you've been having with your experimental data. I'm sure that our people can help you, once they've reviewed your findings. We're all on the edge of our seats here, waiting to see what you've come up with."

Translation: the only way you'll get anything published is to cooperate with Cytex.

Mariella has been expecting this, and reverts to plan B, sending samizdat copies of the paper to her colleagues and to every news organization in the United States and Europe. Most ignore it; a few publish an annotated precis; the *Guardian* and the *Washington Post* publish the whole thing.

More furor. Mariella fields dozens of interviews, emphasizing the same point in each one: not only will biological control fail to work against the slick, but it could also unleash fast-mutating lethal plagues. Someone hacks the email filter, and for more than a day the spacecraft's intranet is swamped by messages ranging from the anodyne compliments of well-wishers to the babble of conspiracy nuts who claim they can prove that the virus is part of a plot to destroy all Caucasians, or that an underground Martian civilization changed the virus, or that the Chi is itself intelligent. Howard Smalls sends an angry message, telling her to keep quiet. Cornish Brittany sends another video clip, a mixture of wounded reproach and icy threats. Mariella asks her how research is progressing on the samples sent via the *Beagle*, and when she gets no reply threatens to sequence the Chi herself, although she knows she doesn't have the resources to even begin to discover the conditions under which it grows.

The paper serves its purpose. Under international pressure, the Chinese government says that it has no further plans to use biological agents against the slick; a day later, so does the United States, which also issues a brief account of the destruction of the original slick by application of metabolic poisons and spraying with napalm. A cosmetic treatment that will not have affected the particles shed into deep water, and that is unlikely to be effective on larger slicks, such as the one drifting at the equator, which satellite surveys suggest is more than a thousand kilometers across. Meanwhile, marine biologists report massive falls in fish stocks in the Indian Ocean, almost certainly the result of displacement of phytoplankton by slicks, and there is tension between India, Bangladesh and Mozambique over disputed fishing grounds. A gene hacker in Colombia publishes a partial sequence of the slick, and claims to have developed an effective control, pricing it at ten billion dollars. It's a crude scam, but other gene hackers begin to post their own sequences, and the Australian and New Zealand governments publish sequences on their official web sites, setting off a small trade war with the United States.

Howard Smalls sends a terse video clip, telling Mariella that she will be arrested as soon as she returns, for disseminating information that could be used to construct a terrorist weapon. "I'm sorry to be so blunt," he says, "but the President feels that your actions have serious implications for the security of our country."

This could be pure bluster, except that Mariella's data vault, the escrow account in Bermuda where she stores her files, guaranteed as confidential and unbreakable as a Swiss bank account, is hacked and plundered. Mariella has been expecting something like that, too. She sends a sound file to the Bushor Report, using a clandestine address and an encryption program she downloaded from one of Barbara Lopez's contacts, a hacker on the run for producing and then disseminating programs that, according to the National Security Agency's warrant, "could threaten U.S. technological superiority." She explains the circumstances of the recording to the Bushor Report, asks them not to use it just yet, and asks for their help.

Now she is on the run too, a fugitive from Cytex, the Chinese biotech companies, and the U.S. government. She begins to make plans. NASA has already uploaded a software patch that rewrote the navigation program in the descent capsule, to ensure that it will splash down beyond the Florida Keys rather than in the South China Sea. While Anchee Ye sleeps, Mariella sends a copy of the patch to the hacker, who alters a couple of lines of code and sends it back. Her skin tingling with nervousness, Mariella runs a simulation to satisfy herself that it still works, and then uses it to overwrite the original patch.

The mirrored radiation shield was discarded four days after the Venus flyby, and the spacecraft's external cameras give access to a three-hundred-sixty-degree view around the ship. Mariella habitually checks this panorama every day, watching the double star of Earth and Moon dim and brighten through three-and-a-half phases. In the final week of the approach, there is a growing barrage from the world's press. Anchee Ye hides behind statements issued by NASA's press office; Mariella does not know how to begin answering the one question everyone is asking.

Anchee starts to talk of what she will do when she gets back. Vacations, building a new deck in the yard of her house, and most of all starting a family. She and Don planned everything before she left. Her ova and his sperm are safely frozen in the NASA fertility clinic. They want to have two girls and one boy, spaced a year apart. No modification, only the statutory screening of the preimplants. A natural family, an ideal family, growing up free from harm in their gated, time-capsule suburb.

Anchee stays awake for every one of the seventy hours of the delicate aerobraking maneuver, in which the spacecraft skims the upper edge of Earth's atmosphere at each cusp of an increasingly regularized elliptical orbit, shedding velocity like a pebble skipping over a lake. Control is crucial: a minute increase in the steepness of the angle of attack could cause the spacecraft to bite too deeply into the atmosphere and break up, but if the angle is too shallow, its orbit could widen beyond the range of its almost-depleted fuel reserves. Anchee uses up the pharmacy's stock of proprietary caffeine pills, and twenty hours into the maneuver Mariella catches her injecting herself with a Syrette.

"I'm maintaining," Anchee says grimly. Her eyes are red-rimmed, her pupils pinpricks. She stinks of sweat and ketones. What is left of her hair is lank string fanning away from the flaking rawness of her scalp. There is a minute tremor in her hands. Mariella plucks the discarded Syrette from the air. According to the English portion of the label, it is mostly methamphetamine sulphate.

"I can keep watch while you sleep," Mariella says.

"I'm catnapping at every apogee," Anchee says in her harsh whisper, with a stare as fierce and cold as death. "Don't worry."

"Do NASA—"

"I tell them I'm getting enough sleep. What do they know? The only downlink is through my slate. They're not plugged into the systems. I am. Don't worry. *It's under control.*"

After sixty hours, the spacecraft is finally inserted in a circular, three-hour equatorial orbit about a hundred kilometers above the Earth. Anchee tumbles through the crew module, collapses into her cocoon, and sleeps around the clock. When she wakes, she finds Mariella and tells her, "The people at Goddard FCC think they can modify a docking collar. They want to send up a shuttle and transfer us across. It'll take about ten days to organize."

"I thought we were going for an old-fashioned splashdown."

"They don't think I'll be able to do it," Anchee says.

Although she is as strung-out as a junkie three days into cold turkey, she holds herself quite still in midair, and her gaze burns like black ice.

Mariella says, "You want to do it."

"I know I can do it. I'm going to bring us home. You think I'd risk everything now?"

It is as if she has read Mariella's mind. Mariella says, "Of course not."

"I'm doing this for my unborn children."

Her voice is an unraveling whisper. Her stare is steady and defiant and desperate.

"Yes. Yes, of course. Can I help?"

"Pack up the samples. Destroy all the cell cultures. Then stay out of the way."

"It's a deal."

"In twelve hours. I need more sleep."

Mariella tries to sleep, too, but with little success. At last, with three hours to go, she disentangles herself from the cocoon, scrubs herself down with moist tissues printed with the logo of a Nanking paper mill, and, for the first time since they left Mars, dons her sweat-stiff thermal undergarment and wriggles into her pressure garment. Then, following a checklist Anchee has printed out, she begins to shut down the systems in the crew module. Anchee is already in the descent capsule, running through a systems check.

Mariella feels an airy nervousness as she goes through the mechanical process of system shutdown, like a small-time criminal waiting to start her first bank job. All will be lost if Anchee discovers the changes to the software patch; and there is also a chance that the altered code might fuck up the navigation software. She uses the glove box for the last time, breaking open a vial of sodium fluoride solution and injecting an aliquot into every one of the cell cultures. The stainless steel thermos that contains what remains of the frozen samples taken from the borehole has already been sealed and packed away. Anchee Ye is probably watching the sterilization procedure on the TV camera up in one corner, and Mariella finds it hard to suppress the urge to give her the finger.

Anchee's glance passes over Mariella as she swims through the air into the descent capsule, an unfathomable gaze, but perhaps a little calmer now. Eyes dry in bruised sockets, face mottled with a subdermal rash. Her snoopy hat hides her crusted scalp. Mariella does a neat tuck-and-roll in the cramped space above the acceleration couches and dogs the hatches, first the one to the spacecraft's crew module, then the one for the capsule itself, and vents the atmosphere in the short connecting tunnel. Anchee Ye insists on checking the seal latches, then drags herself back to the right-hand acceleration couch while Mariella straps herself into the one on the left. The empty couch between them bears the contours of Dr. Wu's body. Ranks of switches with grubby handwritten labels slope above them. Ads blink with insistent brightness on various tiny screens, cycling through Chinese and Korean and English.

With gloves on her hands and goggles over her eyes, Anchee

pecks and pokes at the virtual keyboard of her slate, which is linked to the control system by a hair-thin optical cable. A cheerful American voice comes through Mariella's earpiece. A man's voice, hearty, lively, beef-fed.

"Okay, we have a go for the next orbit."

"Copy that," Anchee says, and tells Mariella, "Remember your training. This is going to be like landing on Mars, but about twice as hard."

The cheerful voice says in their ears, "Two minutes until separation."

"I hear you," Anchee says. She pecks at the air, then opens a cover above her head and pulls out a mechanical trigger. A cluster of lights turn red and start to blink. She says, "Explosive bolts armed. Thrusters are nominal," and tells Mariella, "We're committed. Lie back and enjoy the ride."

She exchanges jargon with the NASA guidance controller, who suddenly says, "On my mark. Three. Two. Mark."

An explosive thump rattles the capsule. Briefly, the couch presses against the length of Mariella's body.

"Burn successful," Anchee says.

"We're acquiring your profile," the ground controller says. "Stand by. . . . Okay. You're looking good. In the pipe. Five by five."

"I'm separating now," Anchee says, and squeezes the trigger switch.

There is a little thump above their heads, a muffled pop like that of a cork easing out of a champagne bottle. The descent capsule has separated from the rest of the spacecraft. They are in a wingless casing three and a half meters long and five wide, falling toward the Earth's atmosphere and impact in the ocean.

No way back now. No way but down.

And there is no way of knowing if the altered software patch has caused an imperceptible retardation in the burn until they are down.

Anchee blows the capsule's shroud; raw sunlight streams through the triangular windows above them. There is the rest of the spacecraft, a fat white cylinder with the stiff, angular wings of its solar-panel arrays extending on either side. It is doing a slow, forward roll, the bell of its motor flashing in the sunlight. It slides out of view as Anchee works the four-way thruster controller, adjusting the pitch of the descent capsule with little squirts of gas until it is riding with its nose about sixty degrees down. Earth rises in the little window, a brown-and-purple map dotted with white specks and streaks of cloud. They are somewhere over Asia, running backward into night. The sun sinks beyond the thin blue shell of the atmosphere, setting light to layer after layer of air.

If the Chinese are going to do anything, they'll do it now, as the capsule swings over their territory. A missile. Smart rocks flung into their path, shredding the capsule's skin, air dispersing in a freezing puff. To keep her mind away from these thoughts, Mariella looks for the Great Wall but fails to find it. Already they are passing over a coastline where clouds pile up like breakers on a beach. There is a chain of islands half-hidden by cloud, Japan surely, but it is getting too dark down there to be sure; the sun has set behind the curve of the Earth's limb, although its light lingers in the thin skin of the atmosphere.

Anchee Ye is swapping acronyms with the NASA guidance controller. She suspects nothing. Or perhaps the patch hasn't worked . . . or perhaps it has gone horribly agley, will dig them in too deep and burn them up like a match head scratching down the sky. . . .

The capsule falls backward over the vast darkness of the Pacific. The giant slick is down there somewhere, spreading inexorably. There is a patch of silver light on the face of the waters. Mariella tries and fails to work out what it is, and asks Anchee Ye if she can see it.

"Moonlight," Anchee says. For the first time she seems relaxed, absorbed in the routine and the jargon that define the narrow parameters of her fate.

"I had this crazy thought it was the giant slick."

"It's a cloudless night down there. We'll get an attitude check in a few minutes, when the Moon sets behind the Earth."

"Four minutes, twenty-eight seconds," the guidance controller says.

"Copy that."

The silver streak of the Moon's reflection elongates and drifts away as the capsule falls further and further and the horizon climbs higher; at last the Moon itself appears just above the dark limb of the Earth, a sliver of bone jabbed into the black sky.

"Now I see it," Anchee says.

"Not for much longer," the guidance controller says. "One minute, twelve seconds."

"Copy that."

The Moon's sliver swings down toward the curved black wall of the horizon. Mariella's fists are tightly clenched as she silently counts off the seconds.

"Fifteen to go," the guidance controller says.

"I don't see anything yet."

"Now?"

"Not yet."

"I'm closing out the clock down here."

Is there a note of anxiety in the man's voice?

"Still nothing," Anchee Ye says. "No, wait. Wait! There it is."

The sliver of white light has sunk imperceptibly, and a nick, the shadow of the Earth, has appeared in its lower quadrant.

Is that delay significant? Has the capsule been nudged from its track by just the right amount? Mariella still doesn't know, but now she has a grain of hope.

"That's good enough for me," the guidance controller says. "You're so close to re-entry now we can hardly see your track above the horizon. We're going a final round down here. Okay. All on go. It's a fine sunny morning at the target area, a little sea haze but nothing to worry about. I understand they're getting ready to cook up your steak breakfasts."

"I might be able to manage a bite," Anchee says.

"Don is waiting for you."

"Tell him I'm coming home."

"I can patch you guys together."

"I'll be down in a few minutes. Thank everyone for the outstanding job."

"Glad to welcome you back. Signal loss in about a minute. Good luck."

Now Mariella glimpses what she thinks is sunrise outside the little triangular window. A faint pinkness laid against the black night like a feather brush of watercolor, slowly deepening to orange. A hand presses her against the ill-fitting contours of the couch and continues to press down inexorably. Gravity. It is not so bad. It is pressing down hard, but she can still breathe.

The fiery orange beyond the little pane of the window darkens to red, red flames filled with incandescent flecks. The capsule begins to judder, pitching this way and that; the air is growing hotter. They are burning up, scorching down through the atmosphere at the center of a ball of fire and ionized gases. Glowing chunks fly past the little window, layers of the capsule's heat shield, burning away just as they should. Mariella remembers the heat-stained Mercury capsule above the lobby of the NASA hotel. This is the way the first people to venture into space returned, falling out of the sky in a burning chariot. Everything is normal. The capsule is still juddering. Static hisses like the crackle of flames in her headset, and the weight pressing down on her grows until for a panicky moment she can't breathe at all and thinks her ribs might snap like the staves of a rotten barrel.

And then the moment is past and the weight lifts and she feels only a tremendous lassitude, the pull of exactly one gravity. She is too tired to even turn her head and see how Anchee is doing. In the window above her, the flames have burned away to a clear blue sky in which a wild white contrail snakes.

The capsule has fallen through night into day and is now plunging down in free fall toward the surface of the planet. There is a bang and a thump and it swings violently around and steadies. The parachutes have deployed.

A voice in her ear is asking if she is okay.

"I'm fine," she says.

It is horribly hot in the capsule, and it is swaying in wide arcs beneath its parachutes, but she is okay.

"From down here, it looks like there might be a slight glitch in your track," the voice says. It is the guidance controller. There is a note of caution in his voice, the merest glimmer of a question mark.

Mariella rolls her head to look at Anchee Ye, and feels for a moment as if the whole capsule has swung over and around her. Across the empty couch, Anchee Ye lies motionless, her head turned away.

Mariella says, "I think she passed out."

"Who am I talking to here?"

"Dr. Anders. The biologist."

"Okay. Listen up, Mariella. We think you're about four hundred kilometers short of the programmed track. That places you as coming down somewhere in the Gulf of Mexico instead of in the Atlantic off the Florida coast. Do you copy that?"

"Yes. Yes, I do."

"Don't worry. We can have someone out to pick you up in a couple of hours. They're scrambling now. Just lay back and it won't be a problem."

The capsule is still swaying beneath its parachutes. Through the window Mariella can see blue sky, the contrail's scrawl of white vapor, blue sky again. She feels elation and relief. "No," she says. "No, it isn't a problem at all."

Limanes, Mexico:
June 4–September 14, 2028

Mariella is told that Anchee Ye is dead ten days later, after she has been moved inland in a battered RV. She is driven along ungraded trails that climb past farms and hamlets, fields of maize and sugarcane and rape, the sun burning in a sky hazed white by dust blowing off the ruined farmlands of the high central plains, burning through the RV's half-polarized windscreen. The wipers scraping back and forth, sweeping away arcs of talc. The driver and his burly companion silhouetted against white glare, both of them *zapatistas*, part of the cadre of soldiers detailed by one of the ministers of the revolutionary government to help her. Other soldiers, heavily armed, follow the RV in two unmarked cars.

The descent capsule splashed down in Campeche Bay off the

Gulf Coast of Mexico, and a fast boat (hired, she learned later, from cigarette smugglers) picked up Mariella and Anchee Ye, sank the capsule, and sped away before American navy helicopters could arrive from Brownsville. After reaching land there was a complicated operation entailing several changes of vehicle, always beneath underpasses so that satellite surveillance couldn't spot them. Mariella, exhausted by the drag of gravity, made horribly nauseous by motion sickness and the hot, humid, reeking air, clutched the thermos and her slate with stubborn strength.

At first, Mariella and Anchee are hidden in a rented villa over-looking the shore near Burros, north of the estuary of the Tamesí river. Mariella's father worked there thirty years ago. The smell of dry scrub and sunbaked earth brings back memories of riding with her parents in a rented jeep to the beach. The jeep was driven by their bodyguard, Emil, a burly man with shoulder-length black hair who habitually wore a safari jacket and chain-smoked unfil-tered Camels. She was six or seven. It wasn't safe to play in the water; the sullen waves cast dead fish and lumps of tar on the sugary sand. Offshore winds whipped the polluted foam into sticky balls that washed up in great drifts along the strandline. A few kilometers down the curve of the coast, the cracking columns of the Pemex oil refinery glittered like cheap jewelery, shrouded in their own haze. Sometimes you got a sulphurous whiff of those vapors.

The people who rescued her are a group of exiled rad greens on the run from the U.S. authorities and sheltered by the revolu-tionary government of Mexico. There are perhaps twenty of them living in the villa, but it's hard to tell because people come and go at all hours. They are very young and enormously idealistic, and treat Mariella with the kind of reverence given a holy relic. There is always a TV or a slate on somewhere, locked into the flood of media interest about the missing Mars astronauts.

Mariella is heavily sedated and spends a lot of time asleep. Her muscles have been terribly weakened by her time in microgravity; she can't walk without help. Gravity is an intense ache in her joints, an agony of grating vertebrae. Her inner ears are so hyper-sensitive she gets dizzy looking down at her feet. She is given massages and hydrotherapy, is placed on a high-calcium diet by the greens' doctor, Ellen Esterhauzy. All this time, Anchee lies in a coma, horribly pallid and thin inside an oxygen tent's shroud.

On the morning of the ninth day, a woman in a business suit arrives and talks with Mariella. She is a representative of a senior member of the revolutionary government, and has an offer to make.

The next afternoon, Mariella is driven away in a van with an escort of half a dozen greens and their leader, Jade. She is transferred to the RV in the middle of a dense pine forest, dopily half-aware of a big argument about who will go with her. Ellen Esterhauzy refuses to leave her patient, and Jade insists that some of his people must come with Mariella too. The *zapatistas* shout and make hasty telephone calls, and then Jade draws a gun on them and starts shouting that this is all fucked up, he has permission to ride along. The *zapatistas* disarm him efficiently and bundle him into the RV, where he calms down instantly. Smiles and handshakes all around; one of the *zapatistas* even gives Jade his gun back.

Mariella asks for Anchee; Jade kneels beside her and tells her that Anchee Ye has gone on ahead, that it isn't safe to travel together. The leader of the *zapatistas* adds that American agents are looking for them, and it is probable that many of the local police are in the pay of the Americans or their right-wing antirevolutionary lackeys.

The RV's air-conditioning isn't running because it would waste precious fuel; instead, all its windows are cranked open, letting in a little hot breeze and a lot of dust. Mariella lies on one of the bunk beds, an IV drip in her arm, the lurch and sway of the RV adding to her continual nausea. Jade and Ellen Esterhauzy tend her patiently, holding a cardboard basin under her chin when she has to be sick, feeding her sips of warm, sugary, flat Coke, wiping her forehead with dampened cloths, helping her to the RV's tiny bathroom. Her slate is under her pillow and she cradles the stainless steel thermos flask. In all this time she hasn't let anyone take it from her, frightened that, despite their reassurances, one of the rad greens might open it, cook the precious chips of ice in a microwave.

The new hiding place is high in the folded foothills of the

Sierra Madre mountains, an old estancia converted into an agricultural research center. The main building is whitewashed and has a red tile roof. It stands on the ridge of a little valley, overlooking steeply sloping fields where coffee and sugar and maize alternate in a neat checkerboard down to the cottonwood trees that grow on either side of the river.

The American boy, Jade, tells Mariella about Anchee Ye's death the next morning. He holds her hand and looks her in the eye and speaks softly in his doped-out voice. He is very young, nineteen, twenty, with a rangy surfer's build and long blond hair streaked white by the sun. Handsome in a square-jawed generic American way, with rings in his eyebrows and nose and ears, and little animated tattoos that wink and sparkle on the tanned skin of his arms. A trust-fund kid rebelling against his parents, who are something in Hollywood; he was genetically tweaked in the womb, one of the first so-called superbabies, and is on the run after firebombing a fertility clinic.

"She died on the way here," he tells Mariella. "She didn't feel any pain. She never even woke up."

"It was her heart," Ellen Esterhauzy says. She is a brusque, pugnacious woman of German-Mexican descent. She smokes little cigarillos and has dyed her long black hair even blacker, the shiny black of a raven's wing. She says, "Her heart enlarged in zero gravity, and here on Earth her fluid balance changed and it could no longer cope."

Mariella tries to take this in. The drugs she has been given to counteract her nausea and vertigo make everything seem slightly remote, like a program on a TV playing in the next room. She says, "Where is she?"

Jade looks at Ellen Esterhauzy, who says, "We have the body. It is in the cold store."

A pause. Mariella realizes that they want her to tell them what to do. As if she has, by traveling all that way with her, become Anchee Ye's next of kin. She says, "She has a husband. Had. In Texas. Houston, Texas. You have to get her back to him."

"That will be difficult, I think," Ellen Esterhauzy says.

"Perhaps. But you'll have to find a way. It's the only decent thing to do."

"Of course it is," Jade says. "But it might not be safe. Not yet. And the zaps are nervous about it. The North knows about the pickup and it's caused plenty of trouble. If the Mexican government officially hands over Anchee Ye's body, things will get much worse."

"Poor Anchee. I knew she was ill, but I didn't realize how ill. She got me home. She stayed alive for that. She didn't believe in what I wanted to do, but she got me home." Mariella turns her head. The stainless steel thermos flask stands on the heavy oak credenza by the bed. She says, "You should have taken her to a hospital."

"She had the best medical attention," Ellen Esterhauzy says stiffly. "Her heart was very damaged. Not only her heart, but her entire circulatory system. There was much muscle wastage, there was fluid in the lungs, her pericardial sac was enlarged, and she was suffering from Dry Lung Syndrome, presumably caused by the low-pressure recirculated air of your spacecraft. She was not strong enough to live, and not strong enough to survive any treatment."

"She was too ill to exercise properly," Mariella says. "She should have been taken straight to a hospital."

"I gave her hyperbaric oxygen," Ellen Esterhauzy says. "It is true she could also have been attached to a heart-lung machine, but the muscles of her own heart were too badly damaged to regenerate, and she was too weak to survive a transplant operation, or wait for growth of replacement muscle. She would have lived perhaps a few more days in a hospital, but still she would have died."

Jade says, "We did all we could."

"She would have died whatever was done," Ellen Esterhauzy says. She means it kindly.

"She might not have died if she had returned on the *Beagle*," Mariella says. "Barbara Lopez should have tried to get her back to Lowell. I didn't even want her to come with me. Shit. Well, I'm responsible for her now, and I want her body returned to her husband. That's the least of my obligation toward her."

Jade says, "We can't—"

Mariella raises herself up, her heart suddenly racing, muscles cramping down her back. "No. You can. You will."

Ellen Esterhauzy helps her settle back on the bed and says, "We will try to think of something. Now you must rest."

A brief coldness on her arm. The room sinking away on all sides.

Jade wakes her early the next morning, holds her head while she is sick into a cardboard basin, pours her a glass of soda water and sits at the end of the bed while she sips it. White curtains stir at the tall windows; the noise of a tractor is distantly receding.

Mariella says, "I'd kill for a ginger biscuit. Or a Bath Oliver."

"Which is?"

Mariella sips soda water. Bubbles fizz on her tongue. She says, "It's a kind of cracker. You might be able to get me a packet from the Scottish Embassy."

"You're kidding, right?"

"Yes, of course I'm kidding."

Jade takes a breath and says, "Listen, Mariella. It's done."

"What do you mean?"

"I took care of your friend," Jade says, and explains in a rush that he dressed Anchee Ye's body and drove it all the way to Monterrey, stole a car and put the body inside it, left the car and the body in front of the American consulate in the Plaza Zaragoza, and then called the U.S. consul.

"It went real well," Jade says. "The consul called the police, and the police called an ambulance. I watched from a smoke shop on the other side of the square. She's in the right hands now."

He grows more and more animated as he fills in the details, like a naughty schoolkid reliving the details of a particularly exciting dare. He has a boyish enthusiasm for conspiracies and the illicit thrill of undercover work; to him, it is a sport no more dangerous than snowboarding or open ocean surfing. He describes how the police approached the stolen car with drawn pistols, wary of boobytraps. Traffic was blocked off at either end of the square, sunlight flaring from windshields, angry drivers sounding their horns, leaning out of windows to try and see what was going on. People gathering in the square, crowding around the car and trying to get a glimpse of the dead astronaut, parting for the ambulance when it briefly sounded its siren. The American consul arguing with the senior police officer. The black bodybag, women crossing themselves, Jade watching everything behind mirrorshades as he lounged at a table among brightly dressed, half-stoned Australian and Canadian tourists, a cold beer in front of him.

Mariella is still too doped up to feel more than a flicker of anger at the thought of Anchee Ye's body being treated like an unwanted side of beef, an inconvenience abandoned in a hot car in a crowded square. She says, "It's a poor end to a difficult voyage."

"It was the only way," Jade says. Truculence clouds his handsome face. "It was for the good of the cause. We couldn't just hand her over. The police are more or less at war with the government. They were never properly purged, and they're massively corrupt. A lot of them are in the pay of the North."

"You should have let the government handle it," Mariella says wearily.

"No way. We can't be obligated."

"Yes, a touch of responsibility would spoil your silly little games, wouldn't it? Leave me alone now. I'm tired."

Ellen Esterhauzy gives her tablets to help her rest; Mariella sticks them under her tongue and spits them out when the woman has gone. She totters across the big airy room they have given her and sits in a patch of sunlight by the open windows, thinking about all that she has to do. It is as if she is recovering from a long illness, and rediscovering the health that she has always taken for granted.

The director of the agricultural research center, Juan Flores, is a slightly built man about Mariella's age, with slick black hair, a neatly trimmed mustache, a narrow face seamed and darkened by the sun. He invariably wears a white shirt and blue jeans and a bolo tie. His calf-length leather boots are highly polished. He has a great admiration for Mariella's work, and an endless reservoir of tolerance for the intrigue his political patron, Oscar Villegas, has inflicted upon him.

Juan Flores regards Mariella as a colleague, and when she is well enough proudly gives her a tour of his research center. The cinderblock laboratory wing, the greenhouses, the tobacco-drying sheds, the weather station, the microwave dish that links the farm with the university in nearby Jalapa because the phone lines are too unreliable, the experimental plots. He pushes Mariella's wheelchair along dusty paths between geometrically planted plots of maize or cotton varieties where assistants are hand-pollinating the plants or breaking up the hard red earth with mattocks. Shows her the solar panels and the windmill turbine, the reed bed that filters the farm's sewage, the system of permeable pipes, made from recycled tires, that trickles the treated water into the soil of the plots.

"We are as self-sufficient as possible," he says. "Part of our purpose is to educate the peasants, and so we must set a good example. It is the only way forward."

Juan Flores is a passionate supporter of the socialist government and a fierce opponent of what he calls the colonialist agribusinesses. He fought under the command of Oscar Villegas in the war of liberation in the south that eventually toppled the old, corrupt, capitalist government, but he is a very pragmatic revolutionary.

"We learn to use the tools of those who would exploit us," he explains, after he has shown Mariella the genetics laboratory and its treasure, an ancient microprobe gun which, powered by compressed helium, fires gold microspheres coated with naked DNA into cultured plant cells, which are then grown up into calluses in sterile medium before being used to create explants. It is an old-fashioned, laborious technique, but effective. At the moment, most of the work, supervised by a cheery seventy-year-old Dutch dopehead with gray hair in ropy dreadlocks that swing at his waist, is devoted to improving tobacco and marijuana. Much of the agriculture in the state of Veracruz is given over to growing these crops, and to manufacturing resin and cigarettes that are smuggled into the North.

"What else can we do," Juan Flores says, "with the embargoes your government impose? Before the revolution, most of our trade went to the North—our shrimp, our oil, our steel, the sweated labor of the maquiladoras. But now our oil is almost gone, and will be worthless once the fragments of the Murchison asteroid arrive. And the maquiladoras along the border have either been seized by the Americans or have been nationalized and shut down.

We can only rely on tourism and drugs to earn dollars. It is an irony, I suppose, that our cigars are as fine as those of Cuba, which now trades legitimately with the North. Meanwhile, the agents of your agricultural department release insects carrying tobacco mosaic virus, or drop feathers drenched with the spores of modified bacteria and fungi from high-flying aircraft, so that they drift across the border and carry infection to our crops. We must work hard to develop resistant strains to counter this clandestine biological warfare."

"The gene-for-gene hypothesis at a state level," Mariella observes.

"Indeed," Juan Flores says seriously. "We must also contend with the smuts and viruses of maize and sweet potatoes and cotton and peanuts, all of which originate in the monoculture farms of the North. We have solved these problems by transferring genes derived from a wild species of perennial corn to our food crops, but it is not easy. The North forbids access to retroviruses that transfer genes, and to other advanced technologies, so we must rely on our faithful old gun."

"I'm beginning to see why Oscar Villegas is interested in the Chi."

"We are fighting a clandestine war when we should be developing good strains of staple crops that are disease- and drought-resistant, that can grow well in the aluminum-rich soils which comprise forty percent of our farmlands. And what we are able to do is nothing compared to the power of the monstrous thing you have brought back from Mars."

"Monstrous? That's pretty emotive, Juan."

"Many in my government would call it that."

"Would you rather Cytex held exclusive rights to it? If they did, you'd never keep up with what they could do."

"It will change all the world," Juan Flores says. "Oscar Villegas sees that clearly. And so, God help me, I must help you grow it."

Mariella sets up her laboratory in a concrete blockhouse that was previously used as an equipment store. Workmen spray the floor and walls and ceiling with a slick polymer sealant and install a filtered ventilation system and big glove boxes. The next week, a whole truckload of smuggled supplies arrives. Riding with the driver and his mate is the woman who ambushed Mariella in the Biological Reserve — the short, dark, businesslike woman who calls herself Clarice Bushor.

She greets Juan Flores in flawless Spanish, and turns to Mariella and says, "I hope he's been looking after you, Dr. Anders, and hasn't been trying to infect you with socialist cant."

"Hello, Anna."

"Clarice," the woman says, without missing a beat, "Clarice Bushor."

She wears blue jeans and a short white jacket over a black T-shirt. Slashes of bronze and purple eyeshadow, bright-red lipstick, immaculate, glossy red fingernails, a heady floral perfume. She does not look like an ecorevolutionary cadre at all. The secretary of a small town politician, perhaps, or the kind of realtor who calls a house a home.

Mariella says, "I don't care which name you use, frankly, as long as you keep out of my way."

Juan Flores says, "We are on the same side, I think."

"We're in agreement about certain things," Clarice Bushor says. "That's about as far as it goes."

Mariella asks her, "Why are you here?"

"I've brought you stuff you're going to need," Clarice Bushor says. "My boys will unload. There's some expensive and delicate equipment in there, and I'd hate to see one of your peasants drop any of it. It cost a great deal to buy, and it cost even more to smuggle it across the border."

"My people are very used to handling scientific equipment," Juan Flores says. "And I believe that it is the property of the government."

"That's one way of looking at it," Clarice Bushor says, squaring up to him. "Another way would be that we've pumped a lot of money into Mexico in one way or another, and this is just a fraction of the vig. You know, the interest? The government helps us just as we've helped the government." She winks broadly at Mariella. "Especially when it was recovering from its revolution. We gave a lot of expertise then, and a lot of money, too. Not to mention embargoed technology that is put to uses we don't always approve of."

Mariella says, "So you're not just an information clearing-house."

"We support many different groups within the green move-ment, Dr. Anders. You might say that we are into wealth redistri-bution."

"I see. You hand out your dead sister's money, but you don't get your hands dirty."

"Not at all," Clarice Bushor says, with a bright smile. "I'm here, after all. We move in all sorts of areas. Information, human resources. Special cases like yourself."

Juan Flores says stiffly, "I hope you will take lunch with us before you leave, Señorita Bushor."

"Leave? I'm not leaving. I'm here to facilitate Dr. Anders's work in any way I can. Right now she's about the most important resource Clarice Bushor has."

After lunch, the woman insists that Mariella give her a tour of the laboratory, although she shows no more than a superficial in-terest.

"I'll be honest," she says. "I don't approve of this. I think you've already given us enough evidence without having to grow this Chi."

"I entrusted the recording to you so that it could be used at the proper time. The Chi must be sequenced first. Then you'll be able to prove once and for all that it is the root cause of the slicks."

The woman runs her fingers over the plastic-coated benchtop, like a housewife checking for dust. She says, "Let's speak honestly here. At a gut level, I'd like to see the unnatural monstrous growth you've brought back from Mars destroyed right now. But that is only my own personal opinion. We are a collective, and I've been persuaded to take a longer view. We've agreed that unusual mea-sures are called for because this is a huge scandal, one that could ruin the biotechnologists for good."

"The work is important in any case," Mariella says, annoyed by the woman's presumption, "not just because it might cause a scandal."

Clarice Bushor smiles and says, "Many in my collective believe that it has become necessary to use GM organisms to destroy the slick. In my opinion, Gaia is perfectly able to regulate herself, and so She will, sooner or later."

"I deal in facts, not opinions. The slicks have already destroyed about half the phytoplankton productivity in the Pacific. People are starving because there's no more fish to be caught, and things will get far worse if nothing is done."

"Perhaps that's why Gaia allows the slicks to grow."

"Really? And what if the Earth becomes uninhabitable as a result?"

"There have been major extinction events before. Gaia will still exist, in a new form. A *purified* form, you might say. We shouldn't question Her ways."

So the woman is that kind of green, one of the misanthropic radicals who insist that nothing less than the removal of the entire human race will cure the Earth's ravaged ecosystems.

"There's another problem," she tells Mariella. "You really shouldn't have chosen to stay here."

"I didn't have much choice."

Clarice Bushor doesn't seem to have heard her. She says, "I'm sympathetic to the Mexican cause, up to a point, but I have no doubt that Oscar Villegas is covertly supporting you because he wants to make use of the thing you have brought back from Mars. I hope you won't allow that."

Mariella manages to hold the woman's bright, mad gaze. She says, "The truth won't be altered, no matter who is helping me."

Clarice Bushor's laugh is unnervingly shrill. Mariella thinks of old glass breaking underfoot. "Perhaps not the truth, but certainly the perception of the truth. You are a rogue scientist, Dr. Anders. You are on the run with something you stole from NASA. You stole a *spaceship* from the Chinese government, and now you're in league with the Mexican revolutionary government. You must have seen something of the news coverage. They're painting you blacker than Typhoid Mary."

"I'm not really interested in what other people think."

Which isn't strictly true. Mariella has kept up with the media speculation about her whereabouts, and knows that it is waning due to lack of anything concrete. And she has printed out and stuck to the wall of her new lab the latest series of Little Iva cartoon strips, in which Little Iva makes miniature robot replicas of herself and her trusty calculator to fight off the Martian bacteria that have invaded her bloodstream.

Clarice Bushor tells her, "Everything you do will be colored by what people think of you. And at the moment they're being primed to think some pretty bad thoughts. Don't kid yourself that you don't need our help, especially as Oscar Villegas wants a piece of what you have. You can bet he isn't really interested in using it to find a way of destroying the slicks. For all their rhetoric, most of the *zapatistas* aren't true greens. You only have to look at the crimes against nature they're perpetrating in this so-called research center."

"They're developing better crops, that's all. They have to feed their people."

"Yes, I might have expected you to be sympathetic. The fact is, though, that the people could feed themselves if only they were given land and seeds and tools. Science has taken that basic right away, even in the so-called green countries. You can't right that injustice with more science."

"The fact is that I don't need your help," Mariella says. "There are dozens of groups like yours, so you need me more than I need you. I bring credibility to your cause. I have the proof you need of a massive misuse of biotechnology, but without me it's not worth very much."

The woman bristles. "You think very highly of yourself."

"I'm one of the scientists who solved the Firstborn Crisis. I've been to Mars and brought back something wonderful and strange. If it wasn't for my reputation, I'm sure that Oscar Villegas would have taken the Chi away from me by now. Of course you need me."

"It's hardly wonderful and strange. Horribly dangerous, certainly."

"Not at all. It's wonderful because of what it is. Life closely related to life on Earth, but with three or four billion years of separate evolution."

The woman smiles. She has dimples. She says, "You are a curious mixture of arrogance and romance. You think yourself a free agent, but you are not. For one thing, you cannot do your work without the equipment we have brought, and you can be sure I'll be keeping a close watch on what you do."

"Yes, I've already put myself in your hands," Mariella says, "but now you must put yourself in mine. Maybe you can help me out in the lab."

The woman refuses, of course. She will not soil her hands with the techniques she wants to ban. Instead, she spends a lot of time lecturing Juan Flores and his workers about green practices, claiming to be appalled that the *zapatistas* have compromised themselves by playing with the hellfire of biotechnology. Even Jade resents the way she naturally assumes she can take charge of all she sees. He starts patrolling the perimeter of the farm, a big nickel-plated automatic tucked in the back of his blue jeans, despite Juan Flores's protest that it is completely unnecessary. Which is certainly true. At least half the field workers — the well-fed muscular ones with good teeth and well-cut jeans and T-shirts, the ones who handle their shovels and mattocks so unskillfully — are soldiers, and there are army patrols in the countryside around the research center. But it gives Jade something to do, an outlet for his nervous energy.

The political patron of the research center, Oscar Villegas, pays a visit a few days after the arrival of Clarice Bushor, appearing one afternoon without warning. Mariella is summoned by a flustered soldier in dust-stained jeans and escorted to the terrace, where Oscar Villegas is drinking wine with Clarice Bushor and Juan Flores.

Oscar Villegas was one of the original *zapatistas* and, although now a senior minister in the government, still wears ordinary olive-drab fatigues and highly polished army boots. A green canvas baseball cap is jammed onto his exuberant black hair, a brass badge of a fist grasping a lightning bolt pinned above its bill. When he sees Mariella, he stands, sweeps off his cap, bows and says around the fat cigar clenched in his white teeth, "Here is our genius, who wants to save the world for the second time."

His tone is entirely without irony, and his smile seems genuine. He has a round, nut-brown face, with thick black eyebrows and a bushy beard. He is full of an infectious, good-humored energy.

He says, "I must see at once this miracle you have brought back from Mars! Truly a wonder that it should find a home in our country, right under the noses of the North."

Mariella is still setting up the laboratory, and says that she has little to show him, but he is insistent. She asks him to put out the cigar before they enter the half-empty room, and he hands it without a word to the sergeant who follows three paces behind. He listens quietly and patiently to her explanations of what she plans to do, and asks several intelligent questions about the procedures. Clearly, he has been well briefed.

They return to the terrace, where a table has been set up with china and cutlery and glasses from Juan Flores's house. The kitchen staff, starched full-length white aprons over their jeans and T-shirts, serve half a dozen courses to Oscar Villegas, Mariella, Clarice Bushor, Ellen Esterhauzy, and Juan Flores and his family. There are toasts to the success of the venture and to cooperation between radical greens and the revolutionary government. Oscar Villegas questions Mariella closely about the expedition to Mars. He is particularly interested in the details of what the press has dubbed the Battle of the 83rd Parallel.

"You are a true revolutionary," he tells her, and jumps up and proposes a toast, holding her eyes with his as he speaks. "You are blooded in war, and you have won a serious prize from the forces of international capitalism. I am honored to be of help to you. This is a great thing. When we demonstrate the true power of what you have brought us, when we provide a cure for the slicks that choke the oceans, we will spread the spirit of our revolution across the world."

Everyone at the table drinks to that, with the conspicuous exception of Clarice Bushor. Mariella looks at her, looks at Oscar Villegas, and says, "You expect a lot from me."

Oscar Villegas sits down and says, "You do not think your work will have serious implications?"

"I'm a scientist, not a politician."

Oscar Villegas grins, showing crooked but very white teeth. He smells strongly of wine and sweet cigar smoke. He says, "Even scientists must live in the world, just like everyone else. You cannot deny that simple truth. And the world is a more complex and dangerous place because of what you scientists do."

"It always was complex. Life is complex. But the rules that underlie that complexity are simple."

"Life should be simple, I agree. Good food, good drink, good friends, a happy family. We have had to fight hard for these things, and so we enjoy them all the more when we can. The North is different. Its people do not fight. As long as their supermarkets are full, as long as they can drive new cars and live in big houses, they are happy to sell their souls to the companies that eat up the world. Companies whose wealth is built on the bones of children in countries like ours. In the North, children go to school, to university. They remain like children even after they grow up. Here, before the revolution, our children had to work in the maquiladoras or in the farms owned by Dole or United Fruit. We fought for the right of our children to determine their own lives. We fought to free them from economic slavery. You will help us in that fight too."

"I'll tell the truth about what I find."

Oscar Villegas takes a long drag on his cigar and exhales a plume of smoke with a flourish. He says, "Many people want to talk with you. We have reporters searching the country. Some are CIA spies, of course, but most are genuine. From all countries of the world, and all desperate to interview you. So you see you are important to me."

He seems genuinely pleased by this, and takes another luxurious drag on his cigar and beams at everyone at the table.

Mariella says, "Perhaps I could talk with one or two of these reporters. I know people who can be trusted. Good science journalists, not sensation mongers."

"No! No, no, it is not possible. This is our secret for the time being. Until I know what you have."

"You know what I have."

"You must grow it up. I must see it. Perhaps then you can talk with a sympathetic reporter. Meanwhile, I play games with them. They follow wild leads into the country. They look for secret laboratories that do not exist, or look for you in laboratories in which you do not work. It's a serious business, of course, keeping you hidden, but also much fun. A good thing my friend Clarice Bushor chose to stay here after she brings the equipment, for otherwise I might have had to have her killed, for the sake of security."

"I'm here because I want to be sure the truth comes out," Clarice Bushor says.

"Yes, why not? This will make both our causes strong. Together, we will liberate Texas and Arizona and New Mexico, perhaps even California."

More toasts to this. This time Mariella does not drink; nor, she notices, does Ellen Esterhauzy. The woman stands with the others, but only touches her wineglass to her lips.

Although Mariella is well enough to begin to think about starting work, Ellen Esterhauzy stays on at the research center. Perhaps Oscar Villegas was not joking about security measures. She helps out in the lab, first as a bottlewasher, and then making up the culture media on which Mariella is trying to grow the Chi.

Mariella learns that Ellen Esterhauzy's husband, an American doctor, was killed in the superstorm that devastated Central America in the middle of the Firstborn Crisis, the same superstorm that was the indirect cause of Forrest's death. Although they do not speak of this again, it binds them close. After her husband's death, Ellen Esterhauzy began to work in the barrios, among refugees from the dustbowls of the central plains and workers from factories and steel mills that closed after the U.S. economy caught cold in '16. She also opened her house as a way station for rad greens and revolutionaries and gene hackers traveling through Mexico on their way to Central and South America.

Ellen Esterhauzy is more pragmatic than most greens because of her work, although she will not allow the use of any biotech in her clinic. She says that there are more fundamental problems than curing genetic defects or prolonging life. What is the good of devoting precious resources extracting stem cells and growing neural material to cure a woman of Parkinson's, when her children are starving to death or dying of cholera or malaria? What is the use of applying gene therapy to a child who has only a one-in-three chance of surviving to adulthood? These and other treatments—embryo screening, somatic cell regrowth, continuous monitoring via implanted chips—are luxuries of the rapacious First World. In Mexico, many of the refugees from the central plains have not even been inoculated with the cure for the Moses virus: their family histories are of healthy daughters and miscarried sons.

Ellen Esterhauzy champions preventative measures that can be taught to women, based on good hygiene and a proper diet. Triage in the battlefield of poverty. In her spare time, she does research into use of medicinal plants by Mexico's indigenous Indians. Herbal infusions to ease malarial fevers. Extracts boiled from roots of unregarded weeds that purge worms from the intestinal tract. Poultices that promote healing of sores and ulcers. Biotechnology can identify and isolate the genes that produce the active compounds in these plants, insert them into bacteria or yeast and use industrial fermentation techniques to churn out vast quantities of pure product, but the expense of copyrighting genes and pushing a single pharmaceutically active chemical through the complex testing required before it can be licensed puts an unfeasibly high price on medicines that can be gathered for free from the fields and forests, and prepared by soaking or boiling.

Triage. Appropriate technology. While she washes and rinses out flasks with meticulous care (for an invisible film of detergent can inhibit growth; a single speck of dust can contaminate a fifty-liter batch of carefully prepared nutrient solution), Ellen Esterhauzy tells stories about the people of the barrios. One in particular stays with Mariella, that of an old woman who by day sits at a street corner in the business district selling loose cigarettes one at a time, and by night sleeps at the railway station. Waiting her turn at a standpipe to wash after she has eaten. Perhaps soup and bread from one of the charities, perhaps a taco from one of the vendors if she has had a good day and sold enough cigarettes. She does not talk to anyone. The poor in their multitude are each all alone. They survive by ignoring the swarming press of people that constantly surrounds them. So the old woman takes her turn at the standpipe, drinks a mouthful of water and washes her feet and head. Takes her blanket and unfolds it on the ground, meticulously squaring it and patting it down, smoothing out wrinkles, choosing with great care stones to anchor its corners before lying down to sleep. Possessing almost nothing except dignity and the desire to make a patch of ground her own. What can you give a woman like that? A woman who lives her life day by day, and a good day is one that yields enough money to buy a taco. An extra hundred years? An injection of tailored white cells that will devour the cataract that frosts her left eye? Or a place where she can grow her own food, a place within the web of a community, dignity on her own terms?

Triage. Appropriate technology.

One day, Ellen Esterhauzy is contacted by the American blind trust that supports her clinic. They need a doctor to treat two astronauts. The two women who had been in and out of the news for more than a year. The women from Mars. Ellen Esterhauzy thinks it will take no more than a couple of days out of her work at the clinic, but then one of the women dies of severe congestive heart failure — really, a collapse of her entire circulatory system — and although there is nothing that could have been done, Ellen Esterhauzy feels she has failed her. So she stays with the other woman, to make sure she is safe. Not because the woman is Mariella Anders, who identified the virus at the heart of the Firstborn Crisis, who helped develop the cure, but because she feels an obligation to help the woman whose friend died in her care. And then something Mariella says strikes her as a hammer strikes a bell. A resonance clear through her being.

"You shouldn't take any notice of what I say. I don't mean half of it."

"You make light of something that to me is important. That is I suppose your prerogative — the prerogative of genius. But you do not realize the effect you have on other people."

"I'm sorry. Please, tell me what it was."

"It was I think a throwaway remark, but it meant something to me. You said it to Jade, who had made some silly remark about

Martians destroying the world. You said that the world was more subtle than our imagination. That most people did not bother to look closely at the world, that they peopled it with monsters to excuse themselves from thinking hard about the way things really are."

"Jade's a silly boy."

"Like most young people he knows he has to live in a world wrecked by the previous generation. Unlike most, he wants to do something about it rather than wallow in cynicism or hedonism. But yes, he is also naive, and very shallow in his understanding of the world. And so he is easily exploited, poor fellow. He didn't understand what you said, but I did. And so I am here."

"I appreciate the help. I really do."

"You must not put your trust in Oscar Villegas. By keeping you here, he has contained you at very little expense to himself. If you succeed then perhaps all will be well, although I think he will want to take the Chi from you. But if you do not succeed, then he will certainly dispose of you without a qualm. And this woman who has taken the name of her dead sister is I think even more dangerous. She is a fanatic. Her principles tell her that she should destroy the Chi rather than make use of it. She could publicize your work before it is finished, and force Oscar Villegas to choose between his status in the government and his support for you. And I also think that she does not want you to succeed."

"She doesn't know me very well."

But the work is difficult and frustrating. Mariella can make only educated guesses about the conditions that will allow the Chi to grow, and there is a huge range of environmental variables to play with. Temperature, pressure, pH, reductant supply, types and concentrations of micronutrients, carbon dioxide concentration. . . . She can make rough estimates of some of these from analyses of the Martian water, but it was almost certainly contaminated when the borehole was drilled, and change in one variable can easily affect others. A small shift in acidity disturbs the carbon dioxide/bicarbonate balance, precipitating some nutrients and increasing the concentration of others by leaching from the rock. And so on. There are dozens of variables to be cross-tested against one another in thousands of combinations, a complex $n$ch-dimensional field with only a few scattered domains which will support growth. And the amount of material available to test all these combinations is very limited. Mariella spends two weeks programming models of conditions within the Martian bedrock on the farm's antiquated mainframe, working out which sets of variables are so inimical to Martian life that they can be ignored, before she sets to work in the laboratory.

She starts from the assumption that the Chi will grow in conditions much like those in deep terrestrial rocks, where a huge variety of microbes flourish. Liquid water as a solvent for micronutrients and for carbon dioxide, hydrogen as a source of energy for the fixation of carbon dioxide into organic molecules. Mariella sets up gradients of temperature against nutrient concentration at fixed rates of carbon dioxide and hydrogen supply, and when that doesn't work varies carbon dioxide and then hydrogen concentration, but still gets no growth. All this working at one remove in tabletop incubators inside big glove boxes, with strict sterile procedures. Dull repetitive work, the kind of work she rebelled against as a student. And, through Juan Flores, Oscar Villegas demands daily reports, while Clarice Bushor is ever watchful. Mariella feels like a butterfly enslaved by ants.

Five weeks pass. Clarice Bushor and Juan Flores fight a cold war around her. The amount of Martian ice left is halved, and halved again. And nothing works. She is missing something. Or there are no living cells or spores in the ice, which will make the task of obtaining a complete genetic sequence almost impossible because of contamination with the virus the Chinese injected into the borehole, the same problem the immense resources of Cytex must be attempting to overcome, using the samples Mariella spiked with caustic dust.

Mariella's lab assistants work twelve hours a day, six days a week, but like the rest of the staff do not work on Sundays. Mariella studies geological maps of the area, and one Sunday asks permission to borrow a jeep, telling Juan Flores that she is feeling strong enough to do a little hill walking, that it will relax her and help her think. Although he makes it clear that he believes she is testing the limits of her freedom, he does not raise an objection.

She goes with Ellen Esterhauzy and Jade. The army captain in charge of the security detail drives their jeep, with two more jeeps following, each carrying three beefy men in civilian clothes. The captain's name is Hector Vierra. A tall man in a black T-shirt, its sleeves rolled up on his muscular arms, and new blue jeans with a white crease down the middle of each leg. His black hair is cut close to his skull, with an upturned fringe at his forehead.

They drive south along unpaved roads, past fields of maize and tobacco bordered with eucalyptus, black locust and acacias. They speed past trucks, crowded buses, carts pulled by mules or oxen, are waved through police checkpoints. Little villages every two or three kilometers, adobe houses hugging the ground, solar panels gleaming on their flat roofs. The fields grow smaller as the road climbs the long slope of an ancient volcano, terraced one above the other with broad swathes of scrub between them, the road winding higher and higher among bluffs of weathered basalt.

Hector Vierra stops the jeep in the shade of a crescent-shaped stand of stunted pine trees. The land spreads north and east under the heat-hazed sky. Turkey vultures turn with lazy ease above a knob of rock a kilometer away.

While the others eat lunch, Mariella potters about on the long slope of weathered rocks below the trees, her cheeks and nose striped with vivid green sunblock, a broad-brimmed white hat on her head. There are stones of every size in long slides stabilized by mosses and tussocks of campion and dwarf lupins. Mostly a red-brown basalt the color of dried blood, but with some darker material mixed in. Amphiboles, pyroxenes, olivines. She collects samples and sits down on a warm ledge to rest her legs; the exertion has made her as tired and unsteady as an old lady. Presently, Ellen Esterhauzy comes down and sits beside her and remarks that this must remind her of Mars.

"A little, I suppose."

But it is not like Mars at all, not with air to breathe and plants growing wherever pockets of thin soil have accumulated among the stones. Even the bare stones have thin glazes of gray or yellow lichens.

"You are starting a rock collection."

"I thought I might try something new. A stupid idea, probably."

"The work is very difficult."

"I fear that I'm keeping you from your own work."

"This is important, I think."

"Yes. Yes, it is."

"Perhaps I dare ask how close we are."

"I don't know."

"It's a stubborn thing."

Mariella plucks a stem from a tuft of dry grass, turns it around and around. "All life is stubborn. This grass clinging to this inhospitable slope, waiting for the winter rains to come, so it can begin to grow again. Cyanobacteria just under the surface of rocks in Antarctic dry valleys, unfrozen only a few days a year, taking in a molecule of carbon dioxide every ten thousand years, making sugar and antifreeze, spitting out a molecule of oxygen ten thousand years later. The Chi, surviving deep beneath the Martian polar cap for billions of years. I know it's in the ice. We just have to find a way to wake it."

On the slope above them, beyond the trees, a faint and irregular popping sound starts up. Mariella turns to look, and Ellen Esterhauzy says, "Jade at his target practice."

"What does our brave captain and his soldiers think of that?"

"Perhaps it amuses them. We should go back, I think. Here, let me carry your treasure for you."

That night, Mariella is awakened by a thunderous knocking at the door of her bedroom. As she sits up, groping for the lamp, the door crashes open. "Don't switch on the light," Juan Flores says, and briefly shines a flashlight, holding it away from his body. "You must get dressed."

"What is it?"

"Intruders at the perimeter. Please, get dressed. Captain Vierra's men will certainly catch them, but we must take precautions."

The dusty rug is warm under Mariella's bare feet; the stone

flags beyond are cooler. By touch she finds the chair where she draped her clothes, and pulls on her jeans, cinches their belt under the T-shirt in which she had been sleeping. She says, "I need the flashlight."

Juan Flores says, "You need to come with me."

"I need to get the samples."

"The soldiers will take care of that."

"The fuck they will, Juan. They know nothing about sterile procedures."

She steps back when he reaches for her arm, and turns and runs to the open window and swings through, banging her shoulder hard against the frame as she tumbles onto the terrace. The sky is cloudy and the land all around dark, but vivid flashes stutter among the trees at the bottom of the valley, where men are shouting each other amid festive firecracker pops, brutal chainsaw rips, something that makes a horribly gleeful whoop.

"Wait!" Juan Flores calls, but Mariella is already running across the terrace. She feels her way down the steps and hurries down the gravel path to her laboratory, which looms like a ghost out of the darkness. She codes the lock and nothing happens, is trying again when Juan Flores catches up with her.

"The soldiers switched off the generator," he says in a whispered hiss, and she realizes that he is very frightened.

"I have to get the samples." She feels quite calm, and everything has an intense particularity. The gunfire down in the valley and the nearer sizzle of insects, the dry scent of weeds growing by the path, the crunch of gravel as Juan Flores anxiously shifts from foot to foot. She says, "Do you have a gun?"

"Yes. Of course."

"Then shoot out the lock."

"I will not. It is government property, and besides, the intruders might hear the shot. Mariella, please. You must come back with me to the estancia. It is the most defensible building here. You will be quite safe. I swear it."

"You go," Mariella says, aware that her stubbornness is foolish but unable or unwilling to overcome it.

"My orders are to stay with you. And I will, although I have no wish to make my children orphans."

"I won't leave the Chi, Juan."

"I confess something. I took a small part of it yesterday, while you were in the mountains. So you see it is not necessary to be here. Now, please come."

But as they begin to climb toward the estancia, the gunfire dies away. A long silence, then a single gunshot, and then silence again. When Mariella and Juan Flores regain the terrace, two jeeps full of soldiers speed up the road, headlights blazing. It is over.

Hector Vierra insists that Mariella look at the dead men. There are three of them, lying in pools of blood on oilcloth sheets, ghoulishly lit by the shifting glare of the flashlights held by a dozen black-clad soldiers. Hector Vierra tells her that one of the intruders shot himself through the head to avoid capture.

"I don't know any one of them," Mariella says, as steadily as she can. She feels very cold now, and wraps her arms across her breasts.

"I would think they are Chinese," Hector Vierra says, "don't you? Certainly, they were not reporters. They were armed with machine pistols firing caseless ammunition, and tasers of the kind that deliver a deadly voltage. That is how they got across the perimeter. They ambushed and killed two of my men."

"I'm sorry."

"They were soldiers, doing their duty. I hope you do yours, Dr. Anders."

The next day, Hector Vierra makes a speech about security to the entire staff of the research center. Mariella misses it because she is checking the integrity of the freezers where the samples of the Chi are stored, but Hector Vierra finds her and tells her that although the three intruders entered Mexico on Australian passports, they were almost certainly ghosts.

"They will have identities taken from dead men. Very common in security work. But I cannot prove it without asking the Australian authorities, and that is not possible."

"So they could have been Chinese agents."

"Perhaps. Or perhaps they were employed by someone who wants us to think they are."

"Cytex."

Hector Vierra passes a hand over the back of his head, his palm rasping against his scalp. His pockmarked cheeks are unshaven and there are bruised pouches under his eyes; Mariella guesses that he has not slept since the attack. He says, "It could be anyone anxious to secure the Chi and to blame the theft on the Chinese. Cytex, the U.S. government, or someone else. I do not think," he says, "that it is a coincidence they came here immediately after your picnic."

"How did they spot me?"

"Many people are looking for you. Most likely it was a policeman at one of the checkpoints. Now that your cover has been compromised, Dr. Anders, there will be no more picnics. You must stay inside the perimeter."

"So I'm a prisoner?"

"It is for your own safety," Hector Vierra says.

Mariella returns to the laborious process of varying conditions in the Mars Jars with a renewed sense of the desperate importance of her work.

Nothing works. Not even her stupid idea.

Clarice Bushor says one evening that perhaps it is fate, a corrective lesson applied by nature to curb Mariella's presumption. "If you were meant to grow this monstrous thing, you would have succeeded by now. No one could do better, according to you. That you have not succeeded means it is not meant to be."

"Nonsense," Mariella says. "It simply means that I don't yet know enough about it. I realize that it's a human failing to see everything in purely human terms, but I can't forgive it."

"Indeed," Juan Flores tells Clarice Bushor. "You seem to think that some entity ordains our successes and failures. God perhaps, except I doubt that you believe in Him. Or, forgive me, Her."

They are sitting at table after supper, on the terrace. Mosquito netting encloses them like a ghostly tent. Candles add to the heat trapped by the stone flags. The dark valley flickers with the will-of-the-wisp lights of insect traps. There's the sound of a jeep moving somewhere across the valley, but no headlights show — the guards use infrared lamps, and wear wavelength-shifting contact lenses.

"Not your God," Clarice Bushor retorts. "As you well know. Not the paternalistic desert God of organized religion, but the goddess of the world. The force that drives the green fuse. The sum of all life on Earth."

She and Jade sit together at one end of the table. They eat only vegan food cooked by Jade, who gathers wild greens on his rambles along the perimeter to spice up the warm salads and polentas and risottos he prepares using utensils he purchased in Limanes; he will not use any of the knives or pots and pans in the station's kitchens in case they have been contaminated by contact with meat. Vegans' dietary requirements are applied with the same rigor as those of Muslims or Jews, and a commitment to veganism is often the first step on the path to active involvement in green radicalism — a renouncement not just of use of animal products but of the values of the culture in which that use is so ritualized it is hardly ever given any thought.

"Gaia's more than just the sum of everything living," Jade says, smiling dazedly. He is on his third joint of the evening. "She's like an emergent pattern. That's why you scientists can't define Her. But She's real. You go out into the desert. You can feel Her there."

Juan Flores shrugs. He is as tired as Mariella of the meandering arguments of the two rad greens, but he feels that it is his duty to refute them. A truly Sisyphean task. He says, "Surely she is either everywhere, or nowhere. Why is one place better than another?"

Clarice Bushor tells Juan Flores, "You scientists can't see that a crime against nature is a crime against the whole world. Because you can't see that everything is linked together. It's all one great, slow dance," she says, holding her cupped palm before her face and slowly turning it back and forth. Her blouse is crisp and immaculate despite the wilting heat, her lipstick and eye shadow just so.

"Ah, nature," Juan Flores says. "But what is nature? It is not a person. It does not think. It does not plan. Surely we can agree on that. What can it be, then, but the personification of the blind forces that shape evolution?"

"We can't begin to define Her," Jade says. "That's the point."

"But if you can't define your God," Juan Flores says, "how can you believe in her?"

Mariella only half-listens to the argument. Juan Flores should realize that there is no point in talking to people like Jade or Clarice Bushor. Their beliefs are derived from faith, not observation. They need no proof of the existence of Gaia because for them it is an irreducible fact that lies at the root of everything else. They find it easier to put their faith in their god than to open their eyes to the world, to realize that there is no omnipotent power to care for them and to forgive them, no personal salvation but that which you make for yourself. To realize that the world is, yes, so much stranger than human imagination. Why make things up when all around are wonders waiting to be unriddled?

There are no mysteries, Mariella thinks, only unrevealed truths. If people will only do a little work, will subject themselves to a little discipline, a little effort, then they too can understand, they too will be amazed not by mystery but by truth. But they don't. Science has built a vast edifice of thought that reaches out to the furthest ends of the Universe, all the way back in time to the first femtosecond of the Universe's creation, all the way forward to matter's final end in the dissolution of protons, a hundred billion years from now. A cathedral of thought built by the cooperation of hundreds of thousands of minds, the greatest achievement of humanity. But most will not even acknowledge it, much less try to understand it.

She still remembers the casual slights and sneers of certain pompous arts students at Cambridge. The moneyed as oblivious to their wealth as fish to water, interested only in maintaining the status quo, with braying upper-middle-class students their eager collaborators. Proud in their ignorance of science, yet scornful of those who were not interested in the minutia of Renaissance art, opera, or the intricacies of their social seasons. Mariella knows now that their scorn was based on fear. To them, scientists are useful but dangerous, and so must be kept in their place, like Morlocks in the engine room of the world. And most people take their cue from their leaders, believe that science is a conspiracy only the initiated few can understand, something to be feared. It is partly the fault of mediocre scientists, of course, who react to criticism like spoiled priests fearful of defrocking, but it is mostly the fault of those who in their ignorance set themselves as the legislators of science, and those, their prejudices set in stone, who have declared themselves to be its moral superiors.

Those like Clarice Bushor, who has returned to her original point, and is saying now that the project seems to be going nowhere and perhaps it is time to wind it up. Staring boldly at Mariella, trying to provoke a reaction.

Mariella says, "We won't know if it will succeed until it does."

Juan Flores says, "I may not agree with everything Señorita Bushor says, but I must admit that she does have a point. Perhaps there is no life in the sample you brought back. Or perhaps it is not possible to grow it in laboratory conditions, no matter how you rearrange them."

Mariella wonders if those are his own words, or if he is parroting Oscar Villegas. She says, "You should know that these things take time. Especially in the conditions here."

A mistake. She has pricked his pride. He says, "You are working in a well-founded laboratory, with assistants and the latest equipment. It is in fact better equipped than my own laboratories. But if you have any complaints, perhaps you could put them in writing. I will be sure to deal with them at once."

"Exactly," Clarice Bushor says. "We've put a lot of money into supporting this scientific mumbo-jumbo, and there's been no return. And the longer the project goes on, the greater the danger that it'll be discovered."

"This isn't magic," Mariella says, feeling heat rise in her face. "This is science. It takes time. Yes, I have good equipment, and yes, I have assistants, but I have only two—three if you count Ellen here—and I had to train them before we began work. Go do a little historical research. See how long it took to discover the structure of DNA, or isolate penicillin. Then come back to me."

"Well gosh," Clarice Bushor says, with an air of sweet disingenuousness. "It isn't as if we're asking you to do anything that complicated, Mariella. Just grow up some bugs, that's all. We know the Chinese managed it, and you have told us that you could do it too, and that's why we helped you. Forgive us for being a little impatient with your excuses."

"It's because you can't see the difficulties that it isn't worth trying to explain them to you."

Clarice Bushor leans forward, her pale face seeming to float above the flickering shadows of the candlelit table. She says, "Perhaps you have another agenda. Perhaps you are working on something else, something you're hiding from us."

Mariella stands, pushing against the arms of her chair. Pain nips at the joints of her spine. For a moment the plane of the table, with its freight of plates and wineglasses and dancing candle flames, seems to tilt away from her. She has not yet fully recovered from her long stay in microgravity. She says, "I won't dignify that with a reply. Excuse me. I have work to do."

She is in the habit of going back to the lab last thing at night. Standing by the incubators and glove boxes, not thinking about anything in particular, breathing in the familiar odors of warm plastic and hypochlorite, the faint tang of methanol and the yeasty must of nutrient concentrate, allowing them to calm her. Numbers slowly scroll upward on the monitors that display conditions inside the Mars Jars. Green lights blink on the control panels of the benchtop incubators. The autoclave ticks as it cools after the final run of the day. It is pleasant to stand there in the quiet half-dark, as a mother might fondly watch her children sleep in their nursery beds, letting thoughts flow as they will.

One evening, she came into the laboratory and found the lights on, Clarice Bushor turning from one of the Mars Jars as bold as you please. The woman had somehow gotten past the security lock. She is sly and clever, not to be underestimated. Mariella bawled her out, telling her that she had endangered weeks of work by breaking into the lab, her anger sprung from fear that the woman could have been planning to sabotage the experiments or even to make good her threat of destroying the Chi. There is no trust between them, and now it was clear that both Oscar Villegas and the greens want immediate success or an end to the work.

Mariella stands in the half-dark for a long time, and at last something on one of the monitors snags her attention: a minute change in the partial pressure of carbon dioxide inside one of the Mars Jars she set up a couple of weeks ago. She sawed cubes from the rocks she had collected from the hillside, sterilized them in the autoclave, put them in two Mars Jars. A jumble of red and brown and black dice under an atmosphere of carbon dioxide and nitrogen, water vapor at saturation, a trickle flow of hydrogen, temperature just above freezing. A wild shot, a diversion from the slow, tedious, painstaking variations in experimental conditions. Done without really thinking about what she was thinking. She inoculated one of the jars with a drop of Martian water and hooked them up to detectors and left them. She hadn't expected anything to come of it, but now it's clear that something is using up the carbon dioxide in the inoculated jar.

She stifles her excitement and methodically scrolls back through the records, telling herself that it is probably nothing, a leak or an unexpected chemical reaction causing a disequilibrium so subtle she has failed to notice it before now. She graphs the fall of carbon dioxide partial pressure against time and discovers that it is increasing exponentially, doubling and then doubling again. A period of just over an hour in fact, which is impressively fast. There are plenty of bacteria that can divide every hour if given a rich and easily usable energy source like glucose, but the Chi—if it is the Chi and not a contaminant—is growing just as quickly using a thin trace of hydrogen as an energy source to fix carbon dioxide into organic compounds. A tough organism all right, as long as it has porous rock in which to grow.

Mariella goes for a walk in the warm dusk, absentmindedly brushing mosquitoes from her bare arms, absentmindedly greeting one of the soldiers standing watch among the cottonwoods by the river.

As she walks back uphill, passing between dense stands of tobacco plants, a voice behind her says, "It's alive, isn't it?"

Mariella's heart leaps in her throat. She turns and tells Clarice Bushor, "I told you not to go into the laboratory without my permission."

The woman is a sketchy shadow in the darkness. Her floral perfume is strong in the warm air. She says, "You've succeeded in growing the Chi. Oh, don't bother to deny it—I've known for some time. Jade really is a very versatile boy. He reprogrammed the computer that monitors the Mars Jars. We had the real readings all along, while you saw only faked data. Until tonight."

Mariella steps right up to the woman. "You admit to fucking around with my experiments? Hiding data from me?"

"And from your two lab assistants. Really, it was for your own good."

"For my own good. Right. What exactly is it that you want?"

"I'm here to help you," Clarice Bushor says calmly. "And you do need my help. What do you think Oscar Villegas will do to you, once he has live samples of the Chi?"

"I don't know if I've succeeded in growing anything yet, much less whether or not it's the Chi."

"You need to get to the States as quickly as possible. I have been making the necessary arrangements."

"Do you really think I'll help you pursue your fantasy of smearing the biotech companies?"

"All you have to do is tell the truth."

"That's all you ask."

"Nothing more."

"I'll have to sequence whatever's growing in the jar before I can decide what to do."

"No. Absolutely not. It will take too long. Juan Flores will tell Oscar Villegas what you are doing, and Oscar Villegas may decide that it can be sequenced without your help."

"Some other test then. I need to know that *something*'s alive in that jar before I agree to anything."

"Something is fixing carbon dioxide."

"I can't rule out a chemical reaction. I should have set up proper controls, but this was such a wild shot. . . ."

"This is what you must do," Clarice Bushor says. "You must think of some excuse to visit the university in Jalapa. Tomorrow, or the day after that. My people are already in position, and they cannot wait too long."

"Even if I am allowed to go, I'll still be under heavy guard."

"Leave that to my people."

"No guns. I don't want to find myself in the middle of a fire-fight."

"I can't promise that."

"Then how will you get me away from Captain Vierra and his soldiers?"

"The people I have hired are experts."

"You *hired*? Christ. And are these people to be trusted?"

"They are all ex-Marines, veterans of the Border Wars. They have no love of the Mexican government."

"Christ. To be frank, I'm not sure if I'm ready to trust my life to a bunch of mercenaries."

"What choice do you have?"

"Ellen must come too."

"For someone who has no bargaining position, Dr. Anders, you have a lot of requests."

"She comes with me," Mariella says firmly. "She has strong links with the radical green movement and she'll be horribly vulnerable if she is left behind. If she doesn't come then neither do I, and you know that without my validation, the Chi is just a bit of exotic biology."

"I will have to ask my people about Dr. Esterhauzy. Meanwhile, you will think of a suitable reason to visit the university," Clarice Bushor says, and walks away into the darkness.

Mariella returns to the lab, places the Mars Jar inside a glove box, floods the box with simulated Martian atmosphere, and carefully extracts a single cube of rock. She puts it on the stage of the glove box's binocular microscope and examines each of its six faces under 25X magnification. Perhaps the fugitive flashes of something darkly reflective deep in the pores of the basalt are the Chi; perhaps they are no more than flakes of quartz.

After some thought, Mariella drops the cube of rock into a Pyrex tube and seals the tube with a rubber cap. Takes out a vial of sodium carbonate labeled with radioactive carbon-14, does a back-of-the-envelope calculation and, using acid to flush carbon dioxide out of the carbonate, injects enough to enrich the atmosphere in the tube by 0.01 percent. She repeats the procedure with a rock taken from the uninoculated control jar and then, as a precaution, takes tiny chips from several of the other inoculated cubes of rock, inserts them into a glass straw under carbon dioxide, and seals the straw by melting its ends in a Bunsen burner flame. Then she goes to bed and for the first time since she has returned to Earth sleeps deeply and easily, and does not remember her dreams.

The next day, Mariella extracts both the inoculated and control cubes of rock with seventy percent ethanol, and runs a couple of aliquots of the extracts through the station's liquid scintillation counter. There is radioactivity only in the extract from the inoculated jar, which confirms that something is definitely fixing carbon dioxide. She prints out the results, finds Juan Flores, and tells him what she has done.

"I wondered what you were doing, working so very late last night," Juan Flores says.

"You're the first to know. But the work isn't finished. Martian soil chemistry gave false positive results in the very first tests for life carried out by the Viking landers more than fifty years ago, and I'm not satisfied with a single piece of evidence. Extraordinary claims require extraordinary proof. If I have succeeded in growing the Chi, it will have fixed some of the radioactive carbon dioxide into organic molecules. A GCMS machine can separate out the organics and identify which, if any, have radioactive label in them. I believe that the nearest is in the university at Jalapa. I need to go there."

Juan Flores studies the printout, then says, "But surely that will not prove it is the Chi. We should begin to sequence it immediately."

The glass straw that contains the chips of rock is inside a foam-packed stainless-steel tube the size of an old-fashioned fountain pen, in the pocket of her jeans. Mariella can feel the steel tube against her hip. She says, "We have to do this step by step, Juan. This will be the subject of intense scrutiny, most of it hostile. The evidence must be impeccable. Once I have the GCMS results, and if they confirm the presence of radioactively labeled organic molecules, then DNA sequencing will be the very next step. Will you instruct Captain Vierra to arrange an escort?"

The Secret of Life   329

The Secret of Life   329

Secret of Life

"It is not be necessary for you to go. I can take the samples myself."

"No. The chain of evidence must be unbroken if I am to have any credibility. Besides, these are my experiments, Juan. Don't I have the right to be the first to know the results?"

Juan Flores nods solemnly. "Of course you do. I would not take that away from you. But before I speak with Captain Vierra, I must talk to Oscar Villegas."

"I'd rather be sure of my case," Mariella says.

"He will find out anyway," Juan Flores says. "I will be candid. He is beginning to lose patience with your project. These results could not have come at a better time. I think we should section one of your rocks for electron microscopy."

"As soon as I get confirmation from the GCMS results," Mariella says, "there's no end of work to be done."

"Yes. Yes, of course. I will talk with Captain Vierra at once."

It takes a day to arrange things. Hector Vierra insists on speaking with Oscar Villegas, kicking the decision up the chain of command so that his ass won't be toast if things go wrong. Clarice Bushor is furious that Mariella has revealed so much, but Mariella tells her that it is the only way she could get out.

"Juan is a scientist, and I appealed to his sense of scientific honor. He understood at once my need to see the results come through; I don't expect you to. I hope your people are in place."

"They will be."

"And Ellen Esterhauzy will come with me."

"They know what to do," Clarice Bushor says.

They go in convoy: Mariella, Ellen Esterhauzy, Clarice Bushor and Jade riding in the jeep driven by Hector Vierra, two jeeps full of soldiers in front, two more behind. At the university, Mariella and the others are greeted by the head of the biochemistry department, Professor Martínez, a fat, effusive man in an old-fashioned three-piece suit. He ushers them into his untidy office, which overlooks a square where, beneath the shade of pepper trees, students sit and read or talk. Slogans are painted on the white concrete walkways and on the walls of the buildings. The next generation carrying the revolution forward. A secretary serves coffee and tiny, piercingly sweet cookies. Clarice Bushor and Jade leave theirs untouched. Mariella hands over the extracts and politely declines Professor Martínez's offer of a tour of the department, saying that she has a little business in town. The professor accepts this white lie, tells her that the results will be ready in three hours, and adds that it is an honor to help her.

They eat at a restaurant recommended by Juan Flores, its shady terrace one floor above a busy commercial street. The soldiers wait outside, smoking as they lean against their jeeps and watch girls go by. Jade and Clarice Bushor insist on inspecting the restaurant's kitchen, and then refuse to eat anything. Jade lopes off down the street, coming back a few minutes later with a carton of nopal juice he has bought from a street vendor. Mariella knows that he will have contacted the mercenaries, and feels her stomach tighten another notch. She drinks two bottles of Carta Blanca beer, smokes a cigarette she has bummed off Hector Vierra and stubs it in her untouched food, while Ellen Esterhauzy and Captain Vierra demolish their plates of huevos con queso. Ellen Esterhauzy knows about the plan, but shows no nerves.

"You have nothing to fear," Hector Vierra tells Mariella. "My men look after you and your friends."

"I know," Mariella says. "But this is a big day for me. I guess that stage fright has robbed me of my appetite."

As they walk downstairs to the jeep, Clarice Bushor tells Mariella, quietly, "We're going to do it at the university. It's too open here."

"Are you sure?"

"Absolutely."

Hector Vierra drives fast, using his horn judiciously as he weaves through the traffic at the head of the little convoy. The beer and the cigarette have made Mariella a little dizzy, and it might not be Glory Dunn she sees as they slowly drive through swarms of students heading toward classes after the end of the siesta, it might be another tall, African-American woman in a business suit who leans against a black car and smiles at her as the jeep goes past.

"Stop," Mariella tells Hector Vierra. "Stop the jeep."

But the black car has gone by the time the jeep has pulled over. Hector Vierra turns in his seat to look at Mariella, and she says, "I thought I saw someone I know."

"Yes? Who exactly? A colleague perhaps?"

"An American," Mariella says, and adds, feeling foolish, "A Secret Service agent."

"You are certain?"

"Not absolutely, no."

"What does this Secret Service agent look like?"

Mariella describes Glory Dunn. Hector Vierra picks up his military-issue cell phone. It has a black metal casing and is the size of a shoe. He talks in rapid Spanish to someone in one of the other jeeps, then tells Mariella, "Some of my men will search for this woman. The rest will escort us back to the farm."

"This is bullshit," Clarice Bushor says, giving Mariella a furious stare. She is sitting in the back between Mariella and Ellen Esterhauzy, with Jade riding shotgun beside Hector Vierra. She tells Hector Vierra, "Dr. Anders must have those results."

"Maybe tomorrow," Hector Vierra says, putting the jeep in gear, "when we have checked things out."

Clarice Bushor says, "We don't even know what she saw. Your soldiers—"

"I do not take risks," Hector Vierra says flatly, and pulls the jeep around. Two others follow close behind.

They are driving around the elevated ring road toward the Limanes exit when Jade stirs and says, "You're going to do something for me, Captain Vierra."

Everyone in the jeep looks at him. He holds his silver automatic in his lap, pointing it at Hector Vierra, who smiles and says quietly, "What is this bullshit?"

For a moment, Mariella thinks that it is happening after all, but then Clarice Bushor says, "What do you think you're doing?"

"Shut up," Jade tells her, his voice flat and hard. "Captain Vierra, you're a prisoner of the U.S. Marines. Cooperate, and no one will be harmed. We're here to take Dr. Anders home."

Clarice Bushor says, "Don't be a fool," and in a smooth motion Jade lifts his gun and shoots her in the chest, the noise very loud, the jeep swerving for a moment, a car in the lane next to it sounding its horn. Clarice Bushor slumps against Ellen Esterhauzy, blood all over the front of her white blouse. The air is filled with the smell of blood and cordite.

Ellen Esterhauzy puts her fingers to the side of Clarice Bushor's neck to check her pulse, and Jade says calmly, "Is she dead?"

Ellen Esterhauzy gives him a frosty stare, then closes the woman's eyes with thumb and forefinger.

Jade says, "I'm not sorry for it. She pissed me off from the start."

Hector Vierra says calmly, "You will not get far, my friend."

"That's Lieutenant Cooley to you, Captain. I don't think your air force will be able to scramble in time to intercept us, and I know your radar can't track our stealth helicopters. How about you give me your gun? It's clipped under the dash, right?"

Hector Vierra hands it over, butt first.

Jade drops it out of the window and says, "Now you need to lose your escort, Captain Vierra. Think you can manage that?"

The big cell phone rings. Jade tells Hector Vierra, "Don't answer that. Just do as I say and no one else will be hurt." He is pointing his pistol at Hector Vierra again, sitting sideways with his back against the jeep's door.

Mariella says, "You waited until I grew it." Her ears are ringing. There are little spots of blood on her face and shirt.

"We were pretty sure you had nothing except the Chinese virus, but hey, you came up with the goods after all. Agent Dunn got the results of your tests while you were eating, and my people moved on the research center."

"This is bullshit," Hector Vierra says.

"All those nights I was pretending to goof off, Captain Vierra, your men never did notice what I was doing to your perimeter security and your communications. My people took out that microwave dish, took out your soldiers, walked right in and got what Dr. Anders grew up in those jars. You want to know if I'm lying, you call up the center right now."

"Fuck you," Hector Vierra says.

Jade leans forward and lifts the cell phone from the dash and switches it off in mid-ring. "Whatever. You'll do what I want anyway. I need you to lose your escort. Do it now, or I'll shoot the two women."

"You need Dr. Anders alive," Hector Vierra says.

"It would be nice, but it isn't important. There's an exit ramp coming up on the far side. Take it. Do as I ask, or I shoot Dr. Esterhauzy, and then I shoot Dr. Anders."

Hector Vierra does it. He drives straight over the center divider, swerves around an oncoming truck, which thunders past with its air-horn blaring, then stamps on the brake and wrenches the steering wheel hard over. The jeep swings right around, almost stalls, recovers. Then they are driving down the ramp the wrong way, past cars flashing their headlights and sounding their horns, down onto the surface street that runs parallel to the elevated ring road.

"You drive pretty good," Jade says.

"Not really," Hector Vierra says, and lets go of the steering wheel. Jade fires one shot as the jeep runs into a support pillar with a tremendous bang. Mariella is thrown forward and hits her forehead on the headrest of Jade's seat and is thrown back. At the same moment airbags blossom out of the steering wheel and dash. As Jade struggles to free his gun, Hector Vierra rears up and, with the small revolver that slips down his sleeve into the palm of his hand, shoots Jade under the chin and shoots him again, the hair on top of Jade's head lifting and a sleet of bloody matter spraying the windshield.

Hector Vierra uses a knife to cut the airbag that pins him, and tries the jeep's motor. It grinds over but doesn't catch. "Fuck it," he says, and sits back. "The bastard shot me in the stomach. We will sit here until my men find me."

Ellen Esterhauzy jumps out of the jeep, opens the driver's door. Hector Vierra protests, but she tells him not to be stupid and rips open his shirt. The man grunts as she probes his bloody abdomen. She tells him to lean forward so that she can look for an exit wound. People are watching from the other side of the street, and she shouts at them in Spanish, asking for help, but no one moves. She turns back and tells the captain, "You're lucky. It went right through."

"I know. I felt it. It's okay. We wait here, for my men."

"Get my bag," Ellen Esterhauzy tells Mariella, who is glad to climb out into the sunlight, away from the two bodies.

Hector Vierra's face is very pale. Droplets of sweat stand out all over it. He says, "I fought two years in the revolution, and now I am shot by a kid."

"He was not what he seemed," Ellen Esterhauzy says. She tapes cotton wadding over his wounds, then looks up at Mariella and says, "You have a piece of what you grew?"

"Yes."

"That is good," Ellen says, and stabs Hector Vierra in the neck with a disposable Syrette. The man looks at her with suddenly unfocused eyes. She lifts his gun away and kicks it under the jeep, drops two Syrettes in his lap. "These are morphine, Captain. Jab another in your thigh if the pain gets bad. If you get prompt treatment you will not die."

"Wait," Hector Vierra says dazedly. "Wait. Stay here."

"Thanks for your help," Mariella says, stepping backward slowly, hoping he does not think to reach for Jade's gun.

Hector Vierra tries to get out of the jeep, but can't figure out how to operate the catch of his safety belt. A sleek black helicopter passes high overhead with a muffled fluttering, like sheets shaken in the wind. As it makes a wide turn and starts to come back, Mariella and Ellen Esterhauzy chase each other into the shadows beneath the elevated ring road.

Monterrey, Mexico:
September 14–15, 2028

They catch a bus into town and try to buy railway tickets at the station, but the clerk tells them that there are no more trains that day. A military exercise has closed the railway line.

Outside, the sky is flushed with evening. Two silver jets rip overhead. Ellen Esterhauzy takes a firm grip on Mariella's wrist and marches her down the row of taxis outside the station. They climb into the car at the head of the line, a battered Lexus with the shine long gone from its silver paintwork. The driver is reading a newspaper spread on the hood. He slowly folds it and with the same slow deliberation, as if ineffably weary of his duty, gets behind the wheel and lays a hairy arm across the back of the passenger seat and asks them where they want to go.

"Monterrey," Ellen Esterhauzy tells him.

"Not possible," the driver says.

"Of course it is possible. I am a doctor and it is a matter of urgency that this poor woman gets there today." Ellen Esterhauzy holds out a fan of creased notes; after a moment, the driver takes them and folds them into his shirt pocket. "Twice that when we arrive," she says.

The driver pulls away from the curb, blatting his horn to clear a way through the crowded plaza. He glances in the rearview mirror and says, "I'm an honest man, doctor. You have already paid enough."

"That's all right. She is an American. She can afford it."

A 3D postcard of Christ is taped over the hole in the dash that once housed a CD player. Christ reaching into his chest and pulling out his bloody heart in a laminated flicker, His long-lashed eyes brimming with stoical pity. Suffering for the world. Mariella suddenly understands the iconography of Barbara Lopez's cockpit decorations. Dedicating her life to Mars so that others might follow.

A little while later, watching the sun set over an open field, she asks Ellen Esterhauzy, "How many were killed at the research farm, do you think?"

"It is best not to think of it."

"They were all killed, Ellen. All killed and what do we do now?"

"We do what we are already doing. You must trust me, Mariella."

"Of course. After all, you didn't take me to Clarice Bushor's people. But where are we going?"

"To meet some friends of mine."

They spend the night in a Motel-6 at the edge of Monterrey. The parking spaces are full of battered Japanese pickups and American jeeps and 4×4s. People come and go at all hours. Headlights stroke the cheap curtains of the room, turning their weave into a translucent grid. It is very hot. A dog barks monotonously, as if barking is the only idea it has left. Mariella lies awake, fragments of the day replaying in her head while Ellen Esterhauzy snores beside her on the double bed like a ship steadily making its way toward morning.

While they are eating breakfast in a café across the road from the motel, there's an item on the TV news about army action against smugglers in the region of Limanes. Ellen Esterhauzy tells Mariella, "They're covering it up. Only a few years ago this government would have made enormous capital from incidents like this. Now they use them to get better trade terms from the North. Listen, Oscar Villegas will have lost prestige over this, and will no longer be able to protect you. We must not contact any of the people who set you up in the research center. We cannot trust them to be on your side."

"I wouldn't go to them anyway." Mariella feels very tired, but her nerves are better. She has drunk three cups of coffee and eaten most of her heuvos rancheros, has recovered enough to be fascinated by the sight of two men who are casually smoking as they sit at the counter. She says, "Without a lab there's not much I can do except give myself up and try to make as much fuss as possible at my trial."

"Would there really be a trial?"

"You're right. Of course there wouldn't be a trial. They'd want to keep me away from the media. It's all about control, isn't it? Controlling information. Making sure that when it flows it generates money. I need to get out of the country, Ellen." Mariella beats a tattoo on the table with her coffee spoon. She says, "I need to get back to the States. Perhaps I can do something there."

"You have a sample of this Chi. You can make use of it?"

"Yes."

"I have many favors owed. Enough, I think, to get you back to the States. After that it will be up to you."

"There are some people I know. . . ."

"First we must get you to a safe place."

There is a pharmacy next to the café. They make some purchases and go back to the motel room. Mariella uses instant tanning cream to darken her face and hands, lets Ellen dye her hair jet black and braid it into a tight pigtail.

"We should have bought you tinted contact lenses," Ellen says, "but as long as you wear the sunglasses you will pass I think."

They check out of the motel and catch a bus into the center of town, passing an abandoned steelworks where refugees from the countryside have made a tent town among piles of rubble that were once blast furnaces, and buy new clothes in a big department store that anchors a decrepit shopping mall. Jeans and a plaid shirt for Ellen, a flowery print dress for Mariella. They pack their old clothes in plastic bags and abandon them at the curb. Ellen makes a phone call in a piss-stinking booth at the bus station. And then they sit at a wrought-iron table in an outdoor café on the other side of the big square until their ride arrives.

Laredo Free Zone:
September 16–18, 2028

She is an old acquaintance of Ellen Esterhauzy's, an aging punk who calls herself Darlajane B. It is her stage name from the 1980s, when she was lead singer in an East German thrash metal group, The Thalidomide Babies. After four years of playing the semilegal clubs of East Berlin, everyone in the group was thrown in prison by the Stasi, but they were let out a year later, just in time to celebrate the fall of the Berlin Wall. Several times, while Mariella and Ellen are waiting for the cross-border ride to fall into place, Darlajane B. plays them a fuzzy video clip of herself dancing on top of the Wall, her T-shirt and Lycra cycle shorts soaked by the play of firehoses.

For a year, Darlajane B. made a good living selling pieces of the Wall to gullible American and Japanese dealers ("So much we sold, a wall they could have built from Stockholm to Beijing"), along with Stasi torture equipment, Soviet military uniforms, badges and weapons. She gave that up after someone with a high-velocity rifle took a shot at her as she was crossing a St. Petersburg bridge, minutes after leaving a hotel room where a couple of Ukrainians had offered her two kilos of red mercury.

With finely tuned empathy for the zeitgeist of the end of the twentieth century, Darlajane B. migrated to Prague. She set up the city's first coin-operated laundry, lost the profits from that in a beer-exporting venture, then moved to Amsterdam and got into the marijuana-growing business, which was where, just after the turn of the millennium, she learned about gene hacking. She took up with a young Englishman, Alex Sharkey, and a few years later, when the European Parliament passed its comprehensive ban on gene engineering, she and Alex moved to Colombia.

"Where the real money is," Darlajane B. says. "The cartels pay gene hackers well. Someone like you, Mariella, a lot of money you could make very quickly. Much more than from this Martian nonsense. The cartels are heavily into somatic re-engineering right now, rewinding telomeres, modifying lymphocytes as plaque-busters, or to target cells with replication errors. They want to live forever. I fix you up in a good research facility. Take only a fifty-percent cut of your first year's salary."

Darlajane B. looking coolly at Mariella, her face unreadable. She is reclining in a nest of cushions, a little old lady encased in black leather, a five-centimeter crest of glue-stiffened hair spikes running from front to back of her otherwise shaven skull, her eyes kohled, her fingers knobby with rings.

Mariella plays it light and says, "I'm almost tempted."

"But of course you are not. I got bored working for those people and so would you. But that's where Alex is. And he doesn't even care for money, just the work. He makes smart drugs, viruses tailored to target specific parts of the client's brain, very intense, very clean. So new they are not yet illegal."

Darlajane B. lives on the top floor of an abandoned clothes factory at the edge of the old industrial district of the border town of Laredo. Steel I-beams coated in thick red paint hold up girders that crisscross beneath the high ceiling, where pigeons come and go with a flutter of wings. The windows are covered with layers of aluminum foil; lights burn day and night. The air is thick with the smell of joss sticks and dope. Display mannequins with the features of turn-of-the-century movie stars, tricked out to look like aliens or horribly mutilated corpses, line one wall like the cast of an old-fashioned disaster movie. Persian rugs and cushions and battered beanbag chairs make a nest at one end of the room; benches laden with computer equipment stretch along the other. Some of the equipment is very old—bulky cathode ray monitors, alphanumeric keyboards, disk drives of every kind. A helical staircase climbs up to the flat roof, with its clattering wind turbines, satellite dish, and cluster of plastic greenhouses in which huge marijuana plants grow in hydroponic racks.

"Here, I am a tourist," Darlajane B. says. "That is what it says on the visa of my real passport. Which is not, you understand, the one I use. I am just visiting. I do not stay in one place too long. But here there are birds, and I like birds."

Mariella thinks that she means the pigeons that roost in the girders, spattering everything with pigeon shit.

Laredo is one of the border towns that was seized by the U.S. government at the beginning of the Mexican revolution, to protect the investments of American companies. Although under martial law and patrolled by U.S. Army troops with ineffectual U.N. observers riding along, it is a lawless, desperate place, full of displaced people working in the maquiladoras for slave wages, tourists who come to sample the bars and whorehouses and gambling palaces, and counterrevolutionary groups fostered by the United States and the multinationals.

Mariella doesn't ask what Darlajane B. does, but it involves people coming and going at all hours. Some stay for no longer than it takes to complete their transactions; others lounge around all day. One of the visitors is a jovial police sergeant who collects what Darlajane B. calls her insurance premium. He tells Mariella that people are looking for her, but she is safe here because the ordinary police have a long-term investment in Darlajane B.

Darlajane B.'s place is, among other things, a way station for radical greens fleeing south from the United States. That is how she came to know Ellen Esterhauzy. It takes her several days to set up the route north, and to contact all the people on the list Mariella gives her.

"Although your Martians we could sequence right here," Darlajane B. says. "No need to go north when I know so many good gene hackers."

"I think they might have the wrong idea about what I want to do."

"You are right not to trust them, of course. And in any case, you cannot afford their services, I think."

"No, and they'd probably sell me out to the Secret Service or the CIA or whoever else is trying to find me."

"They do not try very hard to find you, or I would not let you stay here."

"Because they already have what I have."

Ellen Esterhauzy says, "American soldiers stole the rest of the Chi when they raided the agricultural research center."

Darlajane B. thinks about that, her ring-heavy fingers clicking as she rubs them over each other. She says, "Then to continue with this you are either very stupid or very clever. I suppose you have some plan, but I do not see how it will make you any money."

"That's not the point. This is about a principle."

Later, Ellen Esterhauzy says to Mariella, "But this isn't just about a principle, is it? It is about your pride also."

"What do you mean?"

They are sitting at the edge of the roof of the factory, drinking beer and watching the sun go down over the smokestacks and cracking towers of the chemical plant to the west. Windmill generators spin and hum in the hot breeze. The air smells of burnt rubber.

Ellen Esterhauzy takes a large swallow of beer and rolls the bottle back and forth between her strong, square fingers. She's uncomfortable, and won't look Mariella in the eye. She says, "This is a race. A race to learn about this Chi. And you can't bear to be out of it."

Someone else once accused Mariella of this. Anchee Ye—the memory clutches at her heart. She says, "It will revolutionize biotechnology, Ellen. Change everything. To begin with, it is the key to finding a way of destroying the slicks."

Ellen Esterhauzy says, "So you want to save the world."

"Many things are destroying the world, or changing it in ways we don't like. But yes, the slicks are very dangerous. They have to be destroyed, or at least brought under control, and so far no one seems to have made much progress."

"You are mostly a good woman, I think," Ellen Esterhauzy says, "but you are not a modest one. You hold most people in contempt because they do not understand what you do, the power that is yours to command. The question you must ask yourself is this. What do you want to do with that power?"

"It isn't power, Ellen. It's knowledge."

"But knowledge is power. It is not neutral. You are like a magician in a fable, Mariella. You release things into the world and expect others to deal with them. But you are of this world too. You have responsibility for what you discover. I think you know this, but you have not yet faced up to it."

"Faced up to it? I've nearly *died* because of it!"

Mariella's anger is sudden and strong. She throws her half-empty bottle of beer over the edge of the roof, throws it hard and jumps up before it has smashed on the rubble below. She walks about, blood beating in her head.

She says, "I could have refused to go to Mars. I could have come back on the *Beagle*, handed over all of the Chi to Cytex, or stayed on Mars and helped NASA. But I didn't. I didn't because I knew both of those options were wrong. I don't take responsibility? That's exactly what I've done. For the Chi, for Anchee, for the whole fucking world. . . ."

She's amazed to find that she's crying. "Fuck," she says loudly, and knuckles her eyes.

Ellen Esterhauzy says, "My fairy godfather, as he calls himself, makes the arrangements you asked for, but if you cannot face up to your responsibility perhaps you should not go."

"You don't think I can?"

"What you must do is hard. You must be sure you can bear it. You have other choices I think. Go to one of the multinational cartels, or to the Chinese. Or give yourself up. Or you can throw away what you have, and let the world go on without it. Darlajane B. has an autoclave. Put your fragment of the Chi in there, boil it dry, and you will be free."

"At this point, I don't think I have much choice about what to do. I have to do what I came here to do."

"Yes. Yes, I think now I see the quality that helped you solve the Firstborn Crisis."

"What is this, some kind of test?"

"Sit down," Ellen says calmly. "There is more beer. We'll watch the sun set together. It is courtesy of Dow Chemical, but isn't it magnificent?"

A woman arrives an hour later. She cuts Mariella's hair short in front and gives it a fashionable asymmetric wave in the back, then gives her a manicure and a pedicure.

"We make you look a billion dollars," Darlajane B. says.

"I look like an asshole," Mariella says, turning this way and that as she stands in front of a tall, cracked mirror.

"Yes, a corporate asshole. You go back in style."

"Who am I supposed to be?"

"A sex tourist." Darlajane B. cackles. "For the bullfighting and the cockfighting you come across the border into the Laredo free zone. Find yourself a nice matador in those tight pants maybe, with a big scar. Go to the bars where the girlyboys hang out. Do drugs, fuck yourself senseless, exploit the hell out of poor oppressed Mexican people, go back to your white-bread job in Dallas or Houston or wherever. Thousands like you do it every day."

"Can't I be a normal tourist?"

"A woman traveling on your own? No. You could be on a business trip, but then you would fly, and that is harder. Airports are full of security. The border is difficult, but it is not impossible. No, don't argue. Already it is in motion. Two days ago, Leviticus brought into the country someone who looks like you, and borrowed her passport. You leave in her place."

Leviticus is Darlajane B.'s current lover, a plump, young, well-manicured Nigerian with glossy black skin and cheeks nicked with tribal scars.

"On my own? Ellen, you aren't coming?"

"I am not licensed to practice in the United States. Besides, you are almost recovered."

"And you have your work."

"I will always have my work."

"I've been thinking about our conversation."

"I can't tell you what to do. You must find that out for yourself."

"Enough," Darlajane B. says. "In each other's arms you will be weeping. Some dope we will smoke and you, Mariella, will tell me about Mars. And then we will get you ready."

Mariella leaves two hours later, in a limousine driven by Leviticus. He has exchanged his usual tight shorts and embroidered shirt for a chauffeur's gray suit. Mariella is wearing dark glasses and a yellow business suit drenched in someone else's perfume. Her right eye is blackened, and her lower lip is split and puffy, fabricated evidence of a hard and dirty liaison. The local anesthetic Ellen Esterhauzy applied before she clinically inflicted the damage is beginning to wear off. The glass straw, with its chips of Chi-infected basalt, is concealed in an antique Cross fountain pen Darlajane B. dug out of a drawer full of water-swollen notebooks.

Mariella looks back through the rear window at her friend and Darlajane B., standing in the shadow of the clothes factory among the burnt-out shells of abandoned cars. Then Leviticus turns the corner of the block, and they are gone.

The Invisible Country:
September 18–22, 2028

A kilometer from the border, Leviticus reaches back, hands Mariella a bottle of tequila, and tells her to take a couple of good swigs. The booths and barriers of the border crossing are brightly lit. Armed guards stand on platforms above rows of idling cars and

RVs and trucks. A huge spotlit Stars and Stripes is raised against the night. One soldier leads an eager sniffer dog around the limousine; another shines a flashlight in the trunk. Mariella pushes the bridge of her dark glasses down her nose when the immigration officer checks her passport. The woman looks impassively at her bruised eye, hands back the passport and tells Leviticus to move on.

They drive thirty kilometers up I-35, and then Leviticus pulls over and tells Mariella to get out.

"What do you mean?"

"This is where you'll be picked up."

"By whom?"

Out-Englishing Leviticus's impeccable Oxford accent.

"Well, I have to say that I don't know and I don't care to know."

"I don't mean to be pushy, Leviticus, but Ellen and Darlajane B. didn't really explain what would happen."

"That's the way my woman works. You don't worry, someone will be along."

"Are you going back to Darlajane B.?"

"I have a job to do, but you don't want to know about that. Good luck, Dr. Anders."

Mariella stands alone in the warm dark, watching the limo's taillights disappear. It is a country road turnoff, a stand of cedars at one end and a row of mailboxes nailed to posts at the other. Traffic zips by in a glare of headlights, continually lifting swirls of dust.

Mariella sits on dry fragrant needles in the shadows under the cedars, taking little nips from the tequila bottle. She has thrown away the dark glasses, wishes she could strip off the rest of her disguise. She is tired and her eye is sore and she tastes blood on her lip. She is back in the United States, but she does not feel that she has returned home. She has lost everything but the flecks of life hidden in the pen in the pocket of her borrowed jacket— and there is no guarantee that the Chi is still alive, much less that she will be able to sequence it and understand its secrets.

But this is no longer about the Chi. It is about a principle that has been greatly diminished by companies that want to preserve commercial confidentiality, and governments desperate to limit the availability of biotechnology. It is about the kind of covert science that killed her husband.

Forrest left for Central America at the beginning of October, part of a team that was going into the field to investigate what no one was yet calling the Firstborn Crisis. He and Mariella kept in touch by email. He wrote vivid and funny and touching descriptions of the places his team visited. He confided to her that something fundamental had happened to the ratio of male/female births. The sex ratio of embryos at conception was as expected, roughly 1:1, but more than half of all male fetuses spontaneously aborted at two months. It was almost certainly a sex-linked factor.

Maybe a virus or a prion, maybe something else. We're pretty certain it isn't another thalidomide situation. Medication is pretty haphazard here because biomedical companies dump all kinds of weird stuff on the aid charities: you should see the wild pharmacopoeias of most of the doctors. There's no consistency in treatment of even basic infections. We're taking a lot of blood samples and cervical smears and sending them north for analysis, but it will be a while before the results are in. Right now I'm concentrating on mapping loci of infection—if infection is what it is—and could use your keen analytical mind. And of course the other comforts you bring.

That was the last message Mariella received from her husband. The next day, a superstorm smashed through Central America and dumped torrential rain across the region. More than fifty thousand people were killed in floods and mudslides. Three million were made homeless, with thousands dying each day from the resulting famine and waves of disease.

And Forrest was murdered by bandits who burst into the clinic where he was working, killed everyone but a native Indian orderly, took all the medical supplies and all the food, set fire to the clinic, and vanished. None of the bandits were ever caught; the authorities were too overwhelmed by the storm's destruction.

The U.S. embassy returned Forrest's body in a closed casket. It had been badly burnt in the fire, and had lain for more than a week in the ruins before it had been found. Mariella went through the routines of teaching and writing up her work on the primeval genetic code with a curious detachment, as if she was observing herself. She did not weep at the funeral, although most of Forrest's family wept. She refused the sympathy of friends. She worked.

Two weeks later, she was walking down Melrose Avenue. It was a hot sunny Sunday morning. She was looking in shop windows, thinking about getting a coffee at the bookshop at the end of the block, when she saw a display of Hawaiian shirts. *Forrest would like one of those*, she thought, and then she was crying and could not stop crying, because Forrest was dead and wanted nothing of her any more.

The next day, she made six phone calls and formally tendered her resignation from her tenured position at UCLA. Four weeks later, she left the little house and its garden in the care of a pair of postdocs and flew to Brookhaven, to start work with the hastily assembled Human Fertility Task Force. Where she helped find the cure for the so-called Moses virus. Where she first encountered Penn Brown, where she met most of the people who would form the Second Synthesis group. Where she learned the temptations and costs of fame.

No one knew when or where the genetic disaster that became known as the Firstborn Crisis had first started. By the time enough was known about it to be able to frame the question, most of the principals were dead and the damage had been done.

Mariella started work with the Human Fertility Task Force a few weeks after the funeral of her husband. The task force was badly named, it turned out, because it was not fertility that was the problem, but survival of male fetuses. To begin with, the project was poorly funded, working out of cramped offices and laboratories on one floor of an ancient brick building with an inadequate electrical supply and dangerously leaky containment facilities. But in a year, as the nature of the crisis became apparent, the number of people working for it doubled and then doubled again, and funding became open-ended.

It was as if a war was being fought, although the weapons used were microscopic, and the battlefield lay within human germ-line cells, in the jungles of coiled and supercoiled DNA. For Mariella, it was the most exciting period of her scientific career. Surrounded by her peers, she was devoting her every waking moment to a difficult and important problem. She was doing what she did best, and slowly learned to be happy again.

She was allowed to join the task force's primary research group because, in collaboration with Forrest, she had published a key paper describing an algorithm that predicted the wildfire cascade by which certain infectious diseases suddenly blossomed, and because the screening process being used to find the causative agent was based on the method she had developed in her salad days in David Davies's laboratory to speed up the tedious process of DNA analysis. When she arrived at Brookhaven, screening of maternal and fetal blood and amniotic fluid samples was already in progress, but so far nothing consistently unusual had turned up. Mariella helped organize a more intensive search, using material from spontaneously aborted fetuses and sperm samples.

The plague of spontaneous abortions was clearly sex-linked, since it was expressed only in male fetuses. All male mammals are more vulnerable than females to sex-linked genetic defects because they have only single copies of certain genes; the genetic complement of females includes two X chromosomes, but in males a solitary X chromosome is partnered with a truncated Y chromosome. The genetic lottery predicted that, if the cause was linked to the X chromosome, some female fetuses would be unlucky enough to have parents who both carried copies of the defective gene. However, statistical studies showed that, with the exception of those twinned with a male sibling, there was no increase in spontaneous abortion of female fetuses. Thus, the dominant hypothesis that emerged from the initial study was that the causative factor must be associated with the Y chromosome. Something had infected a high proportion of men and linked itself to the Y chromosomes of their germ-line cells; it was not expressed in the generation infected by the disease, but in the male fetuses which received a copy of the defective Y chromosome.

The obvious assumption was that it was an RNA virus able to insert itself into the DNA of Y chromosomes by reverse transcription. And although sequencing and cross-matching of hundreds of thousands of samples failed to provide any evidence of extraneous DNA sequences in the Y chromosomes of spermatocytes of men from the areas affected by the plague, this hypothesis still held sway a year later, simply because no one had put forward a workable alternative. By now, the epidemiologists had refined their surveys and were charting the spread of spontaneous male abortions north and south of Central America, with outbreaks in Spain, Portugal, the United States, and other countries in which travel to and from Central America was common. In that year, live male births in the affected regions had been reduced by more than ninety percent; the next year, the plague had spread across most of the world, and less than twenty percent of all live births were male.

The media called it the Plague of the Firstborn Crisis. Although inaccurate, the label stuck. There was apocalyptic talk of the end of the human race. Half the countries in Central America were being torn apart by civil war. Women who gave birth to live sons were murdered by jealous neighbors. Charlatans advertised ineffective herbal "cures," or treatments with magnets, lasers or colored lights guaranteed to purify sperm.

And then Mariella had the idea that led to the discovery of the Moses virus.

Afterward, neither she nor anyone in her research group could quite remember what led to the breakthrough. The idea had been raised several times in seminars, but it had failed to stick in anyone's mind until one Sunday in June 2011, when Mariella suddenly realized that the Y chromosome might be only part of the puzzle, the activator rather than the operator.

Men uniquely contribute a Y chromosome to their sons and mothers uniquely contribute an X chromosome, but a second path of inheritance proceeds through the maternal line. Every cell in the human body contains mitochondria, semiautonomous powerhouses that transform sugars into useful chemical energy. In humans, mitochondria are inherited via the cytoplasm of the egg; the mitochondria of the spermatozoon are discarded at fertilization. Thus, descent down the maternal line can be traced backward through slight variations in the sequence of very highly conserved mitochondrial DNA; indeed, these variations can be used to measure population affiliations and to reconstruct patterns of human migration through bloodlines that converge upon the mistily glimpsed woman who was the ancestor of every modern human.

Like all good ideas, Mariella's insight was completely obvious in hindsight. She contacted several members of her group. They all immediately realized that she had remembered something which had been discussed and discarded before, for maternal mitochondrial DNA is inherited by sons and daughters alike, but they also realized that involvement of the Y chromosome could be a crucial factor.

They met in the laboratory and worked all night, not on sperm or spermatocytes or fetal material, but on eggs taken from the ovaries of some of the first women to have been affected. It was painstaking work, but the techniques were routine. The minute amounts of mitochondrial DNA in each egg were extracted, purified, and amplified into millions of copies, and these were sequenced and compared with library sequences of human mDNA.

The inserted sequence of viral DNA stood out at once.

It was half past seven in the morning. Someone rushed out to a liquor store in a nearby mini-mall and brought back a bottle of domestic champagne; against lab regulations they cracked it open and toasted their discovery. They christened it the Moses virus, and composed a brief which they presented to the entire research group that afternoon.

Once the problem had been given a name and a cellular location, the vast machinery of medical biochemistry could be brought to bear upon it. The Moses virus sequence turned out to be already known, a component of something called Colombian flu. Like the common cold, it was spread by sneezes and skin contact; its only apparent symptoms were a brief fever, a scratchy throat and sniffles as the virus made millions of copies of itself. But like a multiple warhead, the DNA virus that caused these minor symptoms contained a sequence coding for manufacture of a separate RNA virus. The RNA virus spread through the body and entered mitochondrial DNA by reverse transcription, and there it lay dormant. In somatic cells it did nothing else, but in ova it became active if the egg was fertilized by a spermatozoon that possessed a Y chromosome. At around the seventh week after fertilization, when the cortex of the indifferent gonad of the embryo began to regress in the first stage of testicular formation, transcription of the virus was activated in the mitochondria in every one of the embryo's cells, massively disrupting their function. The resulting cell death caused toxic shock in the placenta, and spontaneous abortion.

Many of the details of this process came later. What was quickly developed was an artificial gene which the World Health Organization tried to make available to every woman on the planet. Nothing could remove the Moses virus from the human gene pool, but inoculation with the MT54a gene effectively suppressed its transcription.

Mariella's insight was only the capstone of a long and arduous process, but it drew the attention of the press because of the widespread belief that scientific progress was entirely driven by individuals struck by flashes of inspiration. She was briefly the focus of the attention of the world's media. Desperate parents asked her to cure their children of inheritable syndromes that had not yet yielded to gene therapy. A movie company proposed to dramatize her life story and offered her a stupidly huge sum of money to act as a consultant. She turned it down, and luckily the project soon foundered in preproduction. A food company wanted her to endorse its products; a car company gave her a top-of-the-line model that she sold at once, donating the money to a medical charity. Hundreds of magazines and newspapers and journals wanted her to write or referee articles, or to join their editorial boards. She was asked to appear on TV programs, to attend conferences, to accept honorary degrees from more than a dozen universities. At the height of her torment, Mariella thought of the famously blunt form letter Francis Crick had devised after winning the Nobel Prize, with its checklist of things he was not prepared to do. And there was much talk of the Nobel Prize, but in the end the committee decided that it would be invidious to select only one of the many people who had been involved in the research program.

Slowly, Mariella's fame dwindled. She was briefly involved in the search for the origin of the Moses virus, but it came to nothing. There were rumors that it had escaped or had been released deliberately from one of the black biotech laboratories Central American drug barons had set up to develop new narcotics and opiates, or that it was a bioweapon released by accident, or that it was a blackmail attempt that had gone wrong, or that it had been designed by secret U.S. laboratories to destroy the black population, or by the Australians to destroy the Chinese, or by the Chinese to destroy Caucasians.

There was an inevitable backlash against biotechnology and science in general after the end of the Firstborn Crisis. The human genome was now permanently polluted by a virus that could only be cured by deliberate infection with a second virus. There was much wild and inflammatory talk about the dangers of scientific hubris. Governments all around the world cut back their science budgets; the member states of the European Community, long dominated by green politics, voted for a permanent ban on all genetically modified foodstuffs and medical treatments. As a result, Mariella's mother died needlessly before her time.

Mariella's father had died two years before the beginning of the Firstborn Crisis. He suffered a series of small strokes, and although his company's medical policy agreed to pay for restoration of the damaged portions of his brain with grafts of cultured stem cells, he was felled by a massive cerebral hemorrhage before the treatment began, and died in bad circumstances in a National Health Service hospital.

Mariella arrived from the airport on the evening before his death to find him in a bed in a small side ward in the intensive care unit. The beds were so close together that the oxygen cylinder feeding her father's respirator was pushed against the neighboring bed, whose elderly occupant was suffering from dementia and kept hammering at it because he believed he was at home and it was a burglar. Mariella's mother had been at her husband's side for more than twenty-four hours. Mariella persuaded her to get some rest in the patients' day lounge, on a tatty recliner with a broken mechanism; they had to turn it on its side to get at the lever.

Mariella's father died the next morning, amid the clatter of orderlies serving breakfast.

Mariella's mother had already suffered from thyroid cancer. Radioactive iodine treatment and surgery had destroyed the tumor, but a few months after the end of the Firstborn Crisis, the cancer returned, growing aggressively along the nerves of her shoulder and neck. An effective treatment was available in the United States, involving insertion of a plasmid into cultured white blood cells which, after they had been returned to the patient's bloodstream, enabled them to secrete a toxin upon contact with cancer cells. The treatment destroyed all but the most intractable and widespread tumors, but it was banned in Europe because it involved genetic engineering, and Mariella could not persuade her mother to make the trip to the States. "I don't want my genes muddled up at my time of life," she said. Mariella fantasized about smuggling out some of her mother's blood and returning with a culture of modified white blood cells, but it was no more than a fantasy. Her mother suffered a six-week course of radiation therapy, and died in the same hospital as her husband. Her mother's death broke the last tie Mariella had with Scotland, and the funeral was the last time she visited the country where she had been born.

Now, tired and half-drunk in the dark under the cedars in the turnoff by I-35, she thinks that all that she has is built on her dead.

Presently, a light appears a long way off in the desert scrub, and swings around toward her. It is a pickup truck with a big balloon of methane tethered in its loadbed, wallowing down the rutted unmade road like a ship in a choppy sea. Mariella stands, transfixed by its headlights. A door opens behind the glare and a woman says, "I'm your ride, honey."

Mariella stays overnight in a green community near San Roque Creek. Nuevo Llano del Rio, a cooperative named after an early Southern Californian experiment in socialism. Its people grow sugarcane and soy, organic vegetables and fruit. They have a solar farm and their own artesian well, which feeds a complex and efficient irrigation system, run their vehicles and machinery on methane or fuel alcohol distilled from sugarcane. Children are educated in a one-room schoolhouse. Lessons in the morning; labor in the workshops or the fields in the afternoon. The cooperative cobbles shoes, ships exotic fruit, makes custom-designed slates, prints books and pamphlets, launders clothes and cuts hair, codes and maintains hundreds of web sites, runs a touring theatrical company.

Mariella learns all this at the informal reception held to welcome her, a kind of cross between a late-night picnic and a town meeting. Long tables of food and kegs of beer and cider, children running among the knots of adults, a dance band playing Western Swing in a grove of walnut trees hung with lanterns. The next morning, most of the people are out in the fields or in the many small workshops by first light. Mariella eats bran flakes and a peach in the empty commissary, watched by the woman, Courtney Dowd, who drove her here last night. No coffee, only water or herbal tea. Mariella's hair has been cropped short and she wears brand new workboots, blue jeans and a blouse made from undyed hemp.

They drive west in another pickup truck. Courtney Dowd is in her sixties, her face tanned and lined, her long gray hair woven with ribbons into a fat pigtail. A Celtic knot tattoo on her shoulder, rings in her nose and ears. "Other places too," she tells Mariella. "I was a wild child in the nineties."

Mariella says, "I had to take mine out when I joined the Mars program."

"Those tight asses. Honey, you should have told me before we left. I would have found some nice pieces for you. I love the space program, but, shit, I hate the white-bread mentality of the people who run it. They should let us go. They want people to live there, we're the ones who could make it work. Pack us in rockets like that Bradbury story, let us loose on the land."

"Bradbury's Mars got filled up with hamburger stands. And the Martians died out."

"But people like us, we know how to do it right. I bet you'd go back in a New York minute."

Mariella thinks of Barbara Lopez. She says, "Perhaps I should never have left Mars."

"You've a job to do right here. This thing of yours, it really is as dangerous as you say? You weren't bullshitting us last night?"

"All knowledge is dangerous in the wrong hands," Mariella says. She feels a fraud, that people like Courtney Dowd are helping her for the wrong reasons. Not for the first time, she wishes she could see the world as they do, in the absolute terms of black and white, good and evil, that make decisions easy.

"I remember the anti-GM protests thirty years ago," Courtney Dowd says. "We lost the argument then, but we're not going to lose this time. Right now, you're the most famous scientist on the planet. That has to count for something."

"The most notorious, perhaps. Well, I certainly appreciate your help."

"A little excitement like this," Courtney Dowd says, "is just what I need. I thought I was going to end my days burning weeds in the cane fields."

They drive along I-10 for most of the day, through the high plains of west Texas. Courtney Dowd regales Mariella with scandalous stories from her New York days. Sunflowers are in bloom along the shoulders of the road; skinny cows the size of antelopes graze on threadbare grass in pastures that stretch into the distance. The two women glimpse one of the shepherd dogs, modified to be as intelligent as a chimpanzee and fiercer than a tiger, standing proud on a rock ridge against the sky. Courtney Dowd says that it looks as big as a bear.

Thunderstorms rumble along the wide horizon in the afternoon, and it is raining when they turn off the interstate at Odessa and drive north along a two-lane blacktop. Past half-abandoned towns, Sharbauer City and Andrews and Gains and Hobbs. The land raw under the dark sky, deep gullies cutting across bleak moorlike stretches of dead mesquite punctuated by nodding pumps left to rust after the last of the oil was pulled from the ground. Berms of bulldozed mud rise on either side of the road. The ecology has collapsed here, along the southern edge of the Llano Estacado, and the land is washing away.

And then they are climbing toward the Trans Pecos range, and leave the rain and the ruined land behind as they drive across rich farmland divided into big square fields of soy and corn, cotton and rape. Courtney Dowd tells Mariella that the water is drawn from artesian reservoirs two kilometers underground. A factory with gleaming steel chimneys vents white smoke on the horizon, rendering oils pressed from GM rape seed.

They stay the night at an organic fruit farm run by half a dozen women, none of them over thirty. A hundred acres of walnut and peach and apricot trees hemmed between two vast cotton fields. Small children chase each other through the rooms of the Carpenter Gothic house. Hand-dyed rugs on polished wooden floors, candles in wall sconces. The women have a small menagerie of GM pets; people have a habit of abandoning them beside the desert roads. Most are afflicted with metabolic disorders. An adult albino tiger the size of a labrador, pathetically tame and prone to epileptic fits. A very smart but highly neurotic pot-bellied pig. A half-bald pygmy mammoth the size of a Shetland pony, with a skin condition like psoriasis. As in Nuevo Llano del Rio, Mariella is questioned closely about what she found on Mars. She talks for hours with the women, at the big table in their basement kitchen, under a beam hung with copper pans and bunches of herbs. She is happy to talk about the Chi and what she intends to do with it. She is beginning to realize that Ellen Esterhauzy wanted her to learn a lesson on this journey.

The next day Mariella and Courtney Dowd drive north and west in a battered four-by-four borrowed from the women of the fruit farm. The desert reasserts itself after they cross the Pecos River. It is one of the last National Parks. A north wind bends dry, spindly ocotillo stalks. Nothing else grows more than waist-high. Mariella amuses Courtney Dowd by naming the plants. Prickly pear and mesquite, barrel cactus, hedgehog cactus. Devil's pincushion, catsclaw, sage. Greasewood, joint fir, creosote bush. A blooming, buzzing profusion of life. Yet even here patches of engineer grass are strangling the desert plants: the women of the fruit farm are campaigning against agribusinesses that want to introduce GM antelope and cattle into the park to "manage" the spread of the grasses, because the animals will almost certainly graze on the native plants too, until the area becomes worthless as a refuge and is turned into farmland.

PaulMcAuley

The road cuts through the Sacramento mountains, a river tumbling over boulders beside small meadows, the sun shining on vivid green pine and spruce trees that grow up the steep slopes on either side. Mariella reflects that after Mars she has become extraordinarily sensitized to the presence of running water — rain and rivers the unacknowledged miracles that drive Earth's biosphere.

They make a pitstop in the small, picture-perfect hamlet of Cloudcroft, at a little roadside café with checkered tablecloths and wildflowers in jelly jars. Courtney Dowd sucks down her Dr Pepper greedily; it is her first sugar hit in more than a year. Mariella pays the check from the slim roll of dollar bills that Darlajane B. gave her, and they drive on, the road descending through a narrow twisting gorge that suddenly opens up to display the wide desert of New Mexico, the gypsum dunes of White Sands glittering like the ice blink of the Martian polar cap at the horizon and the town of Alamogordo stretched along the highway.

And suddenly things go very wrong.

They drive through tract housing to the International Space Hall of Fame. Ancient one-stage rockets, their paint faded by desert sunlight, stand at the edge of a weedy parking lot, like primitive technological monoliths erected by the priesthood of the Cold War. The glass- and stone-clad cube of the museum is abandoned; space-age history is no longer a tourist draw. The lower parts of the museum and the dome of the observatory next to it are covered in graffiti; half the windows are patched with fiberboard.

Courtney Dowd tells Mariella that this is where she will pick up her next ride, but as soon as they climb out into the baking dry air an amplified voice barks out, ordering them to drop to their knees and clasp their hands behind their heads. The echo clatters off the patched, paint-spattered front of the museum. Mariella and Courtney Dowd look around wildly; the amplified voice repeats its instructions and the off side tires of the 4×4 explode.

"You're next, assholes!" the voice roars. "On your knees!"

The two women kneel on hot concrete. Half a dozen figures in black jeans and black T-shirts, masked with mirrored visors and armed with rifles, stand up around the perimeter of the parking lot. One of them has a bullhorn; another is speaking into a headset microphone.

"It wasn't me," Courtney Dowd says. Tears spill her wrinkled cheeks. "You have to believe that it wasn't me."

"Hush," Mariella says. "It's all right. It's all right."

Strangely, she feels a kind of relief. The worst has finally happened. Her enemies have caught up with her.

The men in black slowly walk toward the two kneeling women, rifles at the ready. There's a familiar clattering sound in the sky, and Mariella turns her head a fraction, sees a little Bell helicopter swooping in.

"It was quite simple," Cornish Brittany tells Mariella. "We thought you might be using the underground railroad to get back into the States, so we spread the word that there was a reward on your head. And someone in the chain gave you up." She turns her brittle smile on Courtney Dowd. "For all their talk of ideals, the greens are as human as the rest of us."

Now they have met in person, Mariella has had to revise her original estimate of the Cytex VP's age. The woman is easily seventy. It is evident in the taut mask of her face, the stringiness of the skin under her jaw, the grain of her muscles. She is wearing white, tasseled cowboy boots that add ten centimeters to her not-very-considerable height, white silk shorts and a matching bolero jacket over an orange T-shirt, and shades herself from the noon sun with a fringed parasol. Her skin is so pale the maps of her blue veins show through; her teased and waved blond hair looks as fragile as spun glass.

"It wasn't anyone I know," Courtney Dowd says. "I swear."

"Don't kid yourself," Cornish Brittany tells her. "Everyone has their price." She turns to the man who is carefully picking through Mariella's and Courtney Dowd's possessions, which have been spread out on the hood of the 4×4. "Haven't you found it yet?"

Mariella says, "Are we under arrest?"

"Oh, I don't think you want to involve the law, dear."

"I think I do. And I think I should talk with someone from NASA, too."

"You'll listen to our offer first," Cornish Brittany says. "Christ, at last."

The man is holding up the barrel of the antique Cross fountain pen. His visor blackly reflects the three women and the wide desert vista behind them.

"Be careful with that," Cornish Brittany tells him. "We don't want a Class Four on our hands."

Another man, wearing white plastic coveralls and elbow-length black gloves, uses forceps to withdraw the glass straw from its casing, sets it within a foam plastic block that fits inside a stainless steel thermos.

When the operation is complete, Cornish Brittany turns to Mariella and says, "You really did grow it."

"Really."

"That's my girl. I always had faith in you."

"If you let my friend go I'll tell you all about it."

Cornish Brittany's smile is no more than a brief tightening of her lips. "Oh, I think she must come with us. After all, I don't know what you told her."

She turns away when Mariella starts to protest, ordering the men to pack up and be fucking quick about it, one of the locals might think to call the cops. The helicopter's motor starts. Mariella and Courtney Dowd are manhandled into its hot cabin. Their wrists are cuffed to the frames of the bucket seats, harnesses are assembled around them, ear protectors are set on their heads.

"I'm sorry!" Mariella yells to Courtney Dowd, but the older woman simply shrugs, already stoically resigned to her fate.

Cornish Brittany climbs in beside the pilot, filling the cabin with her acrid perfume, and carefully fits a helmet over the spun confection of her hairdo. The ground drops away with shocking suddenness, the roofs and yards of the housing tract, then the highway and the white desert tilting a hundred meters below as the helicopter scuds westward. Mariella is settling into her seat, her bones full of the vibration of the helicopter's motor, when there's a flash in the talc-white dunes below. Sun on glass, she thinks, but then something strikes the roof of the cabin with a muffled bang. Brown foam spatters the top of the canopy and the subliminal flutter of the rotors slows. Stops.

With only the tail rotor working, the copter begins to spin

slowly and sedately, fluttering down toward the white dunes like a sycamore seed. Cornish Brittany is clutching the stainless steel thermos and shouting at the pilot, who bends tautly over his control stick and gains a measure of control, skimming the swell of one dune and trying and failing to clear the crest of the next. One of the helicopter's skis digs deep and with a tremendous shock the frail craft slews and topples, the tail rotor whipping up a storm of sand before it jams. Mariella falls against Courtney Dowd, wrenching her cuffed wrists, and sees through the scratched Perspex of the canopy figures scampering toward them out of the shimmering glare.

There are five of them, all ultra-rads, all young men. They are naked except for shorts and tool belts, covered everywhere in fine, dense black hair. Hard callused feet and hands with retractable claws like stout black thorns, mirrored contact lenses capping their pupils. The tips of their enlarged upper canines dent their lower lips and give them bad lisps. Cloned muscles have been grafted to their lengthened femurs. Carrying the three women, they run fast and far from the downed helicopter, the hub of its rotors cased in thick worms of hardened brown foam, its pilot, battered unconscious and still strapped in his seat, left to be found by his buddies.

Mariella is gripped in a fireman's carry by one of the ultra-rads. They run through the hot white glare of the gypsum dunes, long feet barely leaving a trace as they scamper across wide stretches of level hardpan dotted with dry bushes, thread between swell after swell of the dunes. At last, they scramble into the entrance of a narrow tunnel camouflaged by a huge creosote bush, urging Mariella and Courtney Dowd ahead of them, dragging Cornish Brittany behind.

Someone breaks open a handful of biolume tubes. The dim green light reveals a square cave lined with weathered gray wood: the bones of an ancient cabin dismantled and reassembled underground. The five boys sprawl on sandy boards and drink an enormous amount of water before they begin to explain themselves.

Their leader calls himself Devilboy. He says that the man who sold out Mariella told them what was going to happen at the rendezvous in the museum parking lot. They barely had time to organize the hit, using an antipersonnel micromissile tipped with a load of sticky foam, the kind used by police to immobilize rioters and small vehicles.

"Maybe he had a fit of conscience, but it won't save him," Devilboy says. "He took off with the down payment from our friend—" he nudges Cornish Brittany, who lies bound and gagged at his feet, and she glares at him—"but we'll find him."

Mariella says, "I'd rather you let him run."

"He's our problem," one of the others says. "We'll deal with his sorry ass." *Thorry ath.* "Count on it."

"We'll deal with your friend, too," another says, and they all snicker.

Cornish Brittany makes noises behind her gag.

"You silly fuckers could have killed us all," Courtney Dowd says.

"We've used the foam on park ranger jeeps half a dozen times," Devilboy says. "But I admit the 'copter was a first." He sets the stainless steel thermos on the sandy planks in front of Mariella, and adds, mashing every *s*, "I guess this is what it's all about."

"Do you know what's in there?"

"We have an idea." Devilboy grins. All his teeth are pointed. "You take it. Go on, don't look surprised."

Mariella says, "It's just that some of your friends were working for people who want this destroyed," and tells them the story of how a pack of ultra-rads snatched her from under the noses of FBI and Secret Service agents so that Clarice Bushor could talk with her.

The five young men howl appreciatively. Devilboy says, "If that was Tucson it could have been the Diamondbacks or the Red Coyotes."

"Or the Crazy Moon pack," someone else says, a rangy boy surely no more than fourteen. "They'd do something like that for the hell of it."

Devilboy nods. "Plenty of packs around Tucson, all with different affiliations. Lots of game there. The pickings are harder here, only the tough and crazy can survive. Don't worry, we're not going to sell you out. We're on your side."

Courtney Dowd is sort of hunched in one corner, her arms wrapped around herself. She says, "You don't have any side. You come in and raid our livestock when you feel like it, piss off the authorities so that they come down on hardworking people. You just look after yourselves."

"Well, that's true." Devilboy nudges the thermos with a foot, claws ticking steel. "I don't deny we're very interested in this. Even if it does only half of what we hear it does, it'll change the world, right? I mean really change it. We're changed, sure, but only at a somatic level, with surgery and gene therapy. This could help the gene hackers come up with a way to really change us, to evolve all kinds of different human beings."

"Maybe even deer people," one of the boys says, giving Courtney Dowd a hard stare. "They'd be fun to hunt, don't you think?"

"Shit, deer are more fun to hunt than people," Devilboy says. "This isn't about other people, it's about us." *It'th about uth.* "Changing us so we can really live off the land, so we don't have to go after sheep or cattle in bad times. Genetically modifying our germ cells, so our kids don't have to go get tweaked by some black lab, so they can live along with us in the wild places, in the wild way, as soon as they're born. Changing us so we become a new kind of human being."

Mariella and Courtney Dowd talk with the five ultra-rads through the afternoon and into the evening about this and other possibilities. The ultra-rads bolt handfuls of jackrabbit jerky, and cook up jerky with canned beans and brew coffee on a little camping stove for their two guests. They give Cornish Brittany only water, loosening her gag and pouring it into her mouth so that she splutters and snorts it from her nose, tightening the gag again, patting her on the head and telling her that she's a good old girl, she's going to be a lot of fun to chase.

"We don't need to hear her harsh words," Devilboy says, when Mariella suggests that he ease up on his prisoner.

"If you hurt her, you'll probably be in big trouble."

"Shit," Devilboy says amiably, "you think downing a 'copter

won't already have caused trouble? Don't worry about us. We're having more fun than we thought possible."

As the ultra-rads begin to settle down for the night, Mariella and Courtney Dowd go outside to pee. The black sky is thick with bright stars; starlight glimmers like frost on the white dunes. Fugitive rainfall or dew has formed a duricrust over the powdery gypsum, and the way it gives under Mariella's feet, creaking like new snow, reminds her at once of walking on Mars.

Courtney Dowd points at an orange glow at the horizon and says, "I think that might be Alamogordo."

"Those Cytex goons will still be looking for us. And the local police too, I shouldn't wonder."

"I know it. Don't worry, I'm not thinking of running away. This is almost fun."

"I think I've gotten you into a lot of trouble."

"Honey, I've been in trouble all my life."

The ultra-rads are up at dawn. Devilboy shakes out a sheet of e-paper and the others hunker down around him as he studies aerial views transmitted from a couple of balloon drones. In the year and a half Mariella has been away, someone has developed e-paper that can display color images. After a whispered conference, three of the ultra-rads go out to scout the land; an hour later, two come back and report everything is clear.

The ultra-rads haul Cornish Brittany outside. When Mariella and Courtney Dowd crawl out after them, the four young men are already ripping the woman's clothes with swipes of their claws, laughing and whooping as she staggers back and forth in their loose circle. Mariella barges in, pulls one of the boys away, gets between them and Cornish Brittany.

"It's not what you think," Devilboy says, showing all his pointed teeth.

"We're gonna let her go," the youngest says, and a third adds, "Let her find her own way back."

"You're making yourselves like her," Mariella says angrily, staring at Devilboy until he looks away.

Cornish Brittany, unbound but still gagged, is holding the tatters of her bolero jacket across her ripped T-shirt. "Fuck it,"

Mariella says, and works the gag out of the woman's mouth and tells her, "Just go."

Cornish Brittany stares at her for a moment, and then the youngest of the ultra-rads charges at her, whooping and flailing his arms, and she squeals and runs from him with a knock-kneed gait, floundering up the powdery white slope of a dune with the boy scampering alongside. When she disappears over the dune's crest, the boy stands against the sky and howls after her before turning around and running back to the others.

Devilboy says, "We wouldn't have done anything."

"She's too old," someone adds, grinning widely.

"Too tough."

"Too stinky."

"We would have killed her right off," Devilboy says, "if we were that way inclined."

Mariella says, "You've had your fun with her. Let it go."

The four ultra-rads guide Mariella and Courtney Dowd to the shoulder of the highway. It is more than two kilometers away, and Mariella finds it hard going. Her muscles are stiff from her uneasy sleep on the bare boards of the den, and her manacled wrists were badly bruised when the helicopter crashed. And even now she has still not entirely recovered from the effects of her long spell in microgravity.

There are two vehicles waiting on the shoulder, the 4×4 Courtney Dowd borrowed from the fruit farm women, and a battered Blazer with a gun rack and a candy green paint job. The fifth ultra-rad jumps out of the 4×4 as they approach, slaps palms with the others.

"Easy pickings," he says. *Eathy pickingth.* "I guess those fuckers didn't bother to tell the cops. There was but one guy guarding it, but they didn't bother to put any tracking devices on it. They even left the card in the ignition."

Courtney Dowd talks briefly with the driver of the Blazer and then hugs Mariella and wishes her good luck and drives off. Mariella shakes hands with the ultra-rads, their claws pricking her palms, and climbs into the Blazer. It is driven by a young man with skin the color of old oak. Beads and colored metal tags braided into his long black hair. He is half African-American, half Puerto Rican, it turns out. He calls himself the Elk.

"You don't worry now," he says. "We gonna get you back on your path."

"Cytex has a lot of resources."

"We know it. Quite a few tourists suddenly appeared yesterday evening, but they don't know the desert too well, and people have been telling them you're on the way north, east, south *and* west of here."

The Elk wears a sweat-stained black Stetson with a dried-out rattlesnake skin around the brim, a cut-off black T-shirt that shows off his heavily muscled tattooed arms, tight black jeans shiny with grease on the thighs, battered cowboy boots. The boots are made of pony skin, he tells Mariella, when he sees her looking at them. He is just her type, but his presumptive manner and the insolent way he studies her as he drives are something of a turnoff.

Mariella says, "Where are we going?"

"Just down the road a ways to begin with. Your friend told me where to go after that. You had some trouble, huh?"

"Just a little."

The Elk touches his eye, his lip. "Really?"

"That's just part of the ruse I used to get across the border."

"Those wild boys took care of things for you."

"Yes. Yes, they did."

"We get along with them," the Elk says, "although they're too crazy for some. But you don't need to worry now. We'll take good care of you. You're a part of the invisible country right now. The real U.S. of A., not the puppet show run by the federal government and big business."

They make a wide detour along desert roads to avoid Alamo-gordo, then cross the railroad and the highway and, trailing dust, rattle up a steep winding track into the high tree line.

Pueblo-style buildings are clustered beneath the low terrace of a cliff, adobe cubes stacked on top of each other like a tumbled pile of bricks. Solar panels gleam on every roof. The people here are survivalists who partly live off what they can hunt and gather, partly live off money they make taking corporate parties into the desert for bonding retreats. The women seem to do most of the work around the place, cooking, washing clothes in a big stone cistern, dressing an antelope skin stretched on a frame. Mangy dogs and naked children chase around underfoot. Men tinker with their motorbikes and dune buggies, or sit around drinking beer and shooting the breeze. It is the most untidy green community Mariella has ever seen, a cross between a Boy Scout camp and a Hell's Angels den.

The community is dominated by the man who greets Mariella when she steps down from the Blazer: John Pardoe, a sixty-year-old muscular giant dressed in black jeans and biker boots and a leather vest, his gray, greasy, elf-locked hair bushed around a red bandanna. A true alpha male who seems to be married to half the women. Silver and gold and bead and string necklaces are tangled on the gray pelt of his broad chest; a big skinning knife is sheathed at his belt. He founded the place ten years ago and runs it, he tells Mariella as she wolfs down a late breakfast of corn mash and deer sausage, by virtue of his immense strength of character—although silvery knife scars on his arms and chest suggest that he has beaten off a fair number of contenders.

Pardoe has one of his wives treat Mariella's bruised wrists and her minor cuts and abrasions, lets her sleep on his big bed under a cover stitched from coyote skins. When she wakes from muddled dreams, fuzzy-headed and dry-mouthed, it is evening. Pardoe's people have dug a barbecue pit and are roasting an antelope hunted down with bows and slingshots ("The Native American way," Pardoe explains, "so that its spirit and its strength will pass into you"). Many of his people are blooded, mostly a sixteenth or an eighth, and extremely proud of their heritage.

They build a big fire that night, sit around it and pass bottles of oily homemade mescal back and forth as they eat. Some of the men set up a drumming school, tirelessly hammering out polyphonic rhythms. Mariella surprises them by joining in for an hour or so, pounding away until her wrists hurt and her shoulders are sore and her palms are scraped raw from the hide drumhead.

But it feels good and she stays up later than she means to, sipping store-bought beer, eating antelope with mesquite-flavored barbecued corn and a porridge made of yucca root, and talking, mostly about changes in the weather and Pardoe's involuted theories about conspiracies between federal government and big business. Conspiracies to drive people off the land into cities, where, Pardoe says, they can be regulated by chips interacting with their nervous systems, subliminal messages inserted in TV and Musak, endless surveillance from CCTV and the Internet and geosynchronous police satellites, and now genes inserted by nasal spray or via proprietary aspirin to make everyone docile. Pardoe, who has read up on the slicks, gets excited after Mariella explains their potential to ruin ocean ecosystems and tip the global climate into a new equilibrium. He says that it is all part of the big picture.

"After they've ruined the seas and the atmosphere, everyone will be forced to live in cities. Domed cities or underground cities full of people eating their own recycled shit. That's the future they want. And of course they'll regulate who they'll allow in, and you can bet people like us will be left on the outside to die."

How he loves his theory. It is a huge meme that has eaten up his higher thought processes, a junkyard construction into which he wedges and hammers and jams new facts wherever he can, full of disregarded loose ends, impossible to contradict because any objection is part of the conspiracy and therefore valueless.

"Hell, John," someone says, "maybe we'll just build our own domes."

Pardoe chuckles. "Maybe so. But then all we'll have done is build our own prison cells, and the land will still be fucked forever. See, it's all about control. Destroy the land and you destroy freedom."

"Maybe we can move to Mars," someone else says, looking across the fire at Mariella. "You met the Old Woman of Mars, right?"

Everyone is interested in how Barbara Lopez lives, and Mariella is hard-pressed to answer their detailed questions. But then the conversation slowly drifts back to conspiracy theories. Mariella tries to convince them that government is as disorganized as any large human communal activity, with different factions pulling it in different directions and a huge bureaucracy acting as a mod-

erator; that any apparent conspiracy is really an accidental conflu-
ence of corruption, stupidity and cupidity.

"The problem is not that we know too little but that we know
too much," she says. "We have too many facts floating around, and
it's in our nature to try and connect them up, the way we join up
stars in the sky to make pictures of lions and bulls and bears.
Someone plants a rumor or gossip starts going around and those
act as kernels which attract unrelated facts, and pretty soon a story
grows like a snowflake growing around a dust grain."

But none of the men are convinced. Roswell, capital of the
UFO industry, is not far away, and fantasies of government control
are part of the community's social glue. At the heart of Pardoe's
theory is an imaginary but powerful common enemy, a personification of everything his people despise in mainstream culture, the
Other against which, lacking any properly thought-out philosophy,
his people define themselves. It is all very last millennium, Mariella thinks, but for once tempers her criticism and allows the
rambling, increasingly drunken discussion to find its own direction.

The Elk has a boyfriend, it turns out, a raggedy young white
guy with a long forked beard and a shaven head. It surprises Mariella: like most women, she's convinced that she is infallible at
detecting gay men. The Elk and his friend are among the first to
walk away from the group around the big fire, but Mariella stays,
taking sips of mescal as several bottles circle counterclockwise, not
realizing how drunk she is until she tries to stand.

Then she's somehow dancing in the dimming light of the fire
with a man about her age, a mechanic with broken fingernails and
skin grained with grease and oil, a chipped tooth in one corner of
his easy smile. Tattoos on his shoulders and arms and a whorl of
little knots of flesh on his back like braille under her fingertips:
scarification done with cactus needles, the man tells her. It is her
first fuck since the debacle with Jed. She is too drunk to come,
but it is slow and enjoyable and merges into a deep sleep.

She wakes late. Her partner for the night, Mook ("My real
name is Anthony, but there's no Anthonys in the desert except
saints, and I'm no saint. So call me Mook. Everyone does"), leads

her up steep steps carved in the rock face to a big hot tub in the shade of fragrant junipers, filled with salty water drawn from a deep artesian bore and warmed by solar energy.

John Pardoe is already wallowing there with two of his wives, and rears up like an elephant seal to greet Mariella. She allows herself to trust these people, sets down the thermos flask that contains the flecks of Martian life, and clambers into the tub. The hot water steams out her hangover; she lets Mook scrub her back. She soaks in the hot water for a long time, with birds singing all around and scraps of blue sky caught between the shaggy green tops of the juniper trees.

Pardoe bids her a formal farewell after a lunch of tacos filled with beans and cold antelope meat, and coffee as black as sump oil, boiled camp style in a galvanized bucket with a couple of egg whites thrown in to clear it. The patriarch winds a long loop of beads three times around her neck and pronounces what she supposes to be a Native American blessing. Just before she climbs into the Blazer with the Elk, Mook comes forward and shakes her hand with an awkward formality and tells her to watch out for herself.

Mariella and the Elk drive north for most of the day, along a winding road parallel to the old Santa Fe railroad. Its tracks, although buckled and unused for a decade, with a ragged mane of creosote bush growing in the clinker of the roadbed, gleam like clear water in the sunlight. The Sacramento Mountains to the east and the tawny Oscura Mountains to the west.

At noon they stop in a bar in a tiny community that is no more than three buttressed adobe shacks, a filling station-grocery store, and a handful of trailer homes in sandy lots set between the railroad and the highway. The bar is one of the oldest in the state, small and dim and cool, as windowless as a cave. The counter is polished mahogany with a footrail, the kind John Wayne might belly up to and ask for a bottle of red whiskey, and a hundred different kinds of liquor bottles are racked on the irregular shelving behind it. Antelope skulls are nailed to the walls; the ceiling is papered with bills from dozens of defunct currencies. While Mariella sips a Coke, the Elk drinks beer like ice water and talks with the bar's proprietor, a stooped old woman with a fall of white hair and a shrewd gaze. At last, he passes her a block of hash resin swathed in Saranwrap and says she can pay him when he swings by on the way back.

"She's a good old girl," he tells Mariella, as they drive off. "Been there like forever. Inherited that bar from her brother in sixty-three, and he had it from their father. Desert people are the best in the world. Keep nothing back, like the land. Everyone helps everyone else around here, because in the desert everyone needs help sooner or later."

"You grow dope up in the woods. I might have guessed."

"All kinds," the Elk says, not at all abashed. "John surely loves his drugs."

Silence for a couple of kilometers, the railroad floating by on the left, dry pasture strung with barbed wire on the right, and tree-clad mountains rising against the hot white sky. At last, the Elk says, "One day John'll get sick or some buck'll cut him bad. Then it'll end."

"What will you do?"

"Fuck, move on. What else is there? If there's any place to move on to. It's getting harder and harder as it is, and now you say these slicks might make the climate changes even worse. . . . Well, I'm glad to be helping you. We aren't as pious about the land as some greens, but this is where we live and we don't want to see it fucked up."

A couple of kilometers pass by in silence. Then the Elk says, "Those wild boys who get themselves changed? We leave some of our killings out for them. John says they're the new spirits of the land."

"You gave them the missile, didn't you?"

"They had a missile?"

"You know they did. The one that brought down the helicopter. They had balloon drones, too."

"Maybe I did hear something about a Fireant antipersonnel missile," the Elk says. Another kilometer passes, and he adds, "There's a ton of ordnance went missing after the Border Wars, and a lot of the people who've taken to living out here are veterans. You can pick up all kinds of stuff at the moots. You could get a missile like that in trade for an antelope hide, and since all the wolves and the mountain lions in these parts have been poisoned or shot by cattle ranchers, there are plenty of antelope and deer. And there are people who just like to give those wild boys stuff, kind of an insurance deal. After all, if someone wants to inconvenience some government snooper, it's no good one of us doing the deed because the feds know where to find us. But the wild-boy packs don't stay in one place more than a night."

"I'd just like to thank whoever gave them that missile, that's all."

"Goes without saying," the Elk says.

The road climbs a long rise in the land. All afternoon, thunderstorms flick whips of lightning in the far distance. Wind skirls up dust devils among the sage and tussocks of tough engineer grass. They turn west at I-40, then north again along I-25, anonymous in the heavy traffic (but Mariella can't help thinking that the cool, unsympathetic eye of a satellite might be tracking the Blazer), the lights of Albuquerque twinkling to the west in the growing dusk. They skirt the center of Santa Fe, moving in stop-go traffic along wide streets bright with the neon of sprawling motels and generic restaurants, and then in darkness take a country road across the Rio Grande and turn off this into a meadow where two Airstream trailers gleam in the moonlight like a pair of grounded spaceships.

"These people will take you on, so I guess this is where I'll leave you," the Elk says, and reaches over and shakes hands with Mariella. Clutching the thermos flask, she climbs down into warm, eucalyptus-scented air. The liquid sound of a river running off in the distance, the song of crickets. People step out of one of the trailers as the Elk noisily reverses the Blazer and drives off into the night.

Little Iva's Refuge for Rational Thought:
September 23–October 6, 2028

Mariella doesn't realize that the five old people are Shakers until the next morning, although she does wonder at the sleeping arrangements, the two men in one trailer and the three women and herself in the other. Wonders too at their reserved politeness and their gentle, old-fashioned way of calling each other brother or sister, although this custom is no stranger than many she has encountered in other green communities.

She wakes on a thin pad of foam to sun shining through the uncurtained curved rear window of the trailer, and the distant sound of frail voices raised in song. The other mattresses have been rolled up and put away; the trailer is as spartanly neat as a room in a capsule hotel.

Outside, she finds her five hosts standing in a circle in knee-high, sun-dappled grass. They all wear simple white shifts over loose white trousers. Hands joined, singing a simple, instantly familiar round.

When the true simplicity is gained
To bow and to bend we shall not be ashamed
'Till by turning and turning we come 'round right.

They are the last of their congregation. Sister Lia, Sister Katherine, Sister Heather. Brother Larry, Brother Newton. Sister Katherine is their leader, a tall graceful woman with a papery complexion and white hair pinned up under a sunhat. Brother Larry is the oldest, hunched like a turtle, his bald pate freckled with benign tumors.

They are all artists, but only Sister Katherine and Brother Newton are still working. Sister Katherine paints exquisitely realistic flowers in acrylic against vividly contrasting background washes;

Brother Newton uses a battery of miniaturized robots controlled by an ancient Macintosh computer to shape sand grains into flowing organic forms. His lifework, he says with a gap-toothed smile, can be held in the palm of a hand and dispersed with a breath.

They own a hundred acres of prime riverside land, and allow most of it to grow wild. They tend vegetable plots, weave their own clothes on a handloom, throw unglazed pots and plates on a foot-cranked wheel and bake them in a solar-powered kiln. They have honed self-sufficiency to a Zen-like minimalism, although they are troubled by the increasingly dry summers and increasingly severe winters, and are debating about selling their land and moving south. Fifteen years ago, they lost all of their shade trees in a drought that lasted three years; the Rio Grande dried up for the first time since records began. And then there were years in which snow lay two meters deep for three or four months, and they could walk down the frozen river to Santa Fe.

"But we've been discussing it for five years now," Sister Katherine tells Mariella, "and I expect the last of us will still be arguing with herself after she's buried the rest here."

They breakfast on water, fresh bread baked in the kiln in which they fire their pots, and honey from a dripping honeycomb taken from one of the wicker hives that stand here and there among young fruit trees, honey that is peppery and fierce, distillate of the desert's wild heart. Sitting on hand-turned stools at a table weathered silvery gray, in the menthol-scented shade of a eucalyptus tree, Sister Heather naming for Mariella the birds singing around them.

"Can you ride, dear?" Sister Katherine asks.

"Sure."

Remembering, with a sudden pang, Twink. It is almost two years since she rode her horse up the ridge above Oracle, filled with fierce exultation because she had been told she was going to Mars. Two years is a long time in the life of a horse. And Lily, who promised so fervently to take good care of Twink, is almost grown up now. Mariella has seen plenty of photos and video clips, of course, but it isn't the same. She could drive there in a day. But not yet, not yet.

Sister Katherine says, "We don't have an automobile, you see."

Brother Larry stirs and says, "Had one. A nice one, but it broke down."

"That was twelve years ago," Sister Katherine says.

"A nice little Daewoo pickup," Brother Larry says. He is eighty-five, a testament to the amount of change that can be packed into the span of a single human life. He was born in the middle of the Second World War and grew up in the false calm and prosperity of the Cold War, in one of the suburbs that were spreading out from the hearts of cities like colonies of mold. Ranch houses, Danish furniture, gasoline-powered automobiles big as boats and twinkling with chrome trim. Watching Buck Rogers on a Bakelite TV warm as an oven from the heat of its vacuum tubes. Cycling along sidewalks beginning to be buckled by the roots of young shade trees. He was the rhythm guitarist in a minor rock 'n' roll band that reached its apotheosis just before Woodstock, marched on the Pentagon with ten thousand others and tried to levitate it by the power of thought, married and held a low-grade job in state government in Sacramento for thirty years, saw computers get smaller and more powerful, TVs get larger and flatter, giving up on his big collection of LPs when he could no longer buy a stylus for his record player, replacing them with CDs. Retiring just after the turn of the millennium to become a snowbird, buying an RV and driving north in the summer, south in the winter. Making music again, selling it to fans of his old band—fans mostly as old as he was—over the Internet. And then, after his wife's death, and in the same year the death of a son and a grandchild in the Big One, getting religion.

Brother Larry says forcefully, "Red. It was red, as I recall. Slow as a June bug. We had to charge it for two days before it would go any distance. And they call it progress."

So on the last leg of her journey, Mariella and Brother Newton ride out together on a pair of small, docile painted ponies. Pioneer tufts of engineer grass are flashes of vivid green in the dry brush. The sky is a dome of perfect enameled blue, the air so clear that Mariella can see the snowy top of Wheeler Peak floating far off in the distance. A profound, timeless quiet broken only by the whir of insect song. They might be Spanish missionaries from two centuries past, riding out to bring God to the Hopi, except they must wear sunblock against the UV, and many of the native plants and animals are gone.

Mariella and Brother Newton talk very little, although when they stop to eat lunch she learns that he was a computer hacker in the eighties, was caught cloning mobile phones and tweaking commercial databases.

"I did ten years," he says, "which was a heavy sentence. But I was the first black hacker they'd ever brought to trial in Los Angeles, which has always been oppressive to people of color. Whites had it worse in prison because they were the minority, but it was a white man that helped me find God."

Newton volunteered to be a hospital orderly to escape the gangs in the main population, nursed prisoners dying of tuberculosis and AIDS. And befriended a multiple murderer with a thousand-year life sentence, a born-again Shaker who taught classes in divinity.

"Dead a long time ago, but I'll always remember him because he changed my life. I worked in a hospice when I was out on parole, and started hacking again—it was still in my blood. I would have been caught again, I think, and served at least another dime, but then there was the Firstborn Crisis, and I went south to help out with refugees from the civil wars and the superstorm. I first heard your name in a camp outside Caracas, that you had found this wonderful cure."

"I was just part of a team," Mariella says, but Brother Newton ignores this.

"And now a little bit of your thought lies in every woman on Earth," he says. "It must be humbling, I guess, to feel a little like God."

"Yes," she says. She's never thought of it like that before. "Yes, I suppose it is."

They ride for most of the day. Forty kilometers north, along the top of the Cañón Rio Grande toward Taos, although Mariella only realizes that she knows where she is going, that she has been there before, at the end of the journey.

The landscape has changed. The twisted yews that once lined the long approach road are gone, along with the yuccas and mesquites which were once scattered through the scrub. Gullies that notch the edge of the canyon have been deepened by flash floods and snowmelt. New sections of road have been patched in around them; the bridge that once arched above a narrow ravine where a stream ran over red rocks has vanished.

But there is the long, waist-high wall of casually piled stones, and the big gate with a rusted iron statue of the coyote trickster god on the left and a colored resin figure of Little Iva, with her thick-framed spectacles and her baggy jeans and her big-buttoned talking calculator, on the right.

Mariella's heart lifts up. She has been here before. It is Little Iva's Refuge for Rational Thought, the conference center where the scientists of the Second Synthesis group held their second and last meeting. It is part of the desert estate owned by Dolphus Pasternack, the man who writes and draws the Little Iva cartoon strips, who famously said that he liked having scientists around because they were crazier than he was, so crazy that they were almost always right.

The conference center is at the end of a long trail that winds through a desert garden full of oddities. Here is a circle of half-buried Cadillacs, like a post-technological megalith; there a faux ruin of the Statue of Liberty—for some reason, Lady Liberty has the face of an ape. A huge self-assembling sculpture, all humps and flows and half-melted spires, like a cross between a coral reef and a Max Ernst painting; a flying saucer guarded by a silver robot, which turns and salutes Mariella and Brother Newton as they ride past. Statues of black ants as big as horses atop a vent as big as a Martian ash cone. Things like animated tin cans scuttle over stony sand between patches of nopal and cholla. A few birds circle in the blue sky; perhaps they are the hawks Dolphus Pasternack has had trained to snatch the balloon cams of journalists and net tourists.

The road passes through an archway in an artfully arranged fall of huge sandstone boulders, and there is the conference center, a half-sunken concrete blister painted ocher to match the land around it, a scattering of cabins beyond. The parking lot is full of vehicles, and people are coming up the road to meet the two riders. They start clapping and shouting as they get closer, and reach up to shake Mariella's hand as she goes by. Mariella laughs and slaps palms and returns high fives, full of amazement and joy. It has all come together. There is her research student, Tony May, grinning from ear to ear. There is Maury Richards. There is Bridget York, who defended her against Penn Brown's attack at the first meeting of the Second Synthesis group. There are Randy Gilmour and Verne Ward and Stan Stansky—and others she does not know, postdocs and grad students, everyone cheering and clapping as she and Brother Newton ride in jubilant procession up to the glass wall of the center's entrance.

The evening meal is held outside, an informal barbecue lit by flaring torches that do not much dim the starry sky. Mariella shows everyone the slivers of rock that contain the Chi, explains its history. It takes a while.

They break up after midnight, are awakened at dawn by a man blowing an off-key reveille on a battered trumpet. It is their host, Dolphus Pasternack. He is naked under a golden, unbelted dressing gown whose wings are sustained by the desert breeze. A very large and hairy man, with an untrimmed beard and a big belly, a burlesque cherub who blows exultant raspberries at the rising sun and vanishes before the delegates are up and about.

Over breakfast, Mariella and her colleagues begin to work out task assignments and a timetable for the research, an intense, detailed discussion that lasts through lunch. When it is done, Mariella takes Maury Richards aside and says, "I want to thank you for all your help. I hope it didn't get you into trouble."

Maury grins, adding more wrinkles to his wrinkled, weather-tanned face. He has tied his long white hair back with a black ribbon. "A canceled Navy grant. Petty stuff. You look good with black hair, Anders, even if it is kind of short."

"I hate it, but I think I'm going to need it a little while longer. Come on. Let's get to work."

The postdocs have already set up a dozen Mars Jars. Mariella cuts up the slivers of infected rock, using state-of-the-art micromanipulators in a glove box, and distributes them between the four separate research groups. Then it is a matter of waiting while the Chi grows, a few days spent as if this really was the symposium which is the cover for this clandestine research project.

There are talks in the morning, followed by lunch and a siesta, the postdocs playing volleyball on a sand court, their supervisors botanizing in the desert or sitting in the shade and talking. Then a keynote presentation in the evening, and a long, talkative supper. Mariella gives several seminars on her work on the Chi and the virus that the Chinese engineered to try to destroy it, and sits in the audience and listens to presentations by others on the ecological damage caused by the slicks and on DNA sequences published on the Internet, speculative papers on possible selective agents against the slicks, and on what is known about the chemical agents both the Chinese and American governments have used, either with little success or with massive collateral damage to the ecosystems they were trying to protect.

In all this time, they see nothing of their host except for the ragged reveille he blows each dawn. Pasternack's house is several kilometers away, sunken into the rimrock of the canyon, a bunkerlike retreat for the man who has defined and dissected the postmillennial neuroses of the nation.

The three men and two women who look after the catering and maintenance of the conference center are all of the same Native American family and refuse to talk about their boss. Other workers patrol the perimeter and tend the thousands of hectares of the desert ranch, but do not come near the center. At last, Mariella writes a note to thank Pasternack for all he has done and gives it to the woman in charge of the front desk. Early the next morning, she's awakened by a muffled thumping; when she investigates, she finds a piece of paper nailed to the door of her cabin like one of Luther's doctrines.

It is a cartoon. As Little Iva contemplates a horde of big-eyed grays advancing from their flying saucer, her pocket calculator comments tartly, "I don't know why you're so afraid. They're much more like you than I am."

That day, Verne Ward gives what he calls his personal summary of the aims of the meeting. He is the oldest of the Second

Synthesis group and has mostly given up research for administration, but he is an accomplished essayist, wrote what is considered to be the definitive book on the new approach advocated by the group, and is widely respected, even by his enemies. He is a tall, thin Yankee with a prominent Adam's apple and a long, solemn face, and he habitually wears a stump preacher's shapeless black suit.

"What we're doing here isn't important because it's new," he tells the meeting. "We know that the Chinese have already sequenced most, if not all, of the Martian genome, and we must guess that by now the government and Cytex have done the same. What is important is that the government has tried to prevent unaffiliated scientists doing similar research on the slicks—it has put a major area of biology off-limits. It is not the first instance of government interference in scientific research, of course. There have been so many parallels made these past few days between the Chi and the atomic research program in the mid-twentieth century that I'm embarrassed to bring it up again. But it is important, so I will.

"The atomic age gave us mastery of the fundamental particles and forces that make up and drive the Universe. At the time, many commentators speculated that perhaps we were too immature as a species to hold such power, and that it would destroy us. And although we did indeed come close to the brink several times, so far we have survived. We are still coming to terms with that power, but perhaps we know ourselves better because of it.

"And now, in what everyone tells us is the century of biology, evolution is not only directed by selection acting on a population of slowly mutating genes over millions of years, but also by active intelligence. Of course, humans have selectively bred crops and domestic animals since the invention of agriculture, and in the case of dogs, if I might drop in a bit of research I once did, for at least one hundred fifty thousand years. But genetic modification allows us to change in a generation what would take millions of years to change by natural selection, or thousands of years by selective breeding. Perhaps we will destroy ourselves in the process. Perhaps we will destroy all life on Earth—or utterly transform it.

"And now we have access to the even greater power contained within a different branch of evolution, a branch which in the distant past has evolved the ability to genetically engineer its own self in response to changes in its immediate environment.

"The Chi is the nearest thing we have to an alien. And yet because it has the same genetic code, it must have arisen from the same universal ancestor as life on Earth. And that's at the root of the problem. Because life on Earth and life on Mars share the same genetic code, the Chi has been able to co-opt genes from terrestrial organisms, either by itself or with the help of genetic engineers—we do not yet know.

"What the Chi does not share is the same evolutionary history as life on Earth. Not only are the solutions to the problems imposed by Martian and terrestrial environments different, but Martian life and terrestrial life have existed in complete isolation from each other for between three and four billion years. But now these evolutionary paths have been mingled. The Chi was released into the Pacific Ocean after a silly bit of industrial espionage went wrong. It co-opted genes from plankton to help it survive, and produced what are commonly called the slicks. We've heard many presentations about the consequences of that, and we've heard plenty of speculation about the mechanisms behind the Chi's unique ability. We've had to use our imaginations until now because we have been denied the privilege of working on the Chi. Perhaps privilege is the wrong word, a weak word. For we have a right to intellectual freedom.

"Those who campaign against science, who believe that scientists are meddling in things best left alone, would like to prevent us from working in certain areas because the consequences of such research might destroy humanity or damage it forever. Some of us see these anti-science campaigns as Luddite, others as a necessary reminder that as human beings, scientists must make ethical decisions about their research. But those campaigners are as nothing compared to our own government, which has decided that it must completely control research into the biology of the Chi and its products. It has passed a bill limiting all research on the slicks to government-licensed laboratories—and I need not tell you that so far only one license has been granted. Nor has the government allowed access to material returned by the expedition of which Mariella was a part. Out of fear — perhaps. To assuage public opinion — perhaps. Because the unique abilities of the Chi could herald a new and immensely profitable age in biology — almost certainly. And I don't need to add to the conspiracy theories about government being in bed with a certain biotech company.

"Well, bad laws passed because of cupidity and stupidity are still laws. But there's no legal restriction on work on Martian material, and what we have now is an opportunity that we must not fail to grasp. What I'd like to throw out for your consideration is the question of what we should do with what we find. As scientists, we might think that sequencing the Chi's genome is sufficient unto itself. But we're also human beings, with all the moral responsibility that implies. We must also think about the power that knowledge about the Chi may give us."

In fact, there is very little discussion of anything but the immediate practical problems of sequencing the Chi's genome. Most people, especially the postdocs, think that Verne Ward's speech is well-meant but too airy. Research is research. It isn't the job of scientists to foresee the consequences of what they find — forecasting the technological applications of fundamental scientific discoveries is a task better suited to science-fiction writers than scientists. The problem is not what to do with DNA sequences from the Chi, but how to obtain them in the first place.

But Verne Ward's closing words strike a chord in Mariella, for they are eerily close to Ellen Esterhauzy's warning. She has plenty of time to think about them, and to plan her next move, once growth of the fragments of the Chi has provided enough material for the sequencing work.

Extracting, purifying and sequencing the Chi's DNA, processes run in parallel by four separate groups of researchers, takes only three days. In only three more, computer analysis has stitched the sequences into the correct order and determined the reading frames from which the codes for proteins are transcribed.

"We've already identified twenty-eight genes," Bridget York tells the group, on the morning of the seventh day. "All of them are closely similar to highly conserved genes in terrestrial organisms, which is only to be expected. No doubt they evolved very soon after life arose, certainly before the divergence of Martian and terrestrial evolution."

Verne Ward raises a hand. "Do we have a marker for that yet?"

"Before we can do that, we need to identify more genes and match minor differences against known terrestrial evolutionary clocks," Bridget York says.

Randy Gilmour turns in his front-row chair to address the others. "Preliminary estimations give a ballpark figure of around four billion years ago, plus or minus two percent. Which is in the right area, and I'm sure we can refine it further."

"I emphasize that these are very preliminary estimates," Bridget York says severely, "and shouldn't be trusted."

She has not changed much in fifteen years. Her hair is cut shorter and has mostly turned gray, her face is thinner and a little more lined, but she still wears extra-large T-shirts over brightly patterned leggings, and it is easy to see in her the gawky and obsessive teenager she had once been. A mixture of earnestness and defiance, her nerves worn just beneath the skin.

On the big smartboard behind her, the genetic sequence of the Chi is scrolling slowly upward, divided into triplet blocks of As, C's, G's and T's. An interesting sight, Mariella thinks, but not a terribly useful one. She has sat through the presentation with increasing impatience. She has already decided what to do, has already made the necessary calls on Dolphus Pasternack's encrypted phone line. In a few hours she will be out of here, no matter what the others think, but to pass the time she tries to concentrate on their results.

Like the slicks, the Chi is really one huge cell, its undivided cytoplasm ramifying through a tremendously complicated network of hyphae-like strands, its genes carried on thousands of tiny chromosomes that Bridget York has dubbed linear plasmids. It is living proof of the old Poole-Jeffares-Penny conjecture that the genome of the universal ancestor of life on Earth was organized like those of animals and plants rather than those of bacteria: genes strung on straight rather than circular chromosomes, sequences coding for proteins interrupted by introns coding for RNAs or for nothing at all—so-called junk DNA—the whole capped top and bottom with telomeres. The Chi is evolutionarily closer to animals than to bacteria: now Mariella realizes why the Chinese used as the basis for their infective agent a virus that infects mammalian cells.

The linear plasmids are very short, each containing no more than thirty or forty genes, and can be divided into almost a hundred closely related groups or families. Each family of linear plasmids contains variations on a set of closely associated genes, like sentences built from the same small vocabulary, but there are also rogue genes distributed randomly among all the families. The sequences of many genes are interrupted by introns coding for a huge variety of exotic RNAs; despite provocative questions from her audience, Bridget York refuses to speculate whether these contribute to the Chi's ability to appropriate genes from other organisms.

The distribution and duplication of the Chi's genome across hundreds of linear plasmids is clearly a solution to the Eigen limit. Any genome grows beyond its Eigen limit becomes dangerously unstable, because the number of copying errors introduced at each round of replication becomes unacceptably high, but the Chi's genome is a part-work rather than a single volume, and not only is each part small enough that the chance of replication error is very small, but dozens of copies of each linear plasmid are in close proximity to one another. Indeed, it is not even clear if the entire genome is present in the sample; the four research groups obtained slightly different sequences. Randy Gilmour, who supervised the computer analysis of the sequencing, concludes the presentation by suggesting that the Chi's complete genetic repertoire can be determined only by extracting every nanogram of DNA from its entire biomass.

This is all very well, and technically it is of tremendous interest, but Mariella thinks that her colleagues are so carried away with their success that they have forgotten that the sequencing is only part of their strategy. It has already been done by the Chinese, and almost certainly Cytex has done it too, using the samples stolen from the agricultural research center. There is no point debating details when something more fundamental is at stake.

Mariella notices that only Verne Ward keeps quiet during the discussion that follows the presentation. After the meeting breaks up for lunch, he comes over to the table where Mariella and Maury Richards are going over a calculation Tony May has made. He sits right down and says without preamble, "What are you going to do with this, Mariella?"

"Well, I don't think we can publish it just yet."

"But we can talk about it, I hope," Verne Ward says, and gestures to the other senior scientists, who bring their trays over and sit down around Mariella.

"Oh boy," Maury Richards says. "What is this? A delegation?"

"I should go," Tony May says. "You guys probably need to talk—"

"No," Mariella says. "You've done a nice bit of work, Tony, and I want my colleagues to hear about it."

"But first we should hear about what you want to do," Verne Ward says.

"There's no question about what we should do," Bridget York tells him. "We should deposit the finished sequence and the raw data in at least one of the databases as soon as possible. Stan can get it into Scripp's. Right, Stan?"

"No problem," Stan Stansky says cheerfully, around a mouthful of coleslaw. He is a large-framed man with a considerable belly stretching his short-sleeved shirt. The bill of a baseball cap advertising his own software company shades his sunburnt face. He says, "We could start it right now. Upload the sequence. Dump the raw data in a file. Put an announcement out on the web. It could be done in an hour."

"No," Mariella says. "No, not yet."

Stan Stansky shovels up more coleslaw. "But that's what you want, right? That's what all this is about." He washes down the coleslaw with a mouthful of Tang and burps and says, "Excuse me. Freedom of information. Making this available to anyone who wants to work on it or wants to use it to try and find a way of destroying the slicks."

"I'm sure that Cytex is already working on that," Bridget York says.

"Sure," Stan Stansky says, "but they don't have all the answers. The stuff absorbs viruses, and mutates too quickly to be contained by chemical sprays."

Mariella says impatiently, "You could fix zooplankton species so that they can eat the slicks. Or fish. Or even whales. But that's a trivial problem compared with making sure that the whole scientific community has access to the potential of the Chi."

"Screwing up Cytex's commercial advantage," Randy Gilmour says with a wide grin. He is a canny, combative Brooklynite who likes to give the impression that he has an inside edge. In his white silk suit and black silk shirt, a Panama hat shading his handsome, craggy face, he looks like a gangster who's visiting the desert to find out where the bodies are buried. He says, "Mariella's right. The important thing is to fuck over Cytex's exclusivity. Make sure they don't get a lock on this. If they do, then they'll never let it go, because it could be *such* a fundamental shift in the way we do genetic engineering. An organism that modifies its own genes? Anyone who has exclusive rights to that can name their price. And you can bet they'll price it out of reach of noncommercial researchers."

Verne Ward says, "The government would break any monopoly."

Randy Gilmour says, "Yeah, right."

"What about Bell and Microsoft?" Verne Ward says mildly. "And the Thornton Bill overturned human genome patents taken out by companies that did no more than blindly sequence stretches of DNA without defining the function of the genes. This is no different."

"Sure it is," Randy Gilmour says. "This time it'll be the government holding the patents and the licences. Or at least, the government will be in bed with the company which has been granted the patents."

"Well, I don't see what this has to do with the science," Bridget York says, sticking out her chin and looking around, as if daring anyone to take a shot at her.

"Maybe not," Maury Richards says at last, "but it has everything to do with Mariella."

Tony May says, "She wants to go home," and blushes at his presumption.

Mariella says, "Exactly. I'm still on the run. I want to end it."

"Surely this work does end it," Bridget York says. "I mean, isn't that the point?"

Maury Richards says to Mariella, "You should tell them about Tony's work."

Verne Ward says, "There will be endless legal debates about copyright and ownership. The samples were obtained on an expedition financed by NASA and Cytex. Where then does ownership lie? Certainly not with us."

Randy Gilmour says, "The question is, what do we do with what we've done?"

"Well, publish it," Bridget York says impatiently. "Or at least make it available. Why is this such a big deal? Am I missing something?"

"She's right," Stan Stansky says. "The Chinese aren't in a position to complain, because they broke the San Diego protocols. First by bringing the Chi back to Earth, and second, by genetically modifying it. We're pretty sure that Cytex will have sequenced it from the sample Mariella gave them, but so far they've been as secretive as the Chinese, and we all know that's because they were responsible for releasing the Chi into the Pacific Ocean. So let's get the data out right now."

"You're both missing the big picture," Maury Richards says. "Listen to Mariella, for Christ's sake. She knows more about this than any of us, and she's the one with her ass on the line."

Mariella says, amused by Maury Richards's presumption and touched by the sentiment behind it, "Well, the part about my ass on the line is right."

Bridget York tells Mariella, "What if you just give yourself up? The public has lost interest in the slicks. They think they are just another example of science out of control, like the loss of the ozone layer or the Firstborn Crisis. A fifteen-day wonder that doesn't directly affect them. And they've forgotten about you, too.

You were everywhere on the news when you took the Chinese spacecraft, but the media quickly moved on to something else. There was a blip when you came back, but nothing since, so I don't think NASA or the government are going to be too hard on you. They already have what they want. If a couple of their under-the-table deals are compromised, they can't squeal too loudly, or people would start asking questions. It isn't in their interest to stir this all up. There'll be a discreet congressional inquiry, maybe a slap on the wrist. Life will go on."

Mariella says, "You talked with someone, didn't you?"

Bridget York holds her gaze. "A friend of mine at the National Science Foundation had a word with Mae Thornton. To check out the lie of the land."

"That's interesting, because I talked with Senator Thornton just this morning. And with Al Paley, too. They said more or less what you did, Bridget. And I told them I'd meet with them and hand over our results."

Randy Gilmour whistles sharply. Verne Ward says, "I'm not sure if I'm happy with this, Mariella. Shouldn't we try and reach a consensus?"

Maury Richards says, "Christ, Verne. Don't be such a prick."

Verne says mildly, "As I understand it, we agreed to release the data with all our names attached to it."

Mariella says, "That's fine as far as the scientific community is concerned, but I'm thinking of a public statement, too."

"It isn't a good career move," Verne Ward says.

"I'm sure you're right. But my scientific reputation is already, if you'll pardon the expression, fucked beyond all recognition. I appreciate your concern, but I've already made the arrangements."

Bridget York says, "I guess I won't object, as long as we can also upload our sequences to a public database."

"You must make it clear that they aren't complete," Mariella says.

Bridget York says sharply, "Well, of course. It's in the nature of the organism. But we have the complete sequence of what we grew from your sample, Mariella. You can't ask us to do better than that."

"Calm down, Bridget," Maury Richards says. "This isn't a criticism of all the hard work that was done in such a short time. Also, there's more you should know. Tony here has made an interesting calculation."

Tony May takes a while to explain what he has done. He is nervous and in any case not naturally articulate, especially in front of such a challenging audience. He tells them that he has been thinking about the way in which the Chi's genes are distributed among its linear plasmids. In effect, although it appears to be a unitary organism, it is a patchwork mosaic that is continually challenging itself, and every strand contains a slightly different set of genes.

"The center cannot hold," Verne Ward says.

"There is no center," Randy Gilmour says. "That's the point, right? That's why it's so important." He adds, tasting the phrase in his mouth and clearly liking it, "It's a kind of fractal genetic laboratory."

Tony May fumbles with his notes. This is not the first interruption, and he is easily flustered. Mariella suppresses her impulse to take over. This is his work, his responsibility, his glory. He says, "Well, that's not exactly the point. . . ."

Randy Gilmour says, "I've already said that we can't obtain the complete sequence without completely extracting every last nanogram of its DNA. What's new?"

"Let the guy tell it his way," Maury Richards says.

"Well, it *is* about getting the complete sequence," Tony May says. "The way you all set this up was to have four teams working on different subsamples of the Chi. Everyone came out with more or less the same DNA sequence, but the overlap wasn't complete because of the way certain rare genes are distributed between different families of linear plasmids. All the commonly occurring genes were found by every team, but not all of the genes were present in every sample. So I did a probability calculation based on the distribution of the rarer genes. It's an easy arithmetical calculation, something I used just recently to discover how many unfound proofreading errors there were in my thesis."

He takes them through the figures, more confident with mathematics than concepts, and concludes, "Even if you take the lowest estimate, it turns out that we're missing at least forty percent of the total genome. Probably more. It would help to have more samples to find out just how much."

Stan Stansky says, "Well, it's a nice bit of work, but we can't work with what we don't have."

"Maybe none of the missing genes matter," Bridget York says. "Certainly the samples we grew managed without them."

Mariella says, "But it matters legally."

"Because it isn't the complete genetic sequence for the organism," Maury Richards says.

Verne Ward says, touching two fingers to his thin-lipped smile, "And the Thornton Bill means that no entity can copyright partial sequences."

"As if any government lawyers will take notice of a technical nicety," Randy Gilmour says.

"They'll have to," Verne Ward says, "if competent technical witnesses bring it to their attention. It's fascinating, isn't it? An organism which can never be fully defined without completely destroying it."

"All we need do is footnote this in the database entry," Bridget York says. "Which is what we should be doing right now."

"No," Mariella says. "I'm going to present the sequence and the rest of the data first, and I want your word that you won't release it until I do."

Verne Ward says, "If you're going to Thornton and Paley with this, I strongly suggest that the sequence should be made available on a database first. In case they slap an injunction on it."

"Then wait until I'm arrested," Mariella says. "How about that? But first let me at least try and present it."

"Oh, I see," Randy Gilmour says. He shares his broad white smile with all of them. "Don't you guys get it? It's October. She's going to Disneyland."

Anaheim, California:
October 6–9, 2028

The annual conference of the American Society of Cell and Molecular Biologists is the biggest gathering of the scientific calendar. As soon as the fragments of the Chi began to grow in their Mars Jars, Mariella made arrangements to give the keynote speech on the conference's opening day. The conference chair is a former colleague from UCLA who delights in conspiracies and scandals; the neuroscientist scheduled for that slot graciously gave way.

As Mariella drives the borrowed Ford Yahi pickup truck toward the gate of the ranch, Dolphus Pasternack steps out from the shadow of the statue of his creation. She jams on the brakes and jumps out. "Thank you," she says. "Thank you for all you've done."

The cartoonist strikes a mock-heroic pose. Denim coveralls hang loosely on his ursine body. He is barefoot, and a ragged straw hat perches on the long tangles of his blond hair. He looks like a grown-up Huckleberry Finn, lacking only a fishing pole and a corncob pipe.

"You came here for all mankind," he says, assuming a grave, gravelly TV announcer's voice. He is a man of many voices, many masks. They are his shield. He says, "You came to save us from the Martian menace."

"There's a long way to go before that's done. If it can be done."

"Are you sure you don't want one of my people to go with you?"

"I don't want to get anyone else into trouble, and I'm already horribly grateful for the loan of this pickup. Are you sure it can't be traced back to you?"

"I don't officially own it, if that's what you mean. The poor thing was abandoned out on the highway, so we adopted it and fixed it up. And what about you? Can you handle it?"

"I used to drive one all the time."

"You know what I mean."

"I have to use the stealth switch so the highway patrol won't spot me."

"And you'll have to match the traffic around you. Blend in. It won't be as easy as you think."

"If I get it wrong, the worst they can do is arrest me." Mariella wishes that she could feel as insouciant as she tries to sound. "Which is what will happen sooner or later. The best I can hope for is to be able to finish my speech."

"At least there should be plenty of witnesses."

"Thank you for that, too."

Dolphus Pasternack strikes another pose and assumes another voice. "We shall not flag or fail. We shall go on to the end."

"Winston Churchill."

"I knew I'd never slip that one past a Brit. It's not so much, saving the world these days, because the world will keep getting smaller. You can't wiggle a finger without causing an earthquake in Japan or an outbreak of scarlet fever in Tierra del Fuego."

Mariella says, "But there's still plenty of space here. You can go for days without seeing anyone else."

"Is that why you used to live out in the desert, in Arizona?"

"How did you know . . . ?"

"It was on the news."

"Oh. Well, I moved to the desert because I took a job at the Biological Reserve. It was just supposed to be temporary. I was going to buy a house in Tucson, but I never got around to it, and now I can't imagine living anywhere else."

"I love it too." Rolling his eyes, assuming a burlesque Russian accent, striking his hairy chest, bare under the coveralls, with a fist. "Its emptiness speaks to my soul. It is like the steppes, wide and peaceful and completely useless. America is like Russia — they're big countries with absolutely nothing at their hearts."

And in another voice, milder, gentler, "When my father came here, we lived four years in Barstow. He was trying to get back into science, and he had American colleagues trying to help him, but there were no jobs. It was the big downturn after the millennium, when the bubble burst on all the net companies and the stock market crashed. Well, we didn't understand that. We were Russians. We thought that capitalism was the exact opposite of communism. We didn't know that the two sort of meet around each other's back, that both are about robber-barons getting together to screw the little guy, one in the name of profit, the other out of idealism.

"My father couldn't even get a bottle-washing job in any of the labs, so we were living in Barstow. My father was working in a grocery store. It sold comic books and sci-fi paperbacks, too. A lot of media sci-fi shit, but some of the pure quill. So you have to think of this little Russian kid. A Russian kid who's been living in a crappy 1970s brutalist apartment block in Akademgodorok Science City in Siberia, who's now scuffing along a desert track among Joshua trees and creosote bushes in one-hundred-ten-degree heat, with a bottle of Evian water in one hand and a paperback in the other, his head full of galactic empires and futures where stuff actually worked. So that's what the desert is for me, you know. Possibility. A place where anything can come true."

"Even a crazy plan to save the world."

"That too. Why not? Go in peace, Earthling. Knock 'em dead."

It is the first time Mariella has driven after returning to Earth, and the little California-standard Yahi, its gasoline engine converted to run off a fuel cell, is old and slow and heavy to steer. So she takes it easy, stopping that night in a Best Western at the edge of Phoenix's rampant sprawl and driving on early the next morning, skirting Phoenix and its TrafficMaster system, taking a minor road across the border into California to avoid the Agricultural Service checkpoint.

Cacti give way to the featureless creosote bush scrub of the Mohave. Mariella stops at a truck stop beyond Palm Springs, in the shadow of a gigantic purple tyrannosaurus and a yellow apatosaurus, but gets little sleep in her air-conditioned capsule room because of the noise of the big rigs that come and go all night like gigantic creatures at a waterhole.

She is up at dawn, bleary-eyed and full of nerves. She chokes down some scrambled eggs, and uses one of the infobooths to pick up her email, routing through a node in San Francisco to give her some time in case agents on the net are looking for her. The keynote address is set up. Mae Thornton's chief of staff wants to know where the meeting is going to be; Mariella promises to tell him soon.

Nothing left now but to do it.

She drives through Barstow, where as a displaced kid Dolphus Pasternack wandered the desert, dreaming of futures as tremblingly transient as mirages, drives through the pass between the Shadow and Stoddard Ridge mountains. Traffic picks up, funneling down the steep highway through San Bernardino into the brawling basin of Los Angeles. Mariella throws the stealth switch on the hacked TrafficMaster box: now the freeway system will appear to be controlling the falsely identified pickup truck while she drives it manually, a free agent among locked-down drones. If the cops spot her, they can't take control of the pickup or shut it down.

She finds that it is harder than she expected to match the pickup's speed with that of the computer-controlled cars all around her. Free-driving is a sport played mostly by male adolescents; Mariella thinks that its thrill is as limited as any computer game. The need to stay perpetually alert soon exhausts her. Her nervous system is continually jolted by spurts of adrenalin as she reacts a few seconds out of synch to changes in speed of the traffic. She keeps looking around, ready to punch out if a cop car challenges her.

Cars, vans and trucks sluice along like corpuscles in arteries. Sunlight flares from thousands of windshields. The great signs sweep like scythes overhead. The skycars of the rich streak across the achingly blue sky; a line of silver airships moves from north to south in stately procession, like sharks patrolling above a reef. Mariella thinks the dusty pickup truck is horribly conspicuous among the hordes of little candy-colored commuter cars. Hot dry air blasts through the open window. Her hands sweat on the ridged plastic of the steering wheel, sweat pools in the small of her back where it rests against the vinyl seat cover, and her right leg aches as she constantly and delicately manipulates the accelerator pedal.

She is committed now.

From 15 to 91 to 57. The tremendously tall towers of the new downtown far off to the north. Dry brown hills shaken out of shape or marked by the scars of landslides. Block after block of dingbat apartments boarded up or burned out; rebuilt tracts under tents of construction diamond, glittering in the sun like froths of exotic algae; gated communities like medieval castles, each anchored by a shopping mall.

Mariella stops in a mini-mall and makes a phone call to Mae Thornton's chief of staff, tells him where she is going, cuts the connection in the middle of his first question, gets right back on the road. She sees the sign for Disneyland and the convention center, switches through three lanes of slow-moving traffic to the off-ramp, and almost immediately is driving under the arc of a monorail into the convention center's huge parking lot, as if she's dropped into one of Dolphus Pasternack's lost futures.

She leaves the card in the ignition of the pickup truck, as arranged, drops the plastic bag containing her dirty underwear in a trash can. She has brought nothing with her but the slate she borrowed from Tony May, and several dozen slivers of plastic he prepared for her. She hopes it will be all she needs.

There is a demonstration outside the convention center, two or three hundred people kept away from the steps leading up to the entrance by sawhorses, tangles of trophic smartwire that swing to and fro like seaweed in a current, and a unit of bored cops in body armor. The usual green motley, half protest, half street carnival. People in costumes — one man sweating in a half carrot, half fish getup — children in face-paint or animal masks. People holding up banners or penlight projectors. KEEP YOUR FILTHY HANDS OFF MY GENE POOL. DOWN WITH FRANKENSCIENCE.

Inside, conference delegates are milling around in the big lobby, the noise of their conversations a dull roar under the high ceiling. Senior scientists in suits, postdocs and grad students in brightly colored sweatsuit tops, leather or denim jackets, jeans or chinos or baggy shorts. The postdocs and grad students are mostly clustered around the complimentary buffet, freeloading on bad coffee and doughnuts; the senior scientists are talking with each other and hoping to make a good impression on the contract monitors who stand unobtrusively near the long registration desk.

It is a familiar sight to Mariella, and for a moment she feels a relaxation of the tension that has knotted up inside her like a twisted rope. After all, she is here to give a talk, something she's done a hundred times before. She has no notes and no viewgraph files, but that doesn't matter. She is notorious for winging her speeches, for suddenly abandoning the scheduled topic for something else—part of the elaborate game she used to play to keep her colleagues off balance, to stay ahead of the pack.

She is recognized at registration; the conference secretary comes over and pumps her hand and starts asking questions. She disengages herself as quickly as she can, refusing downloads of the convention program and free software and indexes to online journals, and pins her name tag so that it is half-hidden by the lapel of the jacket she borrowed from Bridget York.

The main convention area is as big as an aircraft hangar. Two hundred booths divide it into an irregular grid, like a rat maze. This is where most of the delegates spend most of their time; as well as the booths, set up by manufacturers of scientific equipment that most of the delegates cannot afford, there are two bars, a coffee shop and a pizza restaurant, prime spots for exchanging gossip and schmoozing contract monitors and senior colleagues known to be on grant-awarding committees and the editorial boards of the big journals.

Mariella has arrived with more than an hour to spare. She works her way through the crowded grid, taking a souvenir pen from one of the booths, and finds herself a seat in the coffee shop, where she spends a couple of minutes breaking the pen open and reassembling it. And then she has nothing to do but wait, and brush off the attention of people who want to know where she's been and why she's here. Forcing herself to give polite answers to the more asinine questions, asking permission from those she trusts to give them what she calls a couple of souvenirs from Mars. She feels like an imposter: like someone imitating herself. The rumor of her presence is spreading through the hall. People she doesn't know are openly staring at her. The hour passes, and then another,

and there is no sign of Mae Thornton or Al Paley. Mariella's stomach aches, nerves and too much coffee.

And then her slate rings.

It is Senator Thornton's chief of staff, full of bland reassurance.
The senator's flight has been delayed. She will be there a few hours
later than arranged.

"That's not the deal," Mariella says angrily, and breaks the
connection. Almost at once, the slate rings again. She turns off its
phone function, feeling suddenly cold as a spike of adrenalin hits
her blood.

There is a small chance that it is a genuine cock-up. More
likely, she has walked into some kind of setup. She is sure that
Mae Thornton is on her side, but perhaps the senator is being
watched by people who aren't. Or perhaps she is a political un-
touchable, despite the assurances of Thornton and Al Paley. Who
also isn't here. Shit. Maybe the conference chair has been got at
too—is that why he didn't come to meet her? She realizes that
she can trust no one at all and that her plans may have gone badly
agley.

Well, all she has to do is avoid arrest until she has given the
keynote address. Fearing an ambush, and thinking that a moving
target might be harder to hit, she leaves the coffee shop and wanders at random through the crowded exhibition hall, wondering if
security cameras might be watching her, wondering which of the
people around her might be Secret Service or FBI agents. There
are security guards at the glass doors in the lobby, silhouetted
against the glare of afternoon sunlight. She hadn't noticed them
when she came in. One is talking into his headset mike—has he
spotted her? The noise of the protestors comes through the glass,
audible even above the buzz of the delegates' conversation.

Mariella goes to the registration desk to find out where the
chair of the convention is, but there is now no sign of the conference secretary, and the woman she asks, an employee of the convention center, can't help. Mariella tries phoning his room but
gets no reply, ends up at one of the talks, standing among the
crush at the back of the darkened room. A murmur starts up and
grows as people begin to recognize her. They make space around

her or turn in their seats to look, an earnest postdoc actually shakes her hand, and even the hapless speaker stops for a few seconds before trying to draw the audience's attention back to a viewgraph of an RNA sequence. There is only an hour to go before the keynote speech. Mariella eats a jelly doughnut with a kind of absent-minded fierceness, and is halfway through her second cup of mango-flavored ice water when she realizes that she has to pee.

They get her as she comes out of the stall, two women in neat black suits who pin her arms and hustle her out of the brightly lit restroom. People at the far end of the corridor turn when she shouts that she is being arrested, but no one moves to help her. One of the women swipes a card through a lock and then they are inside some kind of service corridor lit by dim red light, the door closing behind them with a pneumatic sucking sound and the woman who has been waiting on the other side — it is Glory Dunn — taking Mariella's slate.

Mariella feels surprisingly calm, calmer than the two women who clasp her upper arms with trembling tightness. She says, "You found me at last."

"I think you wanted to be found, Dr. Anders," Glory Dunn says. She touches the microphone of her headset rig and says, "We're coming in," and asks Mariella, "Will you be sensible?"

Mariella looks up at the tall black woman and says, "I won't try and run away, if that's what you mean."

"Good."

Glory Dunn nods fractionally, and Mariella is turned and slammed against the wall. Her arms are wrenched behind her, something hard is clipped around her wrists, binding them together, and she is turned around to face Glory Dunn again.

Mariella says, dazed and angry, "I said I wouldn't run away."

But Glory Dunn ignores this and flashes her photo ID in front of Mariella's face and Mirandizes her in a bored tone, asking her, "Do you understand?"

"That I'm being arrested? Yes, I understand. But I don't know why I'm being arrested. Who are you working for?"

"I'm just completing my assignment, Dr. Anders. I must say that it has been one of the more interesting ones." Glory Dunn's red-framed data spex film over for a moment and she adds, "Some-one will explain everything to you. Bring her along, girls."

Mariella finds that with her hands cuffed behind her back it is difficult to match the quick pace of the two women who steer her down the corridor. Robot carts laden with toiletries and towels and bed linen get out of their way, clattering up against the walls with mechanical deference. They ride a big service elevator up twenty floors, go down a long corridor to a door where a man in a black suit, wearing a headset like Glory Dunn's, stands guard. He knocks on the door when he sees them coming, and another black-suited man opens it.

Mariella blinks in the flood of light from the uncurtained window that fills one side of the room. Al Paley is silhouetted against it. Another man sits on the side of the big bed, turned away from them as he watches the big TV hung on the wall. It is showing pictures of the demonstration outside the conference center: a tracking shot over packed heads that ends in a close-up of two children in coyote masks; a brief aerial view; a journalist in a sports jerkin on the steps of the conference center, with the crowd behind a line of police in the distance. The TV's sound is turned off, but the noise of the demonstrators can be faintly heard through the triple-glazed window.

One of the women uncuffs Mariella's wrists; Glory Dunn tosses the slate onto the bed.

Al Paley says, "I'm sorry it had to come to this, Mariella."

"You were a fool to tell them. Or are you in on it, too?"

The man turns from the TV. It is Howard Smalls. He says, "Dr. Paley did what was right. You gave us quite a scramble, Dr. Anders. We only just made it."

Mariella rubs her wrists. She says, "And is Senator Thornton coming to the party too?"

"I don't think she needs to know about this. Where is it?"

"In my top pocket."

Glory Dunn lifts the pen out with scissored fingers and drops it onto the bed, next to the slate. Howard Smalls picks it up and turns it over. His suit is cut close to his slim body, white silk splattered with an off-center sunrise. Beads wink in the cornrows of his hair. His data spex are silver-rimmed, tinted an opaque blue. He says, "You had help." It is a declaration. "No doubt they have samples of the organism too, but we'll talk about that later. We have a lot to talk about."

"Why have I been arrested?"

Howard Smalls stares at her, the cold flat stare of a shark considering where to bite. "There's a whole raft of reasons. Most of them to do with national security."

Smalls unscrews the pen and a half dozen plastic slivers spill into his palm. He looks at them, then looks up at Mariella.

She tells him, "Souvenirs from Mars. Keep one if you like."

Smalls drops the slivers onto the bedspread, and gets up and goes into the bathroom. There is the sound of running water.

Mariella says, "Just the DNA. Quite inert. Nothing infectious. Nothing alive. When you get them analyzed they'll prove that I'm telling the truth."

Smalls comes out of the bathroom, drying his hands on a white towel. "We'll have to check that out, of course. What were you planning to do with them?"

"I thought that some of my colleagues would like a little souvenir from Mars."

Al Paley has been looking out of the window again. Now he turns from it and says to Glory Dunn, "They know you took her."

"Then I'll call up a helicopter, Dr. Paley. It isn't a problem."

Howard Smalls says, "Do it outside. I want to talk with Dr. Anders alone. No, wait, pick up the shit on the bed first."

Glory Dunn hesitates, and Mariella says, "Really, it's quite safe. I'll do it for you, if you like."

The agent smiles and says, "That won't be necessary, Dr. Anders."

When Glory Dunn has fitted the slivers back inside the barrel of the pen, Howard Smalls says, "I'll take care of that."

Al Paley says, "I believe it is NASA property."

"Don't get in over your head," Howard Smalls says, and holds out his hand.

Glory Dunn looks at him, then puts the pen in the inside pocket of her jacket and says, "She's in my care, Mr. Smalls, and so is the evidence."

"I don't think so. And I'm sure your boss would agree."

Glory Dunn drops a cell phone on the bed. "Her number is three on the speed dial. Now if you'll excuse me, I have to arrange your transport."

Al Paley is the first to break the tense silence that follows the departure of Glory Dunn and the other agents. He says, "I'm coming too, Howard."

"I think you're done here, Dr. Paley."

"She's still on the NASA payroll."

Howard Smalls gives him that flat, cold stare. "Really? That's interesting. Well, I've nothing to hide. I'll even let you be in on the formal questioning." He turns to Mariella and says, "You're in a lot of trouble, Dr. Anders. You're an enemy of the state, possibly a spy. Certainly, you're in league with proscribed radical green organizations and the unrecognized revolutionary Mexican government. And of course, you put the Mars mission at risk by absenting yourself from your quarters to seek out rough-trade sex a few days before departure. So far I have done you the favor of not releasing the tape of your interview after that little debacle, although I'm under a lot of pressure to do so."

"I thought you might be keeping that back."

"I kept it back out of respect for your scientific reputation, Dr. Anders. Help me maintain that respect."

"I've been arrested, Mr. Smalls. I don't have to talk to anyone unless my lawyer is present."

"But you want to hear what I have to say," Howard Smalls says.

She doesn't deny it.

"Let's talk about what you did after the raid on the Mexican facility. Obviously you found a place where you could grow more of the organism. If you tell me where that place is, it will count in your favor."

"Cytex still wants exclusive rights to research on the Chi, I take it. And the government is still willing to hand it to them — that is, if you're still working for the government, Mr. Smalls."

Howard Smalls's expression does not change. "Think of your reputation, Dr. Anders. If that video is released to the media, I doubt that you'll be able to work in any laboratory ever again."

Al Paley says, "I really think we should continue this elsewhere, Howard. It looks like there's going to be trouble."

The TV screen shows the chair of the conference at bay, more than a dozen microphones pressed toward him like a bouquet and delegates crowding in behind. Smalls picks up the remote and with an angry motion, like swatting a fly, turns off the TV.

Mariella walks over to the window and looks down. The hotel tower rises from the center of the glass-and-concrete wings of the conference center like an entomologist's pin transfixing a specimen, and the room faces out over the parking lot. The ragged line of the demonstrators has grown, closing off the main entrance. More people are moving across the parking lot, picking their way through the cars jammed in the wide street beyond. Dolphus Pasternack has kept his word. It looks like every green activist in the Greater Los Angeles metropolitan area is converging on the Anaheim Conference Center.

"Oh my," she says, amazed at what she has done.

"You'll get an even better view from the helicopter," Howard Smalls says calmly. "It's of no account."

Mariella looks at Al Paley and says, "Does NASA have anything to do with this any more? Or was *everything* contracted out?"

Al Paley says, "This isn't the time to go into arrangements—"

"I think it's exactly the moment. Cytex has been given all the licenses, hasn't it? NASA has been frozen out. Or have Betsy Sharp and Ali Tillman found the Chi at the south pole?"

"Cytex has always been in partnership with NASA," Al Paley says. "They underwrote the expedition, and after viable biological samples were obtained, they successfully renegotiated a continuation of their research licenses."

"I bet they did."

"It's hardly a secret," Howard Smalls says. His gaze is inscrutable. "Like all transactions between private companies and the government, the contracts and licenses are open to public inspection."

Mariella says, "I know that Cytex and the government tried to steal the Chi from the Chinese. A sample was smuggled out in a diplomatic pouch, aboard a commercial flight, but the scramjet crashed in the Pacific Ocean. That's how the slick got started. Penn Brown told me while we were on Mars, Al. That's why Cytex has a lock on this, why it has been given an exclusive license to sequence and commercially exploit any life discovered on Mars. Penn Brown already had a piece of that, but he wanted more. Cytex conspired to screw NASA, and he wanted to screw Cytex."

Let Howard Smalls think about that.

Al Paley says, "This is getting out of hand, Howard."

"The local police can handle it. Besides, the rabble will disperse as soon as they realize that Dr. Anders isn't here."

Mariella says, "How much did Cytex pay you?"

Smalls stares at her.

"Or perhaps it was blackmail. Some dirty little secret they uncovered."

"Everyone makes deals," Smalls says evenly. "Grow up, Dr. Anders."

Mariella knows then that she has guessed right. She feels a kind of heightened awareness, as if everything in the room is illuminated from within by its own particularity. It occurs to her that most American lives take a crucial turn in anonymous rooms like this, in hotel or motel rooms, in doctors' or lawyers' offices, in rooms lit by indirect "daylight" illumination and furnished from catalogs, with unregarded pictures on the walls, the crackle of static electricity in the siliconized carpet, the subliminal hum of air-conditioning. And yet she has never felt more a stranger in her adopted country than at this moment.

She says, "I'll give all the credit to Penn Brown. He knew what was going on and decided to cut himself into the deal. At the very end, he tried to persuade me to go along with it. We were outside. In our excursion suits, talking over a patch-cord link. I had my slate, and I'd been talking to it because I couldn't use the virtual keyboard. And I happened to record the conversation. You know about it, don't you, Mr. Smalls, because you opened my data vault. But that's not the only place I stored the recording. A radical green collective, the Bushor Report, also has a copy. They'll release it as soon as they hear of my arrest. They've probably released it already."

Al Paley says, "Is any of this true, Howard?"

Howard Smalls is saved from replying by his spex, which ring and extrude a wire-thin microphone. At the same moment there is a knock at the door. It is Glory Dunn. She says, "They're on the roof."

For a moment, Mariella thinks she means the helicopter has arrived.

"Yes," Howard Smalls says into the microphone, and turns to the agent and tells her, "Can't you people do anything about it?"

"No sir. Not without endangering civilians. I have made an arrangement with the police captain in charge of crowd control. He has made several squad cars available. We can leave in those."

Smalls taps his spex; the microphone retracts. He says, "They'd get out of the way if the helicopter came in."

"It's against aviation rules, sir," Glory Dunn says. Is there the ghost of a smile behind her impassive mask? "Sir, I suggest we move downstairs with all speed. The crowd is still growing, and the delegates appear to be joining them."

"Someone will pay for this fucking mess," Smalls says, and the crack in his urbanity speaks volumes.

Mariella is handcuffed again, despite Al Paley's protests. Cornish Brittany is waiting outside the room, flanked by a colorless man in a denim suit, clearly a process server, who tries to hand a fat, buff envelope to Mariella. Glory Dunn blocks his move and, when Cornish Brittany loudly protests, tells one of the agents to arrest her for obstruction.

As she's hustled down the corridor toward the bank of elevators, Mariella asks Howard Smalls, "Did you tell her where I was?"

"I've never seen her before," Howard Smalls says, but it's obvious he's lying.

The half dozen black-suited Secret Service agents make the elevator very crowded. Mariella stands behind Howard Smalls, breathing his cologne. He is talking into his phone again, a curt conversation consisting mostly of impatient yeses and noes. "Do it," he says, and dials another number with his handset as the elevator doors open and they walk out into the roar of the crowd, very loud in the big lobby that is deserted now except for convention center guards. Muffled by the glass doors, the chanting of the crowd sounds like heavy surf breaking against the front of the convention center. One of the agents starts to take out her gun and Glory Dunn tells her to stow it.

A guard opens one of the doors and the noise doubles, and doubles again when the crowd sees Mariella step out into the evening sunlight, pinioned between two black-suited agents. Sun flares on a hundred camera lenses as they swing around to focus on her. Journalists scramble forward, are checked by a dozen cops in white helmets. But the cops can do nothing about the growing swarm of remotes that bob overhead like a school of silver and black and yellow manta rays.

Howard Smalls is screaming, "Where are the cars! Where are the fucking cars!" It isn't clear if he is shouting at the police captain or at someone at the other end of his phone.

The crowd takes up a chant, ragged at first but growing clearer. Three words, over and over.

Let her speak! Let her speak!

Glory Dunn says loudly into Mariella's ear, "Did you organize this?"

"It organized itself! Complex self-assembly! Order out of chaos!"

"It's impressive, whatever it is."

Delegates are mixed with ordinary civilians and green activists in costume, two or three thousand people packing the wide lawn between the entrance to the convention center and the parking lot, and more on the way. All have taken up the chant. Hard echoes rebound from the concrete-and-glass sweep of the conference center's frontage. The horns of frustrated drivers in the street beyond the parking lot make a ragged arpeggio accompaniment.

Mariella sees Jake Boyle, a *faux* wolf's head cap jammed down over his long white hair, bioluminescent lights winking in his white beard like fireflies, his guitar strapped to his back. He is surrounded by his wives and the rest of his extended family and a crowd of greens from Arizona, a hundred or more people Mariella knows by sight if not by name. There are Kathe and Kim, with a slim young woman between them — Lily, all grown up in the two

years Mariella has been away. Someone among the press of journalists at the bottom of the steps is flashing her the okay sign,
thumb and forefinger in a circle: Alex Dyachkov, his beard neatly
trimmed, a camera on his shoulder. The man beside him is slim
and slight and upright.

The moment of recognition is like an electric flash.

Don Ye.

Anchee's husband.

And everyone is chanting.

At last the police captain disengages himself from Howard
Smalls and comes over and speaks into Glory Dunn's ear. "No,"
the agent says. "No, she's under arrest."

"Then you better take her back inside," the captain tells her.

"What does Smalls say?" Glory Dunn asks.

"He wants me to use what he calls due force," the captain
says, "but I don't see any need for it. Most of the science convention is out here in the parking lot. Two Nobel Prize winners, people on every scientific committee in Washington. . . ."

"And this is an election year in California," Glory Dunn says.

The captain is a solid, gray-haired man with a military haircut
and a stiff bearing. He says, "The mayor and the governor have
both expressed their anxiety about the situation."

Glory Dunn says to Mariella, "If you talk to them, will they
let us through?"

"I haven't the faintest idea."

"This is what I'm going to do, Dr. Anders. I'm going to put
my faith in you. And if you don't come through for me, we'll go
back inside and live off room service for as long as it takes."

"In Scotland we'd call that cruel and unusual punishment."

Glory Dunn smiles. "We'll also spend a lot of time watching
extreme gladiators on sports cable."

"Then I really would rather go to prison."

"I don't think there's much chance of that, Dr. Anders. Can I
entrust you with something?"

"I'm not good at keeping secrets."

"I know. But I'll tell you anyway. We know where you've just
come from. It wasn't difficult to figure out."

"You've been keeping watch on my associates?"

"That's our job, Dr. Anders."

"But you didn't do anything about it."

"Well, we didn't tell Cytex, if that's what you mean. The deal was that we shared information with them on a need-to-know basis. But when we found out that they were keeping stuff back, that they'd mounted a covert operation to capture you, my chief decided to be more cautious about what we told them. You go talk to these people now. Good luck."

"Thank you," Mariella says, astonished.

Glory Dunn motions to one of the agents, who releases Mariella from her handcuffs. Those nearest the steps see what is happening and start cheering, and the chanting slowly dies away toward the back of the huge crowd as Mariella walks forward, very conscious of the cameras that aim their lenses at her.

A police technician sticks a patch microphone to her lapel and taps it; a tinny squeal echoes out across the darkening parking lot. Behind Mariella, whether by accident or design, floodlights spring on along the length of the conference center's glass curtain wall. More cheers. A baby is crying loudly. Everywhere Mariella looks, faces are turned toward her. Two helicopters hang like hunting wasps at the periphery of the parking lot, red and green lights winking in the dusk, the throb of their props like slow heartbeats.

She says, "This isn't the way I expected to give my keynote speech."

And is surprised at the volume of her amplified voice, coming from speakers set on the light bars of dozens of patrol cars, rolling across the crowd toward the street beyond the parking lot, where hundreds of people are still filtering through the stalled traffic.

She says, "I think you all know where I have been. Some of you know what I brought back. That's what all this is about. There is life on Mars."

"That's where we should leave it," someone shouts.

"It's too late for that," Mariella says. "It was already here before I went to Mars. And that's why I went there. Let me tell you a little bit about it. I was going to tell you a lot more, but this isn't the place."

"In many ways it is like life on Earth. Perhaps Martian life shared a common ancestor with Earth life. Or perhaps, very early in the history of the Solar System, a fleck of Martian life was knocked off its home planet by a meteor impact. After drifting through space inside rocky debris, it fell to Earth and colonized it. We don't yet know the truth. We do know that although Martian life is closely related to life on Earth, it evolved in a very different way.

"On Earth, we are blessed with a staggering diversity of species which have solved the problem of how to grow and reproduce in many different ways. On Mars, life has been reduced to a single species, which may have absorbed the repertoire of all other Martian species. A version of it has escaped into the seas of Earth, and has changed itself into what we call the slicks by incorporating genes from life on Earth.

"Many of you hate and fear the idea of genetic engineering. This isn't the time or place to debate scientific ethics. But this species, named the Chi by the Chinese scientists who discovered it, is a natural genetic engineer, and its laboratory is its own self. It is a great wonder and a great danger."

Speaking into the absorbed silence of thousands of upturned faces, the hungry camera lenses, hardly aware of Howard Smalls furiously arguing with the police captain and Glory Dunn.

"It is dangerous because we do not know how to control the version which has escaped here on Earth, and caused the slicks that are slowly strangling our oceans. We don't know yet, I should say. That was the reason I went to Mars. To find out more about the origin of this danger. And it is dangerous, yes, but it is also wonderful. Life that is related to us yet which has taken a completely different path."

A murmur in the crowd. She is growing hoarse, and feels that she is beginning to lose the attention of the greens.

She says forcefully, "I came here to do one thing. There are people who want to exploit this wonderful thing. They want to claim ownership. They want exclusive rights to work on it. They believe that they can do what they want without public consultation. That's wrong. Science cannot work in secrecy. People like them have already made tremendous mistakes, and one of those mistakes was the direct cause of the slicks. I'm here to make it possible to try and undo that damage. Not to work in secrecy but openly. To understand the Chi so that the version that has been released into Earth's seas can be destroyed, or at least contained.

"I stand here as an alien in an adopted country. I came here on a scholarship, and I stayed and became a citizen because this country is a place where freedom of speech is enshrined in its Constitution. Because I believe that without freedom of speech, the great democratic discussion of which I'm a small part, the argument about how the world works, cannot exist. We cannot suppress thought without suppressing something wonderful in ourselves, but we can decide whether to make practical use of those thoughts. And we can only do that if all knowledge is available to all, so that everyone can take part in the debate.

"The people who want to exploit the Chi want to take themselves out of that debate. They want to do their work hidden from the public gaze. I say no."

Scattered cheers now, although they quickly die away. Mariella is breathing hard, like a runner at the end of a race.

"I say the only way to defeat them is to make everything we know about the Chi public. Some of my colleagues have sequenced its DNA and because I have been arrested they will have uploaded that information to public databases. And I have given that same information to some of the delegates here. I forget who—there were so many—but you know who you are. Perhaps many of you don't want to use that information, but I'm sure that many more do. If you want nothing to do with it, I understand. But remember that bringing this to Earth cost lives. People died. . . ."

There is a lump in her throat. She can't bring herself to look at Don Ye. She coughs and says, "Too many people died. If you don't want to use the information, find someone who does. Perhaps the people, through the government, will decide that no one should work on it. But I hope it doesn't come to that. We need to learn about the Chi in order to clean the slicks from our seas. But until then, you're responsible for it."

The cheers this time are louder. Howard Smalls is still shouting at the police captain, his rage seeming puny and frail after the amplified thunder of her voice. Mariella turns to him and says, "Are you going to arrest them all too? Are you going to violate their information rights? Break into their data vaults, take away their slates?"

Glory Dunn steps up behind her and says quietly, "I think you've said your piece."

Mariella turns back to the crowd. She says, "I have to go answer some questions. Will you let me do that?"

The roar of the crowd is her affirmation.

Mariella delivers her keynote speech all over again at eight the next morning, in an extraordinary session of the conference. Addressing an audience of her peers and journalists in the main amphitheater of the conference center, and speaking to the world through the ragged hedge of cameras and microphones at the foot of the stage. Every seat in the tiered horseshoe of the amphitheater is taken. Al Paley and Senator Mae Thornton sit side by side in the front row. People sit shoulder to shoulder on the stairways between the banks of seats, and crowd in at the back.

Outside, hundreds of greens still occupy the lawns and the parking lot of the conference center, maintaining a peaceful vigil. Last evening, at Mariella's request, they parted to let the police cruisers through. She was taken to the police headquarters and fingerprinted and photographed, and then driven in a convoy of police cruisers with wailing sirens and flashing lights to a hastily convened court hearing. NASA lawyers organized by Al Paley secured her bail, and she was released into his custody.

"They're holding your slate as evidence," Al Paley says, as he helps her through the noisy scrum in the plaza outside the court building. Men and women shouting her name to get her attention, flashes exploding and camera lights flaring everywhere she turns.

She shouts back, "It's my graduate student's. I'll buy him another. We've won, haven't we? I mean, do you think we've won?"

"That remains to be seen," Al Paley says, but he's grinning

from ear to ear as they dive into the waiting limo. The limo's doors are slammed; camera flashes explode dimly beyond its smoked glass windows. Cops link arms and push the crowd back.

Mariella sprawls on plush velour, utterly exhausted; she feels as if she's just swum the English Channel. "Where are we going?"

"To see an old ally."

NASA has reserved a suite at the top of the Hyatt Regency at the edge of the new downtown. Mae Thornton is waiting for her there, on a curved couch that faces the spectacular view of the Los Angeles basin, a vast grid of lights stretching away in every direction under orange sky-glow.

"I had some dinner brought in," the senator says. She is wearing TV makeup and a spider-silk cerise robe fringed with fractal patterns in gold and emerald. "I hope you don't mind Chinese. It's from a favorite restaurant of mine."

Over crispy duck pancakes, Kung Pao chicken and steamed sea bass, Mariella tells the senator all she knows about the links between Cytex and the government, and Cytex's deal with Howard Smalls.

"There'll be an investigation," Mae Thornton says, "but I have to tell you that it probably won't go far."

"But Howard Smalls was pushing for Cytex's interests all along."

"My dear girl, that will hardly cause a ripple in Washington, where everyone is pushing for someone's interests. It's common knowledge that Howard Smalls is going to run for Congress. He needs to build up his war chest, and because Cytex is the biggest employer in his district, it's hardly surprising that he's been doing favors for them. The whole affair will go before Ways and Means, but probably no further. The business about trying to smuggle the Chi out of Shanghai will be more damaging. I understand that Cytex is already assembling a team of lawyers. You had better be certain of your evidence."

"I have a recording of my conversation with Penn Brown."

Al Paley says, "Our lawyers will want that as soon as possible."

"This isn't the end," Mariella says, dismayed.

Mae Thornton daintily dabs at her mouth with a napkin.

"There'll be a hearing," she says, "but I doubt that it will come to a trial. Cytex will certainly want to plea bargain. It will probably lose its license to work on the Chi, and you'll have to be content with that." She extends an arm, and her chief of staff steps forward smartly and helps her to her feet. "I'm afraid I must cut and run. I have a dozen interviews to give. You should get some rest. It'll be your turn tomorrow."

Mariella sleeps for six hours, wakes to find footage of her speech in front of the conference center on every news channel. It is terrifying and mortifying and exciting. And in the extraordinary session of the conference, after she has presented technical details of the DNA sequencing of the Chi's linear plasmids, she tries to make the same points about freedom of information all over again, and ends by emphasizing that although the material is unique in origin, the sequencing was done in an entirely routine way.

"And if we were able to do it in a scratch laboratory working under tremendous pressure, then anyone with sufficient technical ability and equipment can do it. And both ability and equipment are common enough. You can find them in any hospital, in any birth clinic. And in black labs owned by the former drug cartels, too."

She remembers the name of Darlajane B.'s former collaborator.

"Anyone with sufficient training can do this, anywhere in the world. And I'm sure that they will. Nor is there a lack of material. The slick began to grow a thousand kilometers southwest of Hawaii, but even before I left for Mars it had spread to the coast of Florida, and since then it's spread throughout the world's oceans.

"Any one of us can decide not to work on this. Indeed, it is possible that no one in the United States will be allowed to work on it. But no matter what is decided here, I am certain that many scientists in many other countries will want to do that work, and that is why my colleagues and I released the data. Science is a collective effort. It crosses international boundaries and cultural differences. It must, or else it will wither. No individual, no commercial organization, no government, should have exclusive rights to this organism. It belongs to us all. We must all decide what to do with it."

Afterward, after an hour answering detailed technical questions from her peers and doing her best to give simplified answers to the press, she meets the one person to whom she still owes an unfulfilled pledge.

Houston:
July 23, 2029

There are only a couple of reporters waiting for her at the airport, and Mariella gets past them quickly. She has become ruthlessly expert at dealing with the press. She has been appointed to the post of special advisor to the Office of Technology Assessment, helping to set up a research program to investigate and harness the Chi's potential. She has steered the budget request through the Office of Management and Budget, a monster's lair of malicious obstructionists and ax-toting budget officers where the armor of many an heroic project has proven insufficient, and through the relevant appropriations subcommittee in Congress. After it was passed by the full House, it was referred to both the Energy and Commerce Committees and the Science, Space and Technology Committee, and is presently bogged down in intense politicking by the half-dozen government and private research institutes that want a slice of the pie. Senator Mae Thornton is threatening to add a rider to the trade bill, to force competing agencies to cooperate or face legislation that will embody Congress's preferred framework.

Mariella finds the work intensely engaging, the power that flows within the magic circle of the Beltway heady. Her stature as a scientist and her public personality have made her a serious player. She spends most of her time arguing with her peers in special seminars and symposia and special forums, and writing planning documents and assessments of the latest technical developments. She has discovered a talent for persuasion, an ability to focus her intuition on character judgments, and a use for her fame.

Meanwhile, the legal repercussions of the affair are still playing out. Although the charges laid against her by Howard Smalls and Cytex have been dismissed, she is embroiled in the initial stages of the case brought by the U.S. government against Cytex, and a Congressional hearing into the way NASA planned the mission to Mars's north pole is about to start; it is already filling her email box with hundreds of pages of transcripts and technical reports. She also has to face charges lodged by the Chinese government in the International Court at the Hague, although her condition means that she won't be traveling there just yet. She won't be going anywhere for a couple of months.

All this has taken her away from scientific research. There is so much to be done, yet it is as much as she can do to try and keep up with the flood of research into the Chi and the slicks. There are several treatments that have proved to be very effective in the laboratory and in limited field trials: strains of bacteria that attack the slick's integument; a terminator RNA sequence that inserts itself into every linear plasmid and prevents replication by capping the sequence that controls the unzipping of DNA's double helix; even GM zooplankton which, borrowing a throwaway suggestion of Mariella's, have been engineered to graze on the slicks. But the slicks are now so pervasive that, like the Moses virus, they might never be completely eradicated, only contained. That is good enough, perhaps.

At the rental desk, a solicitous clerk recognizes her and escorts her to the car, hovering anxiously as she squeezes in behind its steering wheel. The route is familiar. She's been back and forth to Houston many times in the months following her acquittal, and has a permanent suite in the NASA hotel. But this time she is here in an entirely personal capacity, and drives two kilometers north past the space center, exiting at last onto a broad street lined by boxy retail units, stopping at a checkpoint and then driving along gently curving residential streets of widely spaced, single-story ranch houses and Tudor-framed houses fronted by immaculate green lawns and shaded by mature oaks and elms. She drives slowly, just under the posted fifteen-kilometers-per-hour limit; the little electric car is overtaken by a gang of children on furiously pedaled bicycles, their excited screams fading as they disappear around a corner.

The Secret of Life   413

Don Ye comes out of the trim little house as she pulls into the driveway and parks behind his lovingly waxed MG. It took a whole month of careful, patient courtship before he could be persuaded that Mariella didn't want to do it out of guilt, but after they had both signed consent and release forms, the implantation procedure in the NASA fertility clinic took less than an hour. There was a fierce flurry of speculation about her condition in the media, but it soon died down through lack of leads—a man in a green community in New Mexico claimed to be responsible, but vanished after an ex-wife appeared with medical records of his vasectomy.

Don Ye helps her out of the rental car and asks, "How is he?"

"Alive and kicking."

Mariella cups the swell of her belly with both hands, like ice fields capping the globe of a fertile world, her gift, her blessing. And realizes how happy she is. All life needs moments in which to pause, to rest, to be rather than to do. For this short time before the birth of Anchee and Don Ye's son, Mariella can set aside all her travails and dissolve in moments like this, new life burgeoning within her, the hot, humid air heavy with the sharp smell of freshly cut grass and the drowsy scent of jasmine, trees spreading their branches above as if in benediction, leaves greedily drinking sunlight, light into life, light spangling the green shade of these fountains of solidified sunshine and dancing over the daylilies that line the drive, and birds singing their hearts out in a ceaseless struggle to define their territories, songs shaped by a ruthless contest between the male drive to spread genes and the imponderabilities of female mate selection, and yet even so (as Dr. Wu, dying, observed), like all of life, rich in accidental beauty.